"Bárcena's [*The Sky over Lima*] is both a love letter to the creative process and a contemplation on the sometimes-blurred line between life and art."
—*Kirkus Reviews*

". . . Bárcena's [*The Sky over Lima*] transforms fact with cinematographic imagination, re-creating the scenery and moods of Lima at the turn of the twentieth century with inimitable precision."
—*Booklist*

"Bárcena's style is both fresh and classic, delightful and mysterious, and his characters—who feel like living, breathing creatures—are sure to captivate even as they break your heart."
—*Library Journal*

"Here's a tale with the subtlest of stings in it, dark wit and telescopic perspective aplenty. And then there's the intoxicating folly of the games that the protagonists play with fantasy and fact, malice, tenderness, ambition, envy and other forces that strike at our most vulnerable selves. I'll be thinking of these characters, what they longed to create and what they managed to despoil, for a long time."
—Helen Oyeyemi, author of *What Is Not Yours Is Not Yours*

"The best heartbreaker novels are the ones that sneak up on you like this one."
—Alexander Chee, *Vulture*

"Bárcena shines where so many writers stumble. His writing about art, of the artifice both in the narrative and implicit in his prose, feels alive, fresh, and important. . . . Against the fascinating backdrop of Lima's burgeoning rubber industry, *The Sky Over Lima* explores notions of class, identity, and friendship, and reminded me of how it first felt to fall in love with writing."
—Sara Nović, author of *True Biz*

ALSO IN ENGLISH TRANSLATION
BY JUAN GÓMEZ BÁRCENA

The Sky Over Lima

NOT
EVEN
THE
DEAD

JUAN GÓMEZ BÁRCENA

Translated by Katie Whittemore

OPEN LETTER

LITERARY TRANSLATIONS FROM THE UNIVERSITY OF ROCHESTER

Originally published in Spanish as *Ni siquiera los muertos* by Editorial Sexto Piso, 2019

Copyright © Juan Gómez Bárcena, 2019
Translation copyright © Katie Whittemore, 2023

First edition, 2023
All rights reserved

Library of Congress Cataloging-in-Publication Data: Available

pb ISBN: 978-1-948830-67-6 | ebook ISBN: 978-1-948830-97-3

Support for the translation of this book was provided by Acción Cultural Española, AC/E

Printed on acid-free paper in the United States of America.

Cover Design by Daniel Benneworth-Gray

Open Letter is the University of Rochester's nonprofit, literary translation press:
Dewey Hall 1-219, Box 278968, Rochester, NY 14627

www.openletterbooks.org

NOT EVEN THE DEAD

The Messiah comes not only as the Redeemer, he comes as the subduer of the Antichrist. Only that historian will have the gift of fanning the spark of hope in the past who is firmly convinced that even the dead will not be safe from the enemy if he wins. And this enemy has not ceased to be victorious.

Walter Benjamin

The world is a vicious and brutal place. We think we're civilized. In truth, it's a cruel world and people are ruthless. They act nice to your face, but underneath they're out to kill you. You have to know how to defend yourself. People will be mean and nasty and try to hurt you just for sport. Lions in the jungle only kill for food, but humans kill for fun. Even your friends are out to get you: they want your job, they want your house, they want your money, they want your wife, they even want your dog. Those are your friends; your enemies are even worse!

Donald Trump

For Marta Jiménez Serrano, who accompanies me inside and outside the pages of this book.

Nicān mihtoa in tlahtlaquetzalli in quēnin Juan quihuāltoca in Juan, onēhuah īnāhuac in Puebla īhuān ōmpa huih Tlacetilīlli Tlahtohcāyōtl Ixachitlān, ce neh-nemiliztli in mani cenzontli īpan yēpōhualli on caxtōlli omēyi netlalōlli caxtiltēcatl īhuān zan cuēcuēl achīc.

Here is the tale of how Juan pursued Juan from the vicinity of Puebla to the United States border, a journey lasting four hundred and seventy-five Spanish leagues and a goodly number of years.

I

The best of the worst – A tavern at midnight – What the viceroy would want, if the viceroy wanted something – A dog's life – A particular idea of home – A rooster's silence – A head, at the bottom of a sack – Fallacy of the strawman – The first last look

The first name put forward is that of Captain Diego de Villegas, a man with proven experience in such nettlesome situations, but Captain Villegas is dead. Somebody suggests a certain Suárez from Plasencia, known for more than fifteen exemplary expeditions, but it turns out Suárez is dead, too. No one mentions Nicolás de Obregón, given that P'urhepecha savages shot him through with arrows, nor Antonio de Oña, who committed innumerable atrocities against the pagan Indians, only to later be ordained as a priest in order to protect said pagans. A degree of enthusiasm momentarily surfaces around the name Pedro Gómez de Carandía, until someone recalls that Pedro had finally received his encomienda the previous year, sheathing his sword and taking up the whip. Pablo de Herrera is imprisoned by order of the governor, the result of certain tithes never having been paid, or having been paid twice, depending on which version you believed; Luis Velasco went mad, dreaming of the gold in the Seven Cities. With no Indians to kill, Domingo de Cóbreces returned to his previous occupation as a pigherd. Alonso Bernardo de Quirós did his best to obtain the viceroy's favor on the battlefields of New Galicia, la Gran Chichimeca, and la Florida, only to wind up hanged in his own home, clutching a letter addressed to the viceroy in his right hand. No one has any doubts about Diego Ruiloba's skill or determination, but neither do they doubt the tepidness of his faith, which is reason enough to discard him from command of this sensitive situation. To find the right name, they will have to dig down deep in the pile of scrolls, grapple with an abundance of human weakness and failure, move from captains to cavalry sergeants and from cavalry sergeants to simple soldiers of fortune; a path paved with men who were too old or who had returned to Castilla, mutilated men, rebellious men, men tried by the Holy Office of the Inquisition, men disfigured by syphilis, dead men. Until suddenly, and perhaps to save himself the trouble of dusting off more dockets and files, it occurs to a clerk to suggest the name of one Juan de Toñanes, former soldier of His Majesty the King, former treasure hunter, former almost everything. The clerk has never met him personally, but Juan de Toñanes is said to have avoided poverty by pursuing those fugitive Indians who escaped from the encomiendas of Puebla. A humble man—unworthy, perhaps, of the enterprise at hand—but with a reputation as a competent person and good Christian, endowed with an almost miraculous ability to invariably return with the Indian in question, shackled and in one piece. May God strike me down, the clerk continues, if his occupation isn't the selfsame enterprise Your Excellencies require someone for; a mission that, excepting the obvious differences, consists of just that, of locating a specific Indian and bringing him back, dead or alive. The clerk falls silent, and the viceroy, who has likewise begun to lose patience with the search, orders the clerk to check his papers for news of this Juan de Toñanes. The clerk turns up a thin, mildewed file, from which they can deduce the following: in his soldiering days, Juan was neither the best nor the worst of the bunch; he bled in many minor skirmishes, never distinguished himself, neither for cowardice nor courage; for years he sent letters to the viceroy requesting—unsuccessfully—to be granted an encomienda; later he begged—dripping in deference—for a sergeant's appointment in the expedition from Coronado to la Quivira; and lastly, he appealed—receiving no response—for a post in Castilla far below his merits. To all appearances, Juan de Toñanes was a common man, but of the most uncommon kind given that over the years he had managed to not defend heresies, engage in duels, participate in brawls or scandals, curse God or His Majesty the King, besmirch the reputations of maidens, or find himself deserving prison or ignominy. Before the clerk was even finished reading the record of service in his hand, the viceroy had decided to suspend their search and summon this Juan de Toñanes of unknown talent and skill, but of

14

whom, like any Spanish soldier, they could expect some facility with a sword and at least a moderate taste for adventure.

Two raps of the knocker wake the dog and the dog's barking wakes the woman dozing beside the hearth. Four men linger in one corner of the tavern, unsteady from drink. By the light of a single candle, they swap cards in silence, indifferent to the knocking at the door and the hammering of the rain on the roof and the sound of the five leaks that drip from the ceiling into five tin cauldrons. Already one of the cauldrons overflows, leaving a puddle the packed dirt floor cannot absorb. She should have emptied it hours ago, the woman perhaps has time to consider, as she lights the oil lamp and goes to answer to the door.

Two men wait outside, sheltering under their capes and sombreros. As soon as the woman turns the key in the lock, they burst into the tavern, stomping their soaking wet boots on the threshold. One of them curses sotto voce; it is unclear if his profanity is directed at the storm, at the night that has caught them unawares in this remote corner of the world, or at the dark-complexioned woman who helps them shrug off their wet overclothes. Their capes are waxy from the rain and when they remove their hats, the last drops splash to the floor. Only after she has hung up their hats and ponchos does the woman have the chance to observe them by the light of the lamp. She sees their eyes and pale skin and coppery beards, she sees the fine shirts they wear, the belts made of thin leather strips, and she sees, above all, their very white hands, clean and most certainly soft, hands made for grazing scrolls or silk and never, ever for working the land. The strangers do not return the woman's look, they take no notice of her, or if they do, they avoid her just as they avoid the attentions of the dog sniffing their riding breeches and leather boots.

The four men at the back of the tavern look up from their cards and jugs of pulque. The whiteness of the newcomers' skin is so extraordinary that the men swivel round, called to attention by the unexpected surprise. The strangers are undoubtedly Spaniards, men of the court perchance, the viceroy's clerks or bureaucrats, and once liberated of their capes and hats they saunter through the tavern slowly and with aplomb.

The strangers finally choose a table. It is surely the cleanest one in the tavern, yet the woman hurries to scrub it with a damp rag. Meanwhile, she recites the list of dishes with which it would be a pleasure to serve the *vuesas mercedes*, Noble Sirs. Your Excellencies must try the house-baked bread. There are two well-ventilated rooms available where, should yYour Graces so desire, you can spend the night. She refers to them in this way, indiscriminately, Your Excellencies, Your Graces, trusting that one of the forms of address is appropriate for the strangers' status. But the strangers don't want food or lodging. Just drink. Two cups of wine. The woman stutters as she informs them that, unfortunately, they have no wine left. They ask for aguardiente, and there is no aguardiente, either. One of the men turns and points to the men playing cards:

"What are they drinking?"

"Pulque, Your Excellency . . . this humble tavern only serves pulque, Your Grace . . . a drink unworthy of your noble palate, sir . . ."

"Pulque, then," the other pronounces.

As they wait, the strangers return to scrutinizing their surroundings. They look at the woman, obviously an Indian, as she enters the galley kitchen to fill their jugs of pulque. They look at the card players at the next table, undoubtedly Indians as well. They observe their callused, dirty hands, their brown skin, their worn clothes, until the Indians in question—unable to withstand the strangers' stares another instant—return, hangdog, to their game. The players appear flustered; they have forgotten whose stake it was. The strangers are satisfied by their discomfort. They look then at the cauldrons strewn randomly on the floor. The hearth. The poorly patched ceiling from which hangs a string of chili peppers and two rather scrawny, unplucked turkeys. A barrel sawn in half to make a seat and a door off its hinges to serve as a table. The row of dirty pulque bowls on the tabletop and the simple wooden cross on the opposite wall, hung out of faith or fear, who knows which, like the hams Jews hung in their shop windows in Castilla. In some spots the floor is laid with round fieldstone; the stone becomes patchier as one advances toward the back of the tavern, and eventually gives way to a simple floor of packed earth, as if someone had once tried to improve the place, but eventually ran out of gold, or hope. On its mat by the fireplace, the dog sighs sorrowfully, in the depths of sleep, subjected, surely, to nightmares.

The woman returns with two jugs of pulque and a plate of fried tortillas no one has requested. Whitish marks from of a pair of lips clearly visible on the rim of one of the jugs. The men stare at the smudge, as if willing it to be erased.

Before she moves off, the woman stoops to perform a complicated curtsy, but one of the men grabs her wrist. There is no violence in his gesture. Just unobjectionable authority, to which she submits with resignation.

"We are looking for a man," he says, and the woman prepares herself to hear.

They are looking for the owner of the tavern, and at the foot of the stairs that lead to the bedchambers, that man finally appears. The strangers watch his approach. They do not move a muscle. They do not stand to receive him. They do not extend their hand in greeting. They do not do, or say, anything. They remain in their seats and from their position judge the man who makes his way toward them, swaying, barely avoiding the cauldrons that catch the raindrops. He appears to be forty or forty-five years old and still has all, or almost all, of his teeth. They look at his messy hair and untidy beard. The blurry eyes. The poorly buttoned shirt. He is, perhaps, a man who has just gotten out of bed, spurred to action by the woman's call, a man who has reached an age when an early night becomes customary practice. He is, perhaps, simply a drunk. The second option is preferable to them: alcohol has always been an excellent companion to difficult enterprises. At least for a certain class of enterprise and certain class of men.

An empty seat waits at the table. One of the men points, with the same imperious hand that grabbed the woman's wrist; now the hand pulls the recent arrival over to the chair, without any need to touch him.

"You are Juan de Toñanes."

It is not a question but a pronouncement, and it takes the tavern owner a moment to respond. In that short span, he thinks many things. He looks at the untouched tortillas and the jugs of pulque, filled to the brim, and the two strangers who haven't deigned to take a single bite, a single sip. The speaker holds his gaze, as if he expects to read a reply there. The second stranger doesn't even bother to glance up. He has taken a small knife from his belt, a gold-handled dagger, not made for waging war but breaking wax seals or slitting the pages of uncut books. He turns to the task of shaping his fingernails, otherwise trimmed and pristine.

"Yes, I am Juan de Toñanes."

And then, attempting nonchalance:

"Of what I am accused?"

"What's that you say?"

"Isn't that why Your Graces are here? To detain me?"

One of the strangers lets out a long laugh. He laughs so long that his companion has time to finish with his left hand and start on the right. No, not at all: the higher ups are very satisfied with Juan. If only he could have been at the palace, hearing how the clerks and the governor and even the viceroy himself spoke of his feats. That is precisely why they have come: to thank him for his service rendered to the Crown, a service noted and recognized by all. And to take advantage of his generosity, perhaps, and request his assistance one more time. That is why they have come so far. And he mustn't be under the impression that he had been easy to find, no. If he knew how many dusty roads, how many towns both large and small, how many leagues they had to deviate from the Camino Real in order to find this godforsaken tavern.

"My assistance?" Juan asks, as if it were impossible to believe that his coarse, scar-laced hands could be of use to anyone. "I regret to tell you, noble sirs, that much time has passed since I last undertook any adventure or enterprise."

The man laughs again. He points to the untouched pulque.

"Well, we certainly haven't come for your wine."

He waves his hand, a vague gesture that encompasses the whole of the tavern. The woman, busying herself in the little kitchen; the four card players, who still appear to be playing, even though they haven't taken their eyes off the strangers.

"All this can be different. The Spanish, as you know, don't go where there is wine, but where there is gold to purchase it."

As he speaks, from his belt the stranger unhooks a wineskin glistening with raindrops. Companionably, he hands it to Juan. Juan holds it for a moment, unsure whether to raise it to his lips or hand it back.

"Come, drink. You're a Spaniard. You know how to appreciate good wine."

Juan takes a long, thorough swig. The wine is delicious: it bears no hint of the stunted vineyards of America, but the rich flavor of Castilla's faraway wineries. When he finishes, Juan wipes his beard on his sleeve and offers the wineskin to the second stranger, perhaps because he assumes the man is thirsty, or to pull him out of his abstraction. The stranger doesn't appear to register the offer. He fiddles with the little dagger, removed from all being said or done at that table.

"Well then, what would the viceroy have me do?" Juan dares to say. The wine has emboldened him.

The second man starts. For an instant, the dagger is still, as if someone had said or done something inappropriate. The other speaks first, attempting to erase Juan's words. Who ever said such a thing? Has he, or his companion, made any reference to the viceroy asking for something, needing something?

Is he insinuating that the viceroy is a beggar who requests charity from his subjects? The viceroy, Juan should know, asks nothing of him. Nothing at all. They are simply relaying an invitation. A mission, he could call it, if it weren't for the fact that the mission will never appear in any record, nor in anybody's memory; neither is anyone ordering or financing it. It is not actually a mission: that must be clear. At yet, if he completes it, the viceroy will heap riches upon him. One could say that it *is* a mission if completed, and that it *isn't* one if—God forbid—it should fail. But even if successful, it can't be called a mission in the strictest sense of the term, since once completed, missions are boasted of in taverns and ports and palace corridors and fortresses, and Juan can never speak of these affairs, no matter the number and class of men who should inquire. Not even in the confessional. Because if God always knows all we do, why bother repeating it? And if He doesn't know, then what are we calling God? Does Juan not agree?

Juan nods. Yes, he says, he agrees, unsure why he is nodding or what he agrees with. His answer appears to satisfy the strangers. The first man continues to speak, more calmly now, and the other returns to tending his nails. Between his fingers, the blade gleams in the firelight, as if he held a miniature sun. Anyway, his companion is saying, now that these questions have been clarified, now that the issue is perfectly understood, we can, for the sake of simplification and instruction, call the mission a mission. And we can even say that it is the viceroy who orders it, though that would be an exaggeration, practically a lie, really. And what the viceroy wants, if the viceroy were to want anything, is very simple, he says, laughing again. It is so uncomplicated for a man with your experience that it almost makes one, well, laugh. You just have to find one specific Indian, somewhere in the Gran Chichimeca. Find him and end his reign, he explains, because they must admit that, as of late, the Indian has garnered a measure of prestige among the savages. You know that's what the Gran Chichimeca is, a savage place, and as enormous as its name suggests. You know it is a wild territory, capable of making the swords of less worthy, less valiant men tremble: a place feared even by the Aztecs, themselves so bloodthirsty—a knowledgeable man like Juan will note that in Náhuatl, the word chichimeca means "dirty and uncivilized dog." But he, the stranger, also knows that someone who, as a youth, took part in the siege of México-Tenochtitlan; someone who pledged his sword to Cristóbal de Olid in the Hibueras and to Nuño de Guzmán in the conquest of New Galicia; someone who made such good slaves of so many on the fields of battle, is not afraid of the Gran Chichimeca or anything else.

At first, Juan doesn't reply. He listens silently, with certain distance, as if the events the man recounts weren't from his very own life, as if they belonged to another man's past. In some ways, this is true: everything the stranger has said seems to have happened to another person. It is difficult to see a soldier in Juan, imagine him with his helmet and arquebus, his own horse and his spoils of war. One could not be faulted for imagining that he had been there forever, serving jugs of pulque and corn tortillas in a tavern slowly rotting away at the edge of the world.

"The Indian . . . is he Chichimeca?" Juan asks, attempting a soldierly tone.

"No. He's from this area. Tlaxcalteca, I believe."

Juan shakes his head. He reaches to tear off a piece of cold tortilla and put it in his mouth, as if the mention of war has brought back his appetite, or courage.

"Then your job is done."

"What do you mean?"

"There is only one thing the Chichimeca hate more than a Christian, and that's the Tlaxcalteca. You can assume your Indian is dead."

The second stranger looks up suddenly from his hands and dagger. His eyes are blue and dead, or the closest thing to death Juan can recall. They are eyes that have only ever contemplated horror after it has been transformed into figures, memorials, files. Eyes that have never seen more bloodshed than a red speck on a hastily-shaven neck, and perhaps that is why this man is so bored of demanding the blood of others from behind his clerkship, not comprehending what it is he demands.

"Not this Indian," that man says, and his voice is so hard, so heavy, that it is proof enough.

For a time, no one speaks. The second stranger has turned his focus back to his dagger and his spotless nails and the other is staring at Juan, waiting. The only sound is the slap of the cards on the table behind him, the *plink* of water on water, the din the woman makes with crockery and pots in the kitchen, where in fact there is nothing left to be cleaned.

"What has this Indian done that so concerns Your Graces? Did he take a maiden by force? Set fire to a church? Go for the throat of the viceroy himself?"

The first stranger shakes his head, a faint smile still on his lips. The reasons, he says, are unimportant. He says they are not going to give him those reasons, but that they do have a thousand gold reasons to give the man who finds him, each one stamped with the likeness of King Juan Carlos, God save him. He says the gold comes from high up and so do the orders and the higher ups are never mistaken, and if they are, then they—those below, that is—are never the wiser. Therefore, if Juan wants to accept the mission, the mission that, strictly speaking, is not a mission and which nobody has ordered, he will have to forget about explanations and settle for the gold. And gold, he adds, encouraged by Juan's renewed attention, is capable of things many men wouldn't believe. Enough doubloons can turn the most ramshackle tavern into a prosperous one; a stop along the Camino Real, even; with fresh horses and abundant wine and Christian customers; no leaky roofs and no Indian maids behind the counter, but good Castilian girls to serve drink without shame or disgrace.

For a moment, Juan observes the mouth that has just issued those words.

"That woman is not a maid," he says. "She is my wife."

A heavy pause.

"I've already told Your Graces that I was done catching Indians a long time ago."

His voice would like to command respect, but only begs forgiveness.

"I understand," the second stranger says, sheathing his dagger.

The men get slowly to their feet, as though they want to give Juan time to regret his decision. But Juan doesn't have regrets, and if he does, he doesn't dare voice them. He stands as well, slowly, with difficulty, perhaps in imitation of their movements, perhaps because so many years with the sword have left their mark.

Before moving to the door, the second stranger turns his blue eyes on Juan. They will stay in the village for three days, he says. Not an hour more. Juan has until then to change his mind. As the man speaks, he rummages in his waist pouch. It looks like he might be about to shake Juan's hand, but no. Instead, he pulls out a coin and tosses it in a contemptuous arc. A coin, nothing but a flash of gold cruising through the air, before vanishing with a white splash into a jug of pulque.

The woman joins them at the door. She helps the strangers into their capes and hats, now dry, or almost dry, from the fire's warmth. Juan thinks he perceives a peculiar glint in the men's eyes when they look at his wife, not unlike the look they gave the jugs of pulque. The corn tortillas. The five leaks in ceiling, ringing in the depths of the five tin cauldrons.

Juan who is seated, again, at the same table. The card players who leave a copper vellon before they depart; Juan who is already draining the first jug of pulque.

The wife who snuffs out the candles and lights the oil lamp and climbs the stairs to the bedroom; Juan who has just started on the second jug. Before she disappears, the wife gives him a look from the stairs, lamp in hand. The look is an invitation Juan pretends not to understand. Finally, she goes. The wife disappears without a word and Juan remains downstairs. Juan and one empty jug of pulque and another one half-finished. Juan and the hearth fire still emanating a posthumous glow; Juan and the sleeping dog and the wind whistling through the beams. Juan surrounded by cauldrons into which the rainless night continues to rain.

The wife who said nothing as she went up to bed and Juan who says nothing when he stays where he is.

There are many things Juan doesn't say. His is a silent and prudent tavern, and a strange one for it. He never asks questions. He serves liquor and tortillas in silence, doesn't inquire of travelers where they come from or where they're headed. It's hard to say if there's anything in the world that interests him. He doesn't want news from the capital or from across the ocean. He doesn't care about the health of kings or popes or their war campaigns. When he's asked a question, he replies with as few syllables as possible, as if each one cost him gold he does not have. That isn't the case, of course. Words are free and the drink served in that tavern is almost free as well, since his customers are poor and in short supply and he can't risk losing them. Sometimes he rents out a couple of damp, gloomy rooms, only countenanced by the most desperate of travelers, two rooms so like ship bunks or coffins or cellars. He charges little. Almost all the guests are Indians. Only occasionally, by chance or negligence, does some Spanish pilgrim arrive at the tavern; someone who got lost in the sierra or wandered off the Camino Real or was robbed by bandits or all three at once.

Whenever he sees one of those Spaniards stamping their feet on the threshold, Juan is unsure whether he should be pleased or sorry. The questions asked by this class of men are always more direct, more incisive. They don't allow for evasion. For instance, they want to know if by chance Juan fought against the Aztecs. I did, Juan replies, hopeful those two words will suffice, and when it turns out they do not, he condescends to add what the travelers have come to hear: a tale so oft repeated that it no longer seems his own. Perhaps it never was. He speaks of the pyramids where the Aztecs performed their fiendish rituals; of the piles of human skulls he saw rise in unbelievable numbers from the base of those temples; he speaks of their battle cudgels and war cries and their terrible feathered heads. What he does not tell, what he will never tell, is that he also

NOT EVEN THE DEAD

saw those same heads severed and skewered on Spanish swords; he saw their bodies shot through by arquebuses or pierced with lances or gnawed down to the bones by the dogs, with a relish not mentioned in the memorials and war chronicles.

If they ask him about Nuño de Guzmán, he replies that the man was a good warrior, the best of all who have trod these lands, because any other response would be an insult to the memory of his many feats. He doesn't say how, in New Galicia, he saw that man murder women and children, nor how Guzmán ordered his native caudillos to be tortured for days, demanding they reveal the whereabouts of implausible treasures.

If, surprised to see him bent over the tavern's accounts, the travelers ask whether he knows how to read and write, he replies that he does, barely. He doesn't say that as a child, in a faraway village in the mountains of Castilla, there was a certain parish priest who, despite Juan's humble origins, liked him or believed in him enough to teach him grammar and even some notion of Latin and theology, in hopes it might lead to a vocation. He doesn't say how there was, in fact, a time when all was hope.

If they are curious about the payment he received for his many services to the Crown, he answers that the war booty allowed him to live well during the years that followed. He doesn't say that he had to beg and plead in church doorways; he doesn't say that he got hungry enough to chew the leather of his breastplate; nor that he raised pigs or dug ditches or cleaned the boots of men who had never fired a crossbow or slept in a tent. He doesn't speak—what for?—of the year he spent in the Veracruz countryside, dealing, by order of the viceroy, with the plague of dogs that had infested the highlands; the sons and grandsons and even great-grandsons of those same dogs that had aided in the conquest of New Spain in earlier years. He doesn't say how, for a year, he was devoted to hunting them down, slitting their throats, putting their heads in sacks and presenting them to the constables: a one-real coin a head; each dog's life worth three hot meals. He doesn't say how, on his last incursion, he faced off against a dog that was ancient but no less terrible for it, the iron collar his last master fastened on him embedded in his neck; a dog that might have traveled to America in the hold of Juan's own ship; suffered with him, perhaps, the rigors of hunger and war and oblivion. And most of all he doesn't say what he did with the dog's corpse: how it didn't cross his mind, not for a second, to cut off its head and stick it in a sack. How he dug him a roomy grave, a worthy grave, a grave that many of Juan's companions-at-arms would have desired for themselves, and he buried him in it, a cadaver that was the last of its kind, as well as Juan's last hope for three hot meals, all covered by a mound of dirt and a cloak of dry leaves and even Juan's tears, because the shameful fact is that he cried, he knelt beside that dog's grave and cried until his sorrow passed or he grew tired; he cried for the dog and he cried for himself and he cried for the stomach that would remain empty another night.

If by chance someone has heard it told that he had, for a time, hunted runaway Indians from the encomiendas of Puebla and asks why he gave up said profession, he replies that the pay was poor. Or that he got too old for some things. Or that he inherited this tavern and preferred the flow of alcohol to the flow of blood. He doesn't say how on his last mission—back when missions were still called missions—he managed to bring in fourteen runaway Indians, heavily-shackled; nor how, as he was being paid the doubloons owed him, he heard the screams proffered by those fourteen Indians as they were whipped and scourged, their bodies branded like cattle. He doesn't talk about the smell of burnt skin. Nor does he say that this tavern wasn't born of any inheritance or stroke of luck, but an unfortunate purchase: he had been told the Camino Real would pass nearby; all said and done and even dusted in the viceroy's palace, he was told, but ultimately the palace made other arrangements and in the end, as was always the case in his life, he chose the wrong path.

If they ask if he is a married man, he replies that he is and turns to busy himself with some task: cleaning the basins, sweeping the tavern, turning the turkey roasting on the spit, hoping they won't ask whether his wife might be that Indian woman on her hands and knees scrubbing the floor.

Juan asks no questions and answers no questions, or he does so with the fewest words possible. This means that, in some sense, he's always alone. And so tonight—while he drinks alone, while he feels alone in the middle of the empty tavern—is no less solitary a night than any other night over the past five years.

He drinks the last drop from the last jug like someone choking down a thought. That's when he sees it: a golden gleam in the dregs of pulque. It's the stranger's coin, and upon it the face of His Majesty Carlos, God save him. Juan doesn't speak. The sovereign's face doesn't speak either. What would a king speak of, if kings spoke. Of what would their laments consist. What does a king remember, and what does he keep to himself. Juan rescues the coin with sticky fingers. Briefly, he weighs it in the air. A gold escudo. Enough to buy this round of pulque and fifty more. Enough to buy a barrel of good Castilian wine.

This is what he thinks. And then, mid-thought, Juan surprises himself with an unexpected action: he holds the coin aloft, featherweight and beautiful—fifty rounds of pulque that a man can lift with a single finger—only to cast it into the fire, in a startling flash of clairvoyance. The momentary crackle of wood and then nothing. The coin does not burn, nor does the king; but Juan does burn, or appears to. The look in his eyes, at least. His face. The hearth-flames igniting his eyes and those eyes slowly filling with flickers of gold.

He climbs the dark stairs, still wobbly from the alcohol. He knocks into a piece of furniture or a corner that hadn't seemed to be there that morning. The wooden stairs creak and shudder under his feet and the door to the bedroom squeaks a feeble lament and the whole house protests unanimously with noise, as if resisting that he should be the one to live in it. Does he live in this house? Has this house ever been his home? He hates its flaking walls and the roof about to cave in with every storm and he hates the tavern when it is full and when it's empty too. He hates the shelter it provides, just like the soldier hates the tent that protects him from the night. Yet while the soldier is cursing the tent, at least he is dreaming of home or at least a certain idea of home. Where would be Juan's home, if such a home existed?

He worries over the question as he slides into bed and settles his body against that of his wife. Home, he thinks at that moment, could be—or could be like—this. Home, he repeats to himself—feeling intense shame as he does—might not be a place but a feeling. This one, for instance: the feeling of his wife's body. Her temperature: the warmth she holds for him every night. A scent: the scent of her hair spread over the pillow. How could he ever confess that at times, in this very bed, under this tumbledown roof, he has believed himself to be the happiest of men. How could he explain to another Castilian that during certain moments on certain nights he has come to feel what many men never come to feel except for a white woman. He cannot. He cannot explain and perhaps he does not wish to. Is this not a woman's way of reasoning? Is he some slut, softening under a few strokes and tender words? No: he is not a woman, he tells himself, as if he has just reached that conclusion. He is not a woman, and he is ashamed of feeling the sort of things he feels and thinking the things he thinks.

Most of his customers believe he married her because there weren't enough marriageable Castilian women in the colony, the available ones being quickly doled out, just like the privileges, encomiendas, and titles were doled out at first. That's what they think. That is, perhaps, what his own wife thinks. After all, the word "love" has never been spoken between them. They didn't say it then and they do not say it now. But there are, generally speaking, many words Juan is reluctant to say. Many are the things he prefers not to recount. He doesn't recount, for instance, what he felt the first time he saw her, bent over a stone, grinding corn. How, the instant he touched her, the thought occurred to him that the skin, darker or whiter, that covers the men's and women's bodies might only be that, a simple casing. That's the rubbish he used to think, still thinks sometimes, when he takes refuge in his wife's lap, contravening the thesis of so many illustrious doctors and men of science. What happens to him then is what is happening to him now: in the darkened room he embraces his wife's shadow, colorless, raceless, and silently begs her forgiveness: forgiveness for wishing with all his might that his Spanish customers didn't ask if his Indian servant is by chance his wife. But these thoughts, he thinks, are also womanly thoughts, and he is no damsel, sighing and fainting before one's own sentiments and the sentiments of others. With that, he angrily swipes them from his head, as if waving away a cluster of flies.

He closes his eyes but does not sleep. The thoughts come so swiftly on his side of the bed that he is surprised that, over on her side, his wife can even close her eyes. He sees his wife, five or six years younger, once again bent over the stone for grinding corn, and he sees a dog's grave, and he sees Nuño de Guzmán laughing louder than the tortured screams of his indigenous caudillos. He sees fourteen Indians arranged in a long line and laden in chains. He sees two strangers at the table, awaiting his answer, and a bag that holds a thousand gold escudos, and he sees an Indian, a single Indian, who is faceless and hides in the brush and weighs the same as the bag. Then he sees the moon. Not in his memory but out the window, illuminating the room with a livid glow and tearing shadows and chiaroscuros from every object. He sees the motionless swell of his sleeping wife. His sleeping wife who is not asleep. The milky shaft of light that falls suddenly and directly upon her open eyes. Those eyes shine with a strange light. A light, Juan thinks, not entirely owed to the moon. She seems about to ask him something, and Juan knows the question well before she opens her mouth. The wife who needs to know, who demands to know, who those strangers were and what they wanted: what proposition did they make and what answer did he give. This is exactly what she's about to ask and Juan knows it, and in the last seconds between silence and word, he tries to decide what he will say.

The wife opens and closes her mouth more than once, as if hesitating. Finally, she speaks.

"Did you remember to bolt the door?"

Silence.

"Yes," he says.

Rising like every morning. With the rooster's crow, as they say, though they have no rooster. Coming down the wooden stairs, prompting the house's first groans in the early morning. The wife who sweeps the dirt floor. The wife who empties the tin cauldrons and sets them out again. The wife who goes and comes from the well. The wife who rinses the dirty basins in a brass washtub and cleans the tables and takes the filth out to the pig while she sings under her breath, a dark song with something of a pagan resonance. And Juan who watches her. Juan sitting in a chair, conscious of her every expression, her every movement. Juan who, in his imagination, undresses her: his wife without her Indian overskirt, his wife without her humble garb and cheap earrings. His wife clad in increasingly expensive attire, mantillas and ruffs, farthingales and gowns, fashion come from afar to hide a little bit more of a woman's body, a woman's skin; his wife who, underneath all those silks and flounces, could be—why not?—a white woman. His wife who no longer feeds the pig or washes pots or needs to set cauldrons on the floor; a recently retiled roof overhead and two servants—three servants, maybe five—bustling to attend to the crowds of guests. And outside, on the other side of the window, her diminutive parcel of land would stretch as far as the eye can see, so vast it can only be covered on horseback; to that end, a horse, two horses, the ramshackle stables rebuilt and in them a horse for him and a horse for her; a dozen horses for their servants and head shepherds. The cobs of corn growing so plump the kernels burst and his wife who is swelling too, his wife's body that once seemed dry as the dirt but no, neither the woman nor the earth were barren, his harvest flourishes and the tavern flourishes and his son flourishes, too; something to watch grow in the midst of life, which slows to a stop. This is what he sees: life, slowing, stopping. His son a fine young man now, with his own horse and his own motivations, giving orders left and right to one hundred, maybe two hundred, overseers. And inside, watching from the window, he and his wife, the two of them still, old but not so very old, eyes young and satisfied with seeing how it grows, this world they built with their own hands.

He sees all this while his wife goes to the cold hearth to light the fire that will warm their breakfast.

"I'll take care of the fire," Juan says.

Before lighting the logs, he burrows his hands in the stiff ash. It isn't long before he finds it: the coin shines with the same intensity, like a hope that nothing and no one can extinguish.

We knew you would change your mind, the first of the viceroy's agents is saying. Don't ask us how, but we knew. Did we say it or not? he asks, turning to his companion. Yes: they said it. It was, perhaps, due to the many years they've been dedicated to this profession. One learns to look men in the eye and know what they have inside. One learns to distinguish the braggarts and louts from the real soldiers. And they knew very well that he is just that: a soldier. A courageous man, determined and valiant. They knew it the moment they laid eyes on him. That he had taken a full day to consider their proposal simply confirms what they already knew: he is a man of straight talk and straight sword, not one of those tavern blowhards whose strength leaks through their mouth. And speaking of mouths, might Juan like a cup of good wine? Because this posada has a first-class wine, a wine worthy of the tables of gentlemen and princes . . . Ah! No? They'd expected no less. He is a decisive man then, one who wishes to make his own decisions, judgement unclouded by alcohol. Another trait for them to celebrate. So, they best get straight to the point, as is popularly said. And that point is, without any doubt, Juan the Indian. Yes, he and the man he will pursue from this day forth share the same name: Juan. It is not for them to say if the coincidence of their names is a question of fate or divine will. The fact is, Juan is here, listening to these words, and Juan the Indian, well, Lord knows where Juan the Indian is. The most recent reports placed him, as they already said, somewhere in the Gran Chichimeca. That's all they know, that's as far as their knowledge goes, as far as their eyes have reached: from now on, Juan's eyes will be their eyes. And now surely Juan will want to know what Juan the Indian looks like; unfortunately, they cannot help with that. Does Juan know what Juan the Indian looks like, perchance? the stranger asks, throwing up his hands theatrically. Well: neither do they. No one knows what he's like, not with any accuracy. Well, there are some who know. They've managed to find a few who knew him a little and even one or two who knew him well. He is referring to the teachers at the Colegio de la Santa Cruz Tlatelolco, where Juan the Indian studied. Because you see, he says, the Indian you must find is a well-educated man: who knows—given past events—why some still insist on educating the Indians. But this isn't relevant at present. The important thing is that before he reaches the Gran Chichimeca, he will make a stop at Tlatelolco. He will visit Juan the Indian's old schoolmasters and he will keep his eyes and ears wide open. Little or nothing is known of Juan the Indian's childhood, how he lived before he arrived at that school. They say he was one of the children taken in by the Franciscan monks of San Francisco Cuitlixco, in the neighboring city of Ocotelulco, but who knows whether that is truth or legend. With Juan's visit to Tlatelolco, they'll have more than enough. What's that? You also want to visit the monastery in Cuitlixco, in the event you might find something useful? Upon my soul, you are a thorough and dutiful man. They can see that the viceroy didn't exaggerate a wit when he recounted Juan's many feats. But honestly, after so long, they highly doubt anyone is left in Cuitlixco who remembers Juan the Indian, or even that the monastery still stands. But if that's his wish, they will guide him there, too. Can Juan read, perchance? Good Heavens! It seems you, too, are an educated man, exclaims the viceroy's henchman, no expression of relief on his face. A literate soldier: now this is a surprise indeed. In that case, they will put down all he needs to know in writing. The route he will take and the people he must see. After that, it will just be Juan and Juan. Well: the Chichimeca and Juan and Juan. Better yet: the Chichimeca and Juan and Juan and God, of course. By the way, does Juan happen to be a religious man, in addition to an educated one? They ask because, for such a mission, they do not want sanctimonious or illuminist-types. If Juan can set aside what he thinks he knows about Christ Our Lord and his teachings, all the better. They aren't hiring a theologian. They are hiring a soldier. Does Juan want to be that soldier? Then enough words. On the other hand, Juan can rest assured that all material aspects of the expedition will be seen to. How much does he think he will need to conclude his enterprise? Two hundred fifty gold escudos? Well, here they are. Juan can do what he likes with them. Perhaps on reaching the Gran Chichimeca, he might find it opportune to hire a dozen mercenaries to join him; as he is surely well aware, the Chichimeca are not fond of receiving guests inside their domain. The Chichimeca mightn't even be men at all: at least not in the strictest sense of the word. There's plenty more to say on that subject, of course. But they won't. They will do just one thing: hand him a bag with two hundred fifty gold coins, and a horse so he can travel as fast as possible. When he returns, he will receive the thousand escudos they have promised. He has their word as soldiers. And the word of a good soldier, as he undoubtedly knows, is worth a great deal. It is not the word of God, but very like it. And speaking of God and His words, perhaps Juan is aware of the latest troubling news arriving from the capital. It seems an epidemic has been unleashed among the natives of this land. Among the Indians, that is. A malady that strikes Indians and shies away from Castilians, as if God had different designs for each population. The symptoms, according to the stories, are terrible. Within two days, the sick cry out in desperation for their relatives to kill them. In five or six days, it's generally all over. What does God mean to say through such signs? the henchman asks, looking up toward the ceiling. They have asked the same themselves, to be sure. Could God be punishing all Indians because of one Indian, as Herod sacrificed a whole generation in order to eliminate a single child? Only God knows the answer to that question. All he can say is that the epidemic has wreaked havoc in certain areas of the viceroyalty. Some encomiendas have had to suspend operations, what with so many dead bodies piling up in the fields. They have seen one of the sick men and can attest that it is not a pretty sight. It is, in fact, highly unpleasant. Unpleasant, he confesses, though possibly useful as a last resort. Because perhaps the epidemic will catch up to Juan the Indian before Juan himself does and then they would all be pleased. But, he clarifies, if that doesn't happen, that's where you come in. What's that you say? Kill Juan the Indian? No: they've said no such thing. Now, has either he, or his companion—such a completely quiet man—said anything of the sort? Would they dare ask Juan to stand in for the course of justice? No, absolutely not: they would not ask that of him. He must not kill Juan the Indian. They repeat it, in case he is hard of hearing: He must not kill Juan the Indian. The instructions are clear: he is to bring him to the competent authorities. Who is the competent authority? Ah! There is much to debate in that regard, as well, the man reasons. In a way, what brings them to this thorny question is a matter of spiritual order, which means that, in this case, the competent authority is or should be the apostolic inquisitor. But Juan will know that, since the unfortunate execution of the Indian Carlos Ometochtzin, the Holy Office has been, shall we say, reluctant to take the Indians to the stakes, so the inquisitor might not be the appropriate person after all. Bring him before the ecclesiastical judge. Or better yet: don't bring him before the ecclesiastical judge. One has to think big. Let's consider this a civil matter, the man resolves. The Indians are also civilians, are they not? Then he can bring him before whomever he chooses. Bring him before the council in the first Christian city he steps in. To the Secretary of the Council of the Indies. The Governor General of the Royal Audiencia of New Galicia is as good an option as any, although quite possibly the Governor General won't know what Juan and his Indian are talking about and will refer them both to the viceroy.

Fine: then they should go to the viceroy. Now, he must remember that the viceroy has not entrusted him with any mission and perhaps won't even remember who he is. A fiendish imbroglio, the matter of competent authorities, and one Juan will have to ponder and resolve while he ponders and resolves the more pressing problem of finding Juan the Indian and getting him in chains, which won't be an easy task either, come to think of it. Because it is known, admits the viceroy's henchman with a sigh, that some men become enraged when they are about be taken captive and will not consent to the chains, especially when they have good reason to believe that what awaits them at the end of the journey is the end of the noose. It doesn't take much imagination, then, to suppose that Juan the Indian might be tempted to resist capture, long before Juan is presented with the dilemma of determining which competent authority will judge him. And in the case of resistance, and only that case, it would be understandable if Juan found himself obliged to draw his sword. Or it might happen that, during the course of the long journey back, his prisoner is tempted to escape, and then nothing should impede Juan from raising his weapon. There are some things a man cannot tolerate, and if Juan the Indian does or even thinks of doing one of those things, who could blame Juan? Under these limited circumstances, wouldn't Juan be the very same competent authority he seeks? Now: the truth is, if such a thing were to occur—it won't, God willing—everything becomes simpler. The head would be enough. A head in a sack doesn't cause nearly as much trouble as a man with two arms and two legs. And he wouldn't have to present Juan the Indian before any viceroy or vicar-general or inquisitor; after all, what an awkward gift for such respectable men. They themselves, the ones speaking to him now, would be as good a judge as any to determine if the mandate had been fulfilled. Perhaps at this point, Juan might be wondering what they, who have never seen Juan the Indian, will do in order know whether he's brought them the right head. Ah! Good heavens, don Juan de Toñanes, you certainly have your own head on straight. How to recognize someone you've never seen? The question is a fiendish one, but the answer is simple. It seems, at least according to information that has reached his ears, that Juan the Indian has in his possession a certain book Their Excellencies wish to be retrieved. A book so notorious they would not expect Juan the Indian to rid himself of it, just as they assume he wouldn't consent to doing without his own head. Well, that's all the proof they need: Juan the Indian's head and the book in question, both tucked nice and neat at the bottom of a sack. Or Juan the Indian walking on his own two feet, laden with chains, and the book under his arm. Those are posed. She doesn't respond. She doesn't remind him of his age, or the illness that kept him in bed last winter for a whole month. She doesn't speak of his inglorious glory days. She simply extends her indigenous hand to help her husband return, after five years, to the saddle. He achieves it on the third try. And then, when it seems they have said all they had to say and Juan is ready to spur his mount, she keeps her hand on the bridle a moment longer.

"What has this man done, for them to be so generous with you? Did he take a maiden by force? Set fire to a church? Go for the throat of the viceroy himself?"

Juan looks away from her.

"I don't know. I forgot to ask."

The dream, the adventure, the fantasy that begins. Juan who sways clumsily on his mount. Juan who has a sense of vertigo, a combination of excitement and grief. Upon reaching the crossroads, he turns momentarily to look at the house growing farther away in the distance. He sees the house that grows ever more distant and out front, the wife who grows more distant as well. Her mouth is slightly agape, as if petrified in a grimace of dread: an expression in which there is no surprise, just the confirmation of something already known but no less intolerable for it. She is looking at him. Inside him. Maybe right through him. She looks in a terrible way, as one looks at terrible things that have happened and the even more terrible things still to come; eyes divested of all volition and all beauty, eyes that have seen horror and are filled with it and therefore excruciating to look at, or perhaps they have seen horror and are empty for that very reason, though that emptiness itself is even more unbearable. Eyes that reflect nothing now, eyes that are what remains of compassion when faith is erased; freedom, when justice is withheld; will, when it lacks hands and a voice. Hope minus hope.

Juan spurs on the horse. He feels the weight of that gaze as he moves away, trotting at first and then galloping, galloping ever faster, and he feels that weight still, much later when, at a bend in the road, the wife and her eyes disappear.

II

The Old World and the New World – Two weeks – A right place and a wrong time – In the beginning was the fire – Child among children – The cuckoo's nest – First manifestation of Christ – Thirty silver coins – A brief return home

There was a time when he was a regular inhabitant of the roads and the posadas that cropped up along them. He doesn't know what to do with those memories now. From his horse he sees things he has seen before and which now, after so many years, appear anew. He sees pine groves and embankments and labyrinthine fields and hills that still bear their pagan names and from which rise Castilian belltowers and villages. He sees, revealed in the light of the sunset, the snowy peaks of Popocatépetl and Iztaccíhuatl, which in Indian memory were a pair of dead lovers and now are but two extinct volcanos. He sees corn crops, but also vineyards and wheat threshing floors and common pastures where flocks of sheep and herds of cattle graze, all come there from the other side of the Mar Oceana. Every so often, there is a small settlement or river bearing a Christian name, as if it sought to conjure in him a kind of nostalgia. He only has to say the name of that village, of that river, of that small mountain, to feel even farther away from home.

Is Castilla his home? Is it the dilapidated tavern he leaves behind? Is his home the woman who waits in that tavern, still fixed in the doorway, perhaps, eyes still rooted on the road down which her husband has disappeared?

Juan tolerates these questions but not their answers. He only has eyes for the world around him. A beggar waiting on the side of the road, his empty palm outstretched to the travelers on foot. A handful of Indians hauling away the shrouded corpses of three plague victims. On either side of the road, poor ranches and remnants of a crumbling pyramid devoured by ivy. Croplands and garden plots stretch on, and in them a few men who give orders and many others who obey. Throngs of Indians hammer the dirt with their hoes and coas as if to demonstrate that the same universal law applies in this part of the world, too: namely, that all things worth possessing have an owner, and that collecting even the remnants of those things requires great effort. Maybe it's just that all land looks alike. Or that the Spaniards have had time to convert the New World into an extension of the Old. Juan observes all of this in silence, the way one observes the sawdust on the floor after a long while spent whittling a hope.

Two weeks. This is how it has been for some time: two weeks left for almost everything. Things he doesn't want to do—or things he wants to do but suspects will never happen—are put off for a conjectural length of time that always lasts two weeks. Two weeks were what the viceroy needed to approve his encomienda request and two weeks for the Audiencia to grant him a small lifetime pension and two weeks for the stroke of luck that would change everything. In two weeks he would finish laying the stones on the tavern floor. And just as he departed, when his wife asked how long before his return, Juan did not hesitate: two weeks, he replied, even though it was virtually impossible; even though he would need much more than two weeks to even reach the lands of the Chichimeca, not to mention the time required to find Juan the Indian, the time required to capture him, to receive his compensation, to journey home. Two weeks, he said, looking his wife in the eye, and she responded to her husband's temporal calculation the way she usually did: with a nod and an attempted smile.

Two weeks, Juan thinks astride his horse, his eyes lost on the boundless horizon.

Just two more weeks.

He reaches Ocotelulco at mid-morning one particular day, it doesn't matter which. There isn't a soul in the main square or on the village streets. Everywhere closed doors and turned latches and shutters that appeared to have been nailed over the windows. The funereal tolling of a bell somewhere. On the street corner, a tavern without a tavern keeper or customers, the tables empty and desolate, the kitchen fires extinguished, not a single horse tied up outside the door. Juan thinks of another tavern and the woman who is now surely overseeing its solitude; she, too, with closed shutters and empty tables and the dregs of pulque that nobody will drink, rotting at the bottom of earthenware jugs. That thought lasts in his head as long as Juan will allow it, which is to say, not long.

The San Francisco Cuitlixco monastery should stand on the banks of the Zahuapan river, and beside it, the outbuildings of the Franciscan school. So say his papers. After much wandering through deserted streets, he finds something akin to an abandoned abbey, and beside it, some crumbling walls that might have belonged to a school. There is nobody in what was once the convent's portico, nor in the atrium. High up, a small belltower holds out, no bell within. Juan looks at his papers at length and then looks at the parched adobe walls and the wooden benches rotting in the damaged nave and back down at his papers. Free of its master's attention, the horse sets off meandering down the atrium passageways, snuffling at the plumes of grass that grow between the tiles, hooves echoing underfoot like the tread of a phantom cavalry.

That's when Juan sees him. At first, he doesn't look like a friar, but a dead friar's soul in purgatory. He lies prostrate in the chapel, before the empty corner where an altar once stood, a hood covering his face. At the sound of Juan's footfall, he ceases his prayers and, with difficulty, gets to his feet. Upright, he still looks ghostly. His body is gaunt and ungainly, and his habit hangs too big on him, as if clinging to air.

"Is that you, Fray Bernardo?" the man asks.

"No. I just . . ."

"I thought you were Fray Bernardo."

And then, motioning listlessly:

"Come nearer the light, where I can see you."

Juan takes one, two, three steps toward the old man. And an old man he is: drawing close is enough to confirm it. Visible under his yellowed, bloodless skin, the skull he will one day become is beginning to show. His eyes are dimmed by an opaque curtain, but still, a sort of light shines in them; a sort of intelligence that studies Juan in the gloom.

"You are a soldier," he says slowly, and it's unclear whether it is a question or assertion, whether his voice contains approval or condemnation or mere curiosity.

"I'm just a man seeking information, father."

stand. How can the friar explain the way that even now, after so many years, he remembers everything that Indian did and said. That Indian who, back then, wasn't more than seven or eight years old. And yet, you see, he remembers. He often slips back to that period: a time when this land was or seemed to be filled with miracles, miracles among which little Juan's existence wasn't the least surprising. The year he is referring to was a year like any other, the friar says. Personally, he doesn't keep track of such things, of the passing time. What are a few years compared to a people's salvation or the eternal nature of the soul? All he can say is that what he is about to tell him occurred very early on, almost at the beginning of it all. At the beginning of what, he might wonder. What else: at the beginning of His work. Does he know that bit about the harvest being plentiful but the laborers few? Wherefore pray to the Lord of the harvest, to send forth laborers. One needn't be learned to understand. The Indians are the harvest. And the Lord of the harvest, of course, is God. And they, the friars, are His laborers. They crossed the ocean to reap the Lord's harvest, to win more souls for Him than for the Devil, who had stolen from Him with his Turks in Europe and his Lutherans in Germany. They sought no other compensation than a few tortillas, some tamales, swigs of water. They didn't even have shoes. Perhaps Juan has heard it told, if not seen it with his own eyes: the monks journeyed barefoot from Veracruz to Cuidad de México. They saw the Indians' bare feet and they removed their sandals. They saw that the Indians didn't have enough to eat and so they suffered hunger with them. They saw they barely had clothing and slept on the ground, so they covered themselves with habits of rough sackcloth and slept on the dirt, a stick or fistful of grass for a headboard. The Indians crowded along the path to watch them pass, lamenting how poor, how forsaken the friars looked. Perhaps that is why they earned the Indians' respect early on. Because they too were poor and they sat at their table, with no lust for gold or silver. The only substance they sought was the stuff their souls were made of. That's what they did, they concerned themselves with the Indians' souls, not their flesh, as it is written that the flesh is like grass that dries out and all the glory of man like the flower of that grass; that gold and silver will tarnish and rot and their moldering will bear witness against us. It was not an easy thing, in the beginning, because they didn't yet speak the Indians' language and had to preach using drawings or signs. It was almost comical. If the endeavor the Lord had commended unto them had not been of such consequence, they surely would have laughed; wandering through the markets, not knowing what to do or say, pointing up at the sky to signify God and down at the ground to allude to the Devil. When they said *Devil*, they crouched like vermin and contorted their faces frightfully, and to personify the grace of God, they mimicked beatific rapture, which came easily to them. The Indians, of course, thought they were mad. Mad or drunk. But the monks persevered, employing some truly astonishing methods, as well as others that are not pleasant to recall. For instance, he once met a certain Fray Luis de Caldera, who passed through villages with a cage full of cats and a kind of oven on a pushcart, calling out and ringing a handbell in order to draw the greatest possible number of Indians. Once the crowd had gathered, he set to lighting a fire in the oven and tossing in the cats. The animals howled and caterwauled terribly during the time they took to die, which, depending on the oven's temperature, could take a rather long time. This is Hell, he would say. The Indians, even more horrified, would look at Fray Luis uncomprehendingly. This, he would repeat, is Hell. And what he meant was, if those animals could barely tolerate the fire's torment for mere moments, what to say of the punishment of Hell and its eternal flame? The scene was repeated in village and after village, and it's worth wondering, muses the friar, if anything worthwhile came from so much burned wood and so many dead cats. If, from that suffering, the Indians learned any lessons about the nature of God. Maybe not, but no one could deny that the Caldera fellow did everything he could. Because here in the Indies, in the beginning it wasn't the Word, as the apostle would have it, but mute silence. In the beginning was fire. In the beginning was the desperate wailing of cats, dying in order to testify: to replace with their cries the words some did not know how to speak.

But again, I digress, says the friar, waving his hand before his eyes. They are sitting under the ribbed vault of the transept, where the wooden nerves of church intertwine and merge, and from there they watch the slow sinking of the sun and the lengthening shadows the pillars cast. Right over their heads someone has painted, with childish ingenuity, several scenes from Christ's life. The paintings are clumsy and imperfect, but the dampness has contributed to the growth of mold and cracks which lend the figures a degree of prehistoric solemnity. The friar observes, or appears to observe, the cave art drawings. The two men contemplating the paintings and the horse contemplating the two men with the same absorption, as if they too were shadows chalked on the wall, not entirely real and not entirely important. But I digress, he says again, I'm still thinking of when we hadn't yet learned the Indians' language, when I should speak precisely of the moment we did learn it. Because with time, thanks to the

Lord's mercy, we learned. This is what the friar says, raising his eyes theatrically to the heavens, as if he were again preaching to his faithful through gestures. Thanks to the Lord's mercy and the children, of course. Playing among them with sticks and stones, being children at their side, that was how the monks gradually learned some words and eventually whole sentences. The children were their teachers. That has always been Our Almighty God's way, has it not: to ennoble the humble and take down the mighty. The mercies He has shown men in His infinite benevolence have always been implemented through low instruments of little regard. Just think of His own Son, in fact. Was anything in the world more scorned and despised than the sacred humanity of our Redeemer Jesus Christ, who was insulted, slapped, spit-upon, mocked in a thousand ways, the friar exclaims; and yet, how simply He chose him to bring about the redemption of the human race, the most magnificent and precious thing He ever made. And so it was in later years, as well, when He achieved the conversion of kings, emperors, and the noblest lords through a few poor and shunted fishermen, unlettered men, with neither power nor worth nor other human favor. It shouldn't surprise us, then, that He would wish to achieve the conversion of this new world—which, with regard to the total number of individuals, has been even greater than the Apostles achieved, he adds proudly—using children as His instruments. Because here, the children taught their evangelists. In order to become teachers, the friar says, first we had to be pupils. In order to speak like men, first we had to speak like children: be children among children. We made ourselves children with the children and Indians with the Indians, phlegmatic and patient like them, poor and naked, gentle and humble and small—small, above all. And none of this would have seemed strange to God, since it is written: Truly I tell you, unless you change and become like little children, you will never enter the kingdom of heaven. The rest, says the friar, dropping his arms and quietening his inflamed voice, you can imagine for yourself. The boy Juan was one of those children, of course. His mouth and hands were instruments through which God worked His miracle. If only you had been there, he says. If only you could have met him. Then you would have nothing to ask me. You would know and understand all. This the friar says with a new gentleness; his eyes stalled in the contemplation of a divine image. Because if the children were without a doubt small, if God once again made use of small and insignificant and even the ridiculous creatures to convey His word, then what could be said of the boy Juan, who was insignificant among the insignificant. He was small in size, yes, no bigger than a Castilian yard, but the friar is referring to something else, at least in part. He was, of all the children who regularly attended school, the only child of mācēhualtin, that is, the lowest and poorest class of Indian. And yet he received doctrine there, in that monastery reserved for the sons of the noblemen and chieftains. They owe that tiny miracle to the Indians themselves and their fondness for trickery and lies. Because back then, the monks gathered all of the region's most important men and staunchly requested they bring their sons to receive instruction; those ignorant and feathered gentlemen nodded with their heads but refused in their hearts. Send my sons to the monastery, of course, to the House of Christ and Mary, by all means, but they did not keep their word, not at the moment of truth. Or they did keep their word, but twisted it, and the children they sent were not their own. So it was that more than a few of those men devised the ruse of sending the disguised son of one of their slaves, dressed in extraordinarily expensive garb and attended by servants and acolytes, as was expected of a highborn child. Such deviousness would be enough to enrage the kindliest of tempers, if it wasn't for the fact that this was how they were fortunate enough to meet the boy, Juan. Later, they learned he was very poor. So poor that, up till then, he had never had shoes of his own. And yet, how natural it was, seeing him in all those clothes and jewels and starch; he seemed to have been made for receiving such lavish attention. If it were possible to conceive of Our Lord God making a mistake—such a thing is impossible, of course—one might even say that the boy possessed the soul of a nobleman, one that landed, through either negligence or accident, in an indigent's body. Because there was something in him. There was, undoubtedly, something. Something, the friar repeats, he wouldn't know how to explain. His eyes, perhaps. Yes: that was it. Something in his gaze, which pierced and disrobed a person; which, in its purity, became beautiful and fearsome all at once. In short, that was the boy Juan: a little child who wasn't the son of any lord and had no status whatsoever, but he seemed to. Of course, Juan wasn't called Juan back then. He had another name, but that name, yes, that name the friar has forgotten. Perhaps Fray Hernando remembers it, but wait, what is he saying, Fray Hernando died many years ago. All or almost all of them have died. And all or almost all of the Indian names sound the same, don't they? He can't recall whose notion it was to baptize him Juan. In any case, it was an excellent idea, because "Juan" means "man who is faithful to God." Did you know that, perchance? the friar asks, momentarily taking his eyes off the painted ceiling. Did you know the meaning of your own name? No matter. The fact is, the name was appropriate, extremely appropriate, because in effect, the boy Juan was faithful to God and faithful to his Franciscan fathers and faithful to all the doctrinal teachings he was taught, no matter how abstract or inaccessible they were to the others. As Juan might assume, it wasn't much, the doctrine the children were taught, at least not in the beginning, when the heathen times were still recent and the friars had to content themselves with little. It sufficed that the Indians learn to bless themselves and make the sign of the cross; to say the Pater Noster and the Ave María, the Credo and the Salve Regina. They had to know that the Devil is under the ground and God is in Heaven and He is one and three at the same time, and other very simple teachings. And of course, they also had to accept that their old gods were nothing but demons the Evil One had beguiled them with, and that in professing faith to Tláloc or Huitzilopochtli, they were worshipping the Evil One himself. But that didn't satisfy the boy Juan. The boy Juan was never satisfied with anything. He learned Latin and Castilian like a child learns the basic rules of a game. He was, according to all opinion, the first native of these lands to devote himself to reading the Scriptures, with a fervor never again witnessed. And that reading didn't fall on deaf ears, as they say, but inspired clever and pertinent questions that the monks couldn't always answer, not without resorting to the authority of the good Doctors of the Church. What questions? Oh, small but exceedingly incisive questions, like a dagger piercing flesh . . . Like how it had occurred to him to think how the Jews paid dearly—thirty silver coins—for Judas's betrayal: after all, it had been completely unnecessary. Why did they need Judas's kiss, if everyone knew who Jesus was and that he'd spent three years preaching openly? Why did Judas hang for fulfilling a prophesy that Matthew attributes to Jeremiah, when it is really a prophecy from Zachariah? Does that mean the Evangelists are capable of error? And if, as tradition and common sense would have it, Matthew is the author of Matthew, how does he know what the Pharisees are thinking, when they are to be found so many leagues away from the Twelve? How does he know what Christ prayed in Gethsemane, when he had already confessed that both he and the others fell asleep? Perhaps, considering the sharpness of those questions, Juan can judge what kind of child the boy Juan was. The kind of man he must surely still be. So pious and so serene and so influential among his people that the friars brought him with them to neighboring villages to preach. At first, they made him translate and recite sermons they wrote on fig tree paper, and later, when they trusted him completely, allowed him to improvise his own sermons. He had no need for translators, or cats, or ovens to burn them in. He carried with him a small, unassuming wooden cross, which he showed to the Indians when he said: In the beginning, this was all I had. Then he brought his hand to his heart and said: Now I have this. I have a soul. He pointed to the sky, pointed to the ground and said: Now I have this. I have God. I have a whole world. That was what he said at the start of every sermon, or at least that's what they thought, because at the time they were only beginning to understand Nahuatl. But his voice. His face. The friar will never forget it, not for as long as he lives—and he has lived a good bit of life since then. Something about those eyes of his, perhaps. Some nights, he still sees those eyes: he senses them gleaming in the dark of his cell, with an intensity only saints and prophets seem capable of. Was the boy Juan, by chance, a saint, a prophet? The friar couldn't say. Theology and metaphysics fall short. He knows only this: when the boy Juan preached, when he undertook to speak the Word, something seemed to burn among the savages who heard him. He—Juan—burned; it was unbearable to look in his eyes, to enter the abyss of eyes that had seen so luminous and so deep, just as sunlight burns even when it is reflected off water. He still sees those eyes, some nights. Has he said that already? Has he told him how, some nights, he believes he sees them gleaming in the dark of his cell, with an intensity only saints and prophets are capable of?

Occasionally the story breaks off. Gaps, long silences fill the old man's words and Juan has to encourage him to go on. And then what happened? he asks. The friar is slow to answer, perhaps because he isn't even entirely aware that he has paused; perhaps because the skein of memories continues to unravel in his mind, but not on his lips. What happened, my son, he says, is a very sad thing. A very sad or a very blessed thing, depending on one's view. Perhaps both at once: Juan can judge. By that time, the seed of Christ had taken root and grown strong in this land, and we resolved to start the battle against the weeds of idolatry. A holy battle, he understands, without swords or bloodshed. A fight that in no way resembled the savagery of soldiers but was like the tenderness of a father who teaches, instructs, and sustains. And punishes, of course. What is the son who goes undisciplined by his own father? Such a son is but a bastard, so say the Scriptures. But I digress, he admits. I was talking about idolatry. Of the extermination of idolatry. Of those hideous dolls the Indians kept everywhere and used to pray for all manner of things, whether a good harvest, a bit of rain, or good fortune in love. The fact is, the moment had come to rid the Indians of those idols, just as the time comes when a child must be separated from the playthings and silly stories that accompanied his first steps. They convened the most important Indians, the fathers of many of the boys who received doctrine at the monastery, and explained this to them. They explained how, up till then, the Devil had tricked them—the Devil always twists what is straight and makes left what is right, and takes pleasure in bearing resemblance to God in a parodic, mocking way—and the time had come for the Indians to turn over all the Evil One's trophies in order that they be purified through fire. And those feathered, ignorant men nodded with their heads but refused in their hearts. Destroy my idols, yes, of course, destroy them in an enormous bonfire, by all means, but at the moment of truth, they did not comply. They offered the monks their smallest, feeblest idols, those they didn't much care about losing, and kept for themselves their most beloved. Is it not written in Isaiah: These people honor me with their lips, but their hearts are far from me? And do the Proverbs not say that the dog turns toward its own vomit, and the clean sow rolls in the mud? Many Indians were still like that: pigs rooting in the mud of their idolatry, which is terribly destructive. They said their statues did not represent demons but gods, and that—for them—the message brought by the Christians was a new and sad Word. Cunningly, they said the Spaniards weren't after the idols so much as the gold and silver and gems those idols were made of. They said so many things, and each and every one of them had the Devil on their lips. But how could those men have guessed, says the friar, his voice gradually revitalized by an ominous echo, that by then their children were more ours than theirs. That in their hearts and deeds they were our sons, and no one was more of a son than the boy Juan. And so it happened that, without being coerced or bribed or compelled, the children willingly confessed who among their fathers worshipped the Devil in secret; where they had concealed their beloved idols, whether underground or in a false wall, in hidden vessels or on the rickety roofs of their homes or under the bases of Christian crosses. The children led the monks to all those places, and the friar can still recall how those children's faces seemed to transform, radiating love and virtue and gratification for the truth as it was revealed. Some of the Indians resisted. Others wept. A few observed the scene at length, and with no reaction, no movement. Absent, they watched how the monks and the children piled those demoniacal statues in the center of the village and set them alight. Recidivists had to be publicly flogged and shamed, of course, because if it pleases God to reveal Himself peacefully among all men, He knows to avail himself of the whip when required. Once they'd performed their penance, the Indians said little or nothing. Just strange utterances, like one the friar once heard spoken: Here is where my own sons break my heart-wings. Exactly that: heart-wings. Perhaps Juan is aware, the friar says with a hint of a smile, that the Indians talk a bit like that, in that flowery, dark way, as if in riddles, or metaphors, as if they didn't entirely want to say what they were about to deliver. For them, veins are snakes and fingernails are pearls; they call the eyes enchanted mirrors, and teeth are grinders, also enchanted; the chest is a fence of ribs and the fingers the five fates and they refer to blood as the red woman. And, just as Joseph could not be entirely worthy of His son's divinity, they called that work, that holy work carried out by their own children, "breaking the heart-wings," as if the heart did in truth fly, and as if faith in Christ Our Lord was not rejoicing, but devastation. Well. The fact is, in time the Indians had so much respect for those children that there was no need for a priest to accompany them. They traveled about the countryside, in gangs of ten or twenty little guardians of the faith, dismantling idols and burning shrines and unveiling witchcraft and Aztec rituals. And who but the boy Juan was the most spirited among them; he led them and innervated them and gave them strength when they lost heart. His audacity knew no bounds. Sometimes he undertook to ransack temples in villages far from the monastery, portions of the world still very tepid in matters of the faith, accompanied by other small angels like him. The monks came to fear that one of those Indians would kill him. I, at least, was afraid of that for a time, the friar admits. Every time he watched him go, he reminded little Juan that, in Scripture, Christ himself says: I send you out as sheep into the midst of wolves; be, then, as prudent as snakes and simple as doves. But the boy Juan would reply with dauntless wisdom. Like how without its spirit the body is dead, and so, father, is faith without works, he would say, citing a particular passage from the Epistle of St. James that even I, an expert in holy things, had trouble placing. And also: If God is for us, who can be against us? The answer was, nobody, of course. Nobody dared to raise a sword against the children of our convent, although many undoubtedly would have liked to—one expected the Devil to oft inspire such an idea. But for the boy Juan, the possibility of being martyred was of little or no concern. If I must die, let it be testifying to my faith, he would say, like Justus and Pastor before the proconsul; like Stephen before the Sanhedrin and Andrew on the cross and Paul in Rome. If he was not a saint or prophet, says the friar, he certainly seemed like one. He was not, however, a martyr. His righteousness was such that he even denounced his own father for the sacrifices of little birds and frogs the man made to Tezcatlipoca. His father was a man of extreme poverty, as destitute of possessions and lacking in intelligence as you

45

can imagine. I think about him sometimes, the friar says after a long silence; a father who, depending on one's perspective, lost his son twice: first at the hands of the nobleman who passed him off as his son, and then when that son was embraced by the brother priests. I think about his end. That's what seems simultaneously both sad and happy: that end. The punishment for a return to the mud of idolatry was hardly a few lashings, he explains; nothing that would trouble the soul of a real man. And he can attest that those lashings were oftentimes delivered with certain lassitude and even apparent indifference, as there was much flesh to flog and the labor of flogging it very tiring. Well: in the case of the boy Juan's father, there hadn't been time to tire. By the time they reached his house, led there by his own son, the man was already dead. He had hanged himself from a roofbeam. Hitherto, naturally, the terribleness. Grievous that, in fleeing punishment for one sin, a man dives headfirst into another, one even more terrible. He is still astonished by the boy Juan's reaction. The child said not a word. He helped take down the poor body and clean his face of the drool still seeping from his mouth, and never shed a single tear. And when they told him he needn't be ashamed to cry, that it was understandable and even natural when faced with a father's death, he turned to them, his face transfigured. Who is my mother, and who are my brothers? he replied, and St. Mark spoke through his mouth. And then: Do not think I have come to bring peace to the earth: I have not come to bring peace, but a sword. Because I have come to set a man against his father and the daughter against her mother. That's what he said, the friar murmured, his voice fluttering with emotion, and it was we, not him, who could not contain ourselves, and broke down in tears of joy . . .

That's as far as he knows, the friar says. Or just about. Because shortly thereafter, they sent the boy Juan to the school that had only just opened in Santa Cruz de Tlatelolco, dedicated to advanced studies. By that time, his own school and this very monastery had already begun to decline and the monks had sought new lodgings in Tlaxcala itself, in the area around what is now the cathedral. The boy Juan left but they remembered him. He, at least, remembers. Like a father must remember and lament a son's absence. Does Juan understand that feeling? Has he ever been separated from what he most loves, in service to a calling higher than that love?

Juan reflects.

"Yes."

The old man smiles.

"Then maybe you can understand this. Because sometimes, after so many years have passed, I still return to these ruins so that I may see his face . . ."

"His face?"

The old man's voice echoes off the vaulted ceiling. At intervals it doesn't even sound like a voice, but a relic, a trace, a ruin of one; one more thing among all the things that surround them, as remote and fragile as they are, exposed to extinction and shadow like the walls that are slowly, steadily crumbling. Juan hears that ruin, that trace, that relic. And he pays heed to the movement of the man's eyes, still fixed on the peeling frescos. Suddenly, the friar's hand. A bony hand raised, pointing upward.

"Look," the old man says. "His face."

Juan follows the line of the hand. The horse, too, lifts its enormous head in accordance with the friar's gesture, toward the paintings on the ceiling. Look, he repeats, his digit aimed at one precise location: not at the scene depicting the Crucifixion or Judas's betrayal or the healing of lepers or the descent into Hell or Mary's annunciation. At first, Juan does not understand. One image comes into focus, one which, at first, appears innocent and serene, almost unsophisticated; yet gradually, the scene becomes vaguely terrifying in the waning light. He sees, sketched on the flaking plaster, the stone pillars of a temple—a temple etched on the ceiling of another temple—and under its archways, a small number of priests and rabbis clustered around a child. What is frightening is the child. The child's eyes. Amid the scene's puerility—the Temple of Jerusalem like a Spanish church; the rabbis painted liked doctors of Salamanca or the Sorbonne; disproportionate noses making the Jews more Jewish—the child's eyes gleam with an unbearable shine, impossible for any pigment to create. They are as hard and blank as mirrors and certain gemstones, and they are perpetually open, as if they had no lids. As if they had no gaze, if such a thing were possible. What do those eyes seek? They do not look at the rabbis, nor at the pillars of the temple. They look ahead, always ahead, in pursuit of the coming Messiah he will one day have to become: little Jesus, who, in adjacent images, watches himself growing up and resisting the temptations in the desert; preaching on the streets of Jerusalem and the banks of the Jordan; suffering in Gethsemane and dying on Golgotha and rising from the dead in Emmaus. He contemplates those future episodes without judgement or agony, with the same indifference with which one contemplates the depiction of another man's life.

The friar, meanwhile, begins to describe the scene. The scene is from the second chapter of the Gospel of Luke, of course. That passage used to fascinate the boy Juan. Though he had questions about it, too, because his curiosity was never satiated: if it had really been revealed to Mary and Joseph that Jesus was the son of God, then why, when the boy tells them that he was in the temple attending to his father's business, did they not understand his words? But setting those doubts aside, it was a lovely passage, perhaps one with which the boy Juan identified. Or perhaps it was the monks who saw the similarities, the friar admits, and that's why someone had the idea of using him as a model for the images in the chapel. Perhaps that circumstance, little Juan being immortalized as the very Son of God himself, might give Juan an idea of the degree to which they came to admire the boy. It is, in any case, a good likeness. The boy Juan had been exactly like that. Brother Jerónimo and Brother Martín and Brother Bernardo would agree, if Brother Jerónimo and Brother Martín and Brother Bernardo hadn't died years ago, God rest their souls. This is what Juan the Indian looks like, or at least how he looked when he had just started to be Juan and still had a long stretch of childhood before him. This is the man you are seeking, says the friar, many years before you sought him.

Night is about to fall when Juan mounts his horse. The friar's eyes are all that shines, two specks of remote light. They have already just said their goodbyes, but the friar appears about to speak. What he has to say, he says with a gesture, reaching out and patting the horse's neck, as if he also wished to bid the creature farewell.

"He seems like a good animal."

"He is, Father."

"How many escudos did he cost you?"

"I couldn't say, Father."

"You couldn't, or you don't want to?"

Juan considers his reply.

"He was a gift."

"A gift."

"Yes."

The old man is silent. His lips pull back into a smile.

"Is this the price?" he asks.

"The price?"

"Your thirty silver coins."

Juan's mouth opens, then closes. The old man continues stroking the horse's neck, never once looking at Juan.

"You know? I don't blame you. One hears things. Even inside the four walls of a monastery, certain terrible things are heard, whether one wants to hear them or not. One must choose whether or not to believe them. You have chosen already. They will have surely told you some of those things and you believe you have an opinion. Or better yet: they may have told you absolutely nothing at all. Sometimes the choice is easier that way. Only it's never that easy. You see, Juan the Indian was my son and yet I am not sure what I should believe . . ."

The two shining specks rise and, for the first time, come to rest full on Juan's face.

"I only ask that you remember this when the time comes. Remember my doubts."

Then he gives the horse's haunch a slap and the animal sets off at a trot. Juan turns to take a fleeting last look at the old man who remains behind, in the dusk, his hand eternalized in a gesture of farewell; evermore the ghost-monk, ever-bound to the place where, for a time, he was happy.

That same night, in an inn on the outskirts of town, Juan dreams of his wife. It will be the last time he sees her, or almost the last. In the dream, he sees his own empty tavern. No clients slumped over the tables, no players exchanging cards or dice. Just his wife. She has fallen asleep in a chair, her face turned toward the hearth. Perhaps she is also dreaming of something or someone. Suddenly, the door. The sound of the knocker wakes the dog, which hadn't been present a moment ago, but the dog's barking does not wake the woman. The woman does not wake; she sleeps on, even as the door swings open. On the other side, a boy. He can't make out his face. He is swathed in dressings and bandages and a kind of veil that looks like a shroud. Beneath the ultra-fine gauze, Juan can see the blood that flows copiously from his nose; the lips parched and smarting from thirst; the tar-black tongue twisting in the half-open mouth. He walks like a corpse. He walks toward the woman the way a corpse would walk if corpses walked. The woman, who does not wake. And then, glimpsed through a crack in the bandages, the child's eyes. His eyes gleam with the unbearable shine of fever; as hard and blank as certain mirrors and certain gemstones; perpetually open, as if they had no lids. As if they had no gaze, if such a thing were possible. The woman's eyes are closed. The woman, who still does not react now that the child is beside her and extending a vile, plague-ridden hand; a hand mottled with red spots, about to graze the woman's skin in a posthumous caress. And when he finally touches her, it is not the woman, but Juan, who wakes.

III

Desires we know not how to name – Poetic license – Not always on earth – A sheep's error – Until when, Catiline – To forget one's own eyes – Preferring to know and not to know – Fable of the farmer and the snake – Kurtz's dream – Death in effigy

The fault lies with the Devil. The fault lies with God. The fault lies with all His creatures, from the most abject to the most virtuous. The fault lies with the climate, drier now than in heathen times. The fault lies with Judgement Day: with the proximity of that day and that judgement. Everywhere Juan goes he finds corpses and opinions; many corpses, many opinions spreading their stink. The fault lies with the Indians, for having reverted to their idols. The fault lies with the Indians, for having betrayed the old gods. The fault lies with all the excesses of these territories: an excess of Indians and an excess of gold and an excess of ambitions. Bodies rotting in hospitals and leper colonies and homes and on the roadsides, and opinions rotting inside one's head. The fault lies with the Spaniards, for bringing unprecedented disease to these lands. The fault lies with the encomenderos, for overwhelming their Indians with tributes and back-breaking labor. The fault lies with the Aztecs, for performing human sacrifices, now the time has come for the sins of the cannibals to be paid by their sons, and their sons' sons. The fault lies with the Aztecs, for having stopped their human sacrifices, now the time has come for hungry gods to claim their rations of flesh.

In the foothills of Mount Tláloc he comes upon a wagon, pulled by an ox and rolling in the opposite direction. In the back sways a pile of human bodies, stippled by a cloud of flies. The fault, the driver says, covering his nose, lies with the times in which we must live: there was once a golden age, when men were made of other stuff and lived to be two hundred and treated one another justly and were healthy and robust as boulders; pity that today we live in turbulent times, times made not for giants but for dwarves, when morals are loose and young people disobey their elders and the gold of our youth has been tarnished and degraded to iron. Beside the ruins of Acozac, he finds an unnamed village, its entire population disappeared or dead, and, as a consequence, nobody speaks or gives an opinion on anything: many bodies and nary an opinion. Some of the houses are in rubble, their roofs recently caved-in, as if when the villagers fled—unable to bury so many dead—they had opted for giving each family its own sepulcher. Shackled to an iron chain a starving dog struggles, no owner, no hope, barking at no one and blaming them all, perhaps. The fault, says an encomendero who travels with him for several leagues, lies with idleness and the easy life the commoners in Aztec society have enjoyed since the Spaniards' arrival: once accustomed to constant warfare and heavy labor and the tyrannies of their own lords, now that they are liberated in Christ they turn to drink, lazing around the fields, nothing to keep them busy, uninterested in working even their own fields, if they had them. On Sunday he makes a stop to hear mass in the hermitage in Chimalhuacán, where before a nearly empty congregation, the priest lays the blame on Aztec witchcraft and while he's at it, German Protestants and the African Moors and English Corsairs and Judaizing converts and future converts and the laziness and fatigue and skepticism of the Holy Office, which no longer pursues the invasive weeds of heresy as determinedly as it should. The fault, a campesino with whom he shares a few gourds of wine, says regretfully, lies only with our ignorance.

Ignorance. Juan thinks of it often. Because may the Devil take him if he knows why so many Indians are dying, struck down by a malady that barely grazes the Spaniards. Or why he himself, a man already on his way to old age, a common man or at least one who has always considered himself common, has been chosen for such a delicate mission. Although to that point, may the Devil also take him if knows why he decided to accept, after years of retirement. Why he doesn't return to be with his wife, lonely or sick or dead. The gold, of course. Gold is a good reason for everything, perhaps the only reason in the world that, once put into words, requires no further rationale. But at the same time, he has the impression that, on occasion, gold can also be a pretext; the excuse some men give themselves to satisfy the many desires they have but cannot name.

Sometimes, mid-trek, he suddenly remembers the last words the friar spoke to him. He doesn't tend to think about them, or if he does, he does so obliquely, like when we catch the eye of a person we want to avoid and so avert our own, yet never manage to entirely evade their gaze. That's how he thinks about the friar. That's how he thinks of his wife without thinking of his wife, of the diseased hands that might, at this very moment, be knocking on his tavern door. His wife, possibly sick. His wife dead. This is also how he eyes—sidelong—Juan the Indian or the memory or fantasy that has been created of Juan the Indian. He remembers the things the friar said he heard. Terrible things. Things he could choose to believe or not believe. Does he believe them? Does Juan believe those things he does not know and which, until recently, he didn't know he did not know? And if it is absurd to believe in what he has not seen and what is not known, then why accept the mission? What are the horrendous crimes for which he is coming to exact payment with his sword? What will he know or believe he knows at the moment he confronts Juan the Indian's eyes with no gaze? He digs his spurs into the horse's flanks. Juan who, while there are no obstacles and no reason to rush, is suddenly galloping in the middle of a plain. The horse races along a stretch of the road, galvanized, ignorant, perhaps, of why he runs. Falling behind them, a ruined house, a stream with no bridge and a mill or the beginnings of a mill arising on the banks of that stream; behind them, too, a dry ditch and his thoughts and the questions those thoughts awaken and a well with no parapet and a grove that hardly casts any shade and his wife's memory and an abandoned cart on the roadside and a solitary scarecrow reigning over a serf-less horizon.

He leaves the sierra's last peaks behind, following a bridlepath that descends in curves and twists not unlike the winding of a river. Someone had the idea of calling this series of peaks the Sierra Nevada, and Juan mulls over the name as he descends into the valley. Here, he thinks, is another example of those words that seek to soothe someone's nostalgia; bear us back in time to a home we will never return to, where the hearth will never again be lit. A new Sierra Nevada for a New Spain.

From above he can espy the path ahead; the remote ruins of Tlapacoyan, whose antiquity is a mystery even to the Aztecs, and beside them Lake Chalco, and further on the Lake of Xochimilco, and even further out the Texcoco, glinting in the midday sun. All those names he remembers with painful exactitude, as one recalls the geography of a nightmare. That landscape was the site of the siege of Tenochtitlan, and the siege of Tenochtitlan is one of those many things Juan would prefer not to discuss, or even remember. Of course, he occasionally finds himself obliged to say something about that glorious event: but he measures his words when he does, selecting images and reflections and even turns of phrase that do not conform to his own memories but to the language of the chronicles. He says, for example, that blood dyed the lagoon, because this is what everyone wants to hear. Or that the Aztec dead numbered in the thousands or even tens of thousands. He does not say, however, that the lake was never bloodred; that image was simply poets taking license. At most, it was tinged brown, a lake of water that looked like sludge and provoked disgust well before it aroused compassion or fear. Nor does he say that he never saw ten thousand dead men, he didn't even see one hundred dead, not even ten. Only captains and kings count the dead by the thousands, precisely because they don't have to look a single one in the eye. He, like every soldier in battle, saw just one corpse, and that was enough. He saw the face of a man who was dying and, on that face, the truncated will to deliver one final utterance; he saw the tremor of agony, eyes closed or open still, the riveting gaze of the enemy whom we kill. And then he slit the throat of another, and another, and another, and each time he saw the same dead man die, a dead man who sometimes had a child's face, or that of a woman, or an old man, but it was always the same dead man, and with every thrust of his knife the dead man's tragedy became more permanent, and his pain never, ever stopped.

Suddenly, he thinks of the epidemic. He realizes that until now—like the captains or God Himself—he has been contemplating the situation from above. He has seen hundreds of corpses, packed in graves and cemeteries, transported by coffin and cart and stretcher, the newly dead and the dead already digested by worms or lime or the elements, but he hasn't actually looked at any of them. God willing, he will never have to, he thinks. God willing, when he returns home—because he is going to return very soon, in just two-week's time—his wife will greet him with a jug of pulque and open arms. Healthy, open, living arms. She will ask where he has been; if he saw the ravages of the epidemic and if he was ever afraid. To her, he will say nothing of fear. He will simply say that, in effect, there were many dead, many, many dead, thousands of dead every-where; so many dead that, for a moment, the lake looked like solid ground for all the corpses he saw floating, adrift, like unmanned canoes.

He spots the capital at daybreak, built on the island that was once Tenochtitlan. It is still reached by the same bridges and roads, still crisscrossed by the same ditches; the same smoke curling in the air from the hearths of houses that look the same; otherwise, however, in little more than twenty years, the Spanish have erased all vestiges of the Aztec, like another quick-spreading plague. We are the plague, Juan thinks, and that thought is but a bolt of lightning that strikes him and then instantly disappears. No trace remains of the shrines and pyramids that once bristled on the horizon, and upon which so many comrades-at-arms were sacrificed. Juan remembers the substructure of one of those temples, and how during the sacking of the city, in one of its many nooks and crannies, he found an inscription written with charcoal that read: Here, the luckless Juan Yuste was prisoner. The Aztecs who devoured the unlucky man ultimately hadn't been any luckier; soon afterward, they saw their children killed and their temples razed and their homes destroyed.

At the top of the ancient ruins, where the Temple Mayor once stood, the Spaniards have built a cathedral and a kind of patchwork of buildings and palaces in the Castilian style, arranged around an immense square. Seen from a distance, the Spanish city looks like a chess board dropped into the heart of an Aztec metropolis, hemmed in on all sides by the Aztec slums, a maze of stinking, tortuous alleys encircled, in turn, by the lake. As he approaches, as he travels the roadway built over the water from pilings and packed earth, Juan wonders if this is the very same path the boy Juan walked so many years before. What had he thought, what had he felt, when for the first time he set eyes on that city the Spaniards had made their own, just as they'd done first with Juan's soul.

He stops three or four thousand varas later, a distance of approximately three kilometers, in the Santiago de Tlatelolco quarter, where, according to his papers, the Colegio de la Santa Cruz should be. It doesn't take him long to find it, imposing and magnificent, with its chapel and belltower and walls of lime and large, smooth river-stones closing off one side of the square. In that very square, Juan recalls, once stood the biggest market in the Indies. But now nothing or almost nothing is left of all that; the square is mostly empty, scarcely a peddler or merchant in sight. Someone has built, with more doubt than certainty, a dozen precarious stalls, and the vendors stand rigidly behind their pieces of fruit, their tamales or small jars of atole; in their eyes, a desire to be anywhere else. Some wear cloth rags over their nose and mouth, and from behind their gags they speak to passersby, who are, at any rate, very few in number and scuttle swiftly across the street. Only a few stay behind to poke around the little booths and food stands, and those few are all Spaniards.

In the entire vacant space of the square, Juan doesn't see more than a single Indian. He is a very elderly man, and has climbed atop a kind of barrel, from which he delivers long speeches to no one, as if he were rallying invisible troops. As he does so, he waves a knotty staff similar to a pilgrim's crook. A madman. At least he looks like a madman. Juan approaches cautiously, leading his horse by the halter. The Indian, the old man, the madman raises his voice even louder. He seems to recite by memory, a text he memorized who knows where, or why.

> The giver of life mocks;
> it is only a dream we pursue,
> oh, our friends,
> our hearts trust
> but he, in truth, does mock . . .
> We come only to doze, we come only to dream:
> it is not true, it is not true that we come to live on the Earth.
> Our body is a flower: some flowers he gives and then dries out.

In the old man's eroded features, he sees the first symptoms of the malady; eyes red and bloodshot; the cracked lips; countenance blazing with fever; nose dripping thick, black blood onto the dirt.

> Only as a flower do you appreciate us,
> so we, your friends, are wilting.
> Like of an emerald, you make pieces of us.
> Like a painting, so you erase us.
> All are leaving for the realm of death,
> the common place in which to lose ourselves.
> Must not we all go to the place of the fleshless?
> Is this place of the fleshless in heaven or on Earth?
> We go together, we go together to his house:
> No one left on Earth!

Around him, the Spaniards circulate wordlessly. They barely give him a glance. For a moment, Juan stands there by himself, until he thinks he has seen enough. Then he walks away. As he heads toward the school, he senses the persecution of the old man's voice, clamoring at his back.

Is it really Earth on which we live?
Not forever on the Earth; just a little while here.
Though it be jade, it cracks;
though it be gold, it breaks;
though it be quetzal feathers, it breaks apart.
Not forever on the Earth; only a short time here.

Juan is an important man, perhaps even a feared one. He realizes this as soon as he crosses through the courtyard entrance and states his reason for coming to the lay brother tending the porter's gate. The boy takes off running, as if someone had cried *fire!* from somewhere inside, and just seconds later four friars come out to receive him, extending honors the likes of which are bestowed on a king. The honors Juan imagines as kingly, at least, but what does he know of sovereigns, Juan thinks, when the closest he's ever been is studying the image engraved on gold doubloons. In any case, the fact is that the Franciscans come running to him, lifting the skirt of their habits with pinched fingers so as not to trip, and bending low in embarrassing bows and kissing the back of his hand as if it were a holy relic. They all introduce themselves at the same time, and a moment later he has forgotten their names: all he knows is that he is speaking to a rhetoric teacher, a philosophy teacher, a music teacher, and a theologian. A lay brother takes his horse to the stables and another carries his luggage and a third comes with a bronze pitcher, in case His Excellency would like to wash his hands. Then they guide him to a sitting room contiguous to the courtyard and pester him with jugs of water and wine, with local fruits and sweets. They call him The Honorable and Your Excellency, and Juan, though slightly unsettled, acquiesces to it. Briefly, he believes he might the victim of some sort of mix-up, since in the course of their first, stumbling words, the monks reference a viceroy's man for whom they have been waiting for weeks. After a few more words, Juan realizes that he is that man, and when he does, he doesn't know what to do with the discovery. We feared a misfortune had befallen His Excellency, says the most resolute of the friars; they even came to think, God forgive them, of the plague. Very few Spaniards have been infected, and in the majority of cases the illness follows a benign course, but one never knows. One never knows, says the second friar. One never knows, says the third. And then they look at him, as if awaiting his opinion.

"One never knows," Juan murmurs, with something like a shrug.

Whatever the case may be, it is fortunate that he is here, even in the unfortunate circumstances that bring them together. This is said by the friar who has just introduced himself as the Rhetoric master, who, perhaps in alignment with his profession, is the most verbose of the bunch. Juan is unsure whether he is referring to the epidemic again or to something else. Oh, no, clarifies the orator, crossing himself; thanks be to God, the epidemic has infected none of their boys. Up till now, it has stopped at their school walls, as if Latin and Philosophy protected them not only from ignorance but the ravages of the illness as well. Or as if God Himself, conscious of the Work performed there, hadn't wanted to whisk away any of the little ones. In short, he continues, when he mentioned certain unfortunate circumstances, he was referring—. He was talking about—. Well, he knows. At this point, it's no secret to His Excellency. When he referred to certain unfortunate circumstances, he repeats, he was talking about Juan the Indian and the recent news out of the Gran Chichimeca. News that has, as His Excellency might imagine, profoundly afflicted every one of them. He fears to sully his mouth with simply naming those events, so sad and so contrary to laws both human and divine. And so he won't. However, what he can do, he and his brothers, is clear up the rumors that have been circulating, as they understand it, in the viceroy's palace and across royal desks and even in the chambers of the Holy Office. Clear up those rumors, he repeats, and take advantage of the opportunity to offer their version of events. Explain to men like His Excellency that this school is not and never has been a hotbed of heresy or machination, despite such heavy words having been uttered in certain unofficial meetings. Rumors spread by enemies of the Order—like the Dominicans—who feel more threatened by Franciscan successes in the Indies than by the advances made by Lutherans in Europe or the Turks in Africa. And yet, what have they ever done inside these four walls but act in strict obeyance of Divine Will. The Bishop of the Diocese and episcopal inquisitor knows it well, since he was present at the inauguration of this noble school, almost ten years ago now. And the viceroy himself knows it, since he was also there, applauding everything they did and said on that venerable occasion. Emperor Carlos knows it too, and his son, Prince Felipe, who have been generous enough to fund the school's costs. They all know, then, the great care that the Franciscans take, the sleepless nights. Even the Dominican brothers, who just one decade ago mocked and ridiculed their endeavors to teach Latin to the Indians, have ultimately been compelled to recognize the fruits of their studies. They recognize it for the worse, but they recognize it. They say that everything the Franciscan order has done within these walls is the Devil's doing: reading and writing are no use to the Indians, except in order to blaspheme and commit heresy. Can His Excellency believe it?

Juan, caught off-guard with a mouthful of half-chewed confection, can but cock his head in a gesture that might mean anything.

No; how could he believe it, the rhetorician continues as the rest of the monks nod in agreement. Imagine them—every brother who gave the best years of his life in order to fortify the Indians' spirit and intellect—turned into agents of the Devil. As he well knows, all they ever intended was to dissipate the darkness in which the indigenous soul dwells, and he mustn't think it vain of them if they should declare that, in many cases, that intention has been fulfilled. While the Dominicans and the Augustines considered it an accomplishment just to get the natives to chant the Pater Noster, or force them to memorize—learning by rote does imprint on the heart—the Ten Commandments of the Holy Mother Church, the Franciscans have given them Latin with which to read holy things, and rhetoric to discuss them, and philosophy as a light so as to not feel about blindly in the halls of reason. And theology, of course; because whosoever calls himself a Christian without knowing Christ's teachings or the disquisitions of a St. Augustine or St. Jeronimo is like a philosophy student calling himself Platonic although he hasn't read the dialogues. Thus, they battled pagan ignorance with spiritual weapons, not material ones. They replaced the encomendero's sword with the teacher's pointer and the shackles with pupils' desks and the whip with the logic of syllogisms, which—outside of Valladolid and Salamanca and a few other important cities—had never been taught in Spain, and much less to men considered useless, almost bestial. He is proud to say that some of their graduates occupy high ranks and posts in the Indian republic already. The majority are translators or work as interpreters during official audiences; others are judges, governors, scribes. It's true, he admits after what feels like a particularly long pause, that in all human undertakings there are mistakes, large and small, and their own noble enterprise, undoubtedly, does not constitute an exception. It is also true—another pause—that the actions which have gathered them together today are of unprecedented gravity and the friar fears he cannot avoid his share of guilt for the sad events. But he has never known any shepherd to be judged for the erring of one sheep over the merits of the flock as a whole, nor for any king to be dethroned for the wickedness of a single one of his subjects. Was not Christ's work worthy, even if it ultimately gave rise to a Judas? Why, then, should they cast aside the essential aspects of their enterprise because of one disciples' defects, doubtlessly grave and unusual but also, for that very reason, unique? He and his brothers would be very sorry indeed if the viceroy, a man ordinarily so judicious and forgiving, were to come to such a conclusion in haste and reconsider his support, which presently amounts to one thousand pesos of annual income for the school. And the fact is, he says, when they saw him arrive, they couldn't help but think that he, His Excellency, Juan, that is, could be just the man to help them avoid that eventuality. His Excellency need only be so kind as to tell the viceroy about what he will see here; he mustn't invent, nor omit, a single detail. What he will see, specifically: learned students well-versed in Latin and philosophy, but above all, docile to an extreme degree, and teachers who are undoubtedly capable of making mistakes, like any man, after all, but sensible enough to correct them. No, no; he needn't respond now; it's best for him to be shown the school first, so he can judge fairly. They want His Excellency to have the chance to see the Work with his own eyes, unencumbered by words or preconceptions. To see their students, that is, their sons. To hear them, above all. To hear them speak.

The school building is large and well-provisioned. According to Juan's estimates, it must be around ten thousand square varas, and to all appearances, recently repaired. Yes, one of his guides proudly explains, barely nine years have passed since they initiated their undertaking and just five since they rebuilt the walls with lime and stone, since the original adobe walls had been on the verge of collapse. They owe the Emperor their gratitude for this, as well; even though he is far away in Spain, the monk murmurs with devotion, his heart is, in all sincerity, very close to the noble work undertaken here by the Franciscan order.

The dormitory is a sort of ample hall, with wooden platforms running along either side, upon which the pupils arrange their sleeping mats and blankets. Beside each bed there is a box with a lock and key where each boy can store his books and belongings without fear of having them pilfered. A cane-carrying watchman makes nightly rounds up and down the corridor, deterring any commotion, racket, or deceitful act; though it is fair to say that, in all these years, nothing of substance has ever come from such vigilance, since the pupils behave with an integrity worthy of the convent's most devout. Because the Franciscan brothers, the same friar emphasizes, take the issues of discipline and decency very seriously. Perhaps His Honor has heard otherwise, the friar hazards, observing Juan's reaction from the corner of his eye, but his brothers—and he himself—are confident this visit will be enough to resolve any misunderstanding.

"I too am confident," Juan says, adopting a serious expression he imagines suitable for a powerful man.

The library is located in an adjacent chamber. It is not very large, just six or seven partially filled stacks, but big enough to constitute the greatest number of books Juan has ever laid eyes upon. Among them are a few gems worthy of consideration, says another of the monks, the one seemingly charged with the books' care. They have collections of sermons and books of grammar and copies of the Holy Scriptures, of course, but also Greek and Latin classics such as Plato, Plutarch, Aristotle, and Boethius, and the Fathers of the Holy Mother Church, like St. Augustine, not to mention unrivaled intellectuals of our time, such as Antonio Nebrija and Luis Vives. All of them, as Juan can see, free of any suspicion of heresy or lassitude with regard to orthodoxy. I see, says Juan. The monk lists many other titles and names of which Juan is completely ignorant, and which, to his ear, sound as fantastical as the Fountain of Youth or the Seven Cities of Cibolo and Quivira. I see, he repeats. As Juan listens, he opens a book at random, trying to feign some kind of intention. He sees pages written in Latin and pages written in Castilian and others written in complex symbols that must be Greek, over which he pauses, examining them a little longer, as if taking the time to appreciate what is written there.

At last, they move to the classroom. When the door opens, the pupils all stand at once, as if with a unanimous will. It is a spacious room, rather dark, with a table and dais for the teacher and several rows of benches to accommodate the students, who narrowly surpass fifty in number. It smells of ink, sweat, old parchment, convent cloisters. There is, in fact, something monkish about the boys, who look to be twelve or thirteen years old. All are dressed in a kind of seminarian's habit and have already adopted the somewhat languid look of the clergy.

The teacher, meanwhile, momentarily neglects his pupils to welcome Juan, bestowing upon him the now-familiar expressions of reverence. Has Juan had a good day, was his trip agreeable, is he in good health? In that case, perhaps His Excellency will grant them the honor of attending one of their lessons, as the students—thrilled to receive such a prominent man in their classroom—have prepared several exercises with which to regale His Excellency. His Excellency nods, unsure what to say. The teacher takes up a kind of baton and the pupils, in chorus, begin, in punctilious, well-tuned voices, to intone a song. It is a beautiful song, sung in a Latin that sounds to Juan more elegant than the Latin once spoken in ancient Rome, but damned if he knows what it means. Then one of the boys recites the Pater Noster. Another lists the classifications of the soul. Others deliver speeches on the complex issue of capacity and acts, material and form, transubstantiation and consubstantiation, the Tyranians and Troyans. The last pupil, seemingly the sharpest of the group, stands up on the bench, as if extemporizing from a kind of dais or pulpit, throws his habit over his arm and recites a Latin speech in a fiery tongue, pointing his accusatory finger in all directions.

"It is, as you can see, Marco Tulio Cicero's *Oratio in Catilinam Prima in Senatu Habita*," the teacher whispers in Juan's ear.

"Ah, Cicero," is all Juan can think to reply.

In the meantime, Juan studies the pupils one by one, with a scrutiny he hadn't known how to give the books. He is reminded, perhaps, of himself; of when he learned to read and write under the tutelage of the priest in his village, a tiny town that might have fit inside this very school. He sees himself at nine or ten, his hand, his still shaky penmanship, as the priest nodded and ruffled his hair and said that one day, oh, one day he would go far. What would the priest say now, if he could see Juan here today, two thousand leagues from his village, a bag of gold at his belt, gold to purchase a man's death? Would he consider this going far?

The speech against Catiline ends and the little Roman senators applaud, ecstatic. And the monks clap, and the teacher claps, and His Excellency claps as well. But he isn't thinking of ancient Rome or Cicero. He isn't remembering himself now, either. His thoughts are reserved for Juan the Indian. All at once he realizes, as if by sudden revelation, that only a few years ago the boy Juan was here, taking notes and singing songs and reciting speeches by dead senators. A man he by no means can kill, but whose head must be brought back at the bottom of a sack regardless. He wore the same habit and sat on one of the benches and obeyed the Franciscan brothers just as docilely. And yet, now. Now what, Juan thinks. He doesn't know the answer.

At some point, the rhetorician leads him to the chapter house. There, the head of school is waiting for him; for health reasons, he was unable join them on the tour. No, no need to fear: it isn't the plague. But he is a very old man, suffering more than a few ailments. It will soon be three years since he went blind; he, who had once been a great devourer of books. And, as Juan might imagine, the news from the Gran Chichimeca has been a terrible blow; even worse than going blind. Juan the Indian, he adds in a whisper, was like a son to him. He hasn't been himself since. Juan, therefore, must pay no mind to what he says or does, since in no way does he represent the feelings of the school community. He doesn't even represent the person he was until very recently. The man who will speak is not actually him, but a troubled soul. Does he understand?

"I understand," says Juan, though he knows not what.

The man who waits is elderly, with a fragile, brittle appearance, his skin as translucid as a Bible page. And he is, in effect, completely blind. He does a reasonably good job of estimating Juan's general location and fixing his gaze on that spot of gloom, but his eyes, white and dead, give him away. He sits on some sort of seat of honor, constructed from wood and reminiscent of a choir stall or the throne of a minor king. The rhetorician positions himself on the man's right side and, in a pompous, vacuous manner, delivers a long and laudatory sermon on the blind man's long intellectual career. Juan doesn't even glance at the rhetorician. He only has eyes for the blind man's lifeless orbs, fixed on nothing, as if there, in the void, he could read the words he is about to speak.

"You must excuse my absence," he says, once the rhetorician has left them. "But the doctors advise me not to move about more than is strictly necessary. I imagine you have had time to see the school."

"Yes, Reverend Father."

"And tell me, what have you seen?"

"I have seen it all, Reverend Father."

"What do you mean, all? To what 'all' do you refer, exactly?"

Juan hesitates.

"I've seen the dormitories, for instance."

"And what else?"

"I've seen the kitchens, as well, and the refectory, and the courtyard. I've seen the classrooms."

"And the boys? Have you seen the boys?"

"Yes, Reverend Father."

"And what did you think of our boys?"

"I thought they were very advanced in their studies."

"Astonishing, isn't it? Almost as though they were students from Salamanca or Valladolid, no?"

"I haven't been to Salamanca or Valladolid, but I expect so, Reverend Father."

"Tell me, which of their abilities did they employ to regale you?"

"On my arrival, they sang . . ."

"Of course! Music. The Indians are great music enthusiasts. And our boys have stunning voices, the voices of angels . . . But tell me, what else did they do?"

"They recited a speech."

"Quintilianus, surely. Or Cicero. Or Boethius. Those boys do love Boethius."

"It was Cicero, Reverend Father."

"Yes, Cicero. And then?"

"Then . . . then they discoursed on various philosophical questions beyond my own knowledge, Reverend Father."

"Ah, Philosophy! Isn't it incredible to see those Indians philosophizing like resurrected Platos and Augustines?"

"Yes, Reverend Father."

"And then? What did they do then?"

"I think that's all, Reverend Father."

"That's all? Are you certain that is all you have seen?"

Juan is unsure of his reply. He studies the blind man's expression for a clue, but the man's face is an unbroken wall.

"I suppose so, Reverend Father. At least all I can recall at this moment."

"Very well. Do me this small favor: forget your eyes. As you can imagine, I frequently forget mine . . . Forget, then, your eyes and tell me what else you have seen."

"I do not understand, Reverend Father."

"Yes, you do. I have been told that you are a pursuer of heresy and the Evil One's machinations. You come by order of the viceroy to apprehend Juan the Indian. And now you are here, in what was once his home, seeking something you hope will help you in your enterprise. Tell me, have you found that something which you came to seek?"

"I'm not sure."

The blind man looks surprised, or disappointed.

"So then, among all those angelic boys who sang and recited the words of wise pagans and deliberated over philosophical questions beyond your knowledge; beneath all that perfection and all that beauty . . . you didn't sense it? You didn't smell it?"

"Smell what, Reverend Father?"

"The Evil One's presence. The smell of sin. The smell of the weeds of heresy."

Juan opens his mouth to speak. Slowly, he closes it again.

63

"I confess they deceived me, too," the old man continues, shaking his head. "Like my Franciscan brothers, I also believed that what we were doing was God's will, not the Devil's. My good brothers will speak to you of errors and lost sheep. But you and I know that where there is a good flock, there are no bad sheep. The Romans following Cicero, from whose example we must learn, gave their language and their lands to the barbarians. They even granted them citizenship; even those who lived at the limits of the Empire and had never seen a marble column in their life. They believed that would pacify them. And how were they thanked for that gift?"

He makes a theatrical gesture of the hands; a gesture, Juan thinks, that seems to belong to the world of senators in togas and tribunes who watched their palaces and silks go up in flames.

"This is what I believe now, at least," the blind man says. "But I believed something else back then. Perhaps I believed too much in myself. A surfeit of confidence in my own opinion and my own pedagogy. And as you know, when one believes, when one firmly believes something, he ignores the signs that counter his faith."

"You speak of Juan the Indian."

"Does the world speak of anything else?"

Juan's eyes and the old man's eyes find each other, they seem to meet in the air, like a collision of two solid bodies.

"What is he accused of, exactly?" Juan dares ask at last.

"Who?"

"That perverse man. Juan the Indian."

The old man cannot stifle a brief expression of annoyance, as if it bothered him to return to a subject he believed dead and buried.

"If you really are the viceroy's envoy, you will have heard the nature of those terrible charges from the viceroy's own mouth," he replies cautiously.

Juan tries to smile; a smile the blind man, in any case, can't see.

"Let us just say that I am aware of the charges, and that the viceroy has asked me to hear them again, from the lips of Your Reverend Father. Expressed in your own words."

Silence. If such a thing were possible, Juan would swear the blind man's dead eyes are staring right at him.

"In that case, I would tell you that Juan the Indian has been accused of heresy and sedition."

"Sedition against whom?"

"Sedition against his Majesty the King, in the person of the viceroy," he replies brusquely, with growing agitation. "Sedition against Spain. Sedition against the words of the Church Fathers and against the sacraments administered by priests and prelates and against the learned teachings he received in this very house. Sedition against all that is good and holy. Sedition, perhaps, against God Himself."

And before he says any more, he makes the sign of the cross.

What follows is a story filled with gaps and silences, as much is still not well-known, and even more is not known at all. It is a story that, to be understood, must reach back into the past, to the moment the boy Juan arrived first at the school, preceded by reports that made him out to be little less than a saint, a new Doctor Aquinas, a person who came to penetrate deeper than anybody into the plan for Divine Providence. It was also said that his father was a poor dead mācēhualli, perhaps to reveal the son's saintliness just as Lazarus first had to die in order to give evidence of Christ's divinity. And come to think of it, posits the blind man, perhaps this is one cause for his present disgrace; perhaps God does not wish for one not of noble condition to be treated or educated as such, just as we don't ask an arm to be a leg or a head to become a pair of buttocks upon which to sit. Perhaps it is precisely the same with the Indians: it is in their nature to dirty their hands in soil, not with the dust of books. In any case, the boy Juan grew up in this school, and at the same time, he grew in sharpness and wisdom. What they didn't know then, what they never could have known, is that such wisdom was perverse, and such sharpness as cutting as a knife, which goes to show that reason does not always produce saints, more often creating monsters. Granted, he cannot say the signs were lacking. If he thinks dispassionately, he must confess that little Juan was already wont to make dangerous arguments during lessons. He was, shall we say, the only student to realize that Moses, author of the Torah, narrates his own death in Deuteronomy; or that the first patriarchs in the Old Testament had multiple wives and made sacrifices to the image and likeness of their God, much like the Indians did in pagan times. It was easy to excuse him back then because he was no more than a child; a boy who asked inappropriate questions, perhaps, misguided by his innocence. But it is equally true, the blind man adds, that under the guise of play, the lion cub or baby snake will reveal the future cruelties they will commit when they grow. In short, he says: the boy grew. He reached the age at which boys turn their attention from holy, high-minded things and sully

65

themselves in the mire of the flesh; inclinations that ruin many called to the vocation over in Spain and even more among the natives of this land—surely His Excellency knows that the Indians are unbridled by nature, as demonstrated by certain shameful episodes that have occurred right in this school. All the same, while one could observe sensual exuberances in his schoolmates that rendered them unsuitable for taking vows, Juan continued to live only for his books, as if the sins of the flesh were alien to him, incomprehensible, even. As if he weren't entirely human. Or as if he were infected with an even greater vice: the arrogance of reason. But, the blind man repeats, how could they have known? Could we? We couldn't. That's what we told ourselves. But perhaps we could have. The world is filled with signs, for those who have the desire and skill to read them. How many times did the watchman catch the boy reading in bed at night, by the light of a tiny candle? He seemed to be praying, moving his lips to give shape to the wise words written by saints and pagans centuries before. And they believed this was good. Perhaps it was, back then. Difficult to judge, now that we know how it ends. These days, some of his brothers beat their breasts, convinced that they might have contributed to his disgrace in some way. They think that perhaps their praise made him vain; they were excessive in their enthusiasm over his wisdom and genius; they were too ambitious with the timeline for their project, too precipitous: instead of teaching the Indians how to be Christians, first they should have taught them to be men. But I contend that if we were too hasty in some way, the blind man says, it was in judging the Indians' condition, and this experience only demonstrates one thing: the Indian is not capable of the spiritual perfection we took for granted; in fact, the livelier his genius, the more dangerous he turns out to be. Naively, my brothers believe that we did not know how to correct his course. And I say, there was no course to correct, just like there is no right way to make a dog speak or instruct a snake in holy matters. Perhaps that's what Juan the Indian already was by then; a dog, a snake, living in their midst but not one of them.

Be that as it may, the blind man repeats, the dog, the snake, grew. He grew as ryegrass grows; blending in among the crop. He grew like wildfire. He learned to speak a Castilian indistinguishable from that of the cloisters of Salamanca, and an extemporal Latin rivalling Horatio or Quintilianus, and even passable Greek. He went so far as to beg his Reverend Fathers to teach him Hebrew, something they undoubtedly would have done, had they themselves not been absolutely ignorant of the language. In light of posterior events, one could say that, ultimately, such ignorance was providential. One day, the boy

Juan presented them with an impeccable and imaginative—maybe too imaginative, now that he thinks of it—translation of Boethius's *The Consolation of
Philosophy*, and another of *Tristia*, written by Ovid while among the Black Sea
barbarians, a translation of such lyricism that all were moved—too lyrical, perhaps, and too moving, if he considers it carefully. Imaginative or not, lyrical or
not, both books were taken to press and sent as gifts to His Majesty the Viceroy, who, he had been told, celebrated them heartily.

"When the snake sets his mind to it," the blind man voice is bitter but his
face impassive. "He can breach even the homes of kings and paladins."

And so it happened. The snake had grown: that's what. By that time, his
insolence was as great or greater than his talent, which is saying a lot. But we
didn't want to hear, the blind man admits; we didn't want to see. How we were
to admit we were wrong? How, even now, can we admit before you that should
Juan the Indian's capture result in bloodshed, that blood will weigh on our
conscience? I recall how during one virtuous discussion of Christ's poverty, for
example, he came to espouse several ludicrous notions, scandalous to all who
heard them. He said, impiously basing his argument on a particular passage
from Matthew, that no man can serve two masters, and that the Church had
to choose between serving the Crown or serving God. The brothers, armed
with wise and stringent examples, reminded him that Matthew himself recognized that one must render unto Caesar what is Caesar's and unto God what is
God's; in other words, their souls were for God, and the Emperor could claim
the worldly—and in some ways trifling—things such as gold. Upon hearing
that rationale, the boy asked maliciously—and it is worth remembering that
he wasn't even fifteen at the time—whether the souls of the Indians who died
unloading their gold from the earth's depths were included in the tribute they
owed the emperor. Here, the blind man says, was a sign. Many and varied were
the punishments they gave him for uttering those words, punishments he completed rigorously but without repentance. He later maintained, based on twisted, false readings of the Holy Scriptures, that not only is it pleasing to Christ
that the Church be poor—an opinion, as you will surely know, to which we
Franciscan friars humbly subscribe—but that any ornamentation or accumula-
tion of goods was actually a mortal sin, whether it consisted of a sack of wheat
or one paltry coin. You see, this was an Indian talking, an Indian who had never
seen a sack of wheat in his life. He said, too, that all brothers in Christ should
distribute whatever they possessed to the poor and set forth to preach with no
saddlebag for their journey, nor two tunics, nor sandals, nor cane. This was an-

other sign. He said he could not find evidence in the Bible for the existence of the Purgatory we preached—you, my son, can judge this for yourself—here was an Indian brat challenging Pope Gregory I, Cyprian of Carthage, and Augustine de Hippo all at once—and he said, too, that the Holy Spirit goes where it will and not where it is told to go, and that the encomienda system was nothing but a way of using Christ as a pretext for enslaving the Indians. Signs, signs, and more signs. Not to mention the day when, perplexed by the fact that no Indian had ever been ordained as a priest in New Spain, he accused all the Franciscan brothers of discriminating in a way Christ never did, not in Canaan, not in Samara, not in any nation on earth. Here, the blind man repeats, was another sign. And if only that had been all. Because if there is a hierarchy of virtue, there must also be a hierarchy of depravation and of sin; and no sin was more terrible than the one he committed every day behind the monks' backs. He is referring, as His Excellency must surely know already, to the translation of the Latin Bible into Spanish; the monstrous project the boy undertook in secret, with nobody's authorization or guidance. Because, at a certain point, Juan no longer accepted tutors or guides. They have reason to believe that he even dared turn his grubby hand to the Songs of Songs, whose translation is expressly forbidden by the Holy Office. That was when he disappeared. The same day they discovered his secret. He fled the school at the darkest hour of the night, they didn't know to where—didn't know then, at least—and his flight was a relief for the pupils as well as the teachers, who no longer knew what punishments or penances to use to rein him. Their only worry was not knowing the whereabouts of that terrible book, which Juan had managed to take with him. Since then, no one knows of its fate, nor whether Juan the Indian had had time to finish it. They only have news, like everyone else, of his wicked sermons among the Chichimeca Indians, enemies of the Spanish Crown; sermons so radical in their form and content that they raised alarm in the viceroy himself. It seems that what they do know is thanks to a single priest or vicar from the recently established villa of Zacatecas, who reported to authorities on the many evils and errors Juan committed. Perhaps, the blind man says, that priest can guide you. What exactly did they consist of, those evils, those errors, those teachings? Ah, wouldn't he like to know the answer. Or perhaps not: he wouldn't like it, really, because it is best to be ignorant of subjects of so little virtue. That is sin's very first victory over our hearts: to make itself known. Hence, he has preferred not to know, and therefore hasn't. Find that priest and ask him—if he's still alive. Ask the apostolic inquisitor. If you're curious and courageous enough, ask the Chichimeca. What he can verify, however, is that not just the viceroy but the very Pope himself would be sorely afflicted if he were to hear those teachings, teachings he, the blind man, knows nothing about. Perhaps he would add something else, now that he thinks of it: if Juan truly is going to confront him; yes, if Juan is—as he has heard—the man chosen to deal with Juan the Indian, then he must be careful. Do not let him speak; above all else, do not listen to what he will want to tell you. Juan the Indian is deceitful, like all Indians, and also highly astute: he will snare you in his net, as he did with us for all these years. What else can they expect from a child who denounced his own father and brought about his death, at nobody's urging? Imagine: somebody who did not shed a single tear for his dead father, at an age when other children cry over a skinned knee. They say even the crocodiles of the Nile cry on rare occasion. They say that even the most wretched vermin do not do what he did: give death to their giver of life. So, when the time comes, do not hesitate, do not listen: let your sword do the talking.

The hour is too late for Juan to depart, so they insist on readying a cell beside the church for His Excellency. Then they accompany him to the refectory, where all the schoolboys are waiting before their bowls of soup. It looks like the meal is about to commence forthwith, but nobody sits, nobody breaks bread or fills their water glass. All eyes are fixed on a kind of pulpit that presides over the hall. A platform with the air of a dais or statue pedestal or sacred throne. Atop it, the blind man. The blind man, who has begun to declaim, in Latin, a kind of sermon, or rally. Who knows what those words mean. The change in the blind man does not escape Juan's notice. His voice is different, suddenly cavernous and terrible. His severe expression is different; the dead eyes appear to have come to life. His gestures are different, brutal and authoritarian, like a sovereign addressing his subjects. His right hand rises to puncture the air again and again.

Behind him, the livid faces of the Franciscan brothers. Clenched jaws. Too-large eyes.

What is the blind man saying?

For a moment, he fears he has asked the question out loud, because suddenly he notes one of the schoolboys approaching, solicitous. A merciful child who has perhaps understood his baffled expression, who stands on tiptoe to whisper in His Excellency's ear: the blind man's words, sweetened by his angel's voice.

The boy says that the blind man says that they are living in difficult times. He says a terrible epidemic is spreading outside and that within these walls terrible events have also occurred.

He says that it is tempting to connect the two facts, but he is prudent enough not to do so; only God has the right to judge the connection between causes and consequences.

He says that tonight they have the privilege of receiving in their home an ambassador of the viceroy; as he says it, the blind man points to the place at the table where he expects to find Juan, but where Juan most certainly is not to be found.

He says that the viceroy is dismayed by these terrible events and begs, suggests, demands that certain things change.

He says some of those things are already changing and many others will have to change.

He says that, perhaps owing to an excess of good faith, many mistakes have been made at this school, but they are going to correct that excess of good faith and fix those mistakes.

That is what the blind man says, or at least what the boy says the blind man is saying. The child translates cautiously in an almost strangled voice, his eyes wide and resigned.

The blind man is going to tell them a story. *Vultis hoc narrare?* Do they want him to tell that story? *Its, si vis.* Yes, we want, the boys respond in unison, something like unease or fright in their voices. The story he is going to tell, the boy says the blind man says, took place many centuries ago, at the time of the ancient Greeks; to be more exact, it took place in the imagination of a Greek called Aesop. It is a fable, and like all fables, it simultaneously contains both a lie and a truth. In any case, it is a valuable teaching, because even though the pagans did not enjoy the light of the Creator, they did possess the light of reason, and with that light they managed to come close, in their fashion, to Divine Providence; so close that it is a pity that, when Judgement Day comes, not a single one of them will rejoice in His grace. But that doesn't matter now, the blind man says according to the boy. What matters is the fable. *Haec facula dicitur agricola et serpens,* the boy says. The fable is called "the farmer and the snake," the boy says. And in the fable there is, as one would expect, a farmer who finds a snake. The snake, as is usual in these cases, is wicked. The wicked snake is almost dead from the cold and the farmer feels pity for it. The wicked snake begs the farmer not to leave it there, since in fables animals always have the gift of human speech. Don't leave me, for the love of God, the wicked snake says—although it can't say for the love of God, the blind man admits, at most it could say for the love of the gods or for the love of this god or that god, since in Ancient Greece men committed the mortal sin of polytheism—in any case, the farmer gathers it in his lap and covers it with a blanket, though the snake is his natural enemy, and brings it inside his cabin. He lights a fire for it. He cleans its skin chapped from the cold. He drips a few sips of milk and honey onto its forked snake-tongue. Thank you, thank you, thank you, the wicked snake says. The wicked snake is pleased. The wicked snake is growing bigger and stronger. Until one day, a day like any other, instead of giving thanks, the wicked snake chooses to give the farmer a wicked bite. The wicked snake is pleased, the blind man repeats, to see its benefactor writhe on the floor. With his final death rattle, the farmer has time to ask the snake why it bit him, for the love of God—for the loves of the gods—why him, he who has given the snake so much succor. And then the reptilian smile, the blind man's smile: Oh, shut up, you stupid farmer! the boy says the blind man says the snake says. You knew exactly who I was when you let me in.

The blind man falls silent. The boy falls silent. The children fall silent. The friars, increasingly restless and stiff, fall silent too.

Haec fabula simplex est, the blind man says. This fable is very simple, the boy says, in a voice that has gradually filled with stammers and shaking. Much simpler than Christ's parables. But he will explain it to them anyway.

The farm is the world.

The farmer is him. The farmer is every one of the venerable Franciscan brothers accompanying him.

The cabin is this school.

The milk and honey are the Word of God.

The snake is all of you. At least, some among you.

This is what the blind man says, and he falls silent again, long enough for the snakes to realize that they are snakes. Children on the verge of crying or screaming or hiding under the table. Children with horror painted on their faces, eying each other, like they are trying to see the scales they do not possess. And yet, they do not cry, they do not scream, they do not hide under the table. No one says a word. Not even the friars, who squirm uncomfortably in their seats, open their mouths. They can hardly muster the will to look up from the floor. Juan sees that they want to make this man stop talking; his words embarrass or sadden or horrify them. They would happily gag him, but they won't. Either because they do not dare or because they cannot. Because that man is their superior and, in their own way, the friars are scolded boys as well, without the gumption to interrupt their Reverend Father. Only Juan the Indian could do it. Only Juan the Indian would dare to raise the loudest voice, so loud it would deafen the world's ears, and perhaps this is why he is no longer a boy and no longer an Indian, either. Perhaps, Juan thinks, that was Juan the Indian's only sin: to speak when others were silent.

You are Indians, continues the blind man, continues the boy, and like the ancient Greeks you were born with the grave sin of polytheism. You were dying of cold on the plains of your paganism and we have come to rescue you from that plain. Can someone who has been saved from winter possibly reproach the fire for tepidness?

Whosoever receives the Word of God, he continues, must be docile as a lamb and simple as a dove.

Whosoever receives the Word of God must not become vain nor complain that the cabin is cold or the milk is sour or the honey not sweet enough for his palate.

Whosoever receives the Word of God must not bite the hand that provides for him. Because to do so is not to bite a farmer or a friar, but God Himself.

So, if there be more snakes among you, if those you hear are not lambs or doves, know that we will never again be naive like farmers, but as sharp as foxes. Implacable as eagles. Careful as dogs that shepherd the flock and do not hesitate to bite the sheep that hangs back or runs ahead, much less the wolf who disguises himself as a sheep.

He says: For some time, this school has neglected discipline, because they believed the boys to be worthy of the great gift they were giving them. But they were wrong. The Scriptures already say that holy things must not be given to dogs or pearls thrown to pigs, lest they be trampled.

He says: The Lord disciplines the one He loves and whips the one He receives like a son. What kind of sons would they be if their Franciscan fathers didn't discipline them? They would not be true sons, but bastards.

He says: Never again shall one who praises God with his lips but bites Him in the depths of his heart be concealed in this house.

He says: We shall make our school great again!

Fiat schola nostra magnum! the wicked snakes respond, their voices uneven, cracking with fear.

The wicked snakes cross themselves. The wicked snakes take their seats in pious silence. Before breaking bread, the wicked snakes give thanks to God.

That night, Juan has a dream. In that place, the very school where Juan the Indian spent his childhood. In that bed, perhaps reminiscent of Juan the Indian's bed, Juan dreams. In the dream there are no words and no human beings. There isn't even any sound. Only a common snail, a snail that absolutely resembles all the other snails in the world, slipping silently along the edge of his sword. That is his dream, his nightmare; a snail that crawls along the edge of his blade and survives. He wakes, and when he does, he cannot say whether that snail was Juan or Juan.

Further on there is a path that disappears into the fields of corn that nobody harvests. Further on are the marshes of Lake Zumpango, inhabited by birds, not men, and a posting station with no horses, no servants, not even an owner. Further on there is a caravan of Indians wandering like sleepwalkers, dragging their tools and rolls of clothing like a ghost army. Two more weeks, Juan thinks, and he will have reached the Gran Chichimeca. Further on there is a river. Further on there are villages that from a distance appear alive but die with every passing step. Further on there is a horse roaming the plain, its tack still hanging from its back. Further on there is a pumpkin patch where pumpkins rot and an abandoned ranch with a hearth where Juan lights a fire. Two more weeks and Juan does not want to use his sword, but he will if required; Juan who will capture or kill that Indian who knows how to read languages Juan doesn't know and write books Juan has never opened. Further on there is an empty village and another on the verge of being empty. Further on there is a flock of vultures patiently circling in the sky. Further on there is a drunk pilgrim spouting nonsense, and a muleteer who doesn't want to talk about what he has seen on the other side of the sierra, and an Indian at a crossroads who prays an Our Father in his scant Latin. Further on there is a dead donkey, still shackled to the grindstone. Two more weeks and he will have reached Juan the Indian and Juan the Indian will return with him, either walking on his own two feet or with his head bumping along in the bottom of a sack. Further on there is a quadrille of Spaniards assigned to pick the encomienda's corn, they sweat in the sun, they curse the dead Indians. Further on there is a dead Indian. Further on there is an abandoned quarantine station; the last patients rotting in an open grave; the windows open and full of broken glass; flies feasting on the dressings darkened by blood and dirty blankets and chamber pots strewn about the floor. Two weeks and Juan will have obtained his gold and his glory; he will be back at his tavern, where, miraculously, the plague will not have reached, or where it has reached but without breaching its walls or damaging any flesh. The dog happily wagging its tail. His wife embracing him in the hall. His wife who will tell him, who is telling him now amid sobs that she was very afraid, if he only knew, so afraid. Further on there is an abandoned Aztec temple and an abandoned Christian hermitage, too. Further on there is an Indian who awaits the coming End Times, and when he tires, begs for alms. Further on there is a village where all villagers sing and dance, fiercely, the drums beat, the kettledrums and sackbuts and bone horn-pipes pulling the Indians into a dance that never ends, some are already touched by sickness but still they dance, they bleed from their mouths and bleed from their noses and bleed from their eyes, and yet still they dance, still they drink enormous clay jars of atole until the jars topple over and the men topple too. Further on there is an empty plain. Further on there is a sunset.

That's where it happens. On that plain where there is nothing to do or see. Under the light of the setting sun.

Weeping. An animal complaint carried on a wind that blows, unfettered by any obstacle that might stop it. It's Juan's horse that stops. Juan shields his eyes with his hand until he spots two little bundles of clothing on the side of the road. The first bundle turns out to be a boy, or what is left of a boy who surely cried and kicked and bawled under his blanket until his strength ran out. The second bundle was, still is, the body of an Indian woman holding out. A woman who tries to crawl along the ditch, imploring hands outstretched toward the child who the sun of the plain has made a mess of offal, to the delight of worms and flies. Her eyes are open, and her mouth is too. She is the one who whines. She cries: her wail reaching where her hands cannot.

Cautiously, Juan dismounts. He bends down to examine his wife's body. Because that body, he has just decided, is that of his wife: the same native features, the same desperation, the same wail; the same need to hold the man she loves, the same failure to do so. The same future, the flesh that wastes and dies. Her eyes: the same eyes, opened to watch him from the past, as if she were still waiting, fixed in place on the tavern's threshold. This woman is also waiting. Who knows what she waits for; what this thing is that keeps her from surrendering. She waits for her son to just sleep. She waits for a miracle. She waits for a doctor to heal her body or a priest to heal her soul.

Juan looks at her lips, blistered from thirst and fever. Her tongue, her tar-black tongue, waggling.

"Water, sir . . ."

So his wife will say, crippled in bed or laid out on the tavern floor. Water, sir, she will say, and there will be no one to hear. Or worse still: there will be someone compassionate enough to hear her and cruel enough to give her the sip that will, for a few more hours, prolong her agony.

"Water, sir . . ."

No, Juan says, Juan thinks, stroking that face consumed by sores. No, he repeats. It's too late. Too late to go back and too late, also, to go on. Too late to save this woman who clutches his breastplate, as if praying to a God that cannot save us. Save her: how could he, if he could not even save his own wife. The wife it is better to never think of again, Juan realizes, Juan decides; her name and her face must never be remembered, because she is dead or almost dead; because right now she is lying on the tavern floor, on that floor there was never enough time to finish laying in the stone. His wife crawling through the same pool of blood, begging for help from anyone who will listen.

"Water, sir . . ."

Juan checks the belt at his waist. The canteen he will not hand to her. The sword he will not draw. He wonders if he will ever dare to draw it again. The gold that rattles in its bag, useless to this woman and to so many other things. The woman's deranged eyes, which glide over the canteen, the sword, the gold.

"Water, sir . . ."

Her mouth is slightly agape, as if petrified in a grimace of dread: an expression in which there is no surprise, just the confirmation of something already known but no less intolerable for it. She is looking at him. Inside him. Maybe right through him. She looks in a terrible way, as one looks at terrible things that have happened and the even more terrible things still to come; eyes divested of all volition and all beauty, eyes that have seen horror and are filled with it and therefore excruciating to look at, or perhaps they have seen horror and are empty for that very reason, though that emptiness itself is even more unbearable. Eyes that reflect nothing now, eyes that are what remains of compassion when faith is erased; freedom, when justice is withheld; will, when it lacks hands and a voice. Hope minus hope.

"Water, sir . . . water, for the love of God . . ."

With a bound, Juan is on his horse. He feels the weight of that gaze as he moves away, trotting at first and then galloping, galloping ever faster, and he feels that weight still, much later, when, at a bend in the road, the wife and her eyes disappear.

IV

Lose the soul to gain the whole world – A Spanish priest, a Spanish doctor, and an encomendero – Putrefaction of a memory – Candles like stars – The best medicine – Neither fear nor trembling – Gold upon gold – Father no church – The Devil is God and God the Devil – As regards to sin – A madman or a brave man – The second coming of Christ

All that remains is to move forward. To not look back. To not ask questions. North, always north. Ahead, always ahead, without changing or questioning the course, because there is nothing left behind him; ahead, only the future can await. Juan rides toward that future. Thoughts and memories farther and farther behind in the solitude of his ride: behind, the ruined tavern; behind, the encomienda he never received; behind, too, that dead woman he has chosen to never think of again. Ahead, only Juan the Indian. Because Juan the Indian also lost everything; he lost his father and he lost his idols and he lost his village and he received nothing in exchange. But Juan does not resign himself to nothing. Someday Juan will return home—but which home is that?—and it won't be with empty hands. To that end—to fill his hands—he needs to find him. To that end—to find meaning—he needs to capture that man who is condemned to be an Indian among Spaniards and Spanish among Indians. He must capture him at any cost, kill him if necessary, even if he doesn't know why. The reason must be found. Invented, if required. A reason, any reason, no matter how unlikely or absurd. Because if that reason doesn't exist, if he's here in the middle

76

of the plain when he could be beside the hearth in his home, then the whole journey lacks any meaning. His wife's death would become irreversible folly; and he, too, would have lost it all—for nothing. Locate Juan the Indian, though he doesn't know if he'll be able to draw his sword; though he doesn't know what he will do or say when he finds him. Locate Juan the Indian and believe that, in doing so, he is saving the world, because only someone who saves the world has a just reason to lose his soul.

A village in the middle of nowhere. An inn at the center of that village. The stable boy, a young Spanish man of no more than fifteen, takes his horse by the halter and leads it to the stables, but not before he has addressed Juan as Your Excellency and Your Grace, performed a complicated bow, and accepted, after much fuss and reluctance, the silver coin Juan handed him.

The cantina is practically deserted. When Juan enters, the innkeeper, a Spaniard, is filling three jugs of wine, and a very young woman, also Spanish, carries those jugs to the only occupied table, where three men converse: a Spanish priest, a Spanish doctor, and a Spanish encomendero. A single window looks over a good portion of the village, and Juan sits down next to it. Through the pane, he sees the empty street and a smattering of Indian hovels in various states of deterioration, rotting slowly into the same mud from which they once emerged. All their windows and shutters are closed and, on some, even the doors have been nailed shut from the inside and any openings blocked by barricades and bulwarks. A dead village, one might say. But a few flickering lights can be glimpsed through the cracks; candles that burn and are consumed slowly alongside their inhabitants.

The girl has come to his table. Close up, she looks even younger and more beautiful, a contradiction, an almost painful juxtaposition, with that crumbling world. Budding breasts swell above the tight-fitting neckline; a neckline that, for the sake of modesty, might well benefit from another stitch, as the priest has just pointed out.

"What will your Lordship drink?"

"A little wine."

"Spanish wine?"

While he waits for his tankard, Juan listens to the conversation underway at the neighboring table. They, too, are watching the deserted streets, illuminated by the last light of dusk. They are discussing it, the village that is either asleep or dead. Apparently, the chief magistrate has recommended that the villagers not leave their homes more than strictly necessary, a completely useless precaution, in the doctor's opinion; Indians will contract the disease whether or not they wall off their huts, and Spaniards won't get sick no matter how they rub their faces against the infected. The solution, concludes the doctor, is that there is no solution, and when a problem lacks a solution, one is free to err however he pleases. Which is why he recommends that everyone live as they see fit, and if they want to join in religious festivities or have a banquet then they should do it, and if they want to kiss their dying relatives, well, they should kiss them, because only Nature knows who will die and who will survive. You mean God, the priest interjects, and the doctor shrugs. Be it Nature's affair or God's, it is indisputable that the Indians and Spaniards are of different quality, perhaps even different material. The case of the horse is illustrative here: no disease is known to wreak havoc on a dun but have no effect whatsoever on bays or sorrels. If a horse dies from a disease, he says, any other horse may die from that same disease. By contrast, even children know that the disease that brings down a horse won't affect a cat or dog or sparrow hawk or snake, much less a man. The conclusion is irrefutable. There is just one conclusion, he says, just one possible conclusion, and it bucks the theories and sermons espoused by men long on good intentions but short on science. The conclusion, he repeats a third time, can any of those present tell him what the conclusion is?

He turns first to the priest and then to the encomendero and lastly to Juan, who has just received his jug of wine.

"You, sir, you too, undoubtedly know what this proves."

Juan holds the man's eyes.

"I suppose it proves we are not horses."

The doctor laughs:

"No, you can bet we aren't horses. We are men. The Indians, on the other hand . . . oh! Who knows what the Indians are."

Juan remains silent. The encomendero, having barely followed the doctor's argument, scratches his head and says that if they were horses, the Spaniards would surely be sorrel steeds and the Indians plain old brown or black horses; mules, perhaps, considering how little and how poorly they manage to educate their offspring. The priest reasons that wits sharper than theirs have already debated the question at length; the humanity of those men native to these lands was demonstrated by the papal bull *Sublimis Deus*, issued by his Holiness Paul III, and as far as he is concerned, a pope's words are more powerful than entire armies of syllogisms and horses. Now, the priest concedes, scratching his beard, it is no less true that, though his Holiness recognized that the Indians were real men, nowhere did he write that there mightn't be differences and grades of quality among them. Such differences surely exist between horse breeds, the priest reasons, and one needn't be an experienced horseman to know that those apt for a team are not necessarily the most appropriate for riding or for war. So, the question should not be whether the Indian is or is not a man, but rather what kind of man the Indian is: if we can rely on him for all types of enterprises—to include self-governance—or for only a few basic things.

The encomendero, ever faithful to his metaphor, is of the opinion that if there is one thing they can be sure of, it is that Indians are not team horses. He has seen Indians work, he himself has suffered their inconstancies and ineptitudes, and he knows full well that even the least strenuous tasks wear them out. A single Spaniard works harder than two full-grown Indians, much in the way that two women do not equal the work of one man; so as far as he can figure it, the Indians have something womanish about them, something almost feminine in their nature. The doctor roundly joins in the encomendero's opinion, because it makes him think about various and obvious indicators: first, the lack of body—and even facial—hair; second, a fondness for wearing their hair very long; third, their inclination toward a certain vile sin of which he cannot speak without revulsion—do the gentlemen know what he means?—a sin that consists of enjoying the body *in malam partem*, not, shall they say, through the normal channel, but another way in. What they call sodomy. But he would go even further: if there is something womanish in every Indian, there is also much that is childlike, and perhaps they should bear that in mind when considering the lack of beard, the high-pitched voice, and the natural innocence with which they believe whatever they are told, whether or not it contradicts reality or understanding. Now that he thinks of it, given their natural weakness, children and women are precisely those most affected by the plague, an observation that could mean everything or absolutely nothing at all.

Silently, the priest weighs his words. There is undoubtedly some truth in both observations, he admits; the Indian's soul is, in effect, mutable like a woman's and feeble and premature like a child's, exactly as he has been given to observe over the course of his sixteen years preaching in these lands. And when all is said and done, that is the only thing that matters: the soul. Doctors might know everything about the body and encomenderos might know something about how that body labors, but only the man who hears confession from his fellow man is truly capable of knowing and studying a spirit's solidity. And if he were to tell them what he has beheld in this examination, how much rot, how many badly-aired, sunless rooms, how many wooden altarpieces shining with gold on the outside but gnawed and even crumbling inside, oh, if he could tell them those stories, the things they would say then. Because he has seen so much. Indians who travel many leagues on foot to confess atrocious crimes, not out of piety but because they believe that, along with absolution, the priests dispense documents that will save them from prison or the gallows. Indians who refuse to accept responsibility for sins they committed while drunk, because, in their ignorance, they believe those errors must be attributed to the God of Wine and no one else. Others make up terrible sins just to assure themselves that the priest will give them terrible penances as well, since it is penance that they actually seek: an excuse to bloody their limbs and whip their backs with nail-studded straps, just like when they bled and whipped themselves for their hellish gods. Even Indians who appear to be exemplary Christians and have for years responded perfectly to the missionaries' questions: Do you believe in Christ our Lord? Yes, I believe; Do you believe in God and the Trinity? Yes, I believe; until one has the notion to approach the question from the opposite flank, and when they asked whether they also believe in Tláloc, in Coatlicue, in Quetzalcóatl, the Indian who calls himself a Christian replies just as naturally that yes, yes, yes, he believes in Christ, and he also believes in the plumed serpent, in the Mother Goddess, and in as many gods as it pleases them to throw in his face. And how many times, when reprimanded, do they still have the gall to say: Father, don't be shocked, because we are still *nepantla*, which in their savage tongue means "in the middle." In the middle of what? In the middle of the past and the present, one understands, in the middle of us and their ancestors, sin and virtue, because they are not yet rooted in faith and they just as soon turn to God as to their old customs and devilish rites, and to them, both creeds seem one and the same.

The encomendero, who hasn't ceased swirling the wine in his tankard, suddenly interrupts. He, too, has much to say on this subject, he says, on Indian idolatry. He might not be an expert in bodies or souls, but he has had the opportunity to experience firsthand the Indians' damned religion. It and only it is to blame for his great misfortune. And that great misfortune, he says, came one morning when he awoke and called for his servants, but the servants did not come, and he left his chambers and passed through the kitchens, empty, and the hall, also empty, and from there he went to the garden and the stables, where the horses were swishing their tails, desperate with hunger and nosing around their empty troughs. He bellowed for his Indians to no avail and galloped the whole length and breadth of his hacienda—three million square varas—hollering just as loud.

He found them at last at nightfall, sprawled about the ruins of an ancient pagan temple turned by time into a nest of brush and brambles. Two or three hundred Indians; all of his Indians, in fact, and all dead; they were fathers and sons and daughters and wives, they were good and not-so-good Indians, obliging Indians and rebellious ones, old people and children and women, every single one of them gathered there, and each one of them had been surprised in a different manner of death: their throats had been slit, they'd been hanged, they'd been bled dry—could they imagine anything so stupid?—and there were some intact bodies, too, dead from something that left no marks, poison, perhaps, or maybe they'd died of fright, because that is what the Indians believe, that a person can also die of fright. And he knew it had all been the idea of a witch doctor, one who had filled their brains with words and curses and ancient spells, someone who still lit secret fires in the ruins of old temples and said the glory days were coming, when the world would end and the winds of their ancestors would blow from the north and sweep across the earth and exterminate whiteness. Who knows what that witch doctor told them. How he convinced them that they had to kill themselves; that it was better to be dead than to continue to work on the encomienda. But the most irritating part was that the blasted witch doctor was still alive, he hadn't poisoned or stabbed or abused himself at all, he was simply there, smiling, says the encomendero, just so he could tell the owner and master of the Indians how much they hated him, how they had wished to abandon him to the land that had caused them so much suffering.

He spent a whole night and day deciding how the man would have to be punished, since the witch doctor told him that death would be nothing but liberation, an irrelevant transition, almost pleasurable, and the encomendero was not willing to allow that. Let's just say that he considered it a point of honor to make the witch doctor suffer and scream before he died, and this small whim became the crucial point, since what else was left for him to hope for? He had no Indians, but at least he'd have justice. The doctor interjects to point out that the Indians are, in effect, capable of proffering terrible screams, perhaps given their resemblance, in some aspects, to animals, whose nature—in addition to that of women and children—they obviously share. The priest, by contrast, says that a scream cannot be used as a measure of a creature's humanity or inhumanity, and if we're going there, it is faithfully documented that Christ himself cried out, screamed a horrible scream, before expiring. Let's leave Christ in peace, says the encomendero, discharging a slap on the table: I assure you, Father: that witch doctor was no Christ. He was the Devil personified, and if even God can scream horribly, I promise you, the Devil can too. And thus, he proposed to make the witch doctor scream, hear him scream like no human being ever had before. Scream, perhaps, like only the Devil can. It was a delicate question; perhaps you gentlemen don't know much about the limits of pain and consciousness, the encomendero says, but the greatest sufferings are often those that most quickly incapacitate us. Pain so terrible it clouds our consciousness and numbs our senses, and the key, he says, the key lies in finding the intersection of maximum pain and maximum consciousness. To retain life inside pain, subdivide it into a thousand deaths. That's the theory, at least. In short, he won't bore them with explanations of how he discovered this tenuous intersection: suffice to say that, after arduous efforts, he hit upon it and achieved his end: the witch doctor screamed horribly before he died, maybe even after he died, and that scream was, in some ways, the encomendero's consolation. Aside from that consolation, nothing. He was forced to abandon the deserted encomienda and beg His Excellency the viceroy for more Indians, but the Indians never arrived, and now the land which had once borne so much fruit remains uncultivated and each month he travels to the capital to make a pilgrimage between offices, studies, and clerks' desks, until someone will take pity on him, the unfortunate man.

For a time, no one speaks. They look out the window, where there is nothing to see; only the night, which has already deepened, leaving very little light. Suddenly, the doctor turns to Juan, as if he'd recalled some long-forgotten thing:

"And you sir, what say you? In your soldier's experience, do the Indians fight like women, children, or men?"

Juan tilts his head.

"I can't make a comparison. I'm afraid I've never raised my sword against women or children."

"Understandable. Then perhaps you can tell us whether an Indian's head is in fact as hard as it is presumed to be. I've heard it from one of His Majesty the King's soldiers that one must take care not to strike them on the head in battle, lest the sword bounce back toward its wielder. Is that true? Is an Indian's head truly that much harder than our own? Harder, even, than steel?"

"You must excuse me. I haven't raised a sword against Christians, either."

The priest sighs and makes a remark about Christians raising swords against other Christians in the very heart of Europe; how, sooner or later, they will have no choice but to exterminate the bloody Germans, and how they will only have themselves to blame. The doctor nods distractedly, as if thinking about something else. The encomendero, however, appears unsatisfied by Juan's answer.

"Perhaps you haven't raised your sword against women, children, or Christians, but you have surely raised it against Indians. Tell us, what's it like, dispatching a hundred of those savages to Hell?"

Juan lingers over the last of his wine.

"To hear you gentlemen tell it, not very different from governing them."

For several moments, the three men are silent, before breaking into laughter. Then, almost immediately, they fall silent again. Someone orders another round. The doctor enumerates the beneficial effects of wine on the human organism. The priest says it is significant that Christ, capable of performing any miracle, would choose to multiply wine at a wedding and, at the Last Supper, make it the vehicle for his blood; two marvels that can only mean Christ himself knew how to enjoy a good wine. The encomendero reminisces out loud about his vineyards with no Indians to work them, and downs half his tankard in a single swig. Outside the window, the last light in the last of the homes dies out.

Gallop farther. Gallop faster. Gallop until he forgets his destination or the actual reason for his journey. Around him, the world dematerializes, blurred by his breakneck speed. Villages in which he does not stop. Secondary roads whose direction does not interest him. Mule drivers to whom he says nothing, poses no questions. This is Juan in the solitude of his journey, a journey that, day after day, is acquiring an element of renunciation, of private cowardice, of secret flight. To pursue Juan the Indian and yet find himself thinking about the man like a fellow adventurer; another solitary rider who has seen the same forests and the same cow paths, who forded the same rivers, who stopped before the same mountains. Two homeless men, advancing because they can no longer go back. To think about Juan the Indian so as not to think about all they both have lost: to forget the world they left behind. And to not achieve this absence of thought, or not achieve it entirely. The gold swinging in his bag like an ever-weightier ballast. The coins' jangle like a nightmare song he can't stop hearing. Juan wants to run more swiftly than time, to a place memory cannot reach.

And then, the first shiver. It happens somewhere on the plain, doesn't matter where exactly. The fever catches up to him all of a sudden, halfway through his journey, as if the disease were a region he had to pass through. Of course, at the time he didn't call the fever a fever. At first, it seems like nothing more than too much sun or exhaustion. A slight dizziness. A metallic aftertaste his mouth, as if he'd spent the night licking coins. Fever like radiance or a creeping clairvoyance or gift that seems to accelerate the things around him, the trees that crop up on either side of the trail and the birds that fly in the sky overhead. He doesn't want to think about the plague: at least not yet. First, he blames the heat and the poor condition of the roads. He blames the wine he drank the previous night. He blames his many years, from which no one is exempt. Then he closes his eyes. Faster and faster his horse advances, breaking into a trot though no one has urged it, and Juan with his eyes shut. Thoughts reach him in intermittent waves, they are and are not, like flares that, for a single instant, illuminate the darkness behind his eyelids. Behind those lids, vertigo. A falling sensation; Juan falling infinitely into an abyss with no anchors or end. That abyss is the horizon, which somehow compels him. That abyss is the journey. The sun still shines but no longer produces heat, and inside his breastplate Juan is numb in the cold soup of his own sweat. A sudden thirst inflames his lips and tongue. It's the plague, he thinks, admits, eyes still closed. It's the plague, he will think later, when he sees his trembling hands; hands hardly able to hold the reins. The plague, he thinks, and feels the chattering of chill and fever both.

The horse's hoofbeats echo inside his skull, but so too do the voices of men who are no longer there. Words he heard in recent days, perhaps only yesterday, but which seem very faraway nonetheless, as if the dust of years or centuries had fallen over them. A doctor says Indians fall ill even when walled inside their homes and Spaniards don't get sick no matter how they rub their faces against the infected. A priest says there is something womanish, childlike, bestial about the Indians. An encomendero explains how life must be retained in pain, subdivided into a thousand deaths. Might he be a Spaniard with an Indian's soul? Is there something womanish, childlike, bestial in his nature? Is this fever one of the thousand deaths that await him?

He spends the last of his strength on opening his eyes and observing the landscape. He doesn't know where he is. With one hand, he unrolls the map the viceroy's men drew for him. He believes he recognizes himself in one corner, one single, small dot on the parchment, but it can't be: everywhere he looks, bridges that shouldn't be there, clusters of ranches, roads that do not exist or did not exist when the map was drawn. An old scroll covered in scribbled names where, today, there is nothing but the uninhabited ruins of villages, and blank spaces where towns seem to have arisen. Only the mountains remain unchanged: on the parchment and on the earth. At some point during the dash, the map falls or is lost. Perhaps he threw it himself. Why? Could it be because he needs both hands to hold the reins? Or because fever has turned his eyes to slits, and without eyes, what good is a map? Or because the very parchment has lost its usefulness; no longer a map but the memory of a map, the cartography of a remote quest, a quest that in no way resembles his.

It's the plague, he thinks with eyes open, eyes closed.

And then he looks up, up where God should be:

Two weeks.

Two more weeks, he begs.

By now the horse is racing where and however it wants, galloping free of any human will. Faster, ever faster, as if something or someone were in pursuit. The horizon pulling at him harder than any whip, any rein, any spur. Juan gripping the bridle as best he can, trying to stop what cannot be stopped. Juan transformed into impotent cargo the horse tolerates on its back, but whose intentions matter naught. What are those intentions? Where is he headed and where is he now? At a certain speed, the earth is or seems to be always the same. A yellow smudge during the day and black at night. So it is: from horseback, he sees nights pass, and days. Months of fever and years of thoughts. The horse wants to run swifter than time; it's no map over which it gallops, but the pages of a calendar.

It's the plague, but not just the plague. This Juan thinks from a nook in his increasingly liquid brain. Because perhaps it isn't just he who is dying. It is the world he knew. It is time. It is his wife who dies as well. Gradually, the flesh has been falling from her memory, consumed by the elements; no one to close her open eyelids or dig her grave. Dawns and dusks occur in succession, swifter and swifter, as if the world were blinking. The world that blinks and his wife's corpse that cannot; his wife rotting, the stinking relic of her, the bones of his wife who will never, ever open her eyes again. Juan waking and sleeping and waking again on horseback. Juan struggling not to think, on nights and not-nights as lengthy as entire lives. Tasteless bread. Odorless earth. The world whitewashed in desert colors. He sees, galloping alongside him, Juan the Indian: Juan the Indian, who is no longer a young man, much less a boy. A man with his own intentions and his own dreams. He sees villages emptying out and then filling up again. He sees the last pits clogged with the last corpses and he sees how trees grow over those pits and how they are felled and sawed to build new houses. He sees, in those trees, nests where birds are born and die. Nests that are, in their way, both cradle and grave. Behind him, in her grave-less death, his wife comes to rest in ash or bone. The tavern he once kept, deserted. He sees the adobe walls begin to dry out and crack. The roof always more rotten, tiles crumbling, no cauldrons to drink up the rain. The dog that barks inside, starving, crying for a master and mistress who will never return. Ever more distant, the tavern and its ruin, a mound of rubble that is, in its own way, also a tomb. Juan who rides over that tomb, erasing it. Juan who has a final burst of strength or consciousness and digs his spurs deep into the horse's flanks, because he wants to gallop faster or because he needs to transfer his pain to another's flesh. Juan who rides over that pain, like first he rode over time.

It's the plague, Juan thinks, says to the darkness. It's the plague, he repeats, and as soon as he does, he realizes that it is night and he is stopped somewhere. He is lying on a very cold, very hard bed; colder and harder as he regains consciousness. Overhead, stars glimmer. And then he sees stars that gleam even closer, constellations of light that are actually candlesticks and oil lamps orbiting him, dazzling him. He cannot see any faces.

"Is he dead?" asks a voice not his own.

"I think so."

Juan nods. He barely has enough strength left to do it: to acknowledge that he is dead. But this simple movement suffices for the oil lamps to bend over him, to come even closer. Hands that struggle to lift him. Faces that appear, now, rescued from the darkness. Eyes that shine in worry and confusion.

"What happened?" a voice whispers.

"His Excellency fell from his horse."

"Almost cracked his noggin."

"Have to call the doctor."

"I think he was drunk."

"Drunk or crazy."

"Looks like he's trying to say something."

"Yes, he's saying something."

And Juan is, in effect, saying something. Tongue asleep, throat dead, Juan speaks.

"It's the plague," he says.

He moves his lips slowly, attempting to form the words, because he must warn them not to come near, not to touch him, not to breathe his air or be infected by his clothes. And above all, not to give him anything to drink: no matter how great his thirst, no matter how he begs and pleads, not to give him a single cup of water.

"It's the plague," he repeats.

By the flickering lamplight, he verifies the effect of his words. The faces hold no fear. Just disbelief. Surprise. Even mockery. Strange faces momentarily deformed by a hint of derision or condescension. Mouths that still move closer. Hands that still touch him. They lift him by his arms and legs, as if carrying a dead body. One of them laughs. Another shakes his head.

"Drunk or crazy," he says.

En route, there is time for Juan to make a slight recovery. The last stretch he makes not suspended in midair but on foot, leaning on the arms of two men who pepper him with questions. They were the ones who saw him bolt past the threshing floor, galloping like a madman down the Camino Real. They saw him jump a ditch, then the stone walls and corrals and fences of the plain, as if chased by the Devil himself. What was he doing? Why was he racing like that? Juan doesn't know what to say. Only a vestige of consciousness remains to him, and he uses it to ask after his horse. Don't worry about him, they reply, he's already been brought to the stables. Juan also wants to know where in the world they are. The men say the name of a town he doesn't know; a name he has already forgotten. Later, he will ask about the distance that remains to Zacatecas. Don't think about that either, the men say: Zacatecas isn't going anywhere.

But what can Juan think about, if not the plague?

In a nearby granary, they lay him down on a makeshift bed. All around, lights come and go, curious children, shadows that ask him this or that. Finally, the doctor arrives, preceded by lanterns and whispering. His is but a grave suggestion of a face, one Juan doesn't dare to look at.

His hands. The doctor's hands opening his mouth. Touching his head. His neck. His chest.

"Is it the plague, doctor?" Juan asks in a small voice.

Laughter again, slightly less restrained this time. Laughter, too, from the doctor, who turns to those gathered, like an actor to his audience.

"At least we know where he got hit," he says, pointing to his head.

And then, raising his voice so Juan can hear:

"The only thing wrong with you, my friend, is exhaustion. Tonight, you must rest and tomorrow . . ."

But then, his voice. His expression. Something rings in Juan's memory, like an echo or a ballad's refrain. The doctor is that repeated verse. Without the priest and the encomendero beside him, the doctor looks like different person. Older, certainly: by five, maybe ten years. Where before there had been a thick, black mustache, now there are whitish wisps; the skeleton of a mustache. Where before there had been the hardness of youth, now there is a kind of softness, a kind of erosion, a kind of capitulation to the world. But he is, without a doubt, the very same man: if one can actually consider a man and the old man he will become the same.

"You're the doctor," Juan murmurs, and he notes how the words stick to each other.

"Yes, I'm the doctor," the doctor says.

The man doesn't recognize him. At least he looks at him as though he doesn't. And yet, just yesterday. At an inn not many leagues to the south. This is what Juan thinks, what Juan now says. You don't recognize me? he asks. You don't remember. Yesterday. At the inn, yesterday. You were talking with a priest and an encomendero. You asked me if Indian heads are as hard as they are presumed to be. You talked about the plague. You talked about horses. But the doctor shakes his head. He checks Juan's temperature with the back of his hand and replies without meeting his eye. Yesterday I was in my house, my friend. He's been in this town for several years: in his house. He was sent here more or less when it ended, the plague Juan is so concerned about. So, Juan has nothing to fear: here in the Indies, one can die from many things, but the plague isn't one of them. And now he should get some sleep.

Then, in a low voice, the doctor speaks to the man holding the lamp.

"I don't know if he's drunk or crazy . . . in case it's the second, give him a bit of wine."

He stands with a certain degree of detachment. Either because he is already old or because he is tired. Before leaving, he turns on the threshold to look at Juan one last time. He seems to smile. A smile in the shadows, but a smile at any rate. Don't be afraid, he says. Drink and don't be afraid. Wine is the best medicine, and it's not just men of science who know it: men of God know it too. Otherwise, why would Christ, who could perform any miracle, choose to multiply the wine at a wedding and make it the vehicle for his blood at the Last Supper; two marvels that can only mean that Christ himself knew how to enjoy good wine.

This is what he says, the white-mustachioed doctor. And then he disappears.

In the dream, Juan the Indian is no longer a young man, much less a boy. In the dream, Juan the Indian isn't all that different from Juan himself. He too has survived the plague. He too has a mission. What is the mission? He smiles. Seems to smile. He no longer fears Juan, if he had, in fact, ever feared him at all. He does not fear him: he is waiting for him. Since the journey's beginning, he has been waiting.

Come, says Juan the Indian, his voice steady.

And without question, Juan gets on his horse.

It is day when he wakes. The sunlight grows stronger on the straw and there is no one in the granary. Just his horse, who turns suddenly, as if alerted by Juan's gaze. Just a pair of chickens pecking at the grain, indifferent to Juan and his horse.

Beside him, there is a bowl of water and another of wine. Juan gulps them down one after the other, until his thirst is quenched and his shirtfront soaked. A dish piled high with tortillas and beans, which he devours using his hands. No one to thank for these gifts. No one to inform that he is again alive and conscious. Minor wooziness when he stands. Some weakness in his arms and legs, but besides that, nothing. The survivor of a shipwreck, momentarily unsteady when he emerges back on deck, only to be a sailor again seconds later, ready to bring the galleon ashore wherever God and the ocean decree.

The stirrups, intact and hanging from his horse's back. The bag filled with gold, which the men who came to his aid had not seen or had preferred not to. The jerked meat and skins of water and wine, anticipating his lips.

With the toes of his boot in the stirrup, Juan requires much exertion and many maneuvers to return to the saddle. Still, he doesn't immediately ride off. His hands rummaging inside the sack and pulling out a gold coin. Landing on the yellow straw, the coin gleams for an instant, gold on gold.

Then he leaves the barn at a trot and circles the building once or twice, eyes clapped on the sun, until he knows which way is north, in which direction lies his journey.

The road wends and falters toward the mines of Zacatecas, traversing the lands of the Otomíes and Guamares; of Guachichiles and Tecuexes and Cazcanes.

The route like a fragile footbridge passing from civilization to civilization, crossing barbarism. If one can in fact call it civilization, the world he comes from and the world toward which he is headed. Sometimes, on this narrow bridge, he meets caravans transporting loads of silver or packs of mules carrying provisions for the miners. Men armed with lances and crossbows who guard the crossing, prepared to face the Indian attack that could come at any moment. But Juan doesn't think about the Indians. Nor does he think about what has just occurred; the plague that perhaps wasn't a plague and the doctor who was most definitely the doctor. Juan who doesn't remember, who struggles not to remember a certain tavern, a certain wife, the bones of a certain dog. The doctor's black mustache. White. His words. Years, the doctor said. Years, Juan repeats. He doesn't want to think about whether he has been on his horse for days or for years: whether the madman, the drunk, was the doctor or himself. Perhaps the world is the madman. Perhaps time is the drunk. Because it is impossible for years to pass in the course of a single night, although—come to think of it—it is impossible, too, for a mustache to turn white overnight; for the plague to be a source of dread one day and laughter the next. Juan, who shakes his head. Juan, who rides. Juan, who doesn't think. He prefers to follow his rescuers' advice: better not to worry. Better not to think. Two weeks, he tells himself, then repeats it out loud; two weeks, in the end. The quest: it is his only thought, his only home. Juan the Indian his only purpose, and after that, nothing.

The road dips and rises and dips again, until it comes to an open ravine between two hills. At the back of that ravine, a smattering of huts scattered over the valley, built with the speed and apathy with which one occupies a territory that does not like feel one's own. It seems ridiculous to call that jumble of wood and adobe a village or town, much less a city. From a distance, it looks more like a caravan about to resume its march; a makeshift camp assembled with the tools of the desert, which are dust and uncertainty and indolence. Nevertheless, this is the villa of Zacatecas, as confirmed by two miners with a beggarly air whom Juan questions on the road. The lucky villa of Zacatecas, so rich in silver deposits that the treasures of the Seven Cities and the Quivera don't hold a candle. At least this is what the miners say, something like pride in their eyes. They are brothers, and they have been there for years, they say, doing their own prospecting. Years tempting luck. Years that nearly—. Years that almost—. Years on the verge of, just a few meters from, days or seconds away from hitting the miraculous vein that would soak them in more silver than they had ever dreamed of. Who knows what separates them from returning to México by carriage. A few meters, a few weeks. They say this, with something in their eyes that looks like pride and is perhaps just madness. Years, they say. Years, Juan repeats. He can discern several of those mines from the road; tortuous tunnels and underground passageways opening every so often among the rocky outcrops, distributed with no real plan or with a plan created by chance. From high up, a torrent of tumultuous, filthy water descends, littered with troughs where workers wash the loads of ore. Juan sees some of these work crews pass by, picks blunt from so much pounding of the earth; many Indians and many Blacks and also some Spaniards with skin equally dark from soot and dust, as if the bowels of the earth made no distinction between rank or race. Men without fortune and without roots who have wound up there, the tomb of the mines, the very edge of the earth, like loose stones rolled and dragged by a river at will. He sees no sick or dead men. Just men working up and down the slope. Just ranches and smelting plants and wooden barracks and a few squat, ramshackle huts. At the highest and most uncluttered part of town, a kind of bastioned fort, with embrasures for arquebuses and crossbows. Plenty of mess halls and just one church with an unfinished belfry, and inside it, a bell not much bigger than the ones worn by sheep.

Juan dismounts at the church portico. An Indian woman languidly sweeps the rubblework floor, like someone who knows all too well that by tomorrow, it will be covered in dust again. Juan tries the door—locked—and then knocks. He also tries knocking on the sacristy door, calls to no response, and lastly, stands on tiptoe to peek through the open window. Inside, in the gloom that smells of staleness and mildew, he thinks he sees an immense armoire, shelves buckled under the weight of papers and files. Behind him, the sound of sweeping stops.

"Padre no church."

Juan turns toward the Indian woman, who still holds her broom with indifference.

"Then where can I find him?"

"Padre no church. Padre tavern."

She points to a shack with the air of a hostel or brothel or both.

"Do you mean the Reverend Father priest?"

"Yes."

"In the tavern?"

"Yes."

Originating inside the shack, he hears a chorus of laughter and then a shout. *Curses on God and the Devil!* the thundering voice replies, so loud it shakes the glass.

"There?"

The woman nods vigorously.

"There."

She resumes her sweeping.

He doesn't see the priest at first. He only sees men who drink, men who shout, men who argue, men who sleep slumped over in their chairs, men who piss or vomit on the dirt floor, men who elbow and shove their way around the gaming table. Men who furiously shake their dice cups, cursing or praying through clenched teeth, during brief, expectant intervals. Men who lean over to see what luck those dice have brought them and who clasp one another and shout or smack their hand on the table or roar blasphemies. By the Virgin's guts, they say. Long live the Lord, for I've lost what my soul is worth, they say. I'd sooner counter God's faith than this wager. Give me a seven, dice, give me a seven; for a seven, I'll declare the Devil is God and God the Devil. I bet three monies in honor of the Holy Trinity and four for Christ's nails and one for the Mother who birthed him and two more for the balls I've got hanging right here between my legs. Among so many men, there is also a handful of women, women who sit on the laps of the luckiest players, chemises shamelessly open. They don't shout, celebrate, or curse the roll of the dice. They are the roll. They are the wager. Little do they care whether it is a seven or a nine or a twelve that is called. They are resigned to being groped, constantly swapping owners and laps, just like the fistfuls of coins and silver nuggets.

Finally, Juan recognizes him, sitting in the opposite corner. From a distance, the man doesn't look like a priest, but a clerk: a clerk with a tonsure and cassock, but a clerk all the same. The table before him is infested with papers and deeds upon which he scribbles furiously with a hen feather. Every so often he dips the quill in the inkwell and every so often, too, he takes a generous swig of wine, his expression coarse and fierce. On the papers several round, purple stains are inked: the many places where that jug has sat before being raised to his lips again.

Juan approaches the man. Before he can speak, the priest stops him, gesturing firmly with his left hand, as he rushes to finish a last sentence with his right. He hasn't looked up once. While he waits, Juan cocks his head and tries to decipher the man's writing.

Sword. Diego Foil. A cutting name, like steel; like the giant warrior he was or appeared to be. That man was there, he says, right where you stand now, asking me the same questions you have come to ask. And I answered every one of them because, back then, I still had hope. What did I hope for? Who knows. Justice, perhaps. What sort of imbecile hopes for justice, in this world? I don't expect it now: somes stones we only trip over once in this lifetime. The world, too, is another stone. God tripped over it just one day, the day of its creation, and then he forgot or tried to forget it. Because it's obvious that not even God seems to expect anything great from his creatures. If you don't believe me, just look around. Can he try to imagine the number of sins being committed at this very moment, in this very tavern? Does God want to do something about that? Should he? And he would go even further: are we even sure He can? Perhaps this is all the hand of God can do, he says, pointing to the bundles of papers stained with wine and ink. Only this: observe. Only this: record what he has seen and stay silent. Bear witness. Testify to all that happens, though that testimony be futile and read by no one; though the world has already become Hell and nothing and nobody can save it. Not even God. Not even the Holy Inquisition. He had faith in the Inquisition once, for a time. Oh! How naive one must be to have faith in the Inquisition, he says, refilling his tankard. Only saints, only scholars, only righteous men fear the Inquisition. Heretics, on the other hand, are perfectly aware that the Inquisition can do nothing. But he didn't know any of that back then. He spent his days and a portion of his nights writing letters and reports for the apostolic inquisitor. He still sends them, in fact. Though they count for nothing: what does it matter. He tells the inquisitor how the world is slowly rotting and how they, the human beings, are the flies on that rot. The larvae, the worms. He writes to him of Zacatecas, because if the world is Hell, then Zacatecas is Hell's very heart; here is where God amused himself, burying silver so men would kill in His name. Does the inquisitor know what is happening at the frontier edge of the viceroyalty, on those lands where the only law is the sword and greed the only spur? Well, if he doesn't know, the priest will explain it to him. Because he has seen many things, so many things; enough to believe that there is no more heresy or ig-nominy to be expected. He has seen many Indian girls baptized against their will in order to ease the conscience of the Spaniards who coupled with them. He has seen encomenderos selling their Indians like slaves, though it is pro-hibited, and branding them with their initials as if they were livestock. He has seen Lutherans disguised as good Christians and he has seen idolatrous and

Jewified and Devil-worshipping men. He has seen Spaniards practicing Indian rites secretly and not so secretly. He has seen encomenderos and gentlemen
and priests of the Holy Mother Church forming a long line outside the door
of old Aztec witch doctor, waiting for spells to give them luck in gambling or
health or love. He has seen a miner ripping out his Indian's eyes and later he
saw how the miner marched the man, still alive, up and down the mountain-
side, since according to superstition, the most prosperous veins are found at
the exact spot a blind Indian chooses to urinate. He has seen hermits taken for
saints mixing Christian prayers with indigenous oaths, perhaps unbeknownst
to them, and paying through the nose for human skulls with which to contemplate life's fugacity and the banality of all material possessions. He has seen
men who blaspheme, men who steal, men who kill. He has seen Chichimeca
savages scalping Christian heads and Christian savages scalping the Chichimeca. Maybe all frontiers are like that, the priest reflects after a long
draught from his tankard: a place where the worst of both worlds come to
meet. He has seen the worst of those worlds. He has heard, has lived so many
things. And he has written to the inquisitor about all of them, lengthy letters
that never receive a reply. Why doesn't the inquisitor answer? Why doesn't he
send his flunkies, why doesn't he erect the gallows, light the bonfires, pull out
his shiny instruments of torture? He asked himself that for a long time, until
he understood or believed he understood the answer. The Inquisition doesn't
exist, he says. The Inquisition is nothing but a word, and behind that word is
nothing. The Inquisition is a story we tell in the dark, to frighten little children. A scarecrow planted in the middle of the plain, to scare off all the birds
in New Spain. That is the Inquisition: a scarecrow that frightens at first, but
actually can only smile, smile stiffly with its ragdoll mouth. The Inquisition is
nothing but fear produced by the Inquisition. It can only burn one soul and
pray for the millions it doesn't burn. Although everyone burns in his own
fashion, of course; we all burn, he says, in this inextinguishable fire that is the
world. Hell, in other words. Is there any difference? If there is, he hasn't found
it, not in all these years. Only a new destruction on the level of Sodom and
Gomorrah could purify the Earth, but it seems God isn't partial to punishments and catastrophes these days. Or perhaps, the priest reasons, this might
be the worst punishment after all: to let us live, to rehearse the hell we ourselves have created. He has waited for that punishment for a long time, as an
answer to his prayers. He remembers, for instance, the plague that hammered
the viceroyalty several years ago now, when the seeds for this villa were, as

some say, recently sown. An epidemic that looked like it would wipe out all the men on Earth. He, at least, had held that hope. He came to believe—what is he saying, *believe?*—he came to wish it would exterminate them all. Clean these lands, like the flood destroyed Noah's world and fire devoured Jerusalem and the plagues decimated Egypt. It didn't happen, of course; these lands might lack many things, but Indians are not one of them. In the end, the plague that was supposed to turn everything upside down eventually passed, leaving naught but the burden of burying the dead. And the Indians went back to dying their usual deaths: flayed by the whip or suffocated by the dust raised by their picks or interred along with the silver under collapsed scaffolding inside the galleries. Not to mention the illogical fact that the epidemic's fury never fell upon the Spaniards, who—by all accounts—are the most mean-spirited, the most wicked, the most abject men to have walked these lands. What was God thinking? If divine fire should burn any race at all, then that race should undoubtedly be the Spanish, wouldn't he agree? God's designs, oh, may whoever understands them be the first to speak. Is this why I drink? he muses as he refills his tankard. Perhaps, but it isn't the only reason. Why do we do what we do? That boy who just placed a bet and lost a month's wages with a single roll of the dice, why did he do it? Why, in order to seal his misfortune, did he just defecate on the memory of Our Lord Jesus Christ, who died on the cross and asked nothing in return? Why, on arriving home, will he beat his Indians, and his wife, too, if he has one? And you, he says turning to Juan, why are you here? Who tricked you into riding all the way to this hell? What does Juan the Indian matter to you, what does he matter to His Excellency the viceroy, what does he matter to the bloody inquisitor? Because of all the letters he sent, only Juan the Indian's preaching has managed to capture the attention of Their Excellencies; blasted Juan the Indian, about whom little or nothing is known. The Inquisition's designs, oh, whoever understands them, may he be the first to speak. Apart from that, there is little he can say. Surely the viceroy or the inquisitor himself have informed Juan of the details of his mission. But if Juan really is interested in what the priest can tell him, perhaps he will be surprised to know that he himself once met the wretch. How long ago was that? Ah, Hell hath no time, my friend. Time does not exist at the center of a drunken stupor and it doesn't exist in Hell either. Perhaps it was during that epidemic he spoke of earlier. It seems, you see, a whole lifetime ago. Is life long or is it, by contrast, very short? Depends on how you look at it. Long enough to taste all the sins in the world and short enough to never be redeemed of them. Let's just say it was a long time ago. Let's just say it was, who knows, five hundred or six hundred letters ago. We can say, then, that it was six hundred thefts, six hundred murders, six hundred blasphemies, six hundred sacrileges ago. Juan the Indian was here then, working on a crew of free miners. For a time, at least. Nobody knew where he came from, nor did anybody ask, that's the truth: here, we all come from somewhere else. We are all fleeing something, the priest explains in an increasingly wine-choked voice, although honestly, we should flee this place more than any other. Well: the fact is, many Indians, both slaves and free men, pass through these parts. Human memory cannot possibly remember them all. If he remembers Juan the Indian it is because there is no human way to forget him. He was a strange Indian. And not just because he knew how to read and write, at an astonishing level for a man of his station. Nor because of that book he always carried with him; the book that was, as would come to be known, actually a sacrilegious Bible. No, that wasn't the reason. Not the only one, at least. There was something in him. Something, the priest repeats, he can't quite explain. Maybe it was his gaze. Yes, that was it. Something in the eyes, his eyes, that pierced a person right through: something so pure it was simultaneously beautiful and terrible. The eyes of a saint or a madman. They looked like the eyes of God, but other times, seen in another light, they turned out to be the eyes of the Devil. Perhaps the difference is smaller than it would seem. If the Devil and God do have eyes, he would swear that those eyes, that gaze, ought to look like two droplets of water. He was, in conclusion, a strange Indian. And he lasted here as long as the mine owners didn't tire of him, which they did quickly, when they discovered that every night he was rallying the hewers and the waste scavengers and the well-diggers, whether they were Indians, Blacks, or slaves. He raised his pick, raised it high for all to see, and said to them: In the beginning, this was all I had. Now, he continued, I have the world. He said this, or at least they say he said it. And sometimes he read to them. Passages from the Holy Scriptures, no less. The one about there being no more Jew or Greek, slave or free man, male or female, because all are one in Jesus Christ. Things like that. Rallying cries that were sucked up by the brains of those poor imbeciles, and which made them feel, momentarily, that they were of the same stature as their masters. Terrible thing, really, because it is always hard to fall, and the higher up one goes, the more deadly the impact. No wonder the mine owners threw him out. What is more difficult to understand is why Juan the Indian didn't return by the same road he'd come, preferring instead to advance into the lands of the savage Chichimeca, devourers of human flesh. Everyone took him for dead. But lo and behold, perhaps sixty or seventy letters later, they had news of him again. He doesn't recall all the details. It seems the information came from a Chichimeca prisoner of war. Yes, that was it: a savage who, at the moment of his execution, asked to receive the sacrament of confession. Confession! From one of those barbarians! Can you believe it? In rudimentary Spanish, He told them that he was a Christian; they all were, in his tribe. That's what he said, that villain, who, months prior, had been carving up Spaniards and forcing them to drink melted silver. He spoke of a prophet they called the Padre, who was not the Son of God but something like His Grandson or Great-Grandson, and to whom they owed all they were. That Padre, the priest says, holding Juan's gaze, you can imagine who he was. What no one can imagine—not even he, who has privileged knowledge when it comes to sin—is the kinds of heresies and monstrosities Juan the Indian preached among them. How terribly he condemned them. Because if the very doctors of the Church often can't agree on their interpretations of some of Scripture's thorniest passages; if many men of good faith have found themselves led into the ignoble river of heresy, what can be expected from a wretched Indian, no matter how astonishing his knowledge? Well, he wrote to the inquisitor one more time, like a shipwreck survivor abandoning himself to a floating piece of timber, and this time he received a reply. The inquisitor congratulated him for his unveilings. The inquisitor urged him to initiate an inquest on behalf of the Holy Office. The inquisitor demanded—for the first time—dates, locations, witnesses, estimates, possible hideouts, strategies for capturing him. As if Juan the Indian were a new Martin Luther or a Fra Dolcino come back to life. Don't misunderstand me, he says, turning to Juan; I am aware of the facts, and of the irreparable damage a false prophet can cause, especially among a people as credulous and simple as the Indians. But you must understand that, not long before, I had written to the inquisitor to inform him that five Chichimeca maidens had been possessed by an entire calvary squadron, by turns and so ferociously that, afterward, there was nothing to do but bury the maidens, and the man hadn't replied. The priest told him about a certain captain of His Majesty the King's troops who wore around his neck—who doubtless wears it still—the skull of one of his most horrible enemies because, according to the captain, the relic redoubled his strength in battle. The priest told him, he couldn't stop telling him, how on one side of the Cerro de la Bufa, he had surprised a group of Spanish miners sacrificing an Indian so that the god Mictlāntēcutli, lord of the underworld and subsoil, would have the good will to spit out his silver nuggets. The inquisitor didn't answer that letter either. He only feared Juan the Indian: only Juan the Indian mattered. Only for him did the inquisitor deign to write to the viceroy himself and only in search of him did they send that Diego Sword or Diego Rapier or Diego Razor or whatever he was called. You, he says, are only here because of him. You have come to Hell, but you are concerned with but one of its many demons. Well: if that is your will, then so be it. But know that if you were to raise your sword and strike down the first man you came across, you would be performing an identical justice. We are all sinners. Do you hear me, rogues? he says, lifting his tankard and turning toward the players, toward the wastrels, toward the blasphemers. We are all sinners. Me, like you: sinner. Me: drunk. I drink because otherwise I would drown in this hell. Or perhaps I'm in Hell because I drink. Wine's designs, oh, whosoever understands them, may he empty his glass in one gulp. In times of scarcity, I've even gone so far as to drink consecrated wine. I have drunk the blood of Christ for my own pleasure. What are you going to do in the face of that? You can denounce me. Write to the inquisitor, if you please. I have done so myself: I have told him of this and even worse things. The inquisitor, steadfast in his habits, never answered. Because, like he said from the start, the inquisitor does not exist. The inquisitor doesn't exist, he says. The inquisitor is nothing but a word, and behind that word, nothing. The inquisitor is a story we tell in the dark, to frighten little children. A scarecrow planted in the middle of the plain, to scare off all the birds in New Spain. That is the inquisitor: a scarecrow that frightens at first, but which can actually only smile, smile stiffly with its ragdoll mouth. The inquisitor is nothing but fear produced by the idea of the inquisitor himself. He can only burn one soul and pray for the millions he doesn't burn: and he has decided to burn Juan the Indian and pray for the rest of us.

The garrison captain receives him that same afternoon. At first, he thinks Juan has come to reinforce the troops, whose numbers are greatly reduced following the most recent skirmishes with the Chichimeca, and he cannot hide his enthusiasm. Many words are necessary to explain that Juan comes to do just the opposite, to take his men.

"But this is madness!" he garrison captain cries, waving the credentials Juan has just handed him. "It cannot be the viceroy's will to leave the city at the mercy of the savages."

"I only need a dozen soldiers. The rest can stay."

"A dozen soldiers, to enter Chichimeca territory! Upon my faith, you are either mad or a man of courage."

Then he takes another look at the papers. He considers.

"How much time are we talking about?"

"Two weeks."

"So just two weeks."

"Yes. Two weeks."

He looks to his assistant, who merely shrugs.

"Very well," he finally says. "Twelve men, two weeks. But I choose the men. And the expenses are to be paid by the viceroy, naturally."

"Naturally."

"There'll be some who put themselves at your service for a single gold escudo, but if you want a job well done, I recommend you pay at least two per head."

"Fine."

The conversation could end there but doesn't. The captain continues to consider the papers and the question he's about to ask.

"I suppose you already know that to undertake this journey is suicide."

"I suppose I do."

The captain simply nods, as if such a reply was to be expected.

"Tell me, exactly what is it that the viceroy wants you to do? What is so valuable as to risk the lives of thirteen good men and the survival of a whole city?"

"I'm looking for an Indian."

"A Chichimeca?"

"No. An Indian from then south. From Tlaxcala."

The captain laughs. His laughter infects his aide and even the soldier standing guard at the door.

"Then they have given you a job already done. There is only one thing the Chichimeca hate more than a Christian: a southern Indian. You can assume yours is already dead."

Juan endeavors to hold his gaze.

"Not this Indian," he says, and his voice is so hard, so leaden that it is proof enough.

The captain shrugs and returns the papers to Juan.

"As you wish. But I wager two to one that they've scalped him by now. Or cut off his crown jewels and stuck them in his mouth. You see, they love that sort of thing. I once saw them perform the very same cruelty on seven of my

boys. It's not a pretty sight, I assure you. But what can one expect from a bunch
of savages who attack our caravans on their arrival rather than their departure,
because they prefer bread and clothing to silver?"

Already he moves to accompany Juan to the door, but Juan remains.

"I would like to speak to one of those men," he says.

"You want to speak with my soldiers?"

"I'm referring to the Chichimeca. Have you a prisoner whom I could in-
terrogate, perchance?"

"Prisoners?"

The captain and his aide exchange amused looks.

"Of course. You want to see the prisoners and by God you shall see them.
Miguel! Take him to the hill. His Excellency wants to have a stroll through our
woods."

From a distance, they look like a clump of trees burgeoning on a treeless horizon. But with each step, the trees begin to transform into something else, revealing their craftmanship, the elaborate carpentry, of human still life, and the
guide, like a diligent pupil, remembers to cover his nose with a handkerchief.
Juan does nothing. He only looks uphill with very wide eyes, up and up and
wider and wider, inhaling the hot stench he's smelled many times before, on a
wind that seems to blow directly from the past.

They come to stop before the first cross. No one speaks; nothing need be
said.

They hear the furious buzz of blowflies that flit from one body to the next,
big and metallic like arquebus bullets. They hear the breeze stirring the dead
men's rags, the tinkling of their necklaces made of bone or shell. They hear
curses from two Spanish soldiers playing dice on a stone slab behind them.
Otherwise, they hear nothing. Not a sigh or snort or whickered moan.

"Going on five days now," the guide apologies from behind his grimy
handkerchief.

The bodies, immobile, frizzled by the sun, look ripped from a dream. But
Juan isn't looking at the bodies. He isn't thinking of the dead: all he can think
about are the crosses. Of the effort it took to build and raise them. The hours
of work chopping and hauling trees from distant parts, from forests he cannot
see anywhere, no matter where he directs his gaze. Wood sawed, sanded, nailed,
and lastly, sown in dirt, just to germinate the seed of war, with great pains and a
dedication that surpasses the other human works he has seen on this Earth. The

settlers' camp, the church, the timber beams that prop up the mine galleries: all have been built in a hurry and with some degree of disinterest, the way one might cobble together a habitat for a wild animal. Only the crosses, carefully selected and cut down and even sanded, appear to retain something of the human, and have been built with something reminiscent of love.

Suddenly, a sound. The crosspiece creaks. One of the dead men shudders with a moan of what could almost be pleasure. Then he begins to intone a song or something reminiscent of a song. The dice players look up from the disputed silver nugget with expressions of annoyance.

Juan approaches the dying Indian. He is a young man, his body completely inked in tattoos and legs splattered in blood and excrement. He swings his head slowly, rocked to the beat of his own song. He appears to smile.

"What is it he sings?" Juan asks.

The guide shrugs. Who knows, captain, he replies. Could be one of his war songs. Could be prayers they dedicate to their heathen gods. Could be just a lullaby his mother sang to him in the cradle, if these devilish Indians have mothers and cradles and were ever even babies, instead of being born ready to stalk their first victims, like beasts.

The Indian who might have never been a baby continues to sing with half-closed eyes and the same smile, drunk from fever and sun, as if, high on his cross, he has seen something the rest cannot. Juan listens to his song. He listens like someone who remembers. Not like someone observing a strange land-scape, but like someone expecting to find an ember warm from his own hearth, though it be on a foreign horizon. He listens long enough to realize that if it is a song, it is a song that repeats. And some time later, in the middle of those incomprehensible spells, he thinks he recognizes something that might be the word father, and then, perhaps, though very distorted, the word heaven. The word kingdom. The word bread.

Only then does Juan dare to examine the man's tattoos, which pulse under the war tunic torn to shreds—Hallowed be Thy name, the Indian could be saying at this moment. Printed on his quivering skin, Juan sees images similar to those that gestate in the wombs of certain caves; he sees reddish bison galloping on the crucified arms and black deer grazing on his legs and little men that come from around the bellybutton to chase them with darts and with arrows—Thy will be done on Earth as it is in Heaven; populating the boy's neck, he spies impossible creatures that appear rescued from a bestiary or the margins of a maritime map; he sees scores of boats crossing the ocean of his abdomen to give birth to little scribbles that look like soldiers, and lastly he sees, outlined faintly on his breast, an enormous black cross, and nailed to that cross, a man who suffers, who agonizes, who prays—and deliver us from evil, Amen.

"Where is Juan the Indian," Juan asks suddenly, spurred by premonition. "Where?"

The guide, who divides his attention between the game of dice and the toes of his boots, looks up and slowly removes his handkerchief. The players sense that they've been summoned and interrupt their game to come over. Only the dying man remains indifferent to everything, eternally arrested in song, eyes closed.

"Where is he? Juan the Indian. Tell me where he is. Where! Open your eyes! Open them!"

And, suddenly, the crucified man does. He opens them so wide that one might say that it is now, precisely now, as he opens them, that he finally dies. But he doesn't die. At least not yet. He only stops his song to look at Juan—eyes yellow and rolled back into his head; a gaze that could only belong to a beast or a god. In a voice between pained and tender:

"Padre . . ."

"That's right! Juan the Indian! Your Padre! Where is he? Where?"

"Padre . . ."

The crucified boy attempts to point to somewhere. The crosspiece creaks. His head moves from side to side, as if refusing. It still takes Juan a second to comprehend. The boy is trying to point north, the same direction his crucified arms have been pointing to for five days and five nights. The whole him a human arrow, driven into the desert sand to show the way.

"It has been *follllfiillt!*" the man wails with the last of his strength.

Only then does the cross cease to shake.

V

The twelve are just barely men, chosen from the youngest, the least experienced,
the stupidest. They do not ask where they are headed, at first; they don't seem
to care. In spite of their youth, their inexperience, or their stupidity, they have
already spent enough time in this land to know that all destinations are alike.
They have also come to understand that they will never be rich and that a hot
meal is a hot meal, even if one has to chew it while roving undiscovered routes
and crushed under the weight of the sun and stars. Perhaps they aren't so stupid
after all, thinks Juan, but they are undoubtedly very young. Three of them look
to be no more than boys and their hands are already skinned from digging in
the mines. There is also a Black boy, who has never wielded a sword or correctly
pronounced the name his first owners gave him: Felipe. Only one called Tomás
has a few hairs on his chin and some experience in the use of weapons. He
always keeps his arquebus at the ready, laid across his horse's neck, and speaks
incessantly of the beautiful and terrible things he has seen happen in this land
as he spits off to either side of his saddle, whether he needs to or not.

The vastness of the plain opens before them, so empty that their eyes and imagination skate to the horizon's edge, never meeting a scrap of reality upon which to cling. The only things that happen do so in the sky: they see, on the unchanging landscape, the shadow of a cloud, the shadow of a bird. Their own shadows, giant at dawn and dusk and reduced to a sliver in the boiling midday heat. Their horses' hooves raise dust clouds that give their figures a ghostly aspect and takes a long time to vanish in the air, like a ship's wake in the ocean. To ride this course is something similar to sailing and there is also something in the land's immensity that is like being at sea, a certain suspicion of being shipwrecked and at the same time some conviction that the horizon is full of routes and any one of those routes is a possibility.

Once they mount their horses, they do not speak, they even manage not to look at one another. Occasionally, their lips appear to move silently, as if they're chewing over an old conversation. They, who at one point felt they were destined for so many feats, to demolish the Aztec Empire or run their own mining concession, no longer wish to waste an ounce of effort on being remembered. Just complete their mission, whatever it may be, and earn the handful of coins he promised them—two escudos per man; one for the Black boy. They will spend their coins in the Zacatecas cantinas, in the Zacatecas brothels, until they forget the reason for their journey or even that they'd traveled at all. But night falls and they wrap themselves in their blankets and in the end, they do exchange a few words, a substitute for warmth from the fire they do not light. By moonlight, they see things not as they are, but as they should have been. They think: if only they had been born a few years earlier. If they had been twenty, twenty years ago. If they had been given to Cortés for the siege of México-Tenochtitlan or to Nuño de Guzmán for the exploration of New Galicia. If they'd been old enough to know the New World before it became an extension of the old. Then they wouldn't be here, lying on the dirt, eating cold mush and coated in dust. Sometimes they just think it, and other times they say it out loud to each other, for comfort. The conversations are slow and filled with tacit understandings, with gaps, with the nostalgia sometimes experienced by those who have barely begun to live. They talk about the Indian-filled encomiendas they don't possess, the silver mines they should have received, the implausible honors heaped on those who were worse men than them, but who had the luck to be older.

Juan, who should be one of those older men, one of those fortunate men, stays quiet. He is too tired to speak. Or because he knows it was always nothing more than a dream: they would have been left without encomiendas and without glory like so many others, because the miser is miserly at any of Earth's latitudes and no continent on the planet is miraculous enough to change that. Thus he limits himself to listening, or not even. He doesn't listen. He doesn't speak. He merely looks at what little the darkness permits him to see. He looks at the shadows of his men and he looks way out beyond, as well. The frozen fire that burns in stars so close his fingers can almost touch them, and below, the dark earth on which another Juan before this Juan once tread.

At daybreak, the horses have to be spurred into walking and, on the descent, they must be reined back with force, almost violence. One would say it made them dizzy to go deeper into this boundless land but that later, once they succumbed to the fever of the gallop, they would never want to stop. Day by day they seem to grow younger, connect with something in the infancy of their species, in the prehistory of every horse, in that time—in that place—where they once roamed like sleepwalkers over immense plains like this one and there was no one to brush their manes or tame them with bridles, horseshoes, saddles, stirrups. But they are only horses, after all, and ultimately they obey. They ride for ten, twelve, fourteen hours if necessary. During the day they ride riven with heat and at night they seek each other out attempting to regain a little midday sun amid the darkness of the frozen plain. No fire, Felipe the Black says with sorrow, almost desperation, every time they get ready to camp for the night and he is prohibited, once again, from knocking together his flintstones. No fire, he repeats, watching the setting sun, and covering himself with all the blankets he has brought, which are not many. And then Tomás must explain to him that the Chichimeca have eyes like they do and that a campfire like the one he wants to light can be seen for ten leagues. And it is preferable, Tomás can promise him, can swear by the Virgin's guts even, it is preferable, he repeats, to shiver from the cold all night than wake up pierced by Zacatecas arrows.

"Do you hear that, you fucking pagan? It's the coyote's whine, the voice of the desert dogs. You don't have to fear them, but you do have to fear the Chichimeca, who attack camps at night without making a single sound and don't start howling until the whole camp is dead and scalped . . ."

Tomás speaks of scalped heads again. He speaks of Indians who bend over their prisoners, be they men or women or creatures new to the world; Indians who slice the crown of their heads while they are still alive, like this, as if tonsuring a friar, leaving the skull skinned and clean. He speaks of their flint knives; of the sound they make when piercing the flesh and scraping the skull. He speaks of huts where he has seen dozens of scalps hanging, hundreds of scalps, maybe thousands of scalps, all the scalps in the world hanging again before his eyes, like the butcher puts out pieces of meat to dry. And some, he explains, the most beautiful, the most terrible, had belonged to maidens of indescribable beauty, long, blonde manes, all bloodstained and shining under the sun like banners in battle.

In the dark, the men sit and listen to his tale. No one denies, or adds, anything. They are words that drop into the invisibleness of night, words sown in their dreams and which oblige them to sleep with hands on the hilts of their swords. Because they do sleep, despite everything. They sleep pressed together, in a circle around a little clearing where nothing is lit and nothing warmed. They eat cold jerky and cold tortillas, and they listen to their horses patiently chewing, the animals silhouetted in the moonglow. In the distance, they see blue-tinged thunderbolts strike silently on the horizon, and they see the scrawny shadows of coyotes, and stars that burn for an instant and are extinguished, and others so bright they look like caldera conveying fire from another world. They see all of this and more, but they do not see light from any campfire. As if the Indians were also invaders in their own land and instead of inhabiting it, they lived by fleeing it, frightened by its immensity or by their own insignificance. For them, home is a desolate plain where the fire is never, ever lit.

At first they believe they have been recruited to cleanse the frontier of Indians, and that seems good. As days go by, they begin to be convinced that they are there to search for silver deposits behind the Crown's back, and that seems even better. Lastly, they decide that their captain is just another madman who is growing old while chasing the gold of the Seven Cities, and even this seems reasonable to them. But, one day, Juan confesses that they are riding in pursuit of one Indian in particular, and they don't know what they think about that.

Mateo asks if the Indian in question happens to be a cacique or head warrior of some tribe, someone whose rescue could demand a ransom in gold or a handshake that would put an end to the war. Bartolomé asks if he might be one of those witch doctors who, according to statements by un-Christian tongues, can find silver veins by simply listening to the sound a coin makes when it falls on the ground. Pedro asks if he is the repository of some kind of immemorial secret or perhaps the only guide able to lead them to the kingdom of the Seven Cities. The Black boy Felipe asks if he's allowed to make a fire.

Juan shakes his head. He says the reasons aren't important. He says he won't give them the reasons but that, instead, he has five gold reasons for each one of them, and each one of those reasons carries the stamped likeness of King Carlos, may God keep him. Yes, they heard right: not two reasons, but five. Five for each man and two for the Black boy Felipe: that's what he says. The gold comes from high up and the order comes from high up as well and the higher ups are never wrong, or if they are, they, the ones below, are never the wiser. So if they want to join him, they will have to forget all about explanations and settle for the gold.

Two weeks, he says.

Two more weeks, he begs.

The men look at each other wordlessly. They accept their captain's silence and they accept their own silence, that silence worth five gold escudos. Slowly they return to their mounts, ready to hunt that Indian who isn't the chief of any tribe, nor the heir to any treasure, nor a man with the gift of magic, resurrection of the dead, or prophecy.

There's nothing left to ask. Or perhaps there remains a single question, who knows whether lucid or foolish, which is a long time in coming:

"And what will we do when we find him, captain?"

They ford a river with a bed the color of blood. They leave behind a plain of cracked earth and a stony area dazzling under the sun and a few humps of rock from which to keep watch over the emptiness. Further out the horizon looks like the floor of an evaporated, prehistoric ocean. They are sailing that ocean. Sometimes, interrupting the tedium of yellow grass, they see a dry tree standing, a few feeble bushes. The Black boy Felipe stops to cut with his machete the prickly pears they come across and drink its raw, thick milk drop by drop. He eats the fruit, which is bitter and isn't normally eaten but turn out in the end to be edible, or the Black boy, at least, sucks them energetically.

Sometimes, when they pass through the vertical wall of a ravine or cross a chute of loose stone, one of them feels compelled to whisper that the land seems to have eyes. He says this while glancing around, as if sounding out an imminent threat. But he does so without real faith, almost as if for convention, because it is what a troop of soldiers has to say when penetrating strange territory. In truth, they have the exact opposite impression. The certainty persists that the world is dead and where they are going there is nothing and nobody left to watch them, not even the eyes of God. The smell of reality is the smell of sun-warmed rock and the smell of their own bodies cooking on that rock, and beyond that, nothing. Finding an Indian settlement behind the next hill would be something of a miracle, a secret relief. They almost want to run into the monstrous mirror—monstrous, yet a mirror nonetheless—that is an Indian's face painted for battle; a way of multiplying their humanity in this part of the world where humanity seems impossible. But they move through the next set of hills and a gravel pit (Cascajal) where the horses buck with caution and an esplanade whose grass grows in raggedy tufts, and the only human handiwork they find is a Spanish helmet abandoned in the middle of the plain. The riders trace several circles around it before daring to dismount. It is new or practically new and it shines so bright in the midday sun that it almost hurts.

"Must be one of the relics from Coronado's expedition," says a boy called Simón, although it is more or less obvious to them all that Coronado never set foot in this place.

"Must be a trophy belonging to the Zacatecas savages, devourers of human flesh," says Tomás, although it is hard to understand why someone would carry an enemy's remains such a distance, only to disregard them in the middle of nowhere.

"Must be the helmet I lost yesterday," says one called Andrés, essentially a boy-soldier on whom all the war fittings are too big. And he says it so convincedly that for a moment it seems reasonable to all, his helmet, his own helmet, yes, of course, the helmet he lost yesterday, while they crossed this same plain fifteen or twenty leagues to the south.

"I dream this place," the Black boy Felipe whispers, making a dark genuflection with his left hand. And it isn't known whether he means that he remembers having dreamt of this moment or that it is precisely now when he is dreaming them all, sleepless and very white under the sun.

They find the first village soon after. They first have to abandon the plain and cross into a mountain range that doesn't appear on the maps and whose gorges have never echoed with the sound of Christian voices. During the night they sense the vertiginous passing of the stars overheard and hear the horses sigh and have dreams on the ground, dreams in which there is only space for more horses and more stars and more desolate peaks. The weight of all humanity resides in their memories, ever smaller on the infinite horizon. The sun at dawn outlines the gap-toothed sierra. From a distance the rocky backbones look like scales on a gigantic dragon, for those who wish to believe in such things. They don't believe in anything. Three days ago they still believed in the gold and in the face of His Majesty Carlos multiplied by five and now they have barely enough faith left to keep riding without asking questions.

At first, they don't even believe in the Indian village. They are slow to accept that it is not simply a pile of rocks, or a hillock tinted gold by the twilight. It is what it appears: a Chichimeca camp, with its straw huts, humble vegetable plots, and deerskins drying in the sun. They hide the horses in a ravine and let hours go by while lying face down on rock, arquebuses at the ready and eyes locked on the deserted village. Because it is deserted: it takes them the rest of the day and an entire night to be convinced. They finally decide to make their approach at daybreak. Not one voice, not one Chichimeca warrior drawing his arrow, not a single sound of a grindstone milling corn. Just a coyote scavenging the meat put out to dry in the smokehouse, who runs from them in terror, howling the way coyotes do when they are afraid. Esteban loads one of the arquebuses. Andrés pulls on his helmet, which, like his breastplate, boots, and even his own sword, is too big for him. Tomás looks at the wind-battered animal skins and the circle of ash where no fire burns and murmurs:

"This village has eyes ..."

They search the huts one by one. Inside they find familiar tools, not so different from what could be found in any Castilian home, as well as implements destined for mysterious—maybe even perverse—uses. The floor is made of naked earth, sprinkled with straw, and from the ceilings hang strings of smoked meat and strips of dried pumpkin, but no human scalps. Braids of red and green chiles and mesquite pods, but none of those long, blonde manes of women's scalps, exquisite and terrible, shining in the sun like standards in battle. Tomás touches a string of dried meat with the tip of his arquebus, perplexed yet resigned.

Inside one of the huts they find a huge clay pot brimming with soup or something that looks like soup. Around the pot exactly three bowls wait, ready for a banquet never to be celebrated. No one leans in to touch them because, as everybody knows, as Tomás knows, the barbaric Chichimeca are capable of going so far as to poison their own food so as to decimate imprudent travelers. Silently they observe the venison steaks, the vegetable soup, the three bowls, empty and ready to be used, and then they move on with their search.

"This accursed village has eyes . . ." Tomás repeats.

And yet, Juan thinks, it's not true now, either. Nobody is watching them. God has closed his eyes or doesn't even have them. Only the coyote examines them from some distance, seated on his back legs. Lit by the midday sun, his muzzle appears to bleed, drip-drop, onto the dirt.

They meet back in the village center. That spot where there should only be a dirt clearing where fires are lit, or war dances performed, or whatever it is Indians do when they aren't murdering Christians. But the heart of this village is not empty. In the place of a circle of cold ash, they find a rectangular cabin, bigger than the others, built with purpose and care that seem un-Indian-like. Through the entwined branches comprising the walls filters a light that is soft, perhaps oscillating, perhaps slightly alive. The men consult each other with a glance, that's between surprised and intimidated. Tomás is already at the door, theatrically brandishing his sword.

"I dream this place," murmurs the Black boy Felipe.

"Well stop dreaming and shut up, fucking pagan," Tomás interrupts. Then, turning arrogantly to the rest, he adds: "Now, let's see who has the guts to go with me."

But it is Juan who steps forward without unsheathing his sword and pushes the door gently, almost as if asking permission. There is nobody inside, or better still, there is less than nobody, that solitude that permeates those places that once held multitudes and now are empty; the clay floor covered with reed mats worn from use, and cuts of wood set out for benches, and a kind of lit lamp hung from the roof bathing a white stone shrine in light. At the back, masked by the gloom that waxes and wanes, a shadow that looks like a crucified man yet is only a wooden statue, a wooden man crucified on an also wooden cross, the dolorous expression savagely carved, as if slashed, and eyes made of smooth white river stone, and the beard and hair tufted with frizzed, curly bristles that look like pubic hair, and an enormous, infernal set of teeth improvised out of obsidian arrowheads, as if the crucified man simultaneously threatened and smiled, and on its head a Spanish helmet on backward, and the stick-body covered by a kind of woman's shawl, blood-stained, and blood daubing hand and foot wounds, like dried tears, and blood dripping a black scab on the ground, as an offering the flies patiently sample. It is a Christ, the closest thing to a Christ that the Chichimeca savages have been able to conceive of, and upon seeing it, the men slowly remove their helmets and make the sign of the cross, as if by condemning its monstrous image they were, in some way, also venerating it.

If each arm of a cross is an arrow, then those arrows point in two opposite directions at the same time. Juan could decide that the Christ pointed southward, to the exact place, in other words, from which they have come, but instead he decides that it is still pointing north, always north. The crosses at the Spanish encampment showed the way to find the Indian settlement and the Christ in the Indian settlement points to an impassable mountain range, on whose peaks neither men nor plants take root. It is a mountain range that cannot be crossed, and they cross it. There are no trails across the bare rock and, like hesitant sleepwalkers, they must invent them. The horses resist navigating the rocky cliffs and must be whipped until both men and mounts are exhausted and ready themselves to withstand yet another night far from fire's warmth. The stone ridges are the color of red ochre and flower on vertical slopes like organ pipes or cathedral spires; they appear to still be growing at their mineral pace, as silently as the hair continues to grow on the dead.

If a cross is an arrow that points north, Juan thinks, then this is the right way, the only possible way.

If this is the only possible way, then Juan the Indian crossed, was forced to cross, this same range. Perhaps be stopped before the same obstacles. Slept curled up in the same rock shelters. He suffered under the same sun and let himself be soaked by the same rain and shivered under the same wintery night.

If Juan the Indian stopped before the same obstacles, if he suffered and slept and shivered under the same rain, under the same sun; if guided by the strength of his faith he survived without food and in absolute solitude on the solitude of the sierra, then that faith had to be immense. Because it was his faith that brought him here. So far and even much farther.

Juan stops to observe his surroundings, the needles of rock that improvise precarious balancing acts against the darkening sky. He observes the bare peaks punished morning and night by sun and wind, devoid of the consolation that a bit of shade, a gawky tree, a stunted cactus. He contemplates nature's resistance to being crossed, to being understood, and in this resistance, he sees Juan's face. Juan's strength. Juan's will, also forged of stone. The way is difficult and the terrain merciless, but he is fortified by the conviction that all he must do is follow the course Juan charted before him: that he is only there to remember what Juan already left behind, the landscape he observed, the chasms where Juan's will, Juan's indomitable will, never flagged for even a moment. The cuts he got on his feet open again, months or years later.

In a way, he is also alone, Juan thinks. Worse than alone. Twenty paces behind him, forming an increasingly elongated column, his men follow. His men who walk like old or dead men. His men who seem to have aged not two weeks but a year, one hundred years; the desert empty of trees and empty, too, of time. The minutes and the hours that hold no meaning for rock and dust, only for life, always one step away from being a corpse, offering of flesh to the sun, bones, dust at last.

His men roasting in the hell of their iron breastplates.

His men furrowing their brows under the raging sun.

His men begging, pleading for the order to turn back.

They say the two weeks promised passed much more than two weeks ago.

They say that Juan the Indian surely found a pass that awaits them, as well, perhaps leagues to the East or leagues to the West.

They say Juan the Indian was murdered by Indians a long time ago.

They say the crosses are arrows that point to, that implore, that demand the need to turn back.

They say the crosses mean nothing; the crosses are only crosses.

They say Juan the Indian never existed but they do, they exist, they are real and they are hungry and cold and afraid they will never see their loved ones again.

They say Juan the Indian is crazy.

They say they are crazy too.

They camp in a dust cloud so white and barren that it looks like a scene from the moon, and when they finally see the moon itself rise and shine on their heads, they feel reflected in it as if in a mirror. They are coated in dust and dirty and they cover themselves with their blankets like an army of nuns or ghosts. They have barely any food left. Their heads are full of it, of the lack of food and drink. No sound is to be heard and the cold feels colder in the midst of the silence. Perhaps that's why they begin to talk: to trick their hunger. To dissolve the cold. But their words dissipate quickly in the air, in hot, dense, puffs. For the first time they do not talk about gold escudos or silver mines or encomiendas of Indians. They settle only for talking about their pasts, that is, the tiny corner of Castilla that witnessed their birth. A past from which few ships and no letters arrive. In their stories, that place seems always the same: a miserable village of narrow horizons and roads that lead nowhere but are also, in their own way, capable of a kind of beauty. And now, in the darkness of these wild lands, they recall that beauty, which requires an entire ocean of distance in order to be seen. They talk about the sun of their childhood, the sun of Castilla, which at that very moment must be warming the other side of the Earth. They talk about relatives who are waiting, they talk about a certain windmill where on a certain night they became men, they talk about humble pilgrimages devoted to humble saints, who died martyrs for reasons unremembered in any other part of the world; they talk about regional songs and local wine and one bed for four brothers. All those images are fixed to the date of their departure, like maps are fixed to a specific time in a determinate corner of the world. Perhaps this is why, in their words, time seems frozen; their little brothers are still children playing, for infinity, on the patios of their homes, they will play and play and never grow, until they return; and their young wives, if they have them, will be eternally young and eternally wives, and they will wait for them with the same patience in the same corner of Castilla, with the table set and honor intact. Even the Black boy Felipe battles with his dark and wavering Spanish to recall his village, his tribe, his barbarous concept of home, and listening to him, one would even say that his village of pagans and cannibals is a good and natural place, almost human.

"And you, captain? Do you have a wife waiting for you?"

Juan does not reply. His eyes are conveniently closed and from the darkness behind his eyelids he simply listens without adding or asking anything. Gradually his men go quiet or fall asleep. Juan opens his eyes and looks again at their faces, or at least what the night permits him to see of their faces. They are children who have aged twenty years and, in the moonlight, their memories seem like real, solid things, on which they could lie down to sleep.

That night Juan dreams of Juan. He doesn't look like Juan from the drawing. He remembers thinking: He's changed so much. He wears a white tunic, and from his hands and bare feet stream fat drops of blood. He gestures with his hand. He wants him to come nearer. He rolls up the sleeves of his tunic and leans over his ear, as if wanting to share a secret. He tells him something. He remembers the sensation of hearing his voice, his words. But when he wakes, he has forgotten the secret.

Simón says that he probably killed a rich landowner, maybe even the governor himself. Pedro is convinced that he is the only owner of the only key to a hidden chamber in the jungle, and in that chamber the minted gold of seven generations. Santiago maintains that he is undoubtedly one of those Aztec witch doctors who, according to reliable testimonies, are capable of bringing down the world with one blow on their bone whistle. Tomás says that it's all a misunderstanding, an enormous, terrible misunderstanding, a poorly-issued order, perhaps, or poorly-understood or poorly-transmitted, someone who believes that another someone ordered something that he never actually ordered or ordered differently or ordered without thinking, because with just a little reflection one realizes that no Indian is worth the life of a single Christian.

Juan shakes his head. He says the reasons don't matter. He says that he isn't going to tell them the reasons but that he has, instead, ten gold reasons for each one of them, and each one of those reasons carries the stamped likeness of King Carlos, may God keep him. Yes, they've heard it right: not five reasons, but ten. Ten for each man and five for the Black boy Felipe: that's what he says. The gold comes from high up and the order comes from high up as well and the higher ups are never wrong, or if they are, they, the ones below, are never the wiser. So if they want to join him, they will have to forget all about explanations and settle for the gold.

Two weeks, he says.

Two more weeks, he begs.

Wordlessly the men look at each other. Then they look at their captain. Not at their captain's face. Not at his mouth, or his eyes. Just the pack that hangs behind him. They look at the pack and if they could have done so, they would look deeper still. Inside. Because there, hung on the horse and in perpetual swing, is where he must keep the gold they are owed. At least one hundred and twenty gold coins—or more. Who knows how much more. With his horse's every trot they hear them jingle, calling out like hope.

Santiago's horse bucks and stops. Bartolomé jumps off his mount and checks the hooves, one by one. Then he turns to Juan and, cupping his hands around his mouth, shouts:

"It's his shoe, captain!"

And then:

"Go on ahead, we'll catch up with you!"

But all the other men go to the horse's aid. Twelve men to examine one horse's foot. Juan is almost an arquebus shot away and he pauses to watch them. They form a furiously gesticulating circle, as if the horse's injured foot made them extremely angry. He cannot hear what they say, but perhaps he can imagine it.

They do not speak of their horses.

They speak, perhaps, of the scarce provisions and the scarce water and their patience, which is becoming scarce as well.

They speak of those two weeks that seem never to end.

They speak of the number of days they have been riding and they struggle to divide them, with their clumsy math, between the ten gold coins they are owed.

They speak of the windmills, humble pilgrimages, regional songs, beds for four siblings; of local wines and children who wait and women who wait as well.

They speak of that Indian who exists only in their captain's mind.

They speak of the madness of entrusting the life of thirteen horses, twelve men, and one Black boy to one man's dream.

They speak of the increasingly cold nights, shivering in desolate snowdrifts, and of a captain who refuses to light the fire even where only the buzzards can see it.

"All set, captain! Wait for us!"

And once again, they set their horses in motion, the twelve of them two-by-two, slow as scolded dogs. They continue to exchange a few words through clenched teeth and a few weak gestures, barely insinuated. They endeavor not to meet the eyes of their captain, who waits for them at the top of the slope.

We are not murderers, they say as they point their arquebuses at him. We are not thieves, they say, their hands already rifling inside his cloth saddlebag. We are not traitors of the Holy Mother Church or His Majesty the King or those lofty papers he carries on him and which they respect as good Castilians and good Christians. But we are definitely not crazy. If he believed that they would follow until the end of the world, until the end of time, then the only madman is him, they say. He is crazy, and so is that Indian he seeks, if he actually exists and has actually survived as they presume he has. They are tired of presuming and believing and they are going to take the only road in which they have a shred of faith: their return. So they are not murderers and they are not going to kill him and they are not thieves and they are not going to rob him, he can rest easy; but if he doesn't keep his mouth shut and his hands still, if he commits any of the crazy things they know he is capable of, if he resists in the slightest, then yes, then they will have to kill him and it will be because he forced them. Do you understand? Look us in the eye and answer us, fiendish captain, do you understand?

Juan doesn't answer or he answers with a gesture. He is still seated on a stone slab, while around him his men—his men?—come and go, searching his saddle and rifling through this clothing. They take his arquebus, they take his sword, they take the dagger hidden in his bootleg. They take his ration of jerky, his half-empty wineskin. The paper stamped by the viceroy's men, papers Pedro shuffles impatiently, searching for who knows what. His bag of coins.

It seems Tomás has made himself ringleader and distributes the loot with pompous movements. They aren't robbing him, absolutely not. They have only come to take what is fair, what they were promised, plus a few extra escudos for their trouble. Enough escudos to empty the bag, no more, no less. This way, each man gets seventeen coins and is happy, and the Black boy Felipe gets four and is even happier, and there is still a handful of small coins of silver and copper that they will manage to divide among them only after grueling calculations and quarrelling. As soon as the gold begins to flow from some hands to others, they seem to lose all interest in him. They hardly look at him. They hold their rapiers and arquebuses slackly, as if the weapons had been suddenly turned into simple shepherd's crooks or farm tools.

Juan thinks about his dream. Again, he tries to remember Juan the Indian's words, but in vain.

"Seventeen escudos," he murmurs, and the men turn around, startled. Only then do they remember to tighten their grip on their arquebuses, their swords.

With slow, calculated steps, Tomás approaches.

"What did you say?"

"Seventeen escudos. The Black boy should get the same as the rest."

The men become very serious and then burst into laughter and then are serious again.

"And why is that?"

"Because he has ridden this far, like all of us."

"So just because he's here."

"Yes."

"And what do you care about this Black boy who points his arquebus at you, like all of us, and who is, by the way, uglier than the rest of us put together?"

"Who says I care about him?"

Again the soldiers laugh, as if it were all a joke. But Tomás is pensive. He has the men circle up again and asks them to hold out their hand and from each man he takes a coin. Then he calls over the Black boy Felipe.

"Tell me something, Negro. The first time you were sold, how many coins did they pay for you?"

"Me?"

"Yes, you, I'm not talking about myself. I might be here on Earth because my father went whoring with my mother, but I didn't come to be sold by the pound at market, like a calf."

"Me, thirteen escudos."

"Thirteen escudos! Well, here you go, eleven. That's what I call making the Americas. Counting the four you already have, that's a total of fifteen. Fifteen for you and sixteen for us. We're not going to fight over a difference of one coin are we, Negro?"

"No, sir."

"Aren't you going to say thank you?"

"Thank you."

"Don't thank me. Thank the captain, you ass, the captain, God knows why he's taken a shine to your black face."

"Thank you, captain."

Before they depart, the horses saddled and the men ready for the return journey, Tomás comes over. He holds a scrap of cloth in his hand. Juan is still sitting on the same rock, his eyes on the ground, so Tomás has to kneel in order for their eyes to meet.

"I'm still asking myself what that Indian could have done to be worth so much money, captain. Did he force himself on a maiden? Burn down a church? Slit the bloody viceroy's throat?"

Juan considers his answer.

"He was a rebel, you might say."

"Another rebel! You know something, captain? In your own way, you're a rebel too. You also want to change the world. If not, go tell it to that Negro."

He waits for Juan to speak, but Juan's mouth stays shut.

"And tell me, who did that Indian rise up against? You, by chance?"

"No."

"God?"

"I'm not sure."

"Then he only rebelled against another man."

"I suppose so."

"And who was right?"

"I don't know."

Tomás smiles sadly.

"You don't know. And do you know why you don't know? Because you, with all your papers and your seals and your status, you are nothing but an errand boy to those illustrious men."

Then he blindfolds him and tells him to count to one thousand, if he knows how, and only then is he allowed to remove the blindfold. If he removes it before, they will kill him. If they discover him attempting to follow, they will kill him. If by some grace he actually finds a trace of civilization up north and has the poor judgement to recount what has just happened, they will kill him. Otherwise, they sincerely wish him luck, they wish him a long life and health and they hope he finds his rebel Indian and metes out his punishment, if that really is what they both deserve. Then they say goodbye. Goodbye, captain! The word *captain* repeated twelve times in twelve mouths, unclear whether it is ironic or a posthumous sign of respect. Juan hears the drumbeat of horse hooves on stone. He hears a metallic tinkling on his right side. He hears a bird's cry. He hears the wind and a voice that is lost in the distance, he hears his own voice repeating numbers, and when he reaches seven hundred fifty-six, he pulls off the blindfold. Beside him, he sees his horse, and on his horse a loaded arquebus and two saddlebags, and in the saddlebags, several days' worth of provisions. On the horizon, stemming south, the twelve black dots of twelve riders moving away. And gleaming in the dirt, next to his boots, a handful of coins scattered on the ground. He cradles them carefully in the palm of his hand; there is no need to count them: he knows that he, too, has been given his sixteen.

Farther north the world is simplified. Everywhere he looks is all stone and sky, above his head or beneath his feet, it's always stone or sky, cliffs that clamber down to the depths of the Earth or crags that descend to the stars. He spends the night in a small hollow in the rock, not much bigger than a coffin, and inscribed on the ceiling he finds a few ancient pictograms, almost erased by time. Juan the Indian also slept in this cave. He doesn't know if he is deciding this or discovering it. Juan slept in this cave. He, too, looked up just before he closed his eyes, to observe the same images drawn in childlike wonder. Juan saw, Juan is seeing now, the outlines of men stiff as scarecrows and animals that no longer or just barely exist. Distant relatives of his horse, galloping over rock since before Christians arrived on this land; even, perhaps, before the arrival of God. All that remains of humanity is summarized in this cave, in this rubric drawn on the skin of the world and on this last man who studies it and then forgets and continues on his journey.

He has decided not to think about anything. His thoughts will have as much thought to them as those doodles have of human beings. A hunter must be like the prey he pursues; he must think like him, he must become, in a certain sense, the hunted, and only by knowing that he is traveling alone and without a quarry can he feel close to Juan the Indian. Because at no point did Juan the Indian stop or turn back. Juan the Indian didn't give up. Somehow, he crossed the river that seems uncrossable and climbed that precipice that is snaking its way to the heavens, even though his horse—did Juan the Indian have a horse?—might have reared, might have resisted another step, like his own horse resists now. Juan the Indian also resisted. He refused to languish at a humble clerk's desk in México or as an eternal servant to the monks in some no-name congregation. He didn't wait for things to fall into his hands. He didn't limit himself to dreaming for the world to change: he simply changed it. He didn't rebel against God or men, as Tomás believed: he rebelled against the world. He came here to build it with his own hands. Perhaps in order to build those things for which he yearned, he had to destroy others. He suddenly remembers the Christ they found in the Chichimeca camp: a grandiose and terrible God, inspired by a grandiose and maybe also terrible man. Is it necessary to be terrible, to be a God in a certain sense, a diminished version of God, an imitation of God made flesh, in order to come this far with nothing but the strength of his faith and his bare hands? In order to cross the world's frontiers and press on?

Juan won't stop either. He won't give in. He is here for something that perhaps has nothing to do with gold and not even with justice. He progresses northward as if guided by an arcane instinct, without making plans or weighing consequences, without rationing his food or water or deciding what he will do when he finds him. Finding him is all that matters. He wants to empty his head the way a rider empties his canteen in the desert, sip by sip. He is that rider and he is also that canteen, slung now from his horse's rump and increasingly lighter. He is that rider and that canteen and he is also Juan the Indian.

Until one day, perhaps two weeks following the desertion of his men, a day, in short, which seemed like any other, the same sun and the same horse, the same stone and the same sky above and beneath his head, Juan's thoughts come galloping back. He crests a peak upon which, without realizing it, he has pegged certain hopes, maybe the last hopes he had left, and from the top he sees more mountains leading north, and behind them a plain that appears to be the same plain as the one he has come from, and upon that plain no fire's glow. A land that looks fresh out of the Creator's oven and numb to human suffering. He dismounts and sits on a rock so as to observe that horizon where there is nothing to see. And then yes, then he finally thinks about the people and the objects that have led him here, he thinks about Juan the Indian who perhaps took another direction or turned back or is long in the ground, and he thinks about the two weeks that were perhaps much more than two weeks, the arrows that were perhaps not genuine arrows, the men crucified for nothing, and he remembers his own home, and other things and other people he doesn't want to think about and only brushes obliquely, as one touches a fever blister with the lightest graze of the tongue.

Night has begun to fall. He senses the first shudder of the last hour of evening. This is, he decides, the last time in his life that he will be cold. Nearby, two hunchbacked mesquite trees coil. It takes a long time to fell them with his sword and much longer to turn them into kindling and light a fire. Tonight, he eats a hot meal for the first time in a long while—how long?—and surrenders to the fire's caress as to the warmth of a wife we thought was lost, and observes the flames that shine like humanity's final thunderbolt, illuminating a land with no master.

Juan looks at that fire burning for no one.

Juan looks at the ashes ascending in the air and later disappearing.

Juan looks at the dark sky and the even darker land.

And suddenly, at a precise point in the blackness, a light that is lit, a light that faintly flickers, then steadies and grows. A fixed light, too, behind him, and another light at a point that seems somewhere above his head, and another on the opposite flank, even closer and more luminous, as if the stars were descending to earth to set the world on fire; as if all of a sudden the night had opened its eyelids to look at him, incandescent and terrible. His horse starts to whinny and kick, and someone whistles or shouts in the distance, and Juan practically throws himself on the fire to stamp it out, but once it's out it is too late, in the blank night the fire seems to have found a mirror in which to multiply, and all around six fires, ten fires, fifteen fires ignite at once, some distant like stars and others so near that he can hear the wood crackle. They are Chichimeca savages; the monstrous, barbaric, bloodthirsty Chichimeca of whom Tomás spoke, the Chichimeca who inhabit inhabitable mountains and who are waiting now, waiting in the night's silence, waiting by the warmth of their fires, waiting for who knows what, but waiting.

He doesn't sleep a wink all night. In the flames' glow he sees the nightmares conspiring, nightmares he isn't dreaming up; he sees trees stalking him and moving shadows that are actually rocks immobile since the origins of time and over and over he imagines the many deaths that await him: his body pierced by arrows, throat slit, mutilated, skewered on a stake, viciously scalped. He begins to pray under his breath, and his own prayer seems to transform into an indigenous incantation. He hears a bush shaken by a wind that does not blow, an enemy hand where there is only air; a coyote howls in the distance, calling to him with its vaguely human voice. Dawn does not yet break, the dawn will never come, and then, at the very moment of this realization, dawn arrives at last: the sun peeks over the rocky crests and spills over his face just as it spills over his horse's hindquarters and over the dying campfires and the Indian horde surrounding him like birds about to take flight, increasingly blue and defined by the light of daybreak. Indians who sleep. Indians who get to their feet. Indians who seem to make signs at him with their bare hands or obsidian hatchets. Indians to the east and Indians to the west, to the south and north. Indians perched on stone pinnacles or up in trees or simply waiting beside their fires, in their ceremonial headdresses and war paint.

Unconvincingly, Juan grips his arquebus. He embraces that piece of iron that will not save his life, that he will not even manage to shoot. He observes the Indians forming columns of three, wielding weapons difficult to identify from a distance, and then he sees them set forth in a disciplined march, solemn, like members of a Rogation procession. On one of the flanks, four Indians bear a motionless lump—their leader? A wounded man?—on a stretcher, and opposite them a dozen Indians carry white torches. They draw near. They do not shoot their arrows or howl furiously or charge from behind the rocks, but they do draw near.

He loads his weapon with trembling hands. He hears, echoing directly from the past, the words a brother in arms whispered to him many years ago, on the eve of his first battle. Never, ever shoot before you see the white of the enemy's eyes: to precipitate is a waste of gunpowder.

But before he can discern the whites of their eyes, he has time to see many other things. With each step, he sees the tribe's leader, the wounded man, transform into a wood carving carried on their shoulders, and the Indians' hands brandishing not weapons but small wooden crosses, and the white torches that become large candles piously lit, and the wood carving that takes the shape of a Virgin covered by a hemp mantle and bouquets of white flowers, and no matter where his eyes land, he doesn't see a single bow or cudgel or shield or stone hatchet; just candles and flowers and the devout who lift their prayers and crosses toward the heavens.

Juan throws his arquebus far from him. He raises his hands in a gesture of supplication or reverence and stands to receive the approaching procession. They are so close that he can see the whites of their eyes and even count the teeth in their smiles. Slowly, he walks out to meet them. He doesn't speak. And when they reach him, when they are a handsbreadth away, the false warriors stop dead in their tracks, they let their crosses and candles drop to either side, and, bathed in tears, prostrate themselves to kiss his leather boots.

"Padre ... Padre ..."

VI

Drink water, eat bread – The first shedding of skin – Throne of a minor king – First apostle of the Kingdom – A man once called Diego – To become a slave of oneself – To ride a bird – A dagger draws the world – Sheep to slaughter – Angel on horseback

The settlement lies a half day's ride away, at the base of a rock formation he has the sense of having camped below days before. He looks at the stony stretches of land that glitter in the sun and the craggy cliffs that rise in precarious balancing acts against the horizon and the rocky spires that look like scales on a gigantic dragon, if one believed in such things, and he feels that each one of the images touches him intimately, in the way that we are touched by the features of a face we have already contemplated. And yet, he's never been here before: how could he have been without finding the hundred or two hundred huts scattered across the slope. A pack of children scamper around him, laughing and shoving. Every so often, they pluck up the courage to come close enough to the stranger to touch a fold of his chamois cape, or one of his extraordinarily white hands, only to take off again, laughing and howling like coyote pups.

In the shade of the huts, young girls naked to the waist mend fabric or conscientiously chew mesquite pods. They glance up from their labor shyly, as if they hadn't intended to. Juan slows in order to observe their faces, their breasts bathed in sunlight. He is surprised to find beautiful women and common women and ugly women, too, just like in all regions of the world.

"All virgins. All María," murmurs one of the old men accompanying him, with a mix of pride and reverence.

Then they guide him inside one of the huts and offer him mouthfuls of strange and not entirely unpleasant delicacies.

"You lots of bread, lots of wine. Lots of bread, wine, bread, wine, bread, wine, bread . . ."

They point to all the bowls one by one, the unfired clay pitchers. They call all the liquid concoctions wine and all the solids bread, whether referring to red beans, venison steaks, or boiled prickly pear. And so Juan eats bread of many forms and flavors and drinks a warm, thick wine.

"Lots of bread, lots of wine . . . Good bread and wine . . ."

The Indians know the words *bread* and *wine* and *good*. Juan hears them surface now and again in their chatter, the words almost unrecognizable in their mouths, mingling with many words that are unfamiliar to him, words that sound less human and more like the bellowing of beasts. He attempts to follow the flow of their conversation, skipping from one Spanish word to another, like the single stones that permit the crossing of a river. He's not certain of having managed. He hears or believes he hears the word *Hell*, and *Heaven* and *kingdom* and *God*. The word *love*. The word *Christian*. That word, above all. Because they are Christians, they say or seem to say, and they repeat it three times, beating their chests with open palms. Christians, not savages.

Savage, for some reason, is the word they pronounce best.

"Who taught you all this?"

"Padre . . . Padre teaches."

But they have questions, too. They speak clumsily, like birds attempting to reproduce the human voice, and their hands are always at the ready to prop up their meaning, slightly delayed after their words. They want to know where he has come from, and to indicate *where* they pretend to scan the horizon in all directions. They want to know if he too is a disciple of their Padre, and with the word *disciple* they remain standing and with *Padre*, they kneel. They want to know his name, the name his mother chose for him, and to accompany *mother*, they mime breasts and briefly cradle the air. And when Juan finally replies, when they hear Juan say the name Juan, they bend docilely once more to kiss his hands, his shirttails, the toes of his boots.

"Padre, Padre," they repeat.

Juan gently moves them off with a light shake of his hand. Yes: he is also named Juan. And he is there to find their Padre, at any cost. Can they help him? Might they be able to tell him where he is hiding?

They are silent for a moment, as if weighing his words. Finally, an old man, his body covered in shells and piercings, steps forward. He points north.

"House," he says. "House of God."

"Take me there."

They gather at the village's center. The area which should have only held a clearing in which to light bonfires, or perform war dances, or do whatever it is that Indians do when they aren't murdering Christians. But the heart of this village is not empty. In place of a mound of ashes there is a rectangular cabin, larger than the others, built with effort and care that do not seem like the work of Indians. Weak light filters through the entwined branches that form the walls, an imperceptibly oscillating light, perhaps. Imperceptibly alive.

Juan steps to the threshold. He looks at the closed door first and then at each one of faces of the Indians who have come out to receive them. Young Indians, old Indians, sick Indians, happy Indians, Indians indifferent to everyone and everything, but not a trace of Juan the Indian.

"Who is your Padre? Where is he?"

"House of God," repeats one of the old men, pointing at the door.

The old man murmurs a few words in his language, and two young men push on the great wooden door. There is no one inside, or rather there is less than no one, there is only the silence that envelopes places that once held many but are empty now; the clay floor covered with reed mats worn from use, blocks of wood as makeshift pews, a sort of burning lamp hung from the ceiling, and an altar of white stone bathed in light. And at the back, obscured by the half-light that comes and goes, a shadow that appears to be a crucified man and is only a wooden sculpture. A wooden man crucified on a wooden cross, his tortured features, carved savagely, as if slashed by knife blade; perhaps a little less savage, a little less tortured than what Juan remembered. Someone has dressed the idol in a threadbare linen tunic and stuck old sandals of Spanish leather on its feet. They are Juan the Indian's clothes. He knows this the very moment he lays eyes on them: even before the Indians wrest them from the Christ and lay them in his hands in a grave, silent offering.

"Padre," they say at last. They smile.

Curious, Juan touches the rag full of rips and patches, so tattered that in some places he sees the shadow of his fingers through the fabric. He touches the blackened sandals, too, their soles almost completely worn through from the chawing of the plains and the sierra. The same plains, the same sierra. And at the end of the journey, Juan the Indian's clothes, abandoned on the side of the path like the first shedding of a snakeskin.

"Padre . . ." they repeat.

They look at him closely. They look at the tunic in his hands and the shirt he has on, covered in dust and dirt. They look at Juan's eyes, Juan's uncertainty, until Juan finally understands. He sits on one of the wooden benches and slowly removes his ragged clothes; the boots where all the smells of the desert have baked. He leaves his sword on the floor, his arquebus, the dagger he hides in his boot shank. An Indian helps him with the left boot, then the right; another is already crouched, sandals ready in hand. Two more men are positioned behind him, directing him to raise his arms—*Heaven, Heaven,* they say—and then the tunic is falling over his body, forming to his body like a sword in its sheath. He senses its heat, the last heat of Juan the Indian, against his skin. Two men kneel beside him, wrestling his boots onto the feet of the wooden Christ.

Adjacent to the altar is a kind of seat of honor, made of wood, which reminds him of the set of seats reserved for a chorus or the throne of a minor king. Two men guide him to it and motion for him to sit. The moment he does, all those present fall to their knees.

"Padre! Padre!" the faithful shout.

But Juan is not their Padre. He repeats it again: he is not their Padre. He bears that name, Juan, because it was what his mother wanted, and he only wears those clothes because it was what they, the Indians, wanted, but all similarities stop there. And he must find him precisely for that reason, because they are not the same person. Do they understand? He must find him. Can they help?

Silent, they listen to his explanations. Look at each other in consternation. Exchange a few words in their language. No one responds. Juan insists with more vehemence. I am talking about your Padre, he says. Talking about the man who taught them all they know. The man who wore those very garments. Where can he find him? Is he hidden there, somewhere in the village?

At last, one shakes his head.

"No . . . Padre village no . . ."

"When did he leave?"

They consult each other with another look, an afflicted air.

"I only want to know when he left! Do you understand? Has he gone? Has he gone or not?"

"Where?" the same Indian asks, on the verge of tears.

Juan doesn't know how to respond.

At first he believes he is just another savage. He hardly notices him at all: a common man leaning against the doorjamb, perhaps taller than the others, perhaps a little more dignified. He wears a frayed doublet, full of mended tears and loose stitches and patches of varying colors, as if someone had wanted to fashion Christian garb by sewing together pieces of rags. He is also wearing an old goatskin pouch, like those used by shepherds and some pilgrims. Atop his head, an enormous straw hat, similar to a cart's wheel, veils his face. But suddenly the common man lifts his head, and then Juan sees a blond beard emerge under the brim of the hat. A blond beard, and white skin scarred by the sun, and a stiff smile that is as if carved on his face.

Never losing his smile, the white man claps his hands twice and shouts a few mysterious words. It is a short, dry message, which nonetheless has an immediate effect on the savages. Before he has stopped speaking, all have hurried out of the church—the church?—and closed the door behind them. Left inside are the Christ dressed in Juan's clothing and Juan dressed in the Christ's clothing and the white man who appears to be dressed in the remnants of the clothing of at least ten men. At no point does his smile fade; a smile so wide and so stiff that it seems to waffle between goodwill and ferocity.

"You must excuse them, captain . . . They are a peaceful people, but also innocent like children . . ."

"What have you said to them?"

He makes a vague gesture, wiping away the words so recently uttered.

"Oh! Nothing important. I might have insinuated that you are tired from your journey, and when you are tired, you don't work miracles, but storms . . ." He laughs weakly, as if in apology. "As I said, they are peaceful people . . . and innocent like children."

"Who are you?"

The man's smile intensifies, or perhaps deepens.

"By no means the man you seek."

"And who do I seek?"

"You seek the Padre . . . Why do you ask me what you already know?"

His smile has disappeared for the first time, but something of its strength seems to have transferred to his eyes. To the shine in his eyes.

"Do you mean Juan the Indian?"

"If that's what you like to call him."

"Then, do you know where I can find him?"

The stranger takes a long pause. He looks at Juan then at his cloth sack. He fidgets with the straw hat.

"And you, do you happen to know where I can find paper?"

"Paper?"

"Yes, paper . . . to write on. Paper, parchment, a bloody clay tablet. Whatever you've got."

Juan rifles in his sack. It occurs to him that the instructions for locating the Padre are perhaps too complicated and must be written down. Perhaps he wants to record a coded message: something that the savages, who might be listening on the other side of the walls, cannot understand. Perhaps he is about to compose a map that will lead him to the Padre's refuge. But when at last he finds his bundle of papers, the man does none of that. He almost rips them from his hands. He kisses the ribbon that holds them together and simply puts them away inside his breastplate, as if stashing a treasure.

"God bless you! You don't know how often I have dreamt of clean, white papers like these . . ."

Juan has no time to ask questions, because in the same breath, as if both subjects were closely connected, the man adds that, unfortunately, the Padre has left. He'd remained there a long time, in that village, waiting, waiting. It seemed he would never leave. What was he waiting for? He was waiting for you, he says. Just for you.

"For me? The Padre, waiting for me?"

"Yes, you. But rest assured, I will help you find him. I will tell you where he went . . ."

Juan looks at the man's hand, his index finger, which seems about to point somewhere.

"You still haven't told me who you are," he says, not looking away from the hand.

"Oh! I'm nobody. Just one of his children . . . We are all his children, didn't you know? Perhaps even you, as well . . ."

A boy has climbed up to the nearest narrow window in order to peek inside the church. Juan sees shining round eyes, spying from the gloom. His smile. He looks happy, as only particular moments in particular childhoods are.

"They believe that I am the Padre, is that so?" he says, indicating the narrow window. "The Padre's envoy, at least. That's why they have dressed me in his clothes."

The man tilts his head. First he says no, and then yes, and then that he isn't sure. After all, what does he know about these Indians? He has been among them so long, he laments, and he is still no more than a stranger. Only He knew how to understand them. Only He could. It is even possible that He was the only one who wanted to. At times it seemed He would be inside their head, inside the heads of all those savages, even without words. If only he could explain, now, what the Padre did. What he was capable of. If only he had the right words. How could he, a simple son, a miniscule man after all, make him understand what he himself has not managed to completely understand? It could be said that He knew how to make them his with a single movement of his hand. All those savages, who, before his arrival, did nothing but eat human flesh and murder each other. It could be said that Padre was capable of penetrating their dreams. Yes, that's what he did; he touched them in their instincts, in their most primal passions, their most irrational desires. And he knew, too, how to rouse those passions with but a single a word. A look. It was all He needed, the man says, turning the hat over and over in his hands: a look. Because in the beginning, He didn't know the savages' tongue, and He had to preach like that, with hand signals, with looks. Can Juan imagine? A man transmitting the mystery of the Holy Trinity with a look. With a gesture. And for that gesture to suffice. To have more force than centuries of arguments between theologians and philosophers. Because even like that, even without words, he managed to reach the bottom of their barbarian souls, their pagan souls, their tormented souls. And there inside, in that dark place, he was able to sow God.

Juan follows the man's reasoning with difficulty. After a time, he isn't even attentive to the words. Only to the way in which the stranger speaks them, as if spitting them out, as if they burned in his mouth. He attends to his brusque and energetic movements, which combined with his ragged clothing, grants him a kind of festive, minstrel-esque air. Juan contemplates his face: the way in which he can shift from joy to sorrow in an instant. It's his passions, not those of the Indians, that appear inflamed. As if before his departure, the Padre had lit a fire inside him that had not yet burned out.

"As regards you," he's saying now. "I suppose they believe you are one of the Padre's emissaries . . . and as you can see, in their own way, they aren't wrong. It's seemed a very serious issue. They weren't the kind of looks that served for explaining the concept of the Holy Trinity to a bunch of savages; they didn't have that power, of course, but they weren't nothing either. There are looks, he says, that command one to the Devil, and he knew how to interpret those looks, and he knew, too, how to contain them: two inches of steel in the chest. That's how it was. That's how he lived. He grifted, he debauched, he wounded, he killed. He didn't know much about religion. Just enough to understand that telling someone that he had a nose like a Jew or the look of a reconciled heretic was reason enough to tempt death; and enough to know that once death was dealt, one should seek sanctuary. More than once, it was his lot to spend a night, sometimes up to a week, besieged by bailiffs in a church in the city of México. He was surrounded by bailiffs outside and priests and friars inside, who tried to convince him of who knows what manner of things. Men who spoke of poverty with golden chalices in their hand; of temperance while those repugnant hands creeped in the confessional's darkness. That was, at the time, his only relationship with the Church. Sometimes, of course, he prayed. He asked God for a dozen escudos with which to change his life, but God didn't listen. At least that's what he believed back then. Because God, the Padre taught him, always listens. He always gives us what we ask of Him, especially when we know how to ask for the things we should. Perhaps God knew something then that he himself only knows now: that neither twelve nor two hundred nor one million escudos would have been enough to save him. To change his life all he had to do was exactly that: change his life. And one specific day, one specific night, in an infectious tavern, it happened. A man he had never seen before walked in through the door. A man who was very rich or had the ways of the very rich. The tavern stunk of piss and vomit and pulque. One of those arrogant gentlemen, belonging to that class of men who know how to cause more damage with their tongue than their hands. That man's hands, says the man who at one time answered to the name Diego, were, by the way, white, clean, prim. They had never given death to a man: he could swear it. But the man's tongue. His words. He remembers him seated across from him at a blood-and-wine-stained table, a table not worthy of Your Excellency, he'd have said, somewhat hurriedly, but the man didn't care or said he didn't care. They talked the entire night. Rather, the man talked. He knew they called him Daga. He knew many things and had many ideas, as well. A job for him. The task, says the man who the worst tongues called Diego de Daga, you can imagine what it was. I had to make it here and talk to him and capture him—or kill him. They never gave me exact instructions. The higher ups never speak clearly! Wouldn't you agree? It's more comfortable for them, not speaking clearly. They keep to telling those below them what the problem is. They tell them that it would be terrible if a certain man kept preaching, continued injecting his poison, that we have to do something, we have to, and the ones below understand . . . what is it they understand? They never say the word kill. They don't want to stain their mouths. They only want to stain our hands. And we do stain them, of course. He, at least, was prepared to stain them. I was prepared to stain them, he repeats. The job took him from México to Zacatecas and from there to the sierra, or what is the same, from there to Hell. He came here. He came here when the Padre's Work was just beginning. How long ago was that? He can't remember. Who knows, and who cares. He arrived, that's enough. Everything is simpler than we believe. Tomorrow comes, yesterday goes: everything is reduced to that. At least that is what the savages think. Do you know, they don't even have a word in their tongue to name such a simple thing as time? Earth and dust and sky: that is all that exists for them. Time is something we walk, he says, like the world. The past falls behind and the future draws near and the present is something we try to hold on to with both hands but can never quite grasp. Earth and dust and sky: that's all that exists. It sounds absurd, he admits, it sounds, perhaps, ridiculous, but could they possibly be sure of the contrary? If now, in the middle of the desert, he was to ask Juan what year they are living in, would his voice not shake with his answer? What importance have they here, the years, the kings, the ephemeris? If he were to tell him that Carlos no longer rules Castilla, but his son, Felipe, what would change things? And if after that, a Felipe who we will call the second, the third were to come? Then what? In short, if he knew all that, what would change? What does he care how they agree to measure time, those who are inclined to measure it? The very notion of a year, of a date, is inconceivable in this desert. Year after what? Year after whom? No Christ ever came here. The closest thing to Christ was, as a matter of fact, the Padre. Maybe that is what the Padre deserves: his own year. His own chronology. Although it is fair to recall that the Padre didn't believe in time. At least not in the way men usually believe. Every day is Judgement Day: that's what he would say. But no matter. The fact is that he met the Padre and he did it, of course, on Judgement Day. He spoke with Him. Perhaps they are still speaking now, right now, in that part of the world where, according to the savages, the events of the past remain. Behind him, always behind him. He told him he had come to kill him. But the Padre was not afraid. He simply sat down and talked and talked. He talked all night and all day: he talked under the sun and under the stars. How he wishes he could recall those words. Everything he says now, trying to remember what the Padre told him, won't be more than the rustle of dead leaves: the drone with which the trees try to imitate wind song. Eggshells, dry and broken, where once there was a bird. The Padre talked a little like that, through images. One could see before him everything he named: see how he pointed to it with the tip of his tongue. The fact is that the Padre talked, who knows for how long, and as he listened he forgot that something called sleep even existed. He told him that the world was rotten and the land, his land, damned. You know the world as I do, Diego says the Padre said, and you know, too, that between the world and Hell there is no longer any difference; flame-licked nightmares are painted on church cupolas in order to terrify the faithful, but in truth, it would be enough to place a mirror; stained glass to reflect all that is monstrous about men. The encomenderos who crucify insubordinate Indians. The men who kill for gold. The priests who live with their concubines, passing them off as mothers or sisters. All of creation moans as one, he said, and as one suffers labor pains. He spoke of that labor that was to come; of the need to bring a new world into being. This is my new world, he said, pointing at the Indians gathered round him, and this new world is only the beginning. And Diego de Daga, the man who lacked the fingers to count to all the men he had killed, decided to sheath his sword and wait. I am going to believe in your words, he says he said. But if you stray from them, though it be by the fingernail on your pinkie, or if you betray but a single letter, I will kill you. The Padre simply smiled. Can Juan understand what kind of person the Padre was? Someone who, when threatened with death, smiles? That was what the Padre did: smile. And he never strayed from the meaning of his own words. Or, depending on how you look it, he strayed so many times that he couldn't manage to count them, because he was constantly assaulted by new ideas, brilliant ideas, revelations that blinded him with their fiery splendor and later left him dazed for days or weeks. Following his illuminations, everything in him seemed to burn; it was unbearable to look in his eyes, to enter the abyss of eyes that had seen so luminous and so deep, just as sunlight can burn even when reflected off water. Then he would come back to himself, filled with new ideas and hungry to bring them to fruition. He said, for instance, that they must bury, must return to the bowels of the earth, all the gold, all the silver, all the rubies in the village, because man must only hunger for bread. He introduced a kind of shell found in shallow fords of local river as currency and, after a time, he discarded even those shells, saying that they too were gold, white gold, but gold just the same. He exiled coin from his world, the mere concept of coin, which, according to him, spilled as much blood as iron did, instead making it so that all the land belonged to all the men and that they should live united and in common, and the corn and beans would be distributed according to each's need. He said we came to this world with nothing and with nothing we will undoubtedly leave, so we should be satisfied having sustenance and something to cover ourselves with. Each morning he sat beneath a fig tree to mete out justice, which was not man's justice but God's, as everything he said was no more than an echo of what was heralded in the Gospel. Sometimes, it is true, he denied something he'd said the previous evening or would one day state that every man could do and eat as much as he wanted, then the next, that whosoever does not accept the hoe should not accept bread. These contradictions did not disturb him. He said that we must not be slaves to our own words, nor even our thoughts. Be free of others' opinions, and even of one's own. He said, too, that we could not yet understand it all. He yearned to serve us: he would give us milk to drink, not solid food, because we were not yet men enough to digest it. And it was thus that a man who had once been called Diego de Daga, that rogue who had one night slit a stranger's throat because it had appeared that behind the man's grave expression he was secretly mocking him; that scoundrel, became—can you believe it—his first apostle. He decided to give his life to the Padre, with the same passion with which had taken the lives of others before. And for a long time—how long—he was by the Padre's side, seeing how his Work grew, stone upon stone. That world he was calling in to replace the other. Until one day, one morning that seemed no different from the rest in any respect, the Padre called him to his righthand side. It was then that he told him. Told him that unfortunately his time in that place had come to an end and he must continue on his path. That the moment had come to leave him on his own. And the man who had raised his sword against women and children and the aged lost his composure and for the first time in a long while he appealed to the Padre, grabbing his shirtfront. His voice was desperate. He said he could not abandon them; not now. He repeated what He himself had said so many times: that his job was still far from done. The Padre smoothly released himself from the hook of his hand, as if he were almost immaterial, and cupped his cheek. He said he was right, the world he had brought into being still had to take shape, to grow, but that this was only the beginning. His Work was barely begun, that first village was just the foundation of something, and if someday he wanted to build its walls and tile its roofs then he must

Juan sees men and women kneeling over dirt rows to pick beans and others who weave esparto grass sarapes or leather sandals. A young man hammers furiously on an anvil; another chops woods or hauls baskets or kneads dough. He sees a line of women who are passing a ball of clay and how each one leaves her tiny mark in the mud: one shapes the handles, another makes marks with her burin, another dips the piece in a tub of water. By the time the clay reaches the last pair of hands, it is a pot decorated with geometric shapes and mysterious pictures, and all that is left is to fire it in the kiln. He sees before the House of God a chorus of thirty or forty children singing improbably in Latin, accompanied by drums and bone shawms, and a kind of Indian subcantor waving his staff in time to the music. Otherwise no human sound can be heard: just the hammering of tools and the fluttering of turkeys in their pens.

The Padre's apostle is still talking. He speaks in an ominous voice about the terrible time of their heathendom, when they spent their time getting drunk and shooting arrows at each other, devouring each other, like animals roaming the plain. But Juan is no longer listening. He only has ears for the silence. Only has eyes for the Indians who mill about bringing or taking things in respectful silence, sometimes with a small smile upon their lips, with the haste and discretion of industrious monks. They seem happy. They seem human. More human than any of the Indians he saw working the encomiendas, digging in the mines, suffering on their crosses. He would even say they appeared satisfied; they expected nothing of themselves, nor of their tomorrows, other than what they had in their hands today. And there didn't seem to be superior or inferior men among them: they were simply that, men. Men who work like slaves, perhaps, but do so in a world without masters, in a world of slaves unto themselves and for this reason they are, in some way, free. Watching them he understands what it is Juan the Indian saw here. What it is he wanted to do; what he might have even achieved. A man's dream, which for its ambition and beauty, appears almost divine: to establish a world that, against all odds, keeps on spinning without silver and gold as its fuel. A world in which all that is gained and all that is lost is the human.

He finds his own horse tied to one of the beams in the smithy, snuffling and eating from a wooden trough. Beside the horse sits an Indian, mouth agape, all his attention on the animal's immense head. He makes a move to lift his hand and touch his muzzle, slowly, but doesn't dare in the end. When he sees the Padre and the apostle, he stands abruptly, as if caught out.

The man once called Diego laughs, pointing to the look of shock on his face. They must be understanding, he explains to Juan: it's the first horse the Indian has seen in his life.

"Isn't that so, Marcos? You've never seen a horse before, have you?"

The Indian nods, never taking his eyes off the animal.

"No ... I hear."

"Hear?" Juan asks.

Another vigorous nod.

"Saint Peter ..."

"Saint Peter?"

"Horse fall Saint Peter ..."

The apostle smiles proudly.

"As you can see, these Indians are well-versed in the faith and sacred history. Test him, go ahead, ask whatever you like."

Juan hesitates. He reaches out to stroke his horse's mane, completing the movement the Indian doesn't make.

"Tell me, is this how you imagined a horse?"

The Indian does not turn to look at him. He doesn't even blink. His eyes are two black pins burning in the sunlight, akin in every way to the eyes of the horse.

"No, Padre."

"How did you imagine them?"

The Indian is slow to reply, as if the issue deserved deep reflection.

"Bird," he says at a last.

"Bird?"

"Big bird."

The apostle lets out an exaggerated laugh.

"A bird, eh? Saint Peter riding a bird, no less! They're a little crazy, these Indians ... But they're good. At least most of them are. Marcos, for instance, is good ... You're good, isn't that so, Marcos?"

The Indian nods with conviction.

"I good. I pure. No punish. I Jesus."

And then, before the apostle's undying laughter, he repeats:

"No punish. I Jesus. I Jesus."

At some point, the apostle appears to lose interest in Juan. He has sat down in the dust and taken out the bundle of papers. In deep concentration, he almost seems to draw blood from the page. A Bible with some carelessly underlined passages, some pages with folded corners and some pages ripped out, and among all that writing, not a single blank space; among all those letters he sees charcoal scribbles, bands of figures that pulse between paragraphs, between lines, between words, a torrent of shapes intertwined in interminable latticework. He sees, as if interpreting a religious tympanum, figures he recognizes and others which are a mystery; he sees Indians weaving baskets and Indians harvesting gourds and Indians kneeling in prayer; he sees the interior of a straw hut; he sees a naked woman bathing her naked child in a river; he sees turkeys and feather headdresses and flutes made of bone. In some cases, to round out a figure or create a shadow, the drawing makes use of a sinuous line of text, or even blots out a word: a smudge over the word mercy; over the word love. He sees children scampering, amid laughter and shoves. He sees a man crying over another man's grave. He sees a ripened ear of corn that appears made out of teeth, and a set of human teeth constructed from kernels of corn. A smile. Opened eyes, closed eyes. Lips pursed to kiss or spit or blow out a flame. He sees the cycle of life, a woman who gives birth in Genesis, amid unspeakable suffering, and a child who drags himself on the ground, who crawls, who stands to walk from Exodus on, who becomes a man page by page until he copulates, piously, in the Gospels—his phallus in the shape of a cross; his wife hollow like a sanctum or a tabernacle—he sees that woman again, the same woman, giving birth in Revelations, amid unspeakable suffering. And he sees many other things that he cannot manage to understand or explain. He sees the skeleton of a dead horse, bones worn smooth by sand. He sees a prison or the idea of a prison, and three prisoners crushed together, languishing in hunger or pain or loathing. He sees a mule-drawn cart crossing through the thick of battle. He sees a wooden chapel and then a stone cathedral and lastly a cathedral made of iron, yet devoured by flames nonetheless. He sees a man on horseback, razing the plains and delivering hope and death. He sees a page stained completely black, as if in mourning for something or someone. He sees a cross formed from two arquebuses driven into the dirt and a black horse that waits. He sees an enormous snake slithering through the desert, and hundreds of men and women and even children hanging on to its scales as best they can. He sees a pyramid of dead women rising from the sludge of the earth to the sludge of the sky. He sees the desert and the black scar that runs through it. He sees a man shouting from the heights of a pulpit or stage and below him he sees hundreds, perhaps thousands, of men bearing it on their backs, almost crushed under its weight. And he sees even more: he sees weapons from another time, campesinos, churches, gold coins, dawns breaking, warriors. He sees a drove of demonic gods, the dead idols of the Chichimeca, burning on an enormous pyre; a fire lit in the Acts of the Apostles, never to be extinguished, through all that remains of the book; a fire that burns, that purifies some members of the tribe, who knows whether all the members, men and women writhing amid the flames, and on the final pages he also sees—as if born suddenly of a nightmare—armless men and legless men and men with empty eye sockets and men sliced open from stern to stem and the Enemy slinking among their bodies; he sees knives that travel from hand to flesh and from flesh to sheath, and he also sees beheadings and torture and deaths by arrowshot, men who drown in water and men who drown in flames, as if a Diego de Daga from other times had emerged from the past to torment the present.

Suddenly, Diego himself, the man who was Diego and is now the Padre's apostle, snatches the book back. He turns the pages urgently, fevered.

"This is not what concerns you . . . what concerns you is . . . this."

He returns the book to Juan, open to Genesis. And in it, on a blank or almost blank page, he finds a human face. It fills the entire page. It is the Padre. He knows before the apostle can even open his mouth. He is wearing his own clothes and sitting on a seat that looks like the throne of a minor king and from that throne he reigns with a vaguely terrifying air. It is the Padre who is frightening. The Padre's eyes. They gleam from the depths of the portrait with an intolerable brightness inside which no pigment could survive. They are as hard and blank as mirrors and certain gemstones, and they are perpetually open, as if they had no lids. As if they had no gaze, if such a thing were possible. Eyes fixed ahead, always ahead, in pursuit of the coming Christ he would eventually have to become, or perhaps in pursuit of the figures drawn viciously in the book's margins. The Padre contemplates those dreadful inhabitants of Daga's dreams without a shred of judgement or agony, admiration or rejection, as one might contemplate a future that is already known and simply does not affect us in the least.

Evening falls. The laborers slow to a stop and the kiln fires are extinguished. The Indian women who form the chain of potters suddenly get to their feet, as if unified by the call of an inaudible bugle, and dissolve into the crowd of Indians returning to their huts. The pots lay abandoned in the dirt, half-complete, or rather, there are thirty versions of the same pot in different phases of the process, from its birth as a simple hunk of clay until it is ready to quench our thirst. Only the apostle remains immobile, bent over his papers. He draws the work winding down, the kilns extinguishing their flames, the potters dissolving into the crowd of Indians returning to their huts.

And then, in the increasingly deserted alleyways, Juan hears something that sounds like an animal's lowing, or the suffering of a beast. He looks in all directions until he believes he has discovered its provenance: a pen just visible in the distance, at the edge of the village.

"What is that?"

"The sheep," the apostle replies, his eyes on the paper.

"Sheep? Here?"

"Yes. Sheep."

Juan sets off in the direction of the enclosure, wondering how Juan the Indian could have managed to bring his own flock of Spanish sheep with him. On the way, he crosses the path of an old man who comes along, shaking his head.

"Not pure," he says sorrowfully, pointing back. "No María, no Jesús."

Juan quickens his pace, knowing—perhaps—what he is about to find. A fenced-in enclosure, built with stakes twice a man's height. Two sentinels keep watch at the gate, supplied with bows and lances. And on the other side, through the cracks, in shadows cast by the setting sun, he glimpses bodies. Pieces of bodies. He sees Diego's last drawings made of flesh on earth, as if the margins of the Book of Revelation had at last spawned its gallery of monsters into the world. He sees armless Indians and legless Indians and Indians with empty eye sockets, all still alive, all roaming like sleepwalkers around the same dusty circle, some clustered against the stakes and some crying and some embracing with their tiny bodies or shrinking from one another, surrendering to disgust or shame.

"What is this," he asks. His voice is ice.

There is no question, only condemnation.

The sentinels exchange glances, confused. They are searching for the right word and can't find it.

"This agnus, Padre," says one.

"Agnus," repeats the other, very somber.

"Agnus," Juan murmurs, not looking at them, as if he's miles away.

"Sheep," one says at last. "This sheep, Padre."

"Sheep!" the other man confirms, smiling, pleased to have finally found the right word.

"Sheep," Juan repeats. "What do you mean sheep, you bastards. What the hell are you saying!"

He almost shouts this last sentence. Perhaps this is why the passing Indians start to swarm around him. Some are smiling. They look at Juan, something between amused and perplexed. Others tug weakly on the folds of his tunic, trying to explain to Juan what Juan does not understand.

"Sheep," they repeat with didactic patience. "Sheep. No María, no Jesús."

Juan pushes them away roughly.

"They are not sheep, you villains, they are men. Do you understand me? Men!"

And then a familiar voice, a hard voice, reverberates behind him.

"They are sheep," says Diego de Daga. "Wayward sheep."

He clutches the sharpened charcoal in his left hand, as if brandishing a dagger. He does not look at Juan, nor does he look at the prisoners, who begin to shake and shout at the sound of his voice. He is looking at the sky, the last of the evening light, as if reading in it the words he is about to say.

He says that he doesn't have the gift of letters, but he knows that it is written that the ax is already laid at a tree's roots, and that every tree that does not bear good fruit will be thrown into fire.

He says that God punishes those He loves and flogs all those he receives as His children, and that a son who goes unpunished and unflogged by his father is not a true son but a bastard.

He says: If your hand or foot causes you to sin, cut it off and cast it from you.

He says: And if your eye causes you to sin, pluck it out and cast it from you, because it is better for one of your limbs to perish than for your whole body to be cast into hellfire.

He says: God will judge those outside of you. Expel the wicked from your midst.

He says that the member that sins must be cut off so it does not corrupt the rest of the body and that the member of the Church who sins must be cut off so that they don't corrupt the Church.

He says that land that produces thorns and thistles, it is worthless and about to be cursed, and in the end will be burned.

As Diego speaks, as his voice cascades with the first shadow of night, Juan stops watching the prisoners. He prefers to examine, one by the one, the faces of the Indians who are listening to Diego de Daga. Approving Indians, bewitched Indians, laughing Indians. Indians with their eyes serenely closed, transported or cradled by his words. Indians who sing, even, and drown out the cries and laments with their song. Among all those peaceful, satisfied, tolerant Indians, just two eyes painfully open. Just one expression of horror. A bronze-skinned woman: an Indian woman who reminds him, perhaps—vaguely, painfully—of someone. Her mouth is slightly agape, as if petrified in a grimace of dread: an expression in which there is no surprise, just the confirmation of something which is already known but no less intolerable for it. She does not watch the prisoners, either. She does not watch the Indians. She does not watch the sky. She only looks behind her. She is looking at him. Inside him. Who knows if right through him. She looks in a terrible way, as one looks at terrible things that have happened and the even more terrible things still to come; eyes divested of all volition and all beauty, eyes that have seen horror and are filled with it and therefore excruciating to look at, or perhaps they have seen horror and are empty for that very reason, though that emptiness itself is even more unbearable. Eyes that reflect nothing now, eyes that are what remains of compassion when faith is erased; freedom, when justice is withheld; will, when it lacks hands and a voice. Hope minus hope.

It happens after moonrise, before the rooster crows. Juan dresses in haste. He gathers his sack, his arquebus, sword. He glides over the reed mat in bare feet, boots in hand. He cautiously pushes on the door to the hut, which creaks drily. For what seems an enormous length of time, he stands stock-still beside the door, attentive to the sounds of night. Just the distant crackle of a fire; a coyote's yelp.

He finds his horse tethered near the kiln, vaguely illuminated by the pale moon. He hurries to tighten the saddle straps, to lay the arquebus across the horse's neck, and ties his sack to the pommel on the saddle. Made clumsy in the dark, it takes him longer than usual. He senses every one of his movements is accompanied by noises and rattles; his arms and legs as heavy as stone. But at last he pulls himself onto his horse, and with a light tug on the reins, spurs it south.

He doesn't make it out of the village. He stops the horse at the last hut. He looks at the way back—or what the night permits him to see of it—for a long while. He sees the notched teeth of the sierras and the dust of the plains whitened by the moonlight and he remembers the travails of reaching this point, the men who abandoned him on the mountain, the campfires he never lit, the crucified Indians and the silver mines and all the paths that lead back to his past. And when his thoughts get there, when he is back at the pile of ash that was his home, alone again, waiting—again—for the viceroy's mercy which never comes, he shakes his head and pulls his horse around.

He finds the two sentinels flanking the door to the pen, armed with torches. He approaches them with lordly dignity, or what he imagines is lordly dignity, arrogant astride his horse.

"Open the door and release the men," he says firmly.

The sentinels stutter.

"Padre?"

"Do you not hear me? Release the men. The sheep! Release the damned sheep!"

"They no want, Padre . . . still impure . . ."

"I told you to open the door. I command it."

They hurry to slide back the latch. Juan reaches down to take one of the torches and enters the pen on horseback. He feels the slap of the stench first. Then, by wavering torchlight, he starts to distinguish the first gaunt faces, the tangled bodies, reddened by the glow of the flames and dried blood. Men and women who blink, confused, recently returned from sleep to the reality of their imprisonment.

Furiously, Juan waves the torch.

"Go! Flee!"

Some moan, immobile. Others cry out, terrified, perhaps, of the horse's huge shadow. Others turn their blind eyes and hands toward Juan.

"Padre . . . Padre . . . Forgive, Padre . . ."

"Go! Go, now! You hear me? Go!"

He can hear human voices, footsteps, on the other side of the fence. Through the cracks, he makes out the glow of other torches, bodies drawing near. The captives remain curled on the ground, like beasts groveling before their own insignificance. They don't get up because they can't. Or because they don't want to. Because they don't know how. Because they understand that all has been lost already, or to the contrary, they fear losing something that still belongs to them. But the fact remains, they do not get up, they only cry, shout, roll in the dust, cover each other's faces with their hands.

Juan hisses a curse and spurs the horse with a furious kick. He gallops, hurtling into the night; he gallops, evading the torches that sway in the dark; he gallops, his tunic rippling behind him like the defeated wings of an angel; he gallops northward, northward, always northward, as the last screams die behind him.

VII

Obstacles a man can't jump – Coals of stone – Drink from the bed of a thought – A dream revealing nothing at all – Another dream, more like death – Indians who don't seem Indian – Seven cities and three colonies – Tente en el aire – The king is dead, long live the king – A tongue like a river – Go with God – Wayward monks – A human wine cellar – A cesspit sung in chorus – Still she waits

A man who rides on horseback is a man thinking quickly, thinks Juan rather quickly as he rides. He feels his thoughts crack around him like bolts of lightning, sporadic flashes in an intermittent world. By their light, he sees fragments of blue sky. A lone cactus. A coyote skeleton. A flock of birds forming an arrow or the idea of an arrow. A pile of sharp rocks that emerge from nothing, and with the rocks the doubt that his horse can jump them. In the end, the horse clears both. A picturesque scene of barren plains wasted by the sun, somewhat blurred through eyes that tear as he hurtles ahead. And he thinks he also sees, riding roughshod behind him, flashes of the world he abandons. An Indian who hammers a red-hot iron. A gang of children scamper round him, laughing and shoving. A chain of women pass a ball of clay from the earth's womb to the heat of the oven. An Indian looks in terror at his horse's head, reaches out his hand, withdraws, reaches out again and finally, in a moment of courage or madness, touches it; the same Indian discovers there is nothing behind that touch, no sorcery or marvel. And then, the fence stakes. The two sentinels. The pen. The sheep. The sheep.

Thinking too fast is tiring, dizzying. Every time he stops to check if they are following him—they are not; why would they—he feels his legs go weak. He tries to think of something else: maybe nothing at all. Around him, the earth pulses, vertiginous as a dreamscape. Thoughts, memories fade. All but the sheep, which somehow remain. The sheep again. The huge fence, impenetrable, terrible, like an obstacle his horse can't clear, his memory can't clear, his conscience will never, ever clear. If it were Juan who built that fence, he thinks, if it were he who accepted or tolerated or even inspired that thing happening on the inside, then what? But it wasn't Juan, he decides, it couldn't have been. How could he? He, who arrived full of so many beautiful dreams, he wouldn't have been capable. Or, if he had done it, it was for the right reasons, in pursuit of ends not easily discernible today; not to lock them up, not to punish, not to torment all that withering flesh. Only Diego could do that. Men like Diego who lay waste to the most magnificent aims: they are second fiddle, he thinks, emulators, mercenaries; they are the idiots, the satellites, the blind, the mediocre; the illuminated who do not shine with their own light but can only reflect the sun's splendor, like the moon. He opens the Padre's Bible, lets his eyes roam over the margins full of penitence and torment, and asks himself which came first, the drawings of the crimes or the crimes themselves. If it is the pen that follows the sword or the sword that imitates the scratch of the pen.

From the height of his horse, he observes the horizon. He contemplates the choppy ridges stemming northward. The Padre is out there somewhere. He remembers the words the Padre said, or the words Diego said the Padre said: his Work was just beginning, he had barely laid the foundation for something, and that was why he had to depart immediately for the north. To build its walls. To lay the roof of his Work. Juan has to believe in something and decides to believe in this. He believes in those walls, in that roof: in that dream that has already, somewhere, been made stone. He will find that place. That dream. Someday, he will use it to shelter from the sun, from the cold, from the rain; he will rest in the shade of those walls, under the roof of the Padre's promises. And when he digs in his spurs, he feels as strong as the men he's seen ride after a fistful of gold or a pinch of honor.

Time is something we walk, Diego de Daga had said. Suddenly Juan recalls his words. The past falls behind and the future draws near and the present is something we try to hold on to with both hands but can never quite grasp. Earth and dust and sky: that's all that exists.

Does Juan believe in those words? He doesn't know what to think. He isn't even sure of what they mean. All he knows is that, when he finally reaches the rough, barren lava flows of the badlands, he cannot determine how much time has gone by. Instead, he knows what he has passed: a string of hills, a grove of stunted trees, stony ground like an abandoned ossuary. Dawns and dusks, which in his memory also seem like unmoving landscapes, stops along a route. He remembers, too, a gully his horse nosed from end to end, looking for a trickle of water. There was none. No water, no way to measure the time.

Everything is simpler than we believe, Diego de Daga had said. Tomorrow comes, yesterday goes; all can be reduced to this. The savages, who have twenty-five words for their arrows, haven't required a single word to name such an essential, such an astonishing, thing: time.

Is time really so essential, so astonishing? Juan wonders from the philosophical heights of his horse. Is it realer than an arrow's flight? Realer than the miracle of that arrow piercing the very bird we'd dreamed of?

The badlands stretch before him, like an enormous answer or deferral or refutation of his question. Neither time nor arrows seem to mean much on that boundless, dead land: why measure the time of its desolation, why shoot at the birdless sky? Land, the very word is made useless. Nothing that looks like land as far as the eye can see, just old remains of lava flows, spit atop one another in a kind of inert surf; just bulbs of black rock, fossils of rivers, skeletons of lakes, just volcano cones with their spattered consequences eternalized on the ground. Those rocky coals are the leagues he must travel still: the days he still must cross. And cross them he does, in defiance of his horse, who does not want to go, who rears, who scrapes himself and makes his hooves bleed trying to drive them into the rock. His horse, as if barefoot in a field of glass.

At some point, it becomes night in the badlands. He camps wherever he stops, since in those parts it's all the same, and shivers before a tiny fire sustained by a handful of lichen and moss, the only life that clings to the fissures in the rock. Then the sun emerges from behind the domes of lava and the badlands are, once again, all light and glints and glimmers reflecting, multiplying on the rock crystals, and later, perhaps just a few minutes later, the sun sets again and shadows spread until the world grows dark and there is barely time to light the fire and already it is day again, the bed of the badlands veiled in bloody brilliance and Juan pulling his horse by the halter, the horse reluctant like a soul being led to Hell.

Two weeks, he thinks.

Just two more weeks, he begs.

He traverses fragments of earth, fragments of time. He also traverses fragments of the Padre's life. He sees the man at his side, party to this interval. He stops at the same insignificant spot where Juan stops. He warms himself by the same fire. They take turns drinking from the same waterskin, each draught a cruel contribution to the other's thirst. He sees him sleep or try to sleep, besieged by cold. He sees him squint, blinded by the wind. He tugs at his horse with the same obstinance, the same patience. But no, that's not possible: Juan the Indian didn't have, doesn't have, a horse. He sees him, then, tugging at himself; the bridle of will taking the body further than the body can go.

Juan thinks about his body. About its limits. About whether those limits will be reached in the here and now or beyond the borders of this journey.

He thinks about the journey.

He thinks about the badlands, which do not end. About the land without limits and without dirt.

He thinks about the trickle of blood from his horse's hooves. How hard he has to pull to make the creature take another step.

He thinks about the weight of the saddlebags. He thinks about the weight of the sun. He thinks about the weight of his waterskin, ever lighter on his belt and ever heavier on his conscience.

Hunger is a place that extends as far as the eye can see. Thirst is a landscape of rough contours and concentric paths, a thorn pulsing in his temple. Juan inhabits that landscape. Eyes full of sun and stone, he realizes he will never manage to make it through. The horizon seems to recede with every step, like a fever dilating in all directions. The land unfolding before him is not terrain but the coordinates on a map: an atlas of such ambition that each crease cradles provinces, whole continents, unknown worlds. A lifetime would not suffice to travel its expanse. And yet he must make the attempt. He must pull his horse's halter and drag him over the rock and through the vertigo of thirst and through days and nights as if losing himself inside a calendar. The horse doesn't walk, he's tired, he whickers in sorrow. At some point, Juan throws the empty wineskin far from him, why not, and the horse turns his head to watch it fly, momentarily, in the birdless sky. The then horse dies. It happens that quickly: the animal is watching the waterskin and the next instant, he's dead.

By the time the body crumples on the rocks, not a trace of horseflesh remains: just a jumble of bones sanded down by grit and sun. Juan looks at those bones, illuminated by infinite dawns. The bridle still in his hands, tethering the void. He remembers, suddenly, that he never gave the horse a name. He rode on his back for so many days, calling him horse, just that, and now he is dead. Should he bury the bones?

He looks at the map that extends to the horizon, and beyond, the impossible boundaries he will never reach. A parchment in shreds, tatters, on whose snags and stitches one could stop and die of loneliness. That's all that's left for him to do. Die. He realizes this with cold indifference. Death lies before him and what does it matter. Slowly he allows himself to succumb to the ground, as if he, too, had been turned into a smattering of bones. He digs through his bag in search of the impossible, a last sip of water where no water will be, water to fill a mouth that is all tongue and sand. All he finds are a few strips of jerky that inflame his thirst, and the Padre's book. Lying against the bones of the unnamed horse, he opens it. He tries to read, dazzled by the sunlight. He doesn't look at the drawings: just the verses in tiny, cramped script. Some have been underlined or crossed out or circled in ink, so savagely that, in some places, the paper has torn. They are, they must be, the Padre's favorite passages. Places where his eyes came to rest. Ideas he touched, for a moment at least, with the tip of his thoughts. Swiftly he turns the pages, letting his eyes jump from underlined word to underlined word. He has followed the Padre's steps this far and now he follows the wake of his reading, lets himself slip inside the book in his hand.

He reads: Foxes have holes, and birds of the air have nests; but the Son of man hath nowhere to lay his head.

He reads: Behold, I will send my messenger, and he shall prepare the way before you.

He reads: For here have we no continuing city, but we seek one to come.

As he reads; as his cracked and arid lips separate to repeat Juan the Indian's words, the words of the Lord, overhead clouds and stars and twilights pass. Night falls, day breaks, and it's night again. The sky blinks and with each blink, new words emerge, scratched until the page bled.

He reads: in the world ye shall have affliction but be comforted: I have overcome the world.

He reads: He who will find his life, shall lose it: and he who loses his life for my sake, shall find it.

He reads: Dearly beloved, be not ignorant of this one thing, that one day with the Lord is as a thousand years, and a thousand years as one day.

In his dream he knows he is dreaming. In his dream, there are mature wheat fields to the south instead of the stripped and dead plain he traverses as he progresses northward. Thirst has no place in his dream. In front of him he only sees the Padre and the Padre is speaking to him with his boundless mouth, but Juan covers his ears with both hands: he knows it is not the Padre who speaks, only his dream. He doesn't want to hear and so he does not listen. He looks. He looks at the Padre's hard, ambivalent eyes. His white hands. His tongue. The Padre's tongue turned into a double-edged sword, caressing the world while simultaneously stabbing it, wounding it. Finally, he sheathes that double-edged tongue in his mouth. The Padre falls silent. The Padre is silent and reaches out to Juan with his left hand, holy or terrible. He strokes his closed eyelids.

Go back to sleep, says the voice Juan doesn't hear.

And then Juan wakes.

He hears the whinny of his dead horse. But a dead horse doesn't whinny, and as a consequence, Juan doesn't move either. Doesn't even open his eyes. He stays curled up in a crevice in the rock, hoping, hoping, hoping . . . for what. He hopes his horse will stop whinnying, that he will resign himself to death once and for all. Perhaps Juan should be resigned to it as well. But this last bit he thinks obliquely, the voice of his thoughts muffled by thirst or exhaustion. Maybe this is being dead, the voice whispers. Perhaps death consists of speaking, thinking, whinnying infinitely, only for the other dead to hear us. Perhaps. And then, when he is just about convinced, he hears a voice over the one in his head. Words that don't belong to his horse or his thoughts.

"Ramón! Ramón, come here! He's still breathing."

He hears footsteps. A tinkling of bells, like those worn by cattle or ghosts. Someone kisses his lips. A cold and liquid kiss that makes him cough and spit a slug of water out on the dirt.

Their names are Ramón and Miguel and they are brothers, or more precisely, they share the same mother. Both are ignorant of the identities of their respective fathers. They work as herdsmen on Don Pablo Cigüenza's hacienda, and it is to this job that the señor owes the good fortune of being alive. Because the fact is, they never or almost never use the old cow path; when they have to move the herd, they go by way of the Coyotada or Cuencamé or Pedrero Grande, sometimes even by Tierra Generosa, but never or almost never by the old cow path; and that afternoon, for reasons not quite clear even to them, they ended up on the old cow path they never or almost never take. It was precisely on that cow path that they found him, or rather that their horses found him, suddenly disobeying the reins in order to nose at a dust-coated bundle of rags. He, the señor, was the bundle of rags, Miguel clarifies in case Juan hadn't already imagined it and adds that, in his view, it was luck or providence or simple fate or who knows what that they found him before the coyotes did, doesn't he think?

The three of them are sat around the fire, eating tortillas off a clay griddle. The sheep graze indolently nearby, lit by the last light of evening. Juan looks back and forth between the faces of his saviors and is unable to match them to anything or anyone he has met up until then. He's not even sure if they are Spaniards or Indians. They seem Castilian when they speak, poor Castilians bereft of all predilection and pretension, but Castilians at the end of the day; men who must have inherited their tongue from Castilla and, from the Indians, a certain sorrowful, somber air. Their sombreros are not entirely Spanish, but as far as he knows, they aren't native either. He observes their faces and those faces don't seem to say much, or rather, what they say is contradictory. Some of their features might be found quartered and pasted on men come from Castilla or Andalusia, but the overall result is ambiguous, slightly native, like when a church is built based on plans from Spain but, in spite of it, once the stones are set, the structure still has an indigenous quality. Their words, too, seem to have that same accent; a foreign echo that is at times a kind of musicality in their phrasing and at times a vaguely nasal pronunciation, or particular expressions Juan has never heard and which come from who knows where. Usted, they call him all the time: usted, they say, usted should eat another tortilla, usted will pardon the poverty of our offering, usted is truly a fortunate man, and they refer to him in the third person, as if he weren't present or at least not entirely. Juan asks himself if they forgo the formalities of address, the vos and the vuesa merced, because they respect him too much or because they do not respect him at all.

The men who are half-brothers and half-Indian continue to speak while Juan eats tortillas and takes long swigs from the spigot on the canteen. They say that the señor shouldn't take to walking on the plain like that, with no caution or provisions and, to top it off, no horse. Though to be frank, they've never known any traveler to have gotten himself lost in the badlands, which is, after all, not so large that it can't be crossed in a few days' time. Where has the señor come from, may they ask?

Juan points with his sword. In a voice still choked by thirst and affliction, he explains that the last thing he saw was an Indian village that lay to the south.

"An Indian village, to the south?"

The half-brothers exchange a glance under their hat brims.

"I reckon he's talking about Nombre de Dios."

"How do you figure? No, Nombre de Dios is out that way. And it can't be San Bartolomé either because that's on the other side."

"You're right."

"I'd say it was the old San Juan mission."

"Couldn't be. That mission was abandoned some number of years ago. The village the señor saw was still standing, is that right?"

Juan nods.

"Yes, definitely standing."

"See, Ramón? It can't be San Juan, San Juan has been deserted forever, as they say. Has to be someplace we don't know. Or the señor has been walking around in circles and lost his way and who knows which place he's talking about . . ."

They argue. Juan listens, drowsy from the fire. From time to time, he stretches out a weak hand to take the canteen. He's no longer thirsty, but something like the echo of thirst remains, an urgency to feel the canteen full and cold and within arm's reach. At some point, the men take out two rough wooden pipes and begin to smoke slowly. They smoke the way he has only seen Indians smoke, during their ritual ceremonies. They must be Indians after all, he thinks as consciousness falls away.

When he opens his eyes, it is pitch dark and the men are still awake beside the fire, taking reverent turns with a clay demijohn. They offer it to him with solemn expressions, and Juan holds it in his hands before deciding whether or not to take a drink. It's mezcal, they say. When Juan shows no sign of comprehension, they start to laugh. It isn't scornful laughter; rather, they laugh like small children in the presence of some kind of wonder or marvel.

"Can it be that the señor has really never tried mezcal?"

"Never."

"Oh! How we envy you . . . Who can remember their first sip of mezcal, Ramón?"

And Ramón, dreamily:

"Oh! Who can remember so far back!"

By the blessedness of the Virgin of Guadalupe they swear two things: that he has never tasted something so repugnant in his life and also that a single sip won't satisfy him.

And it turns out to be exactly as they say. The first sip, in effect, is repugnant. The second is like permitting a live animal to climb into his mouth. And the third and fourth and fifth are like sitting down to pet the back of that animal, increasingly calm and quiet in his gut.

"You know what? Me and my brother here were wanting to ask if the señor is gachupín or criollo, but seeing how you've only just had your first go at mezcal, there's no doubt that you, sir, are gachupín."

Juan blinks in confusion. The men laugh again, just as innocently:

"Ah! One must be very gachupín not to know the word 'gachupín'!"

They explain, with coarse patience, that a man who comes from Spain is called a gachupín and the Spaniard raised in the colony is a criollo. And from what they've observed, the señor can boast of being the most gachupín gachupín that they've ever seen; the champion of gachupínes. If it wasn't for where they'd found him, they'd assume he'd just stepped onto the docks at Veracruz, still seasick from his ship's rocking.

Juan is unsure whether this is praise or mockery, so he arranges his face in an expression somewhere between seriousness and a smile.

"And now, if you don't consider the question indiscreet, tell us, what is the señor doing on these God forsaken expanses?"

Juan touches the cover of the Padre's Bible. Momentarily, he considers telling the truth, and then considers the most appropriate way to lie or at least tell that truth only partially. Finally he stumbles into a hazy tale, fragmented and halting, about a dozen soldiers who set off in search of the Seven Cities, then alludes to a set of unforeseen circumstances that separate and disperse them: a turn of fortunes that could just as well be a storm, a mutiny, or an attack by rebellious Indians. Miguel and Ramón watch him, open-mouthed.

"They were looking for the way to the Seven Cities, you say?"

"Yes."

"Excuse the question and the insistence, señor, but which Seven Cities would that be? Do you mean the Seven Cities of Cibola and Quivera, the golden kingdom of El Dorado? That old wives' tale?"

Before Juan can reply, Ramón preempts him.

"What's this about the Cibola, Miguel. Surely . . . the señor must be referring to the Thirteen Colonies, isn't that so?"

Juan gestures in a way that could mean anything, but which appears, in the reddish gloom of the fire, an affirmative. Ramón throws himself into an enthusiastic discussion of the Thirteen Colonies, a place—or thirteen places—of prosperity and riches and opportunities, based on what he's heard, and which do no disservice to the cities of gemstones and jewels dreamed of by the first conquistadors. He mentions a colony called Virginia, and another called Georgia, and two Carolinas, one in the north and one in the south, and even a so-called Maryland, which according to his understanding means "Tierra de María": God knows why the English are so keen to baptize their lands with women's names. And speaking of the English, the worst thing about these colonies are the very English who establish and inhabit and infect them with their Protestantism.

Suddenly Ramón stops short.

"The señor isn't a Protestant, I hope?"

"No. Catholic."

"Not a priest?"

"No. I'm just a soldier."

Ramón and Miguel exchange another glance. They look relieved. His clothes had them confused, they explain.

"My clothes?"

Juan thinks about his clothes for the first time in long time. By the firelight, he examines the Padre's long and dirty tunic, the raw leather belt, his sandals.

"Yes. We thought you were one of those hermits, so poor and pious that they go live in the desert, since the world offers them so little."

"I'm not a monk," Juan repeats, stirring the fire. "Just a soldier."

Not even he knows if he is telling the truth.

The next morning, they say their farewells at the crossroads of the Camino Real. Before going their separate ways, the brothers give him a canteen and a few rations of corn and beans, which Juan insists on paying for with a gold coin. When they go to put it in their pocket, they pause to turn it over and study it again, as if the gold or the image inscribed thereupon were some kind of wonder.

"There is something else I would like to ask you," Juan says when they are about to leave. "Your Graces . . . excuse the crudeness of my question, but are Your Graces Indians or Spaniards?"

The expression "Your Graces" makes them smile, but the rest of the question wipes the smile from their faces. Lamentably, they confess with eyes downcast, they are neither one nor the other. All they know for sure is that their mother was cambuja: what their fathers were is nothing but the sum of conjectures and suppositions, speculations born by studying their features, which, as the señor can confirm, are not very defined; thus, it is anyone's guess. Cambuja? Juan inquires. Miguel smiles sadly. Ah, he says, what a complicated thing, explaining what a cambujo is to a gachupín, but we will try. A cambujo, they say, is the son of a chino and an india; not a chino from China, of course, here there are no chinos from China, as he might imagine; there is another class of chinos, which is what we call the son of a mulatto and an india: they assume they needn't explain to the señor that the mulatto is the son of a pure white man and pure black woman. Of course, here purity is, if anything, a treasure hard to find. The fact is, their mother was cambuja, that's the only incontrovertible fact in the equation: or almost incontrovertible, because according to the tittle-tattle, their mother's father might not have been a chino, but a zambo prieto, or even a black man with unusually light skin, and therefore their mother wouldn't be cambuja, she'd be zamba. But they will assume—as they have done all their lives—that their mother is correct and that she is, when all is said and done, cambuja. The issue of their fathers is another question all together. As regards Miguel's father, all they know is that he was a calpamulato, or at least that's what he said; in other words, son of a zambaigo and a loba, which as everyone knows are the offspring of the union between a cambujo and an india and a salta atrás with a mulatta, respectively. If that were the case, then Miguel himself would necessarily be tente en el aire, although the possibility remains that his father wasn't a calpamulato but actually straight lobo, which would make Miguel . . . let's see, Miguel, what would that make you? I don't know if there's a name for that, Miguel himself confesses, scratching the nape of his neck. As for Ramón, their mother, unfortunately, has never been able to disclose his father's caste. In their case, the act that takes place between men and women had occurred both in a hurry and in the dark, and consequently few guesses could be made as to the color of his skin: but, for simplicity's sake, they chose to believe that the man was calpamulato and agree therefore that Ramón is tente en el aire, the same—most likely—as his brother. Had the señor understood?

"I understand," Juan says, to say something.

No one speaks for a time. The three men on the side of the road, the sheep that bunch together anxiously on the grassless plain: all appear to be waiting for something. Finally, Juan decides to speak again.

"Incidentally, you haven't by any chance seen this man?"

Miguel and Ramón look up from their sheep to examine the strange book Juan holds out.

"Who is he?"

"An Indian. His name is Juan, although he also goes by Padre."

"An Indian, you say?"

"Yes."

They shake their heads in silence, still staring at the likeness.

"Doesn't look indio to me. Look at his skin, his eyes. I'd say he's ladino. Probably apiñdado or zambo."

"You think? I wouldn't put so much Black in the mix. Chino, at most. Maybe even tente en el aire."

Juan opens then closes his mouth.

"Yes," Ramón finally concedes. "You're right. I would swear he's tente en el aire."

And then he looks from the likeness to Juan, an odd gleam in his eye.

"Why are you looking for him? He hasn't done the señor a wrong turn, has he? Tente en el aire are notorious cheats."

Confused, Juan hesitates before answering.

"But aren't you tente en el air, too?"

The brothers nod.

"We are. That's why you ought to believe us, because we know what we're talking about. Take heed: tente en el aire are cheats. Everybody knows that."

Before they depart, the brothers tell Juan that he will find the city two leagues from where they stand. The word "city" makes him smile. He thinks the brothers must be exaggerating, the way men from the country sometimes do, believing the small hill overlooking their village to be a mountain and the chapel that lacks an altarpiece and parish priest to be a cathedral. That's precisely what he expects: a chapel awaiting consecration; a village of recently built straw-and-adobe huts, precariously sown right in the middle of Indian territory like a seed that might well bear fruit or just as easily disappear, swallowed up by the frontier dust. Maybe a Franciscan mission. Maybe the first boring of a humble mine, more fertile still in disappointments than silver. But he travels the two leagues and at the end of them he finds the impossible: a real city, which appears to have been founded decades or centuries ago there on the plain. He sees a few straw-and-adobe huts, yes, but also palaces of dressed stone and iron balconies, convents with limewashed walls, a garden where nature appears either domesticated or at least restrained. Emerging from between the rooftops, the two spires of a cathedral, a Christian cathedral, here, in the heart of unconquered lands, here, surrounded by savages and cacti and paramos that not even Pedro de Alvarado's terrible soldiers had been able to subdue.

It is impossible, he thinks.

It is impossible, he says out loud to no one.

And yet. And yet, he says or thinks, maybe all of this is simply another one of the Padre's signs. Another mark of his teachings. Who but Juan was capable of bringing Christ's message to this land of oblivion? What force of will but his could gather the strength of hands that would suffice to erect this immense church, large enough to house any man's most disproportionate ambitions? And those hands, Juan thinks as he looks around him, are no longer white or Black or Indian, or they are all at once: one need only observe the passersby who stroll up and down the street, men and women who might be Indians and yet at the same time cannot be, not by any means: skin tones he has never seen before, tested alloys of all races imaginable; he sees an Indian with light hair and a Black woman who mightn't be entirely Black hanging out laundry and a white or almost white man with an also-white wig riding inside a carriage, and chasing the carriage are several children with skin the color of a copper vellón, children who could be the sons and daughters of all or none of those people, as if, willy-nilly, God had mixed up the litters of all His creatures and sent them back to Earth.

He wonders whether this is the world the Padre dreamed of; the equality between the races he preached. A world in which, ultimately, Spanish elements had been imposed in some fashion over the foundations of the indigenous, like an echo that resists fading entirely. Otherwise, how does one explain the pipes so many white men carry clamped between their teeth, keeping alive in their tobacco bowls the fire of pagan rites, or those who are carried on the shoulders of their manservants, on palanquins in some ways reminiscent of the stretchers that carried the old caudillos. Otherwise respectable men with graying wigs atop their heads, like Chichimeca archers flaunting their enemies' scalps, and Castilian-looking women on their balconies, drinking saucers of what looks like Indian chocolate. And all of them outfitted in the most implausible clothes, extravagant garb seemingly born of a madman's mind or the court of some distant kingdom; dress coats replete with bows and buttons and capes that drag on the ground and ridiculous marquis-esque hats. He sees an odd patrol of soldiers who have, at some point, abandoned their armor and helmets, and beside them a small group of women who, inside their corsets and overskirts, conversely look ready for battle: it is as if the men had given up protecting their bodies and the women were mounting an even more vigorous defense of their own, armored in enormous skirts and slips, armed with parasols and fans and white gloves. Only the clergymen appeared unchanged. He sees them walking along one side of the street with the same tonsures, the same habits, the same resigned faces. Resigned, the clergymen and the donkey he sees walking in circles around the large mill wheel, a donkey the same as all the donkeys he has ever seen, making the same wheel turn, blinded to the same senseless journey.

He stops before the church portico, flabbergasted by the figures carved into its façade: a vertiginous swarm of bodies and leafy tendrils, so glutted there is no room for a single saint more. Inside he finds impossible columns, slim at their base and widening the higher they rise toward the vaulted ceiling, and an altarpiece replete with gilding and foliage. Even the Christ looks changed: he suffers on the same cross but does so with unfamiliar viciousness, contorted by horror and bathed in blood. Juan kneels at his feet and prays or tries to pray but the words and even his thoughts catch on his lips. He is empty. He can only think about Juan the Indian and that other Christ he saw in a similar state of agony on a hill in Zacatecas, so distant it might well be mistaken for a dream.

A sexton passes him from behind and tells him it isn't the time for soliciting alms: he must come back later. Juan wants to ask what he means, but the sexton is already well past him, busy lighting the altar candles and preparing for the service which is about to begin. A line of women wait before the confessional, linked by devotion or boredom. He feels the liquid weight of their stares. An old woman approaches, keeping her distance. She extends her arm out as far as she can and drops, into the hollow of his palm, a silver coin. There is no brush of her hand. He feels only the lukewarm coin, and after that, nothing; the old lady takes refuge behind her mantilla and returns to the queue. It is a strange coin, with the likeness of a king he doesn't know, a king who also appears to don a species of wig or someone else's head of hair, as if the Indians hadn't been content to impose their barbarous customs on the colony, somehow also managing to sow them on the other side of the ocean.

Juan leaves the cathedral and steps into the light of the portico. It is market day and the square opposite the cathedral has been annexed by merchants and their stalls of wood and canvas. Some men eat and drink amid the smoke from ambulant kitchens and the merchants hawking their wares. Others haggle over the price for a particular bauble or simply stroll the square, fingering the merchandise. Juan avoids the pulque vendors and tamale fryers and finds, finally, what he's looking for, a stall that is little more than four rickety stakes covered with a hemp rag, and on the floor, a trunk stuffed with old clothes. He searches patiently until he comes across a cape, a striped tunic, a pair of breeches, and some well-worn boots, which—though hideous—appear to conform with the singular idea of elegance and decorum in this place.

The proprietor is an old woman, her mouth shirred in a grimace of displeasure seemingly impossible to erase. Out the corner of that mouth, the woman says a price Juan doesn't understand or half-understands; he choose not to ask for clarification, holding out his bag of coins instead. The old woman looks skeptically at his beggar's tunic and the dirty hands that have been rummaging through her wares. She looks even more skeptically at the bag of coins. One by one she takes them out, studies the likenesses, rubs them on her sleeve, bites or tries to bite them with her toothless mouth. She doesn't trust them. What does she trust? Only the silver coin he was given as alms appears to satisfy her.

"This is our king?" Juan says tentatively, pointing at the selected coin.

So it seems, the old woman replies, suddenly softened by the coin's discovery. So it seems, she repeats, but sometimes what seems to be is naught compared to reality. News—not to mention the coins where the kings' names are inscribed—reaches the Colony so late that, in America, it isn't unusual to kneel before a king who, in Spain, has been dead and buried for months or years. So, yes, as far as she is concerned Carlos III still lives and reigns and will be her king as long as the letters and ships continue to say so.

"Like I always say," she mutters with a hint of a smile, handing back the pouch. "If Death came from Madrid, we'd all outlive the last tooth in our heads."

"No," says the atole vendor.

"No," says the water boy, surprised mid-chore.

"No," says a lady from behind her fan.

"I've never seen him in my life," says the proprietor of the inn where Juan spends the first night.

All amend their negative replies with explanations Juan only half-hears: no, I'm sorry you've lost your servant; no, I haven't seen this cambujo, this lobo, this jíbaro, this torna atrás; terribly sorry, all calpamulatos look the same to me. Their mouths full of new words, new expressions, even new gestures; they speak Juan's language, to be sure, yet it is not his language, definitely not his language, just like the water at a river's source isn't the same water where it meets the ocean. And Juan in the market, in the gardens, in the hospitals, on the thresholds of palaces and shacks, churches and pulquerías; over days and nights, in the slums and on big estates, and the whole time, hearing the sound of the river's waters.

"No."

"I'm sorry."

"I bet my wig that the man you're looking for is coyote, not indio."

"I fear you'll need to engage another servant."

And time and again, Juan opening and closing the same book.

"Thank you, thank you, thank you."

A beggar curled at the back of an alley, against a pile of logs that reek of urine. Juan hands him the Padre's clothes wrapped in a reed mat. The beggar examines them with suspicion, going over their many stains and tears as if comparing his own poverty to the poverty of the stinking tunic's previous owner. He appears skeptical of the verdict. Finally, he appears to accept the gift with a brief, courteous gesture.

"By the way," Juan says, already moving away. "You don't happen to know this Indian, do you?" Juan shows the man the book.

"Ah! They already took him, señor."

"Who?"

"Him, who else?? The Padrecito."

"The Padrecito?"

"They already took him away."

"Where?"

He motions vaguely toward somewhere in the city behind him. Juan guesses correctly: the man is pointing north.

"Well, to jail. He was asking for it and, in the end, they gave him the pleasure, señor."

"To jail? Why?"

The beggar seems to stir in his corner, to make himself smaller. I, señor, know nothing. I, señor, am guilty of nothing. It's fair to say that I, señor, am but a beggar as well. Though I am poor, I am not like him; I don't go looking for any trouble, I swear it on the Virgin of Guadalupe. Begging your pardon, señor: I know it's wrong to swear. I don't know what I'm saying. I'm just here, that's all, holding out my hand, like this, I don't bother anybody, I don't shout nonsense or poppycock, I don't make a fuss or agitate the people passing by. I was just sitting here, asking myself whether or not that pouch you've got there is getting too heavy, and if there wouldn't be just one little peso in there that you wouldn't miss. Yes, you say? Well, Godspeed.

The building is an old, cloistered convent, which, with little imagination, has been outfitted as the city jail. The windows are barred with the same grille-work that kept the nuns from making a break for the century's temptations, and its kitchen garden is now a dreary courtyard where the prisoners make their rounds. Juan waits beside the oven that once produced fritters and flaky pastries, attended by a soldier who only consents to call the warden in exchange for a coin. While he waits, he hears voices that echo off the walls of adobe and stone. They are not, as Juan would have expected, laments and confessions induced by the rack, but sounds that might be cries of jubilation, and curses, and invitations to play cards, and mad peals of laughter clamoring in a kind of raging celebration.

The warden is a diminutive old man burdened by the weight of many worries. His eyes are small and sad, veiled by a pair of round glasses. From behind the lenses, he studies Juan from head toe, shaking his head. The little enthusiasm that had at first animated him appears to have suddenly dissipated.

"You, sir, are not the sheriff from the Royal Prison," he says. It is unclear whether this a question or statement.

"No. I'm just . . ."

The warden interrupts him with a wave of his right hand. It's terrible, he mumbles. Terrible. They have been waiting for four months for the sheriffs who are supposed to transfer a specific group of prisoners to Ciudad de México for execution. Four months! And during that time, the prisoners in question have had the absurd notion that they can go on eating, and drinking, and taking up what little free space he has left, and meanwhile, what can he he, unlucky man, do about it? How long will this last? Does the viceroy think that his jail, a dark and modest jail in a dark and modest provincial city, can sustain all the colony's criminals?

For a few moments, he is quiet, staring at his shoes. He looks tired, and the next words he speaks confirm it. I'm tired, he says in his silly little voice. I am a very busy and a very tired man. He addresses Juan directly for the first time: Whatever his reason for coming, he honestly has no time for it. He isn't looking for a jailer or an errand boy and much less a new prisoner. Another prisoner is, in fact, the last thing he needs. The jail is so chock-full that he fears the caging of another soul—if they even have souls, these odious swine—is all it would take for the whole building to come crashing down. Sometimes, he confesses, looking heavenward, he has dreamed of it: the sheriffs of the Royal Prison would finally arrive, within the year or a million years, what does it matter, and they would find nothing where four walls once stood. His jail converted into a pile of rubble. His jail swallowed up by the bowels of the Earth, falling and falling into the very pit of Hell, which is, after all, the final destination of everyone in that place. This is what he thinks of his jail. What he thinks of his prisoners. What he thinks, even, of himself, since in his fantasy, he too is guzzled by the Earth, joining his repertoire of monsters. He sees himself falling infinitely, intermingling with his flock of murderers, brawlers, and madmen; in the company of the drunks and the lazy, the family killers and wife killers and rabble-rousers, the thieves and beggars, bandits and idiots by nature. And that thought, see, doesn't keep him up at night. To Hell with it all. To Hell with himself. So if Juan has come to confess to a crime, he's better off tamping down his remorse for a few more days and venting in a confessional or the lock-up in some neighboring village. They've already got all the miscreants they need in this city, plus a few for good measure.

Juan tries to assuage him. It's true, he hasn't come to take the criminals the man speaks of, but he isn't there to cause the man trouble either. He's just looking for an old friend who, according to his information, is inside, imprisoned on charges of vagrancy and disorderly living. He, Juan, would be very pleased to pay the man's fine.

Behind his glasses, there is light in the warden's eyes:

"Do you mean you have come to take him out of here?"

"Yes."

The warden gives three little claps.

"Guard! This man wants to take one of our monsters! Bring him down before he changes his mind!"

Juan, meanwhile, has opened the book to the portrait page and is trying to show the warden. The man in question is named Juan, he says, but he calls himself the Padrecito; he also answers to the Padre, and Juan the Indian, and as far as he knows, looks more or less like this.

The warden laughs. He doesn't bother to look at the drawing. Does Juan actually think that he knows even half the men inside? If he remembered them all, he would be a wonder of nature: he could leave his post at the jail and make a living traveling fair to fair, touted from the circus booth as the Incredible

Memory Man. If he knew the life or crimes of each of those men, even to a deficient or approximate degree, his head would contain all the world's stories: the most miserable, at least, the most fetid, the most abject. No, my friend, he says, taking Juan's arm and accompanying him to the stairway: you must be the one to go down there and look for your protégé. And for the love of God, he mutters, promise me that you will do everything in your power to find the wretch.

Juan had envisioned a complicated maze of galleries and dungeons, maybe a torture chamber or two, but all he finds is a set of stone steps descending directly to the prisoners' cells. The jailer goes ahead with an oil lamp and a certain air of resignation. Juan hears the increasingly impassioned shouts that are as though caged inside, and when the jailer unlocks the last door, the stench slaps him in the face, an odor so intense it could have a color—the color of a human body consumed by flames—and the consistency of a fist to the gut. Filtering in from both flanks, a sickly light, a madhouse light, illuminating some bodies and eclipsing others, the shadow from the window bars casting a grid on the floor. The place is reminiscent of a ship's bilge, a place condemned to rot and eternal darkness in order to keep the rest float. Or a castle cellar, where what is ageing are not wines and liquors but human beings. That's exactly what it's like, a human cellar, rags of men shrouded in dense air and the damp and cold; hundreds of bodies riled or furious or idiotized or sleepwalking, waiting for the moment to be uncorked and revealed by the sun's light.

Juan proceeds down the corridor, looking to either side at a succession of faces packed together. Some men are smoking cigarettes. Others lie curled in a corner or on a handful of straw, shaking from fever or chill. Some relieve themselves in barrels sawed in half and serving as latrines: casks with moldy staves, fermenting their stink as long as the jailers please, until they consent to empty them. There are also men who energetically deal decks of cards and men who argue and men who laugh and men who hide their wineskin at the sight of the jailer and others who grip the cell bars and exercise or sing or whisper. An old man who plays with a small dog. A scabies-sufferer who furiously scratches. A fat man who holds a crust of black bread aloft and pretends it's the host and expends a thunderous laugh before breaking it into pieces and scattering the crumbs among the faithful. In a cell that is all gloom and straw he sees the white body of a naked young man illuminated, for an instant, on the straw mat, a boy surrendering with abandon and an almost distracted air to the sunlight percolating through the tiny window, offering himself up like a cat or an odalisque. They are grown men and others almost boys and some already old men, smooth-faced and bearded, healthy or one foot in the grave, but always or almost always brown-faced and indigenous in manner. Some study Juan from the depths of their dull and vinous eyes, but most hardly give him a glance or don't even turn his way. They remain absorbed in their games, their sullen silences, their prayers, their jokes.

Slowly Juan makes his way to the end of the corridor, then turns on his heel and, even more slowly, makes his way back. He carries the book open to the portrait page, and after a number of examined faces, looks back at the drawing, like the quill that must, on occasion, be returned to the inkwell for fresh supply. He pauses before some of the particularly crammed cells, before certain bodies that do not turn toward the light. He finds no trace of the Padrecito in any of them. He stops at the entry door, shaking his head. The jailer gives him a mournful look, disconsolate.

"The señor won't be taking any with him, then?"

Before Juan can answer, a voice comes from the cell immediately at his back.

"The señor is looking for the Padrecito?"

Juan turns brusquely. The prisoner who has spoken is one of the men sitting on the casks, pants around his ankles. He has a thick beard and a somewhat fugitive-like face, and he looks at Juan with an expression of either concentration or profound exertion.

"How do you know?"

The man dilly-dallies, as if he had all the time in the world. He does, in a way. He takes a handful of straw and gives himself a vigorous wipe, then uses the darkened straw to point at the book.

"That's what you've got scribbled on those papers, isn't it? The snout of that poor wretch."

Juan presses himself to the bars.

"You know him? You know where he is?"

The man fastens his pants, feigning deep reflection. He looks at the men on either side of him. They smile with a certain insolence.

"And what do my compadres and I get for telling you?"

"I will be happy to make myself responsible for your fines. All three of you."

The men laugh loudly, but there is a measure of sadness, too. They explain that, having reached this moment in their lives, neither gold nor a stranger's intercession can make much difference for them. They aren't there for vagrancy or thieving or bedding girls, all crimes redeemable with a bit of will and bunch of coin, but for engaging in criminal activity along the Camino Real and slitting the throat of a chief magistrate, who had it coming, by the way, and everybody knows that blood crimes are only paid with more blood. Our future, they say, isn't much longer than a noose and the stairs to the gallows. So, what is it they want? Juan asks, expectant. The three bandits shrug. They want what no one but God can give them, and apart from that, nothing. Juan grips the cell bars tighter. Does that mean they're not going to help him? The first man shakes his head slowly, maintaining the hint of a smile. No: it just means that they're going to help him, but they'll do it for nothing. They want to be very clear on that point. They are helping him in exchange for nothing. They are helping him just because. Because they want to and only because they want to, is that clear? Crystal clear, Juan says, and he prepares to listen.

This is his cell. This is the pile of straw where he slept. The lice-ridden blanket he covered himself with. The barrel where he shat. This, the first bandit repeats, is the place where, day and night, he shouted all his nonsense. These four walls were sick of hearing him, and so were we. So were we, the second and third bandits confirm. Especially us. Because they were used to living with good for nothings, with murderers of all stripes, but not with madmen. And the Padre-cito was undoubtedly a madman. Maybe that's why they released him. Because one day they did just that, released him. He didn't seem either happy or sad; he went back into the world with the same serenity with which he'd arrived at this cell. For some time, the first bandit says, they thought he was a lucky man: now they're not so sure. After all, the world he returned to is a garbage dump, a trash heap, excrement. Although, of course, so is this jail. The jail, we could say, is the final cesspit for all the excrement too fetid for even this cesspit of a world. We are the excrement's excrement, the second bandit says. The foulness that filth itself is embarrassed to call its own. We are the shit that shit would rid itself of if it could, finishes the third bandit, if turds had consciousness and something like dignity or a sense of shame. Do we have dignity, consciousness, a sense of shame? Yes and no. Depends on who you ask. There're all types in here: men who have wound up at the bottom of the cesspool because we are contemptible sons of bitches or because the world in which we live is. And there are also those who come here with something like dignity but lose it because the cess-pool that is the world's cesspool stinks too bad. The Padrecito stank, too, at least in a physical sense. His shit stank like the rest of ours; his sweat and urine and mouth stank no less than anybody else's. His words stank, too; he muttered madness that rotted in their ears, and sometimes they had to beat him, yes, they thrashed him with slaps and kicks until he shut up or fell asleep. That's why everyone was a little happier when he was finally released. The cesspit's cesspit that is the jail seemed, at least for a time, to smell a little better. They themselves seem cleaner, although it's abundantly clear that the opposite is true; the longer they stew in the cold soup of their own sweat, their own rancidness, they will naturally smell a little worse. The fact is, the Padrecito left one day. How long ago was that? The first bandit says he can't remember time; that here, within these four walls, time is only measured by barrels of excrement, fuller and fuller until one day, they're empty. The second bandit says that time is a luxury of the powerful. The third bandit adds that time is a luxury of the powerful and the moneylenders. The first bandit intervenes again to say that time is a luxury of the powerful and the moneylenders and the clergy, all of them filth as well, shit born of shit that will bear more shit, although not the class of excrement that will end up in any jail or cesspool. The second bandit says time doesn't exist. The third says that, in his view, time doesn't exist and God doesn't exist and creation is organized in the image and likeness of this jail, that is, according to no law but that of chance. Chance and stupidity, the first concludes. That's right, says the second. Well said, says the third. Anyway, says the first, picking up the thread; all they can say for sure is that the Padrecito was released at some point between the beginning of creation perpetrated by that God who surely doesn't exist and this very moment during which they are speaking. Do the men know why he was jailed? The third bandit nods. For begging, he says. For dragging himself from door to door asking for alms and for sleeping under the city bridge and in mangers and stables. The second bandit doesn't agree, at least not entirely. It was for being a beggar and also for being a madman; because he wasn't content with dragging himself door to door, asking for alms, but had to go around saying that he'd been ordained a priest in the desert, repeating his drivel to anyone with ears to hear him. It was for being a beggar and a madman, the first bandit concludes, but also for being a rebel and rabble-rouser, because the mad ravings that rotted inside one's ears were an attempt, somehow or another, to move men to rebellion or contempt. What did he say? What were those ravings? Juan presses, and those ravings are so many and so varied that, for the first time, the bandits' voices overlap, become tangled, confused. For example, he said . . . If you can believe it . . . They needed a law that didn't differentiate between whites, Blacks, and Indians; that men should only be distinguished by their vice and virtue. He said that His Majesty Carlos III of Spain and Louis XVI of France and all the monarchs he could think, large and small, were degrading justice with their absolute powers, which belong only to God. He said the time had come to break the slaves' chains, chains that could be forged of iron but also of fear, of trickery, of ignorance. Those were the worst, those made of ignorance. You had to break them with hammer blows, but not with just any hammer. That hammer was something the Padrecito called reason, the first bandit clarifies. That hammer, the second bandit confirms, was a thing called science. That hammer was nothing but a madman's nonsense, the third bandit concludes, smacking at the air. There's absolutely no doubt that he was mad; the three of them agree on that, at least. His was a madness that faced in just one direction: toward the future. He spoke of the future the way some men speak of their past: as if they were the pages of an already-written book. In those pages, he read what was to come. Someday, everything would be science and technology and reason, whatever those words might mean, and when that happened, he said, monstrous prisons like this one would be torn down until no stone were left standing. And he didn't think the prison was monstrous because he was in it, they clarified, nor because there were men like us in the world. No, that didn't concern him in the least; it was monstrous only because of how it was built, because of how the prisoners vegetated inside, providing no benefit and no purpose; they left no legacy to society other than the blood of their crimes. That's what he used to say. That it didn't make any sense for nations to restrict associations of fifty people for fear of rebellion and uproar, while in truth, within their prisons there were naturally occurring associations of hundreds, thousands, maybe millions of despicable men who did no good, who were nothing but mouths that needlessly consumed, hands that did not work, backs that carried no load, wasted time, like donkeys that shake off the harness and no longer turn the big wheel that is the world. A day could come, the bandits state the Padrecito said, when prisons would be big workshops where the criminals would give back to society, multiplied, what they had first wrenched from it. They would get a return on every one of their days, every minute, every second, clock time subdivided into every last profitable instant. Oh! What rubbish. Because he spoke, yes, of clocks, not one clock but many, and not only in the bell towers but in the town halls too, the workshops and schools and prisons, prisons most of all, of course, a clock in every home and in every man's heart, many clocks that were actually one single clock, the pulse in a single body. Just as there was anatomy to study the body, he said, soon an anatomical study concerning societies would emerge: every nation would be structured like an enormous body, an army in which every soldier, every member, every miniscule volition, would intertwine to form a single aim. What was that aim? They didn't know, and maybe the Padrecito didn't either. He knew only this: one day nations would be immense workshops, an industry produced by men in order to generate more men, better and better men, and that this, work, would become the measure of modern peoples; it would perform the function of morality, it would fill the void of belief, and it would come to represent the principle of all that is good. At least this is what he said, day in and day out. Work, he said, should be the peoples' religion. Imagine that, the third bandit says snidely. The Padrecito could. He imagined the entirety of New Spain transformed into a workshop of monstrous proportions, in which the efforts of every man and every woman would have a carefully assigned function. Of course, the Padrecito didn't even believe in New Spain's viceroyalty, the first bandit explains; for him, New Spain was a huge mistake in and of itself, starting with the name, what was all this about New Spain, he would holler at times, enraged, why did they have to call themselves Spain, old or new, no matter, but Spain, which slept its siesta so far and so stupid and so white on the other side of the ocean. Spain and its gang of gachupínes could go to Hell as far as he was concerned. They boasted of having reconquered their lands from the Moors—the Indians here must do the same and send back their conquistadors; together they must build their own nation, pursue their own ends, send the whole of Europe to Hell. There was a phrase he always used, what was it? Ah, hell, I remember now. God is very high up, above the king in Spain and us here down below. That's what he said. I have come to redeem you, Mexicans of México, he would cry out, suddenly, at random, generally when we were all sleeping and not in the mood for sedition; I have come to liberate you from the chains of ignorance and the chains of slavery and the chains of the metropolis, and then we'd have to beat him to shut him up. One time, the first bandit laughs, he had the brilliant idea to climb up to the pipe where the jailers dump our shit. Can you believe it? He put his mouth to it like a trumpet, that infectious drain—a metal tube even shit, if it could, would avoid touching—and used it like a sort of bullhorn through which to harangue the city: to tell them that although they didn't believe it, they too were in a prison, they too were prisoners of a faraway Spain and the desires of just a few. He said that there is something of God in the cesspool. What did he mean? All that shouting made us laugh, but after a few hours it also made us very tired and we had to beat him to get him down and let us sleep. It's true, the second bandit laughs. Sure is, laughs the third. Until one day, they simply put him back on the street. Why did they do that? It was because he was a beggar, the second bandit says; because there wasn't enough food to go around and he was one of the few, maybe even the only, who didn't have a sister or a wife or even a daughter to come and share a crust of bread with him. The third bandit doesn't agree, or at least not entirely. It was for being a beggar and being a madman; because if he stayed one more night, they would have to smash his head in, remember what you said yourself: he was pitiful, but pitiful or not pitiful, we were going to kill him. It was for being a beggar and a madman, the first bandit concludes, but also for being a rebel and rabble-rouser: because the jailers realized he did less harm preaching in the streets than trumpeting his nonsense through the latrine bullhorn. Whatever he was, he isn't here now. He left, says the first bandit. He left, says the second. He left, says the third, and there is, perhaps, a small hint sadness in their voices. Might they know where he went? They shrug. What's it to them? It's enough to think about where they'll be in a couple of days, a couple of months at most: drying out in the sun on the Mexico City gallows. Wherever that wretch is, says the first bandit, it'll be a better place than the one that awaits them. Although now that he thinks about it, he might have said something about heading north. Withdraw to the desert, isn't that right, boys? Sounds familiar to me, murmurs the third. Yes, I remember now; he said the world wasn't yet ready for his teachings, how's that? He said we were like children who must be given milk, unready for solid food, because we weren't yet man enough to digest it. That he would go walking in the desert, like the hermits, while we grew up, and he wouldn't need anyone or anything, since reason alone was enough to diagnose and cure the world's weaknesses. He also said that the Devil might send him the three temptations of Christ in the desert. He didn't say that! the second bandit interrupts. He didn't say it, but he thought it, replies the third. It's true: he thought it, the second admits, shaking his head. I don't know if we told you, but the Padrecito believed himself to be a priest; hence the name, of course, Padrecito, he always wanted us to call him that, as if he were the clergy, and we, his parishioners. He said we knew nothing: that if Christ were to be born again before our eyes, the Mexican canons would send him to be burned at the stake before our scorn and our indifference. He often said that a man pursuing him was about to arrive, and that the man would be neither his executioner nor tormentor but his disciple. Might you be that redeemer, compadre? asks the first bandit sarcastically. Are you the disciple he was waiting for? Oh, he was an odd one, the Padrecito. But just notice how, in spite of it all, he managed to make us take his nonsense at least a bit seriously. At any rate, we still call him that. Padrecito. Like he was somebody's father or priest. One might say that he sometimes believed that he was God, the third bandit interjects. But, like I said at the start, God doesn't exist. God doesn't exist and time doesn't exist, concludes the first bandit, spitting a wad of phlegm onto the straw. Time is the luxury of the powerful and the moneylenders and the clergy, and creation is organized in the image and likeness of this jail, that is, according to no law but that of chance and stupidity. That's right, says the second. Well said, says the third.

Returning, at last, to the world. The sudden fear that, from now on, he would always see the world as a giant sewer whose most foul waste somebody has to conceal and bury. Prison as the world's elimination system, Juan thinks, and the world, why not, God's elimination system. But first, a series of hallways and dungeons that seem to never end, the jailer who guides him through a new way, perhaps because he is being led to the back door; perhaps because the prison has continued growing in the meantime, multiplying to the limits of the possible. It is the women's ward. Through the taciturn light of the windows, Juan sees faces appearing one after another on either side, like flashes of white lightning throughout the night. There are women who play cards and women who argue and women who pray the rosary and women who laugh and others who whisper or sing or moan. Two young women pick lice from each other's heads like trained, silent monkeys. Leaning against the bars of her cell, an old woman knits a kind of interminable scarf, a scarf too long for any human neck. In a cell that is all gloom and straw, he sees, illuminated for just an instant, the white breast of woman nursing her child. There are grown up women and others are almost girls and some who are old or very old, with their hair worn long or shaved to the scalp, healthy or with one foot in the grave, but always or almost always dark-complected and Indian in manner. Some study Juan from the depths of their dull and vinous eyes, or blow him an apathetic kiss, but most hardly give him a glance or don't even turn his way. They remain absorbed in their games, their sullen silences, their prayers, their jokes.

In their midst, a single pair of painfully open eyes; a single expression of horror. A brown-skinned woman whose mouth is slightly agape, as if petrified in a grimace of dread: an expression in which there is no surprise, just the confirmation of something already known but no less unbearable for it. She doesn't look at her cellmates. She doesn't look at the jailer. She doesn't look at the unattainable freedom beyond the bars. She is looking at Juan. Inside Juan. Who knows if right through Juan. She looks in a terrible way, as one looks at terrible things that have happened and the even more terrible things still to come; eyes divested of all volition and all beauty, eyes that have seen horror and are full of it and therefore excruciating to see, or maybe they have seen horror and are empty for that very reason and that emptiness is even more unbearable. Eyes that reflect nothing now, what remains of compassion when faith has been erased; freedom, when justice is withheld; will, when it lacks hands and a voice. Hope minus hope.

Juan presses himself to the bars. With a trembling hand, he points not at the woman but at the gaze that is as if sewn on her face.

"How much?"

The jailer stops. The lamp in his hand continues to sway, chiaroscuro thrown across his bewildered face.

"The señor wants to pay her fine? Pay the fine for this trollop?"

"How much?"

The jailer names a ridiculous number. An amount so small that it isn't expressed in gold or silver but copper vellón. Juan slips his fingers into his pouch and, without looking, hands him the first coin he finds.

"Hey, you," the guard says, rattling the key inside the lock. "Come here. You're about to get very lucky."

But the girl, the trollop, doesn't move. She simply makes her look of horror last a little longer, that's it.

"Did you hear me?"

She still doesn't obey. Her look has transformed into something else. There is no horror now, or not just horror, at least: now there is also rage. Indignation. Scorn. The girl does not want to be saved, at least not like this: not for that small bit of coin. Not out of charity or compassion. Perhaps that is the reason she moves away, suddenly, far from the bars that are open at last. She scuttles through the crowd of women until she is lost among them; just another prisoner, no different from her comrades in fortune.

"Your loss, slut!" the jailer shouts, furiously brandishing his heavy key ring.

Then, calm, he turns to Juan. This is how they are, the women who live in the prison, he explains didactically. Most of them, at least. They'd rather fill their bellies on the town hall's tab than sweat, as God intended, at a job. He knows that beggar well, and all the others of her ilk: all money is wasted money when it comes to sluts like her. He'd bet his hand that she'll be back within two weeks, with the same desire to loaf about, another sin on her conscience.

Juan says nothing. Slowly he separates from the bars, resigned. The jailer still holds the coin in his palm. His expression is pleading.

"The señor doesn't want to try for another? I have some who are prettier and less disagreeable . . ."

VIII

*Faceless beggars – Foolishness for God – Inheritance from a dead father – An eagle
fights its prison – Toy for a future child – New flags for an old world – Poor table
and humble roof – Many stones and a few bones – The patrón has just left because
you, sir, have just arrived – Days or years – The patrón and the Patrón – Crucified
peasants – The fire and us*

Just five coins at the bottom of his pouch. He spent the others on provisions
for the journey and new clothes and an airless inn next to the cathedral. He
even got himself a white wig—all true gentlemen have one sometimes even
two extras, sir, the tailor insisted—which he now dons clumsily like a second
head of hair. In all those places—the tailor, the shop, the inn—they bite his
coins before accepting them and shake their head when he shows them the
sketch of the Padrecito. They hardly bother to look. They don't do business
with riffraff or crazy hermits or prisoners in viceregal jails or beggars, they
say, and are certainly not able to remember their faces. Beggars, they seem to
say, have no face. Beggars only have outstretched hands and tattered layers
of clothing and disgusting diseases, the sort one must protect oneself with
a few yards of distance and the intercession of certain saints. Juan puts the
book away slowly, while before him the tailor, the shopkeeper, the innkeeper,
dillydallies a little longer, squinting at the worn face on the coins he has been
given. And now, here he is, saddlebags filled, his wig tilting atop his head, and
just five coins at the bottom of his pouch: not enough to purchase a horse or
other beast of burden. All that's left, then, is to walk, to keep walking north,

always north, dragging his bags behind him. Juan transformed into his own horse, a mount that will never, ever stop.

But, why not stop? Why keep walking, on the trail of a man who is a delinquent, a beggar, maybe insane? Juan doesn't have the answer. Or maybe he does, with a part of his thoughts that he wouldn't dare look in the face—if thoughts had faces. He only knows or thinks he knows one thing: the journey is not over.

At the bottom of his pouch, wrapped with the five gold coins: the Padre's book, and between the pages, between the apostle's fierce drawings, passages underlined or crossed out or circled in ink with such fury that the paper is torn in places. They are—they couldn't be anything else—the Padre's favorite passages. Places where the Padre's gaze came to rest. Ideas that he touched, for a moment at least, with the tip of his thoughts. Juan takes the book and hastily turns the pages, allowing his eyes to jump from underlined passage to underlined passage. He has followed the Padre's footsteps to this place and now he follows the trail of his reading and lets himself slip inside the book he holds in his hand.

He reads: Wherefore, behold, I send unto you prophets, and wise men, and scribes; some of them you shall kill and crucify; and some of them shall you scourge in your synagogues, and persecute them from city to city.

He reads: Let no man deceive himself. If any man among you seems wise in this world, let him become a fool, so that he may be wise. For the wisdom of this world is foolishness with God.

He reads: Yea, and all that will live godly in Christ Jesus shall suffer persecution.

He reads: But God hath chosen the foolish things of the world to confound the wise; and God hath chosen the weak things of the world to confound the things which are mighty.

He reads: Yea, the time comes, that whosoever kills you will think that he does God's service.

He is barely out of the city's slums when a carriage catches up to him. Less a carriage than a pathetic cart, similar to the wagons used by traveling play-actors or puppeteers, with a cowhide cover and a pair of mules hitched to the front. A young boy no more than ten is perched on the driver's seat and steering the reins with aplomb. He wears an enormous hat, a hat in no way intended for such a small head, a hat perhaps inherited from his dead father or destined for a future son. The sun has reddened his skin and he has the look of those children long subjected to the obligations of their elders: a look that harbors no hope of yielding to horseplay or games. Only a faint glimmer that portends something of the old man he will become.

"Where are you going?" the child asks, slowing the mules to match Juan's pace.

Juan, too exhausted to speak, can only point to the horizon toward which he and the cart are headed. The child nods gravely, as if Juan has unwittingly given the correct response. He observes Juan's provisions, too heavy to be hauled by the efforts of one man alone.

"Might the good sir have something to drink?"

Juan digs around in the saddlebags for the wineskin. The child, the tiny hand of the child, takes the wineskin with a remotely authoritative gesture. Then he halts the trotting mules and takes the long gulp of a thirsty man. Before returning the wineskin, he dries his beardless cheeks with his shirt sleeve.

"Get in," he says with the same authority and the same gesture, not bothering to look at Juan.

There are a few sacks of grain in the back of the cart, jugs of pulque and atole, and strings of peppers. Even a hen, asleep in the straw inside her little wooden crate. But there is, in effect, just enough room for Juan to settle his bags and himself, using his pouch for a pillow.

"Where are you headed?" he asks when the young mule driver whistles and animals resume their trot.

"North," he replies out the corner of his mouth.

That is all he will say for the next four towns.

From the wagon, Juan sees sown fields and barren lands, miserable villages, adobe chapels. He sees garb the likes of which he has never seen and men who are, in some sense, new as well; men who are less and less Indian but less and less Spanish, too, if that were possible. When they pass, he has time to observe fragments of their faces, catch fragments of their conversations. Their accent, he decides, is unlike any other on the globe. The land they traverse is different from the land he comes from and identical at the same time: the same wretched hands bearing the same hoes, the same pitchforks, the same teams of oxen; new uniforms and new hats to resist the old sun, always the same sun beating down, flagellation on the men's backs. Each time he sees a beggar or a pilgrim off to the side in the ditch, he turns, avid to study their face. Almost all of the terrain is bare grassland and desert hills and plots of land ravaged by the sun. Wasted worlds where there is nothing to see and nothing to search: just the sound of hoofbeats on the ground, and the wagon wheels bouncing over rubbly stone, and the voice of the young mule driver—a voice that seems to grow deeper, more robust by the moment—murmuring asides in the mules' primitive language. Every so often, the hen opens her tiny black eyes only to close them again, lulled by the torpor of the road. It starts to rain, fine, timid droplets that reverberate on the wagon cover like spadefuls of dirt on a dead man's coffin. The rain stops and the sun comes out and then hides again. A bank of clouds, heavy and blank, forms on the horizon, as if their destination were akin to night, or a storm.

And then, suddenly, Juan hears the pealing of bells that sound very close, though they are crossing an area where there are no villages or churches. The bells clamor and clatter and mixed with the metal ringing a terrible cry re-sounds, somewhere between pain and euphoria. Abruptly, the bells fall silent, and with them the cry. Still, there are no bells, no human throat, to be seen. Around a bend in the road, the wagon meets a squadron of soldiers outfitted in white uniforms and black hats, marching north. They carry loaded muskets—sophisticated, to Juan's eyes—with a kind of knife fitted to the barrels. The first soldier carries a birdcage and inside the cage there is no bird, only a human head that seems to have flown off its body; a head emancipated from that body forevermore. He sees the decapitated man's long, white hair, hanging aimlessly. His features peaceful, as if he had been surprised in the middle of a dream. The open mouth, frozen in a scream: perhaps the very cry Juan just heard, ricochet-ing, amplified by the valley. It looks like the head of a priest, the open eyes of a priest who waits or prays or dreams, and this padrecito, thinks Juan, could be *the* Padrecito. But the mules pick up their pace and the soldiers and the birdcage and the head fall behind before Juan can distinguish its features.

Stop, he tells the driver, but the carriage does not stop. He leans out and repeats the order, but the boy holding the reins doesn't deign to turn around, his eyes fixed on the road where so many things are yet to happen.

"The head belongs to the father of the nation," he explains from under his hat, bringing his cane down unnecessarily across the mules' backs. El Padre de la Patria.

And then:

"It is war."

And still later:

"It is time."

Time for what, Juan would have liked to ask, but doesn't. All of a sudden, he feels a shudder akin to vertigo, the aftertaste of blood in his mouth, the bobbing of the carriage which suddenly seems to be the same bobbing as the head in the birdcage and the birdcage in the soldier's hand, a shuttling of ideas and images and fragments of the landscape that slide by the window, and his head, Juan's head, transformed into the head of the padrecito—the head of the Padrecito?—Juan's open eyes are his eyes now, what those dead eyes would see if they could see, the bars of the birdcage suddenly like the rubblework of the road or the gray of the sky, rocked by the rhythm of the ride. He thinks: I'm drunk. And then: I'm dreaming. I'm sick. Beneath the gray wig—the fake hair, so like the dead man's white mane—his head seems to boil. The land boils too. Rain suddenly, brutally unleashed, stormy and swift; water on the wagon cover and water on the paving stones and on the trees and on his thoughts. Water in front of and behind his eyes. Water vomited from the sky in order to cleanse the world. Rain like radiance or creeping clairvoyance or a gift that appears to accelerate things, the succession of trees on both sides of the road, faster and faster, and the mud puddles bubbling on the ground, the carriage that clatters and rumbles over them and then finally flies, almost flies; the madness of a journey that never ends. Night falling swiftly over his eyes and over the scenery, and on the other side, like characters sprung from a nightmare, soldiers readying themselves for battle by the light of torches or lanterns or flashes of lightning; soldiers in white uniforms and soldiers in blue uniforms and soldiers in no uniform but instead in their campesino clothes. Inside the carriage, inside her crate, the hen finally opens her ferocious eyes and beats her wings, despairing or enraged; wings that seem to grow until they flood the crate and burst the bars, like an eagle liberated from its prison to finally begins its hunt in an unremitting night. Eagles screeching inside the narrow confines of their cages, the cage in the carriage, the infinite cage of the world, no longer denying their nature as birds of prey. Outside, someone dies, assailed by its hooked beak or by bullets. The first shots. The first thunder. Somebody dies and before dying that somebody screams. Death is the sudden eruption of sound. And following the death, many more voices, rallying cries, commands: soldiers come and go along both sides of the road, take their positions, load their muskets, cross themselves. He sees, for an instant, a standard stamped with the Virgin of Guadalupe. He sees a weapon about to be discharged. He sees a dead man. Then he sees noth-

ing. His eyelids close with neither will nor resistance, as if the man's death had
fallen upon them, and inside the sarcophagus of the carriage, the world continues to slip by in the form of sounds that are at once garbled and yet singularly
sharp. He hears shouts. Shouts that spill like rain and water droplets that drum
like shouts. He hears the cry: Viva el Ejército Trigarante and: Viva México,
and: Death to the gachupínes. And the gachupínes die, perhaps, somewhere
outside the car. He hears the buzz of their suffering, crackling in the night like
the crack of the mule driver's whip. Viva Fernando VII, says a strangled voice,
and the voice receives a full-throated answer: Death to bad government, and:
Death to Spain, and: Death to tyranny, voices that reverberate like an echo of
the Padrecito. His words, suddenly, in other men's mouths. The men fight for
land Juan cannot see and in his body there is a fight as well, an intense pain at
his temples, in his chest, his arms, the shaking in his arms ever worse, as if they
weren't his own or were his but just barely, his body a battle against his body
so that from that battle would emerge, the lone survivor, an idea: It is war. It is
time. It is the end. And then finally, suddenly, the mule driver's voice rising in
answer to those thoughts—but how could a voice so deep, the voice of a dour
man, belong to the boy—the driver's voice, in any case, which replies: No, it is
not the end. It is the beginning.

The beginning of what, Juan would like to know. But he doesn't ask.

He had believed he was about to die. He was, perhaps, dead for a time. But
now it is day again and the sky is blue and the carriage has stopped in another
place. A solicitous voice: We have arrived, señor. Juan is slow to comprehend
the meaning of those words. Inside the carriage, the same things: the sacks of
grain, the clay pots of pulque and atole, the strings of tornachiles. The same
hen dozing in the straw, inside her little wooden crate. Juan who is regaining
awareness of his body, his body his own again, the legs that slowly obey and
support him as he gets down. He takes several wobbly steps toward the driver.
He rubs his sun-dazed eyes, like someone dusting off the vestige of a dream.
The mule driver, still holding the crop, points to the front door of an inn. For
what feels like a vast length of time, Juan stares at the driver's face under the
brim of his hat: his puckered countenance, the wasted face, like Bible paper
that might have burned in a fire with no smoke, no consequences. We have
arrived, señor, the old man repeats in his lightly flute-like, childish voice, and
Juan nods vigorously but without conviction. Yes: they have arrived. Slowly,
with creaking effort, the old man turns back in the driver's seat. "You're not

staying, sir?" Juan asks, before the man departs. Oh, no: absolutely not. He is leaving: his journey has come to an end. So many years transporting provisions and travelers, the old man explains; so many years, he says, competing with the gringos who have filled the highways of México with stagecoaches that travel faster and cheaper; those years, ah, they've been more than enough. Because one cannot compete with the gringos. Against the neighbors to the north, he says, against the dollar, against the numbers, against reality, one cannot do a thing. It's time to return, he concludes, goading the mules and, in effect, ordering them to start back. Juan watches him go. He doesn't move, doesn't speak a single word of farewell; a traveler ditched in the middle of the square in a strange city, with a dust-smeared bag and forlorn look on his face. From behind, the old man's hat doesn't look so enormous now, not even big: just a regular old hat, a little antiquated perhaps, like the inheritance from a dead father or a toy for a future son.

The square is deserted, paralyzed by the heat. It is hardly more than a dusty rectangle, where a dry fountain presides. A few adobe and limestone houses; a few wooden porticos. In the middle of the emptiness, a dog collapsed in the sun, abandoned to a sleep reminiscent of death. Not even a twitch of his tail. The only thing that seems to show something like life is a striped cloth hanging from the inn balcony, gently distracted by the wind. It is a faded and battered flag, by turns green and by turns white and by turns red and by turns all the colors at once, at the breeze's whim. In the center, the image of a rampant eagle atop a nogal: an eagle somehow evocative of the hen locked in her wooden crate and the emblems of certain Aztec drawings.

Then, suddenly, in one corner of the square, life. Two boys who are sitting still in the shade of one of the porticos watch every one of his movements with astonishment. Have they been there all along? Juan approaches slowly. He hears their whispers.

"I think he's a gringo."

"Or a British lord."

"Looks like a judge to me."

They're looking at his white wig. Juan snatches it from his head, understanding that, somehow, it has become unnecessary baggage. He holds it tightly and twists it in his hands as he speaks to them, as if it were a living body. He asks if perchance they can tell him the name of the place, which they do, even repeating it once, twice, three times. Then he asks them if perchance they know the reason for the battle he has just witnessed only a few leagues to the south, and the boys exchange perplexed glances before they reply that they don't know what armies, what battles, what dead men he's talking about. Lastly, he asks about the flag. For an instant, the boys' eyes are as if wrapped in that piece of cloth. It's The Flag, one boy says simply. The Flag, the second confirms. The flag of what? They don't appear to understand the question. The Flag is The Flag. The Flag is the flag of the Republic. The Flag is the flag of all of us, they say; the flag of our land. And what is their land? What republic?

"He's drunk," one mutters.

But even so they try to explain to the drunk who looks like a gringo, or a British lord, or a judge driven mad by the desert, what republic, what land they are talking about. They use the word "emancipation." They use the word "justice." They use the word "México," as if they were resurrected Aztecs. So, this city is called México, Juan says at last, attempting to put things in order, and the boys snicker. Oh, he hasn't understood a thing, this judge. They just told him that their town is called this and called that. But México, they say, The Flag over there, is much more than that. It encompasses the town, of course, but the next town too, and the next, and the one after that. México is the name of the highest mountain to be climbed and the deepest depths to descend. México is the horizon as well as the horizon one sees once one reaches the horizon. He could ride for weeks in one direction or in its opposite and he would find only México, México, more México everywhere. Because México is an infinite land, a land that only seems to end on maps.

That's what they say, those boys, and then they are silent. The only sound is the dog's gravelly breathing; a lament that seems pumped from the bottom of a nightmare. Suddenly Juan remembers the Padrecito. The Padrecito's words, whose echoes still seem to reverberate within the walls the of city jail. I have come to redeem you, Mexicans of México, the bandits said the Padrecito said; I have come to liberate you from the chains of ignorance and the chains of slavery and the chains of the metropolis. Juan looks around, the small, miserable square, the walls chipped and bare, the balcony railings hung with scraps of humble rags, and asks himself if this is the kingdom the Padrecito aspired to build.

"I will show you something."

He is already rooting through his saddlebag. As he pulls out the book, as he leafs quickly through the pages, he explains that he is looking for a man. A man who is or looks like a beggar.

"A beggar?"

Their eyes shine with skepticism. Beggars, they seem to say, do not have faces. Beggars only have hands outstretched for begging and threadbare capes and disgusting diseases, from which one must protect himself with a few yards of distance and the intercession of certain saints. Perhaps he isn't exactly a beggar, Juan ultimately concedes; let's call him a pilgrim or a hermit or a humble traveler. He calls himself the Padrecito.

"The Padrecito?" asks one of the boys. "Is he a priest?"

"Something like that."

"Something like that?"

Juan reflects a moment.

"He isn't a priest."

And then:

"But he looks like one."

And even then:

"Perhaps he is a priest in some sense."

By then he has found the page with the portrait. The boys lean over the book with absent and slightly mocking curiosity, ready to take one look and answer no. But that one glance is enough to wipe the indifference from their faces and the rudeness from their laughter.

"It's the Patrón!" the first boy exclaims.

"It's the Patrón!" exclaims the second.

"The Patrón himself!" the first boy insists, as if there was any doubt.

And for a moment, they bring their hands reverentially to their heads, looking to find the hats they do not have.

The señor must excuse us. We didn't know that you. We didn't know that Your Excellency. We didn't know Your Honor was looking for the Patrón. If you had said from the beginning that you were one of the Patrón's men, then we. We wouldn't have laughed. We would have collaborated. We would have helped Your Lordship in any way necessary and even beyond. But we didn't know that. We thought that. We came to think that. But no. We were wrong. Your Honor is, without a doubt, one of the Patrón's foremen, one of the Patrón's collectors, one of the Patrón's representatives. If you had said so. If we had known. But we didn't know. Just tell us what you need and we'll do whatever we can. Find the Patrón? Ah, we'd love to help you with that, and with whatever Your Honor decrees and orders and commands. But the Patrón, you know, Your Excellency knows, Your Lordship undoubtedly knows very well, ah, the Patrón, the Patrón, who can say where he's to be found. Perhaps at this very moment he is inspecting the functioning of one of his many factories. Perhaps he is instructing his foremen. Perhaps he has a map spread on the table and on that map he is looking at this very town, scarcely a dot, not even large enough to put his finger on. How to find the Patrón if everything he is seeing with his eyes is the Patrón. Because, in some ways, this is the case, everything belongs to him, the dirt they walk on, the air they breathe, the water that feeds their wheat beds and cotton patches and cattle pastures. His possessions encompass the town, of course, but the next town too, and the next, and the one after that. His is the horizon as well as the horizon one sees when he reaches the horizon. He could ride for days in one direction or in its opposite and he would find only the Patrón, the Patrón, everywhere the Patrón's domain. A portion of the world not so large as México, to be sure, but just as big in any case. Bigger than what man's imagination can conceive. Bigger than that which they, sons of laborers who are also in some ways the Patrón's sons, are capable of dreaming. And that's why he, His Excellency, His Lordship, His Honor, must forgive them, because after all this is how they are, insignificant as a stone or a tree that grows on the Patrón's land, among so many identical stones and trees. His Lordship must accept their apologies and their poor table and humble roof, if he requires them. And when he finally does find the Patrón he mustn't forget to tell him that here, in this corner of the world that is at your service, in this town whose name the Patrón himself has perhaps forgotten or mislaid or confused with the name of other identical towns, they wait for him and honor him with a fervor of which he is perhaps unaware. Although we expect that the Patrón knows everything already; that not a single hair falls from our heads without his knowledge and permission.

He has found the Patrón and yet the journey isn't over. He has found the Patrón and now the Patrón, the body of the Patrón, extends in all directions. It is possible to camp on one of his fingertips and then spend an entire day trying to reach the hills of his knuckles. He passes through the Patrón's lands like a flea inhabiting the continent of a dog, ignorant, perhaps, that something called dog exists. He travels roads that run through the Patrón and sleeps in the shade of trees the Patrón's laborers planted and under the midday sun he sees the shimmer of the limewashed walls of a town the Patrón also ordered to be sown, like the trees. The town offers, as modest fruit, a cantina full of chipped walls. A few cotton fields. A mill that is also the Patrón, like the river that moves it. In the middle of the road naps another starving dog belonging to nobody, with constellations of fleas on its body and who knows how many roads and woods and towns and sleeping dogs and human beings we will never come to know. Outside the cantina, several villagers swaddled in ponchos wait, hunched over their wooden rocking chairs. Enormous sombreros weigh on each of their heads, and seem to weigh a bit heavier when Juan asks for the Patrón's whereabouts. Silence. The Patrón. The Patrón, those who dare look at the likeness Juan holds out to them repeat in a whisper. They smoke more hurriedly. They keep the cigarettes that are pure coals between their fingers and pass an unfired clay demijohn back and forth between them. The señor wants to know where the Patrón is, they say, and it's a pity they can't help him. They can't help him because the Patrón could be anywhere. He is, obviously, a rich man, so rich that he has never spent two nights under the same roof in his whole life. Because all of this is his. They make a vague gesture that encompasses the dusty roads, the heat-burnt horizon, the sleeping dog. The Patrón has so much land and so many estates and so many laborers that one is hard pressed to know the names of all the towns his holdings contain. At least that's what they say. Once, years ago, the Patrón was right there, at the cantina door, can the señor believe it? He didn't know where he was. Plonked right where the señor is standing now. Right there. They had never seen him before then. They'd been limited to dealing with his foremen, his sheriffs, and his rent collectors. But they recognized him immediately. It was the Patrón and he had gotten lost on his own land. He didn't know how to leave it. He had set off riding on a whim, or perhaps to see what his property was like under the skins of the maps, and he had wound up there, outside that humble cantina, asking directions for the way back. They gave him those directions, he tossed them a gold coin, and then they never saw him again. Just his foremen and sheriffs and rent collectors, who do remember the name of this town and, if required, the names of each and every one of them. The lands they occupy. The pesos they owe the Patrón.

Juan asks them for the road Juan took.

Juan tosses them a gold coin.

Juan loads his saddlebags and follows the path they show him, north, always north.

The town is also the Patrón, he thinks as he rides away, and its inhabitants are the Patrón's calloused hands, his muck-stained shoes. They too belong to the land, like turds that are born and die stuck to the same ground. Only the dog is free, he lives with his beggar's freedom, and for this reason, because no one else can, it sets off after Juan. Its ears are back and there is a certain hope in its eyes, like someone who has received many stones and also a few bones.

The Patrón's land looks like all the lands he has known up to now. A place where the same universal laws are obeyed, namely, namely, that all things worth possessing have an owner, and that collecting even the remnants of those things requires great effort. On the roadside, he sees swindlers and crooks, ruined ranches, a few men who give orders and many more who obey. Women who carry earthenware pitchers of water and cook pots while their husbands, their sons, their brothers bend over the plowed furrows with same old tools and sweat the same old sweat as their ancestors. Their faces are familiar. He has a sense that he has seen them before, days or years ago, like someone playing the whole night with different decks of cards and, as luck would have it, getting dealt the same hand.

But there are certain changes to the always identical land, Juan notes with surprise. In one of the adobe villages rotting on the side of the road he finds a crumbling belltower, and on that belltower an enormous clock with hands; a stopped clock, but a clock to be sure. Every so often, stuck in the ground, wooden posts that sustain extremely long, black wires, like lines for hanging clothes where no clothes are hung and nothing happens. They only serve as a place for the birds to rest. The birds rest above and below the men work, the men suffer. Shining under the sun, a path that looks like an open stitch in the earth; a badly healed scar of metal and wood laid crosswise, slithering toward the horizon. Juan follows that trail. When they see him pass, the campesinos wave their hats in the distance. What are they doing? They tell him to be careful. They say don't be foolish. Get away from there, compadre, they shout. For the love of God, get away. That path, Juan finally realizes, is not actually a path. Like the wires crossing the sky, it is made by man but not for man. And whatever it is that travels that path effectively ends up arriving, caravans of smoke and metal that plow through the earth like a ship plowing through the ocean. Why does the sea belong to no one and yet there is no land too wretched to lack an owner? He moves aside to listen to the almost animal-like snort, its storm of ironmongery, the plume of black smoke and plain dust that rises for a moment to cloud the world.

Smoke on the horizon, too, ascending in slow spirals. They are Juan's chimneys, Juan's factories. One of them, at least. It rises like a brick cathedral, a temple for a new cult dedicated to metal and fire. Juan waits before the entrance archway, hat in hand, like a new devotee. Around him he sees furnaces of faith, fulling mills, plumes; mills moving on their own. Its priests are angry, they are dirty, they are hungry. At a siren's wail, they exit into a square courtyard, with caps soaking wet and aprons smeared in grease. Nervously they smoke the stubs of cigarettes that almost burn their fingers, and that pinch of tobacco is the only thread that links them to the past. They look, by turns, like priests and prisoners. They are, perhaps, prisoners, inhabiting a new jail full of light and purpose, just as the Padrecito had foreseen. They work, forming huge chains where every priest, every worker, every prisoner repeats the same movement unto infinity. For a moment, Juan remembers the way the Padre's Indians molded their clay vessels, in a chain that began and never, ever ended. High up on the central nave, an enormous clock with hands subdividing time down to the last usable instant, which the prisoners look at with resignation or hope. He sees them feed their forges, their rust volcanos, and produce within them strange objects, objects unnecessary, perhaps, or absurd. One would say that the factory's only aim is to produce the pieces that will keep the factory standing. The factory perpetuating itself, as if the iron had a will of its own, its own intent. Is this the Patrón's will, are these his intentions?

But the Patrón isn't there either. Juan, at least, isn't able to find him. He knocks on doors large and small, wooden gates and iron grilles. He hears the sound of latches, horns, bells, brass chimes. He talks with guards and managers, with foremen and workers. He waits beside the watchman's hut; in carpeted hallways and offices. And in those offices, in those huts, in those halls, always the same answers, or depending on one's perspective, always a different answer. Unfortunately, the Patrón cannot receive him. Unfortunately, the Patrón is a very busy man, he cannot hear your request, whatever it may be. The Patrón is not in. The Patrón doesn't know who you are. The Patrón has a very important meeting this morning and must not be disturbed. The Patrón doesn't give work to layabouts or beggars. The Patrón hasn't arrived yet. The Patrón just left. Sometimes, crazy combinations of the same replies. The Patrón is a very busy man precisely because he cannot hear your request. The Patrón isn't in because the Patrón doesn't know who you are, whoever you may be. The Patrón has just left because you, sir, have just arrived, and he will continue to be away as long as you continue to be a layabout and beggar.

And seated in those offices, standing in so many hallways, checking so many latches and bells and chimes and iron doorknockers, Juan waits. He turns the Padre's book over in his hands, always ready to show the Patrón's face to the many managers, guards, foremen, workers. Sometimes he opens it and takes a distracted glance at the verses in his tiny, cramped handwriting. Some have been underlined or crossed out or circled in ink, so savagely that, in some places, the paper has torn. They are, they must be, the Padre's favorite passages. Places that held his gaze. Ideas he touched, for a moment at least, with the tip of his thoughts. Rapidly he turns the pages, letting his eyes jump from underlined word to underlined word. He has followed the Padre's steps this far and now he follows the wake of his reading, lets himself slip inside the book in his hand.

He reads: I know how to be brought low and I know how to abound. Everywhere, and in all things, I have learned the secret of being full and of being hungry; of abounding and of having need.

He reads: The sluggard craves but his soul hath naught: but the soul of the diligent shall have plenty.

He reads: We did not behave inordinately among you. Nor did we take food from anyone for nothing, but with labor and hardship we worked night and day because we did not wish to be a burden to any of you. Not because we do not have authority, but so that we might make ourselves an example for you to follow. For even when we were with you, we warned you of this; that if there were any who would not work, he should not eat.

He reads: And I say to you, make friends with the riches of iniquity, so that when you fail, they may receive you into eternal dwellings.

He reads: Evil and slothful servant! You knew that I reap where I did not sow and gather where I did not scatter. Therefore, you ought to have put my money in the bank. And then at my coming I would have received my own with interest. Therefore, take the talent from him and give it to him who has ten talents. For to everyone who has, it shall be given, and he shall have abundance. But from the one who has not, even that which he has shall be taken away.

He reads: The ransom of a man's life is his wealth, but a poor man has no means of redemption.

And thus, the days or years pass.

Do they pass, the days, or the years? Is it possible to spend days and years like this, sitting in an office, standing in a hall? It is, perhaps, impossible, but it doesn't seem so to Juan. He spends, at any rate, sufficient time that meeting with the Patrón seems like something that is never going to happen. But then it does. There is no reason, at least no reason Juan is aware of, but one day, the same questions, the same people, lead him to an opulent office and not the door to the street. Juan sits down in a red-felt armchair and waits an enormous amount of time, five minutes perhaps. Those five minutes tick by as if they were days or years. Now that he is on the verge of achieving it, his will appears weaker than ever. What is he going to say? Why has he arrived at this point? Has he come to capture him, or throw himself at his feet like one of his disciples?

At last, a man appears on the other side of the table. He is not the Patrón. He is a tiny, ridiculous man with a clipped mustache. The Patrón's secretary, perhaps, who offers him a very small and very cold hand. Then he arches his brow and his face settles into an expression of expectation. I'm looking for the Patrón, Juan explains to those raised eyebrows. I am the patrón, the secretary replies. Behind him, a pendulum clock chimes twelve o'clock on who knows what day and what year. Juan waits those twelve strokes before speaking again, his voice trembling.

"You are not the Patrón."

"Of course I'm the patrón," the patrón repeats.

Juan rifles in his satchel. The patrón's body starts, and stiffens in his chair. While Juan rummages, he noiselessly opens one of the desk drawers and slips his hand inside. He appears to relax only when he sees Juan take out a book with antique covers and iron rivets, which he leaves on the table, opened to the first page. You are not the Patrón, he repeats, and there is something mechanical in his voice; something reminiscent of the clock's voice. You are not this man. The patrón leans over the likeness. He laughs, completely relieved.

"Now I understand," he says, laughing still.

He shuts the desk drawer and opens another on the opposite side. He takes out a gold cigarette case.

"Have a smoke, won't you?"

Now I understand, the patrón says again, the cigarette hanging from his lips. Undoubtedly there has been some kind of confusion, he explains. You are not looking for the patrón. You are looking for the Patrón. Juan blinks in confusion. Is there a difference? Much more than you think, the patrón insists. You want to see the Patrón, and you expected to find him here. But the Patrón is not here. The Patrón has never been here, do you understand? I'd be surprised if he remembers my name. What am I saying? I'd be surprised if he even remembers that this factory exists! Because if you owned this entire region, my friend, would you waste your life here, in this miserable office? Would you sit in this chair? If the Patrón has amassed so many pesos, if he has built this empire, it is precisely because he was never content to sit still in one place. So where can you find him? Ah! Who can answer that question? Only the Patrón, says the patrón. But in order to ask the Patrón, you'd have to find him. And the Patrón could be anywhere. Perhaps at his very moment he is inspecting the functioning of another of his many factories. Or he has a map spread out on the table and on that map he is looking right at that building, which he doesn't even remember having built. He's even heard that Patrón lives on the actual railway line. Does this seem possible to you or not? Well, it's what they say. People in the know. Secretaries of secretaries of men who once shook the Patrón's hand, perhaps. They say he lives on one of his trains, from south to north and north to south. Always moving. And from there he controls everything, controls everyone, as if they were part of his own body. Though perhaps that's just a manner of speaking. Who could ever comprehend what the Patrón thinks; what the Patrón has arranged. This is what the patrón says, his face veiled in smoke from his cigarette: a smoke no stranger than the smoke from the factory or the iron caravans. It is his recommendation, therefore, that whatever the issue he came to discuss with the Patrón, he should give up on finding him. What will he gain by continuing his search? He will gain nothing. He's not exaggerating when he tells him that a century wouldn't be time enough to find him. In fact, if he considers it coldly, he'll admit that it's a miracle that he's gotten so far. How much negligence had to occur for me to be sitting in this office with you! he exclaims. In order for you to be able to meet with me, such a busy man . . . And yet, I myself, listen to what I'm saying, I myself have only seen the Patrón once in my life. It was years ago, but he still recalls. As if it were happening right now, before his very eyes. He remembers it that well. What a man! What a voice! Of course, Juan has never heard the Patrón's voice, and he fears he'll never get the chance to hear it . . . Though something tells me, the patrón says, that you won't give up so easily. That despite his advice and instructions, he is going to keep trying anyway, as long as there is blood in his veins. And he likes that, see, that kind of obstinance. In some ways, he reminds him of the Patrón, the patrón says. So who knows. Perhaps he will end up finding him after all. In some ways, in a very abstract way, of course, he even looks a little like him. Like the Patrón, that is. He too pressed on when everything seemed impossible. Did Juan know that before the Patrón began to amass his fortune, he was practically a beggar with nothing but the empty palm of his hand and nary a peso to fill it with? What does he think about that? The Patrón's hand, begging for alms! Well, it seems that was the case. At least that's what the Patrón himself told him. He showed him his naked hand, his empty hand, and said: In the beginning, this was all I had. Now, and he continued to point to his factories and estates and boundless domains, I have the world. That's what he said. So you might do well in continuing to look for him after all. It's the kind of thing the Patrón would do: never give up. And, if you will permit me, a piece of advice . . . Maybe it's nonsense, what I'm about to say. Yes, maybe it is, but you should try in the old cotton-yarn factory. It's thirty, thirty-five kilometers from here, but . . . Yes: kilometers. In cotton country. They say everything started in that factory. That when they started building it, the Patrón was nothing but a peon laying stones, and by the time it was finished, the factory was his. That's why they say he has a soft spot for it, because cotton gave him his first boost. At least that's what they say. People in the know . . .

Once more, Juan shakes the man's small hand, such a cold hand, which also seems to be made of iron. There is no need to ask anything else. He knows that the factory can only be waiting for him to the north.

On the edge of town, he sees a handful of men sitting under a wall in the shade, clapping and playing a guitar. A girl is dancing among them, her eyes closed, like someone swaying to the rhythm of a dream. Juan is about to ask if the cotton factory is close by, but something in her happiness, in the girl's blind dancing, stops him. He doesn't know that they are the last human beings he will see for the whole day. He touches the brim of his hat and continues on his way.

He comes across more barren villages further on. A dry well, a dry fountain. A creek, also dry, dotted with bones that might have belonged to thirsty cattle. The road slides through lands that were once for sowing, scorched by the heat. A cornless, hopeless horizon, governed by scarecrows that look like crucified peasants. He spends the night in one of the abandoned villages. No ivy or grasses grow in the entranceways, and the walls are clean and limewashed, as if the inhabitants were about to return any minute. He lights a fire in one of the homes and drinks coffee in the gloom of the uninhabited house. He thinks about who its owners might be, and he thinks about the Patrón, about that factory where no one expects him and yet, at the same time, everyone obeys him, just as we pray to a God who showed Himself just once and forever. Lastly, he remembers to think a little about himself, as he finishes the dregs. Just like usual, when he turns his gaze inward, he quickly gives up. He unrolls his mat directly on the floor, warmish from the fire's heat. At dawn he hears the wind whistle through the roof beams and the murmur of what sounds something like old conversations, and the morning comes without a rooster's crow to announce it.

The road pulses in the midday sun. The world's shapes and colors boil on the horizon like figures of melted wax. The heat lays before Juan's eye things that are not there and makes vanish things that are, and when at one of the bends in the road he finally espies another human being, he hesitates to convince himself of it. It is a young man with a bundle on his back and a peasant's blush on his face. He is also headed for the cotton factory. He seems pleased to have found company. This way we can kill the boredom of the trek with a bit of chat, isn't that right, sir? Juan agrees and they fall into step. They walk shoulder to shoulder through land contorted from thirst.

"What happened here?" Juan asks, pointing to another ruined village alongside the road.

"The drought, sir. A bad year came and an even worse one left."

The young man tells him that he was born in one of the towns to the south. That town, he says, doesn't exist anymore either. What happened to its inhabitants is what happens to the guests at a wedding: at a certain time in the early morning hours, the celebration ends and the pulquería or tavern or wherever they've come together closes and each person goes his or her own way, never to meet again. That's what happened with his town. With the townspeople. Of course, they had never known a party, what we call a party, and he isn't sure that his parents or their parents ever did either. What's clear is that the town had seen better years: no one doubts that. But it is a fact that the land never was good, the young man says, and that the government's delegates were no better. They expropriated the communal lands five years ago and gave them to the Patrón, just because they didn't have their papers in order. True, they'd never had papers: what they did have was land. Since the world was young. Since then, that's what they'd had. But they were told the land was not sufficient proof and the Patrón took it away.

Juan stops in the middle of the road. The young man talks to the air until he realizes and turns back to look at him, as if struck by lightning six or seven steps behind.

"Did I say something that made you uncomfortable, señor?"

"No. Only, that Patrón you speak of . . . you wouldn't be referring to this man?"

The young man leans just momentarily over the likeness. He pulls away sharply, as if he were tired of looking at it.

"Well, yes, señor, that is exactly who I'm referring to. You don't know him, by any chance?"

"And you're sure he's the one who took your land?"

The young man looks the drawing over carefully. He answers slowly.

"Pretty sure, señor. It isn't something one easily forgets or jokes about."

Juan hastens to apologize. That isn't what he meant to say. What he's trying to explain is that the Patrón is an important man: a person with many responsibilities. Might this injustice have been perpetrated by someone else, in his name perhaps, but without the Patrón's knowledge? The boy shakes his head. Someone else, without the Patrón's knowledge? He can't speak to that. Although he expects that not a single hair falls from their heads without his knowledge and permission, but who knows. Maybe it's like the señor says. If it was him, or who knows who else, isn't for me to say, he adds. In any event, it was done. All the boy knows is that, if it wasn't the Patrón's doing, they can at least be sure he was the one to reap the benefits. The lands fell into his hands, as we say, because the Patrón had the papers we were lacking.

Then, after a long silence, he says that what hurt most is that the land seemed happy with the change of ownership. That right from the first harvest the Patrón got big, red ears of corn the likes of which he and his people had never seen. Then the drought came and the town died. It was dead from the time their lands were taken, but with the drought there was nothing to do but bury it. Some of the townspeople left for Coahuila. Others for Torreón, for Monterrey. But the undeniable fact is that they left.

"And you?"

"What about me?"

"What are you going to the factory to do?"

"Ay, well, what I have to do, señor. The same as you. Go and beg the Patrón for work . . ."

On the side of the road, they come across a barn with chipped paint and a dozen laborers eating under its shade. Upon sight of them, the men remove their hats and bring them to their chests. One of them, mustachioed and ceremonious, stands to welcome them. Juan observes their mended sarapes, the humble tortillas they unwrap with liturgical solemnity. They are very poor. Theirs is a kind of poverty that is damaged as much by accepting their invitation as rejecting it. Juan and the boy accept.

They are also going to the cotton factory. They too are seeking work. In these times, what else is there to do?

Nothing else. Just walk. Now they are twelve, fourteen who walk together. They take up the whole width of the road, with their bundles and straw mats strapped to their backs. From the turned fields, from the villages still alive, the campesinos stop their work to watch them.

"Where are you headed, compadres?"

"The cotton factory."

"Is there work there?"

"There has to be."

Some shake their heads and continue stirring the dirt. But others lay down their hoes and wheelbarrows and run to catch up. Or they carry their tools on their shoulders, as if instead of heading for the city they were on their way to plant seeds. There are young men but old men too. Twenty, thirty men. Fifty men. Some women are waiting on the side of the road. They give them pitchers filled with water and wine. They give them bread. They make the sign of the cross before the walkers, so that God will intercede and the Patrón will take pity on them. After all, even the Patrón must have a heart and soul. And he must also have, if it is his desire, enough factories to employ one hundred men in a day, without too many questions. One hundred men and a handful of women, because some of them, as soon as they finish blessing the men, bless themselves and set off on the road. They walk shoulder to shoulder. Do they also wish to work in the Patrón's factory? They speak of the Patrón. They speak of their expropriated lands. Of ditches and irrigation canals that come to kiss the Patrón's fields and no others. Of herds no longer permitted to drink from the rivers which their ancestors named. They speak of mills and bridges. They speak of taxes. Of debts. Of indentured servants on the Patrón's latifundia, sown in the dirt like corn that will never sprout. They shake their heads, as if pushing away a bad thought, and say: Let's hope the Patrón has an ounce of pity for us.

They are three hundred men and women. Three hundred human beings. There are three hundred of us, Juan thinks, as it suddenly occurs to him to think in this way, in the plural, so many arms and legs and desires, all headed in the same direction. He doesn't remember Juan the Indian, or he only just barely does. He remembers, by contrast, the Patrón's affronts, the Patrón's handouts, as if he had witnessed them with his own eyes. There are a thousand of them and all have seen the same things with the same eyes. When they reach the next town, men and women come out to receive them amid cheers and applause, and a small group of children scamper around, elated to touch the soldiers' hands. They are not soldiers, they are campesinos, but they march as if they were. A pregnant woman joins their ranks, cradling her enormous belly. She wants work, too, she says. Work for her and work for her son. She says they want to be heard. She says they want bread. The mayor, solemn and dressed in his Sunday best, watches them pass from the height of the balcony of the town hall. He waves his hat and directs a few words to the parading troops. What does he say? No one listens. At the front, a man with the face on an outlaw has climbed atop a wagon and shouts a few slogans, his fist in the air. He is who they are listening to. Who is that man? He shouts: Viva el Patrón! Death to the latifundia! And the voices spread like air or fire. It's the Compadre, someone shouts close to Juan's ear. It's the Compadre! Long live the Compadre! shouts one voice, one hundred voices, and the Compadre, still atop the wagon, continues to shout. The crowd chants his name. They applaud him. Someone fires into the air, a shot that resounds like an affirmation. His hands, the Compadre's flashing hands, seem to dance over their heads: riling or calming the spirits of those who hear him, like a puppet master who knows how to control his marionettes' will. Land and liberty! the Compadre cries in his steady voice, and like an echo, that cry is repeated in two thousand throats. Two thousand throats? Even the unborn child seems to shout. What would that child shout, if he shouted?

Night is falling. They light fires by the roadside to warm themselves. They light torches. Altar candles from church. Oil lamps. Several old women shrouded in their black shawls hand out clay bowls with a smattering of humble foodstuffs. There isn't enough food for all. There is only enough drink: demijohns of pulque and mezcal that are passed from hand to hand and never run out. Eight thousand hands. Ten thousand hands. When they drink they close their eyes, and in their expression there is a kind of innocence, as if they suckled the aguardiente from a teat. As if they were their own thirsty herds, jumping fences and stockades in order to drink from the river they'd so long yearned for. The alcohol that is enough and the food that is not. They are hungry. We are hungry and we are drunk, Juan thinks, wiping the pulque from his chin with his sleeve. Land and liberty and bread, they shout, we shout. Party rockets explode from the terraces of the nearby homes, as if they were celebrating a pilgrimage honoring a local patron saint. Which saint, which patron? Some men aim their pistols, their carbines, heavenward and shoot off salutes in honor of that nameless saint. Where have they gotten their pistols, their carbines? We processioners. We devotees. We soldiers. The pregnant woman says she wants a weapon. She says her son wants one, too. Weapons! the men shout, the men beg. Arms and bread! we shout.

Yonder, we discern the factory lights, glowing like a distant flame. There, lying in ambush, the Patrón waits for us. What is he waiting for? What are we waiting for? If a hair doesn't fall from our heads without his knowledge and permission, then how can He be ignorant of the five thousand heads, the ten thousand heads marching to meet him? Because we are going to meet him. We are hungry and armed. We have alcohol. We have no fear. We have no justice. We travel the countryside visible by moonlight, by fire. The factory lights like a lantern guiding us through the dark. Like moths drawn to the flame. We are the moths and the moths, sometimes, fly too close to the fire. They fly and fly until they too are fire. But death is nothing, death is not the end. It is the beginning. The beginning of something. The beginning of what. The pregnant woman undresses in the moonlight, in the firelight, and screams until she deafens the world. Something that begins. The woman giving birth directly over the dirt and, under her skirts, no human flesh: just cartridges, pistols, bullets. A rifle cradled in her lap. An iron son who comes to be born in a world that is also iron.

More rockets exploding in the sky, igniting the sky. Not rockets. Shots. A man is dead. Are we that man? Soldiers in uniform parapeted in ditches and behind walls. Soldiers who shoot at us. Are we those soldiers? We are not. Not us. They are federales and we are men. We are the people and we are armed and we are armed because we are hungry. There isn't enough food and there isn't enough land but there is enough hunger, there is hunger enough; enough reason to kill a man. This, perhaps, is what we have come to tell the Patrón. We come to plead with him. To beg him to die as well. We call him by his name and the Patrón does not answer. We knock down the entrance gate and the Patrón does not receive us, unfortunately the Patrón cannot attend to our request, and we burst into warehouses and offices to be heard, the Patrón so busy and we so hungry, so drunk, throwing papers we can't read into the air, the Patrón has just left because we have just arrived and he will remain away as long as we remain layabouts and beggars. How long will we be layabouts and beggars? How long will the Patrón be away?

All around, workers who flee. Workers who join us. Workers who defend the Patrón, the immense vacuum the Patrón has left in his wake. Workers who seem to come alive for the first time. Workers who die. Workers who die and we who die and the Patrón who dies, too, the Patrón, at last, the death of the Patrón, at last, a death like any other, just a man, after all, a body huddled behind the desk, holding a silver revolver that won't be fired, the Patrón flat on the floor, the Patrón pleading, the Patrón pissing his pants, see, boys, the courage the Master squanders? someone laughs, someone insults, our arms that drag him down the stairs, drag him back down to the ground; the pleasure of seeing him kneel on land that was torn from us, hearing his old man's voice beg, his already-dead or almost-dead voice crying out under the blows, have a little pity on me, and we who have no food and no land and no pity either, how could we, we have arms, yes, we have mothers and fathers who died without their due, we have debts, thirsty herds, we have hunger; we have hands and on our hands, the Patrón's blood, but we have no pity, his body lifted over our heads and the Patrón's eyes that open for the last time, the Patrón who seems to fix his eyes on all of us, the Patrón who looks at you, too, and his death is not an end, but a beginning. The beginning of something. The beginning of what. The beginning of the fire. An oil lamp thrown against one factory wall and the fire that originates there, but not just there, the fire that comes from all sides, it starts in the barrel of our guns and where it ends, no one knows; it kindles in the warp-weighted looms and the desks and the rugs, it delights in the machines' greased bodies, escalates in the crystal of the chandeliers, and we who must retreat several steps so as not to become fire as well, cautious moths, we who return to the night and from the night observe the flames at work. And in those flames, we see something we had not seen. We see the factory devoured by its own light and we see ourselves recovered from the darkness, reddened like creatures of and for the earth. We see our hundred thousand dirty, sweaty faces. We see an old man gripping a rusty rifle. We see a child or almost-child with a blood-splattered face. We see a woman with a flash of cruelty in her eyes. We see where our bodies begin and end, and our hands, our iron will made up of one thousand small wills that suddenly hesitate or doubt. Men who look at one another, terrified by the magnitude of their own rage, separate again, serfs again. Juan looking at the Patrón's body abandoned in the dirt, expanding and shrinking before his eyes, as if transfigured by the fire's flicker. Juan looking at his own hands. Juan looking at the rifle those hands hold. The weapon that falls to the ground and the factory that still hasn't fallen, burning the whole night, luminous and eternal, and its flames rising to where the men never dreamed they would reach.

IX

The Lord's Crucifixion – An orphaned people and a new father – Ride without horses – Neither peasants nor soldiers – Long live the revolution, death to the revolutionaries – A portrait of the revolution – God's Judgement – What revolutionaries – Collapse of a dream – A town whose name matters not – A page mourns – Posthumous caress – A cross after all – A broken horse

They sleep out in the open, like wedding guests who refuse to abandon the place where, for one night at least, they were happy. Are they happy? The party ends and they wait for something, but they don't know what. Day breaks and the sun illuminates the corpses of peasants and federales equally. The factory's smoking ruins and behind it the horizon, as distant and impossible as always. Riders who gallop back and forth, swarming over the land that once belonged to the Patrón, the body that was part of his body. What to make of that land now, to whom does it belong, upon whose flesh do they sleep and wait?

Because the Patrón is dead, they remind themselves. The Patrón is dead, they repeat, as incredulous as if they were pronouncing the death of God Himself. Now they huddle around God's corpse and observe their work. Men and women who slowly remove their hats, still courteous, still small before the Patrón's stiff and mutilated body. No one says a word. They loiter, leaning on their rifle butts, as if they were peasants again, chins propped on the handles of their farm implements.

One voice that rises. Juan kneeling beside the cadaver, turning the disfigured face toward the light. Juan wiping away the blood with a handkerchief.

197

Stopping mid-motion. This isn't the Patrón, he says slowly, and it's unclear whether there is condemnation or consolation in his words. He must repeat himself twice before the others react: this isn't the Patrón. This isn't the Patrón. The man's murderers frozen with the same countenance, puzzlement bordering on a dream. They don't understand or perhaps it is Juan who doesn't understand. Of course it's the Patrón, one murderer finally says, spitting on the ground. I think it's the Patrón, says a young man, almost a boy, kicking the dead man's leg. The Patrón, the Patrón, that son of a bitch. But still Juan shakes his head, staring at the face of a man who is too old, too white.

He might be the patrón, Juan concedes, getting to his feet. But he's not the Patrón. Of course he's the señor Patrón! a woman shouts, midway between indignation and scorn. The *señor* and the capital P still tied to his name, accompanying him to the grave. I'd know the man who took my land, says another. He burned down my house. My cows died of thirst because of him. He ordered my brother's death; no matter how worm-eaten he is, how rotten his intestines, I will never forget his face. Voices that overlap, that confirm the impossible: this is the Patrón, we killed him, death to the Patrón, Viva la Revolución. Still Juan disputes the evidence, but no one heeds him now. He's drunk, someone laughs. Is Juan drunk? No time to decide: already the peasants are hoisting the bloody corpse onto their shoulders, carrying it to the base of a telegraph pole, like a criminal is brought to the pillory or a lamb to the sacrificial stone. A noose, produced from who knows where. The noose that soars, many hands conspiring in a single effort, and the Patrón's body—the Patrón's body?—rising, rising overhead, until it is left upside down and swinging. Now, even at the moment of death, he rises higher than anyone else. The Patrón who seems, momentarily, to writhe, who swings before his children's impassible gaze, hands clawing at the air, the final death rattle of a crucified man with no cross or compass.

Throughout what remains of the day, the peasants loot the spoils of the factory. They take everything: charred desks, disconnected lamps, a tapestry miraculously saved from the fire. A spool of cable that serves no function and never will. A mechanical loom that requires twenty men to drag it off who knows where. Somebody stripping a corpse to take his dress coat, his boots, his silver watchchain. Men and horses roaming like sleepwalkers through the still-smoldering ruins. And other men, many men, distributing old rifles and cartridge belts and setting off north, in search of another factory, another Patrón, another dream.

Juan sits at the foot of the post, the bullseye at the epicenter of a catastrophe, an immovable rock at the heart of a collapsing world. Above him, the Patrón's body sways, stirred by the breeze. On Juan's knees, the book open to the likeness and his eyes that travel from the corpse to the book and the book to the corpse. Futile diligence, since the dead man's features—what is left of his features—contain no similarity, no ambiguity upon which to build hope's foundation. Though perhaps "hope" isn't the right word, Juan thinks. Because if Juan the Indian really was the Patrón; if Juan's hands, among many others, had participated in his killing, then, then what. What would his journey mean. What sense could he make of all he had experienced up to now, how could he know, in the end, whether he loved Juan the Indian or despised him, whether he celebrated his death or condemned it. There would be no one to tell him whether this world was the world Juan the Indian dreamed of, the building that—in order to be perfected—had needed walls and a roof built over its foundations. Everything is much simpler if the Patrón is just the Patrón and Juan the Indian is somewhere else, above or below ground, but somewhere else; and, simultaneously, much more difficult, because it means Juan must look back, to the south; he must review every choice, every detour on his route, every day spent in the city or the desert, every insignificant assumption, in an attempt to locate the moment he took a wrong turn and Juan the Indian stopped being Juan the Indian.

A boy, removed from the traffic of men who come and go, has sat down beside him. He nibbles on a dry corn cob and looks over Juan's shoulder at the Padre's useless portrait.

"Who's that?" he asks in his soft serf's voice.

Juan opens his mouth. Closes it.

"I don't know," he says at last.

The boy gives an energetic nod, as if not knowing was the most natural thing in the world. But he doesn't move away. He eats his corn and observes the nameless face, nothing but just a drawing after all.

Three or four other boys join them, as if magnetized by the first child's words. One of them has a cigarette in his mouth and a rifle as tall as his body. One glance at the book suffices to make him speak.

"It's the Compadre," he says simply, cigarette between his lips.

Juan looks at the boy and at the book and at the boy again.

"This isn't the Compadre," he begins to explain with all the patience he can muster. "It's . . ."

He doesn't finish the sentence; he has nothing to say.

Suddenly, more men, more women. Peasants who drop a painting in a gilded frame or a pair of practically new boots and come to crowd around the book. The book that begins to travel from hand to hand, no less of a marvel than the Patrón himself. The children who stand on tiptoe and day laborers who touch its covers with illiterate fascination, with muck-stained or bloodstained hands, and finally lay eyes on the portrait.

"The Compadre!" an old man says and crosses himself.

Then, as if the old man's tongue had lit upon a sacred word, all cry at once. "It's true! The Compadre! Yes, it's him!"

The Compadre, Juan thinks, like one receiving a whiplash. The Compadre. He hears the sounds from the day before, the echo reverberating on the plain. The voice of the people chanting his name, Compadre, Compadre, Compadre. He sees him or recalls seeing him in the distance, up on the wagon to commence his rally, so small and so blurry and so far away that he could be any man. He sees him closer up, half his face concealed by his huge palm sombrero; a hat that could hide any face. He sees him, lastly, fighting very nearby, so close that Juan had only needed to reach out in order to touch his body; but by then night has fallen in his memory and the night is impenetrable and that body is not a body but a wild guess.

The Compadre, he thinks.

The Compadre, he remembers.

Abruptly, he retrieves the book. He holds it high overhead for all to see. They say this man is the Compadre. Are they sure? He asks each of them, each one of those men and women who are like in ecstasy over his image, an image no less sacred than the very countenance of Christ himself. Juan, almost shouting. Are they sure? Would they swear it on the Bible? On this Bible, for instance?

The peasants, the soldiers, are momentarily silent. They find his question ridiculous. They no longer look at the portrait; they're looking at Juan. Why wouldn't they be sure of what they saw with their own eyes, they seem to say. They say it: How could we be mistaken about this, señor. They might not know about books or fancy little drawings, a man says, but they know unmistakably who the Compadre is. Because if they won't forget the Patrón's face, no matter how worm-eaten, no matter how rotten, they certainly won't forget the face of the Compadre, God raise him to Paradise. And they can swear that the Compadre has just one face and that's the face they are looking at right now, drawn on that piece of paper before them. Does the señor doubt it? That the Compadre has just one face? That the Compadre is the Compadre?

And then Juan asks the question to which no answer is possible. He wants to know who the Compadre is, where he comes from, what is his given name. If that name isn't, by chance, Juan. But nobody can tell him anything about names or origins. We already told you: the Compadre is the Compadre. He's like us: his only mother is the land and sweat is his only father. His name is everyone's name. The Compadre was born in Monterrey or Torreón, on the Durango agave plantations or the sugar mills of Morelos: what does it matter. There is one land and all men are one as well. The Compadre is the father of each and every one of them. The Compadre is a servant and the served. We, they say, are the Compadre. You're looking for the Compadre and the Compadre is here and here and there. If you shoot a carbine, if you shout long live the revolution and death to the oppressors, then you are the Compadre too. The Compadre has always led the revolution, since long before the revolution began. Maybe long before the Compadre himself was even born. Where is the revolution? Well, that's precisely where the Compadre will be. That, or somewhere like it, is what they say. Then they are silent.

And the revolution, Juan knows full well, can only lie to the north.

To the revolution, one always arrives either too late or too early. It is hard, perhaps impossible, to catch it at the exact moment. At times along the way, Juan comes across a burned-down ranch or a corpse stranded in a ditch and he knows the Compadre has just departed. Other times, there's nothing, no estates in ruins or dead landlords, and that can only mean the Compadre hasn't yet arrived. He'll arrive later or he'll never arrive at all: who can say. The only thing left to do is walk. Walk faster. Never fast enough to catch up to the dream that rides on horseback, over rails, over telegraph wires.

But to try, nonetheless. The dream of the revolution rushing blindly toward the future, like a driverless, horseless coach, if such a coach were possible. And yes, it is possible: at that very moment, Juan sees a stagecoach rush past, a coach that is all machine and all metal, galloping down the road with no engine but human desire. That horseless carriage is the revolution. The revolution is that coach and the horizon toward which it heads.

He leaves a town where they know nothing about the Compadre and another where they know too much. The Compadre, a boy with his arm in

201

a sling tells him, is hope. The Compadre is the Devil, whispers a priest. The Compadre is our redeemer, a woman confesses behind her shuttered windows. And so on, one after another, until he has exhausted all the village faces. The Compadre is a calamity no less terrible than the drought and the Patrón. The Compadre is México, México's soul. The Compadre is a dream, but like all dreams he is made from the stuff of nightmares. The Compadre is the past or he is the future. The Compadre is very handsome, sighs a girl selling lemonade in the main square; the Compadre kills federales and landowners but, first and most of all, he kidnaps pretty girls and I wish I were a pretty girl, or just that the Compadre thought I was a pretty girl, even if it were just for a few days, one night even, I could be beautiful for the Compadre for one whole night, so a brave and handsome boy like his father would grow in my belly. The Compadre, an old man mutters, is nothing but a story they tell children so they'll go early to bed.

Juan keeps walking, never managing to understand. He follows the Compadre because now he cannot do anything else. He has followed him all this time, even when he believed he was condemning or betraying him. But he did not condemn him, he did not betray. He burnt down a factory that had appeared to correspond to the Compadre's dream, but which turned out to be an obstacle the Compadre himself detested. He was hired to destroy the Compadre's world, the Compadre's Work, and yet here he is, converted into his only witness. He, Juan thinks, is the living testimony that an Indian called Juan began a journey that has not yet ended. And now he is here, he has come so far, contemplating his life as one contemplates a road with no forks or shortcuts; a path that has always led to the Compadre, that will, perhaps, always lead to the Compadre.

To walk is all that remains. Walk faster. Never fast enough to get answers to his questions. To know whether the world he sees before him is the Compadre's kingdom or simply the means necessary to forge it. Left behind are the men hanged at the crossroads and the walls shelled by firing squads and the women who raise their white hands to the heavens. Are they the revolution, as well? Sometimes Juan is surprised to find himself observing their sun-bloated corpses as if they weren't entirely real: just the bloody, worthless skin a snake must shed to keep on living. Other times, he can't help but feel infinite compassion for each one of those anonymous bodies, innocent or guilty, and then they don't seem like the simple shedding of skin. Suddenly, he is convinced that the revolution has no skin at all, in other words, that the revolution is just its skin and nothing but that skin: beyond the victims, there is nothing. The revolution is the very corpse the revolution produces.

Where two roads meet, he comes across a dozen men conversing around a campfire. Some wear humble clothes and cartridge belts in an X across their chests and others wear threadbare uniforms, dusted with all the colors of the plain. It is unclear whether they are peasants dressed up as soldiers or soldiers dressed up as peasants. At the sight of Juan, they exchange a few whispered words. One of the men, who could be a sergeant in the federal army or a guerilla fighter with some authority over the others, wearily gets to his feet. He aims his rifle at him, but something in his movement makes it clear that he does so without any real conviction, like someone who grows bored with a prolonged game of cards but is still set on maintaining the appearances of the game.

"Who are you with?" he says, in a voice that attempts a certain challenge. "With the government or the revolutionaries?"

Juan considers a moment.

"I'm with the men," he says.

The half-soldiers, half-peasants—men, in the end—start to laugh.

"Ah, he's a live one, the gachupín."

They ask no more questions. They pass him a wineskin and give conflicting advice. Don't go that way, they say. It's full of soldiers. Then they point in the opposite direction. Don't go that way, either. The revolutionaries have taken it. After a while, they seem to forget him. While the fire lasts, they talk about thwarted loves, recipes for stew, American tobacco, which might be the best or the worst in the world; of corridos that condense all the good and all the bad this life has to offer. Then they stomp on the still-hot ashes, take their carbines and hats and bid their farewells with certain ceremony. Juan watches them decamp for the south. He doesn't know whether they are for or against the revolution, but decamp they do, all the same.

Pursuing the path of the revolution, Juan thinks, is not unlike swimming upstream. First the calm waters, unanimous, all flowing evenly toward the same delta; then the first bends, the first twists, kinks, divisions; the water increasingly energetic and noisy, rushing just as much to where it wants to go as where it can. The same river that sometimes separates into two or three or twenty, in furious, foaming bifurcations, and then the need to decide which course is correct, which tributary and which river are the true ones; how does one know, in fact, that something called river even exists?

Viva la Revolución, cry the Compadre's men.

Viva la Revolución, cry his enemies.

Viva la Revolución, other men cry, men whom the Compadre cares nothing about.

To find the Compadre, it's enough to follow his arrows. A ransacked palace is an arrow. A landowner bleeding out in a ditch is an arrow, as well. Sometimes, on the side of the road, he comes across rows of bodies hanging from telegraph posts, swinging like sacks. Men who were not revolutionary enough. Or maybe revolutionaries who weren't men enough. To their fronts, someone has pinned signs on which the dead men confess their crimes. I supplied grain to the federales. I oppressed my workers. I believed this land was mine. I was not a true revolutionary. For a long time, Juan stands and looks at those bodies and the words suspended upon them, as one contemplates a divine act whose intention cannot be understood nor questioned. The lettering on the signs is all the same. It is the Padre's handwriting. Juan recognizes it immediately. The same fierce, fevered script with which he brought the word of God into Castilian; so many verses in tiny, cramped handwriting, so many passages underlined or crossed out or circled in ink, that only now seem to make sense.

He remembers: Do not think that I came to send peace to the earth. I did not come to send peace, but the sword. For I have come to set a man against his father, and the daughter against her mother, and the daughter-in-law against her mother-in-law.

He remembers: Then He made a whip of small cords and drove them all out of the Temple, with the sheep and oxen; and poured out the changers' money; and overthrew their tables.

He remembers: He who spares his rod hates his son, but he who loves him disciplines him.

He remembers: And the angel thrust his sickle into the earth, and gathered the vine of the earth, and cast it into the great winepress of the wrath of God. And the winepress was trodden without the city, and blood came out of the winepress, even unto the horse bridles.

The Compadre has his own tongue: a language that both friends and enemies have had time to learn on their flesh. Visiting a town means destroying it. A mass means a war council. The campesinos who defend their landlords are

were neither in favor of the revolution nor against it. If only you had been either hot or cold, they say the Compadre told them solemnly before he put a bullet in their heads. They also say he ordered the execution of the man who had been his best friend, General Tagle, all because General Tagle, who was, by the way, a man more courageous and resolute than most, had deviated just a smidgeon from the Compadre's thinking. But how not to deviate from the Compadre's thinking even a teensy bit; how to correctly follow his many commands if those commands were always changing. Because in every town they visited, after every shootout suffered, the Compadre would be assaulted constantly by new ideas, brilliant ideas, revelations that blinded him with their fiery splendor and later left him dazed for days or weeks. After his illuminations, everything in him seemed to burn; it was unbearable to look in his eyes, to enter the abyss of eyes that had seen so luminous and so deep, just like sunlight can burn even when reflected off the water. Then he would return to himself, filled with new ideas and hungering to bring them to fruition. For instance, first he said that the Good Lord Jesus was on their side; that if God had made his son to be born in a stable in México instead of Bethlehem, that same Christ would have fought and suffered in their ranks. Then he said that Christ's silence was suspicious. That was his word: suspicious. That, in the end, all silence was a twisted form of speech: a voice complicit with the powerful and exploitative. Then, following another of his revelations, he added that Christ was not complicit with Evil but Evil itself: he hadn't died to wipe away the sins of men, but to forgive and justify and uphold the sins of the caudillos on Earth, and of those other caudillos, the priests. They even say that, in one village, he ransacked the parish church. Take and eat of Him, all of you, for this is His body, he said, throwing the golden chalice and many precious stones from the sanctuary into the villagers' hungry hands. Then he celebrated a summary trial against the Christ chiseled on the cross. He forced dozens of witnesses to the pulpit to provide testimony against that piece of timber, which, according to His custom, remained silent. And finally, the Compadre himself stepped up to the pulpit, Bible in hand, to recite a few words that a now-silent God had spoken through his servant Paul: the slaves who submit to their masters; who try to please them and do not question them, the Compadre said that Paul said that God said; who does not steal but shows themselves to be worthy of full confidence, will draw praise for the doctrine of God our Savior. He read still many more sayings and passages that condemned the accused, because the Compadre was well-versed in the Sacred Scriptures, like a soldier who knows his enemies' thoughts and strategies better than anyone. They also say he ordered a summary execution of that enemy, under his very own roof; the firing squad squaring off against the altarpiece and blowing Christ's image to smithereens. His figure annihilated in a storm of sawdust and splinters and returned to what it has always really been: nothing but a piece of wood.

Where two roads meet, he comes across a dozen men conversing around a campfire. Some wear humble clothes and cartridge belts in an X across their chests and others wear threadbare uniforms, dusted with all the colors of the plain. It is unclear whether they are peasants dressed up as soldiers or soldiers dressed up as peasants. At the sight of Juan, they exchange a few whispered words. One of the men, who could be a sergeant in the federal army or a guerilla fighter with some authority over the others, wearily gets to his feet. He aims his rifle at him, but something in his movement makes it clear that he does so without any real conviction, like someone who grows bored with a prolonged game of cards but is still set on maintaining the appearances of the game.

"Who are you with?" he says, his voice an attempt at a challenge. "The government or the revolutionaries?"

Juan considers.

"I'm with the men," he says.

Nobody laughs. Not the sergeant in the federal army or guerrilla fighter with some authority, who doesn't relax his stance or lower his rifle.

"We're all men here," he explains wearily. "So if you're one, too, have the courage to give us an answer."

Juan looks at the faces one by one, imploring the men for a sign that doesn't come. In the end, places his trust in the Compadre's memory:

"With the revolutionaries."

They are not satisfied.

"Bloody hell, man, we knew that already. But speak now—where are you headed, to Villa or Carranza?"

Juan considers.

"I'm headed to México."

The half-soldiers, half-peasants—Mexicans, in the end—laugh.

"Ah, he's a live one, the gachupín."

They ask no more questions. They pass him a bottle of tequila and give conflicting advice. Don't go that way, they say. It's full of Villa's men. Then they point in the opposite direction. Don't go that way, either. Carranza's people have taken it. After a while, they seem to forget him. While the fire lasts, they talk about the good men they've seen die and the bastards who are still standing; they talk about northern women, who are undoubtedly more beautiful but less willing than the women in the south; about the Virgin of Guadalupe, who grants her blessings to one side or the other, depending on her mood. Then they stomp on the still-hot ashes, take their carbines and hats and bid their farewells with certain ceremony. Juan watches them decamp for the south, he doesn't know if they are for or against the Compadre, but decamp they do, all the same.

On the hilltop, a burned church: the toppled belltower, the beams like twisted ribs of a wrecked ship, the toppled saints abused and hacked with machetes and riddled with bullets. In the ruins of the apse, it is still possible to make out the defaced table that was once the altar, blackened by fire. In the recess that harbors Christ on the cross, someone has stood a carbine on its end, dressed in a peasant's poncho. This is our new religion, they say the Compadre said as he lit God's house aflame. Because it was the Compadre who destroyed the church, who dragged the pews and the chairs to feed the flames, who shot his .30-30 Winchester at the church bell while it still hung in its gable. Ding. In the beginning, this was all I had, they say he said as he lifted his rifle over his head for all to see: now, he continued, I have the world. And they say that as the flames swallowed the central nave, the Compadre shouted over the fire's roar that God did not exist; that God was nothing but a dream dreamed up by the rich to feed the nightmares of the poor. God is a very old idea, he said, brandishing his rifle before the villagers, and we are here to give you new ones. Ideas like this. Ideas that will be your dreams and their nightmare. And they say that while the church burned—and the truth was it burned for many hours; for a whole night and part of the next day—the Compadre talked and talked, never tiring. He said that, until that moment, he too had believed, and thought, and dreamed: he had felt pity or hope or fury for that corpse yoked to two crossed pieces of timber. Now, they say the Compadre said, I know the truth. The only God, he said, pointing to his belly, is this. The only miracle, he added, raising his right fist, is here. The only Paradise, the only Hell, he said, gesturing to the flaming church—and perhaps the village around it; and to the world beyond the village—is this.

Juan picks his way through the rubble and sees, emerging here and there, a torn cassock or a headless saint or a man's scorched hand. Under the still intact portico, he finds three fallen scarecrows; three scarecrows which are, in reality, three dead priests. They don their ceremonial chasubles, stained with dirt and blood, and though they are sprawled on the ground, their murderers have troubled themselves to stick their ecclesiastical caps on their heads and missals in their clawed hands. Someone has hung a cardboard sign around each of their broken necks, and on them a few blurred letters can be read, as if the priests, though dead, were speaking.

I loved the tithe more than the Church, says the first dead priest.

I loved the Church more than Christ, whispers the second.

I loved Christ more than mankind, confesses the last.

The name of the village isn't important. It is a village like so many others, with little limewashed houses, parish church, and vegetable gardens; a small square, dirt corrals, and adobe walls; a cantina, on whose threshold a drunk like any other drunk is dozing. Juan stops to ask the man the same question he always asks. He opens the book. Shows him the portrait. The drunk barely reacts, blinking once. He looks at him from the bloodshot depths of his vinous eyes and doesn't say a word. Then he points to a specific part of town. The gesture is as natural as if the man were giving Juan directions to the lavatory.

"What's over there?" Juan asks. He hasn't yet understood.

"The Compadre." The drunk closes his eyes and goes back to swatting away the flies that dot his face.

And then he sees him. The Compadre, or the Compadre's men. In the distance, they are nothing but a handful of little white dots, one or two hundred little dots, white and immobile, almost filling the small cemetery. Juan approaches slowly, as if, after so long on the road, he wanted to delay the end of his journey. He sees them more clearly with every step, their carbines like shepherds' crooks. Their peasant clothing crisscrossed with cartridge belts. Some cry silent tears. Others observe the turned earth with remote expressions. All hold their sombreros tight to their chests as they stand in a circle around the fresh grave. They barely look up at Juan when he joins them to pay his respects; his own hat clutched in his right hand.

One by one he studies their forsaken faces, streaked with tears and dust and blood. No sign of the Compadre. Then he looks at the humble coffin, which would appear to hold a fallen comrade-at-arms. Two carbines are lashed together and stuck in the dirt as a makeshift cross.

"Who is the dead man?" Juan inquires, in a whisper, of the nearest mourner.

The man meets his gaze with unhinged eyes, the eyes the newly-orphaned. With that one look, Juan understands.

In the dark interior of his saddlebag, the Padre's book, and inside its closed pages, the darkest page yet, smudged and soaked and dressed in mourning by the Padre and his inkwell. Juan thinks suddenly of the tenebrous page that has so often intrigued him, and of the underlined verses that accompany it.

He remembers: Verily, verily I say to you, unless the grain of wheat falls into the ground and dies, it remains alone. But if it dies, it brings forth much fruit.

He remembers: All flesh is like grass and all its glory like the flower of grass. The grass withers, and the flower falls, but the word of the Lord remains forever.

He remembers: For where there is a Testament, there must be the death of the one who made it.

It can't be the Compadre. That is all he can think as two men spit on their palms and take up the spades to finish the digging. This is not the Compadre's burial. This is not his grave. These four wooden boards are not his kingdom. And yet, the men weep as if it were. And yet, the men, the Compadre's men, whisper how they watched him die in their arms. That corpse is the corpse of the Revolution. Who killed it? No bullet, no betrayal, no battle. The Compadre, explains one of the men, his voice breaking, simply fell from his horse. He points to the animal tied to the cemetery fence. Who would have ever imagined: his own horse. Old Thunder. Because the Compadre had so many enemies and it was reasonable that any one of them should have eventually hit his mark. His enemy was the Church. His enemies were the federales. His enemies were those men who called themselves revolutionaries and were not, just below the surface, true revolutionaries. His enemies were the enemies of the people, which are, to be sure, infinite. And yet it was Thunder who killed him; Thunder who seemed, at times, to be his only friend: the only one who always knew where the Compadre wanted to go and took him there. It's true that the Compadre had been very drunk when he mounted the horse, he could hardly stand on two feet, but, if one considers it coolly, when was it any different? When was the last time they saw the Compadre sober? And it's also true that for some time now, Thunder had become wilder than he used to be, he allowed no one but the Compadre to ride him and even then, he was wont to buck and kick and gallop with such vehemence that the very ground seemed to flee from under his hooves. That horse, progressively fast and mad and wild, like the Revolution itself. The Compadre was the horse that the revolution's riders stopped knowing how to ride. The Compadre was Thunder, and only Thunder could put an end to Thunder.

Juan listens to their explanations. As he does so, he observes the horse beside the cemetery fence. Seen from this distance, grazing with a peaceful, vaguely meditative air, he doesn't look like a wild horse, much less a horse capable of killing a man. There is something unreal in the soldier's words, something of a tale with an air of truth when told around a campfire, but which by the light of day, takes the shape of what it really is: an old wives' tale. The words of the Compadre's men are just that, Juan thinks; Juan decides. Old wives' tales. Because the Compadre cannot be dead. Or perhaps he could be, he admits. Maybe somebody's compadre has died, yes, and this is his grave, and those his sons, but that someone is not, cannot be, the genuine Compadre. There is no way this is the man he is looking for, the man he has pursued through so many villages and deserts and cities. To prove it, he rummages in his saddlebag and takes out the book. The glint of the Bible's gold lettering makes some soldiers' eyes flash with anger or suspicion. But Juan isn't planning to murmur any prayer, any Latin verse: he's only finding the right page to show them the Compadre's portrait.

Five or six heads abandon their scowls of grief to squint at the open book. Their mouths, their voices, swell with shock. It's the Compadre! they whisper. The Compadre's spitting image! A soldier brushes a grimy fingertip over the inked wrinkles of the likeness.

"How much are you asking?" he whispers, like one who covets a holy relic. "I'll give you a peso!"

"It's not for sale." Juan returns the book to his saddlebag.

"I'll give you two pesos!"

"I'll give you ten!"

"Fifty pesos!"

The spade stuck in the turned earth of the burial mound. Four men securing the coffin with rope and lowering it with delicacy, almost loving care. The Compadre's body deposited at the bottom of the grave. And following that act, a long silence. The men look askance at one another. An uncomfortable pause during which time there is nothing else to do: no hymn to intone, no prayer, no sermon.

No hope of future life, since they've made a whole revolution out of proving the meaninglessness of those prayers, those hymns, those sermons. There is no life after this one to justify it. And now, the man who aspired to destroy the dream of religion awaits consecration in the dirt, without a priest and with a cross made of rifles, yet a cross, after all.

Among the men who wait in their white clothes and cartridge belts, Juan makes out a small bundle. It is a very young, very frail woman whose beauty seems to wither inside her mourning dress. She is flanked by two men who look like lieutenants or minor caudillos and who hold her by the arms, as if they feared she would collapse and fall into the grave.

Who is that woman? Juan whispers into the ear of the nearest man. She is the Little Widow, the owner of that ear replies. The Little Widow? Yes; the Little Widow. The Compadre's last sweetheart. Because the Compadre left behind many a widow, he says; many women who are now mourning, inconsolable, and who will mourn their loss for as long as they live.

With new eyes, Juan looks at her. He looks at her eyes: they are dry. Men offer her, continually, a shoulder to cry on, but the Little Widow does not weep. Her humble legs, legs of a fieldworker or maybe a washerwoman, stand inside a pair of fine patent-leather shoes, too fine, perhaps, because to see her is to know that this is the first time in her life that she has worn a pair of dress shoes. Juan observes her body at length; slightly bowed, like a flower with a bent stem. He observes her skin, or what her dress permits him to see of her flesh: the flesh the Compadre perhaps kissed and caressed and licked. He tries to see her through his eyes. To see her just as he saw her for the first time, with the eyes of desire, not pity. He's not sure he has managed.

Someone, at some point, gives the signal. Again, the gravediggers spit on their hands and begin to patiently fill the hole with all the dirt they'd previously removed. Juan hears the spadesful of dirt drum on the wood and wonders what this final rain would sound like from inside; what would the dead think of the manner in which we distance ourselves from them, if the dead were to think anything at all.

All those gathered wait, motionless, before the increasingly small grave, as if they expected the miracle of resurrection. Only the Little Widow refuses to wait for this miracle. The gravediggers have only just begun their task when, abruptly, she frees herself from her companions' arms. The crowd parts respectfully to allow her to pass. Before he steps aside, Juan believes her eyes, the Little Widow's eyes, momentarily alight on his own. A fleeting look, as brief as a flicker of thought; so brief that a second after it happens, it no longer seems real. He watches her move slowly away, almost stumbling in her too-fine shoes. For an instant, he imagines himself walking beside her. Taking her arm, perhaps, like the Compadre surely did so many times. What would he ask the Little Widow? What would they talk about, if they were to talk?

The Little Widow leaves first. Then, their work complete, the gravediggers depart, spades on their shoulders. One by one, the Compadre's sons silently don their hats and leave too, fists tightly closed over the coins they will spend in the cantina. Tonight they will drink many glasses of tequila and many glasses of moonshine, and between draughts they will tell each other stories, perhaps, about the Compadre; orphans who laugh and cry all at once and who won't sleep or will sleep very little before climbing back into the saddle and taking their pain and rage out for a walk in nearby towns. None of them seem to remember Thunder, or Juan. The gravesite becomes more and more solitary, until there is no one is left to watch it. Only Juan. Watching. Only Juan, standing and asking himself whether this really is the end of his journey.

Yes, he says to himself. The journey ends here, in a small village's small cemetery, in an impoverished region whose name doesn't matter. The Compadre chose this place to stop, and here is where he must stop as well.

And yet, he says to himself. And yet, maybe it is nothing, after all; nothing but a huge mistake. He remembers the many times the Compadre seemed dead or defeated or wiped off the face of the Earth, only to keep walking. He remembers the many confusions that brought him, after so many twists and turns, to this very spot. He remembers the Padre surviving, against all odds, among the Chichimeca savages. The Padrecito rotting in a jail nobody leaves, but which he ultimately left. He remembers the dead Patrón who wasn't, in the end, the genuine Patrón. Who's to say this isn't what's happening right now. The Compadre, at least the genuine Compadre, can't be dead. Not just because it's absurd to imagine him falling off his horse; absurd, actually, to imagine him falling anywhere. Not just because nobody but God—a diminished version of God, an animus of God made flesh—could have made it so far with nothing but the strength of his bare hands. He can't be dead because if he were, Juan's journey would be devoid of meaning. And so Juan clings to that handgrip of hope, like one puts his faith in floating driftwood after a shipwreck.

Thunder waits, tethered to the cemetery fence, black coat splendid in the last of the evening light. He waits very still, as if he were deep in thought, or brooding over his grief. Nobody has wanted to take responsibility for him: nobody has loosened his bridle or granted him the grace of a bullet between the eyes. Only Juan goes near, slowly at first. Softly, he rests his palm on the horse's neck. The animal barely moves. Easy, Thunder, Juan murmurs, as perhaps the Compadre did many times before. Thunder seems about to kick, but does not. It seems the horse might turn against Juan, against Juan's attempts, but does not. Finally, Juan dares to climb into the saddle and Thunder accommodates his weight without surprise or resistance, as if he were accepting the company of an old comrade-at-arms.

"Let's go, Thunder," Juan says softly, and Thunder sets off with the obedience of a trained circus animal.

The sun is sinking on the horizon and now its light barely grazes the mound at the gravesite. Juan dons his sombrero, spurs the horse, and chooses not to look back. As he leaves the village, he hears the strumming of a guitar and the first booze-slick notes of the corridos originating from the cantina. From his distance, he can hardly decipher the lyrics, but he knows very well the tales they tell: stories of men and women who die so that the truth of their song might survive them.

X

Living inside a corrido – The empty shell of a pair of eyes – To mount a horse and to mount a beloved – The long road home – A victim of the revolution – Gathering the bullets – The hour of angelus – Forty-eight dreams – Crucifixion of a dream – Through the curtains – A husband's desire – Three bullets in the belly

What comes next doesn't exactly happen in time. It is the story, or not even a story, of a return. Juan retracing his steps, going round and round the place where he lost the Compadre's trail, like a grayhound that turns in ever-widening circles until it collects the missing kill. But Juan isn't going to find anything, and in some sense, even he knows it. Only the towns where he has already been, the same inscrutable faces and the same narrow cots in the same inns, mangers where the Compadre's horse chews the same alfalfa. Coming from the main square, a square that is always rather small and rather sad, the strum of the same songs. And Juan feels himself travel the landscape of those songs, he inhabits the inside of a corrido where the same things come to pass, the bandit dying over and over in the voice of every man, accompanied by every guitar; the always-young and always-lonely girl who mourns her inconsolable and eternal love. And the Compadre continues to be effectively dead in every town, dead or vanished forever, what does it matter: the Compadre is like a dream shared by all throughout the course of a particularly long night. Now it is day again. The sun lights the Compadre's grave, buried in every cemetery. Executed against this wall. The Compadre, you know, was killed by the federales, right here. They were other revolutionaries, Carranza's men; I saw it with my own eyes. The

215

Compadre, listen to me good, the Compadre was murdered by his own men, like Christ was crucified by his brothers. The Compadre was here and there; he spoke of this and that; and at the precise moment of his many deaths, he said a good number of last words.

They can kill me, but they can't stop the revolution.

Or:

I have been a loyal man whom destiny brought to the world to fight for the good of the poor and until today, the day of my death, I have never betrayed or forgotten my duty.

Or:

Don't let me die like this . . . Say I said something.

The Compadre turned into an idea. The Compadre, a scarecrow to shake to scare the children who won't go to sleep: the Compadre will take you away with him, loaded onto the black rump of his black horse. The Compadre as another figure on the altarpieces, a profane saint to thank for the peace that doesn't come, the freedom that doesn't come, the lands that don't come yet but will come, one day very soon: long live the Compadre and long live the revolution and long live the government. The revolution doesn't stop nor does it advance, a wild horse we tie to a worn-out wheel: the horse that turns and the wheel that spins and the illusion of movement that fills the miller's hands with yellow flour. Images of what's been already lived come out to meet Juan on his path: wisps of a revolution that is all word and smile and celebration. Skyrockets instead of shots and promises the peasants gum inside their homes instead of bread. Viva la Revolución! they continue to shout, their backs bent over the plowed furrows, their heads bent under the sun; on their knees in the dirt to pick cotton or sow corn. Death to the latifundia! they shout still, almost aphonic with joy, and the local bosses who never tire of smiling or being happy either. Revolutionaries too, the tax collectors and bankers and government delegates who continue inaugurating bridges and handing out pieces of paper that will someday be pieces of land, and the peasants who still save those small treasures under their mattresses, like one rotting away with hope. Viva la revolución, they repeat, although they themselves are, in fact, already dead: dead men who smile and sing during the harvest and get religiously drunk on pay day.

Until one day. A day that is perhaps not a day, but a night or a fragment of a night: a moment when perhaps Juan can't sleep, tossing and turning in another narrow cot in another narrow inn. Or a dusk when he is camping out in the open in the middle of nowhere and contemplates, as if comprehending the glow of his own fire, the shapes of the fire that change over the unchanging earth. That day, that night, somehow or other, Juan gives up. Hours later, he comes across another peasant, a peasant with a hoe, not a rifle, with a hat but without land or hope, and he asks him a different question. Words in which, for the first time, there is no space for the Compadre. The circle must be broken somewhere and Juan starts with a simple question. And the answer to that question leads him to cross the circle he himself has drawn; a return that is, this time, in some way, a journey and a story. That same night he arrives, like a sleepwalker, at the beginning of that story. It is the cemetery where the Compadre's body rests. It is at a distance of just one hundred paces from the Little Widow's house. Everything in it appears as though stopped in time, expectant: two inanimate hens who sleep as if sunk into their own bodies; a dog tied to the porch, barking indolently. Juan jumps out of the saddle and heads straight for the door. His footsteps are not his own. They are another's, his feet and his eyes that look at everything or everything the waxing dark lets be seen: the humble threshold and the drooping vegetable garden and the girl who comes out in a nightdress to receive him, holding an oil lamp. She doesn't seem surprised. She doesn't seem anything: no expression on her face reveals a human feeling. She motions with her free hand, what could be an invitation or a reproach. Then she disappears behind the bead curtain that hides the door. Still, Juan stands and waits a few seconds, unsure. The dog, which in the meantime has abandoned all pretense of ferociousness, walks to come sniffs his hands. Otherwise, there is no change, no sound. He sees, before him, the steadying of the curtain, the beads swinging ever more gently, until they stop. Only then, when it seems like he won't, does he decide that, yes, he wants to enter.

The first night, the girl asks him not to hurt her. It's all she says, don't hurt me, as she waits for him, already naked, her body exquisite and fragile in the middle of the ugliness of everything, her two hands hidden behind her back and those hands resting on the edges of the cot, as if she were afraid to fall. Who isn't afraid to fall sometimes, Juan thinks, as if in a dream. He wants to tell the girl it isn't necessary, that what is about to happen can happen later or never happen at all, but, set in his face, he still has the eyes of the other, the other's will, his determination, and also a certain sense of return, of doing things twice, infinite times, a stone that sinks endlessly in the water, its fall replicated in increasingly remote circles. His body—Juan's body, which approaches—like the image of another body bouncing off a mirror, a body that doesn't judge nor is entirely free, a puppet of himself, and like this, as if in that mirror, he watches himself walk toward the girl, how many times before has he taken those steps, how many times next to her, he wonders, how many nights and not-nights has he gone near like he goes near now until touching her flesh, which shivers in the warmth and hopeless poverty of her room. The girl's eyes, again, before his own, or the ruins of those eyes before his, her hollow eyes, empty eyes, eyes an empty shell, a gaze that has died and now, perhaps, is revived, eyes open and mouth open and in that a mouth a taste he already knows and the memory of a certain pleasure, the renewal of a certain rite, the sacrificial act of allowing himself to surrender to the bed, in a coming and going of shadows multiplied by the lamplight.

She says it then.

"Don't hurt me."

And Juan obeys. Or perhaps not, who but the girl could say, and the girl doesn't speak, she doesn't moan, she hardly breathes; Juan trying to find in their movements a certain delicacy that escapes, the memory of some tenderness, a vestige of light, the weight of his body like a gesture that imposes itself, that subdues her wordlessly, and the girl who bears it all with her mouth slightly open, all of her body open, her sex open like a wound that never heals, flesh that can be run through and wounded infinite times, and her eyes, open, her eyes, and in the girl's eyes Juan's eyes, and in Juan's eyes the girl's eyes, which seem to radiate and transfer in the room's shadow, a claudication to the blackness in which is no surprise, just the confirmation of something already known but no less unbearable for it. She isn't looking at the ceiling. She isn't looking at the light from the dying lamp. She looks only at him. Inside him. Who knows if right through him. She looks in a terrible way, as one looks at terrible things that have happened and the even more terrible things still to come; eyes divested of all will and all beauty, eyes that have seen horror and are full of it and therefore excruciating to see, or maybe they have seen horror and are empty for that very reason and that emptiness is even more intolerable. Eyes that reflect nothing now, eyes that are what remains of compassion when faith has been erased; freedom, when justice is withheld; will, when it lacks hands and voice. Hope minus hope.

The second night. The third night. Then the fourth and fifth and sixth nights, with their respective mornings, and then their afternoons. And after the seventh night, the seventh day, the days and nights become numberless. Juan who doesn't sleep in the narrow cot of some roadside inn but on the Little Widow's narrow straw mattress, next to her also exceedingly narrow body, so thin it seems he is always looking at her in profile. At daybreak, the girl slips out to light the stove and warm the tortillas, when there are tortillas, and re-steep the coffee, when there is coffee. Juan, still awash on shores of sleep, watches her work in silence from under the covers. Later he will eat the tortillas and drink the coffee while the girl cleans the crockery in a pail with sand or hangs the clothes out to dry or de-kernels ears of corn. They don't speak a word, they hardly look at one another, but in that not-speaking and not-looking there is a kind of communication, like two animals lying together in the sun. Then Juan grunts something, dries his beard on his sleeve, takes his hat from the peg by the door and heads out into the dust of the road. At first he encounters, under the passing hat brims, grim looks, the gachupín, the looks seem to say, only a blasted gachupín would disrespect the Compadre like that, mounting his horse and mounting his beloved, too. But after a few days, not even that matters. They see him sweat in the girl's vegetable plot, chop her wood, repair the dried-out bricks in the walls, take forever with the menial chores full of sweat and shame, and they feel a little placated in their rage. A white man suffering is someone who appears to suffer twice. On one occasion, many days later—how many days?—they even invite him to the village cantina, and Juan makes his glass of aguardiente last with short and reliable sips. They make him talk, and they listen somewhere between enchanted and teasing to the tales Juan carries stuck in his brain, tall tales that have a certain flavor of early colonial chronicles, an old man's legends, and a madman's gibberish. He speaks of Aztecs come back to life and plagues that raze the land and distant viceroyalties and caravels and encomiendas. He speaks of missions that are not missions, since they cannot boast of it in taverns or ports or halls of palaces or fortresses. He speaks of one dog's lonely grave, which he dug with his own two hands. He speaks of a woman who lies buried under the ruins of another tavern which is somewhat reminiscent of this one: a corpse no one bothered to give a proper burial. Those fabulations make them laugh but, after a time, they also make them sad, though they don't know why, their desire to laugh like the contents of a bottle that, sip by sip, also winds up empty, and they listen to the end of the story as if regretful or ashamed and don't look up from their own glasses.

Juan returns with the night. With or without money, Juan always returns. With his shirt dusted or filthy, with something to say or the same silence he left with, once again he is in the tamped dirt entryway, and the girl who waits with the oil lamp in hand and her own silence, a light and a silence that are like an outstretched hand in the dark. Juan grabs that hand to come through the door. Inside, the house has something of a home about it, and also of a temple, and together they nibble some leftovers from lunch, gathered around the domestic altar that is a table where water and bread are shared. From the badly-tiled roof, a few remnants of rain sometimes drip—five leaks, ringing in the depths of five tin pots—but those pots also have something baptismal and sacred about them; four walls to protect them from the storms and the cold and the patrónes. Sometimes Juan brings back a large basket of stones, patiently chosen on the riverbank, and spends the last hours of rest laying them out on the dirt floor, as if living at ground level wasn't enough. The woman watches him from the bed with dry resignation; she sees him sweat and huff and curse, on his knees in unheard supplication. Then they turn out the light, or better still, leave it burning, and they undress and mix with certain human roughness, a certain sense of hurry, a fear of they know not what.

One day—one night—she whispers a tiny loveliness in Juan's ear. Another time, when the thing has finished or appears to have finished, she reaches out to stroke his cheek, his head, his still-heaving chest. Juan looks at length at the hand that has let that tenderness escape. If he is thinking something, he doesn't say it. He arrives so drunk the following night that he can't stay on his feet, and it is the girl who has to take off his boots, his shirt stained with vomit and dirt, his string belt, and it is she, too, who finally climbs atop his body to ride him, without urgency, on a slow and silent journey. From the depths of his drunkenness, Juan sees the girl's body vibrating with its own hunger, her lips parted in something that could be a smile and her gaze filling itself with something, something unknown but which shines like the lamp she lights each night, to guide him on the long way back home.

Sometimes the Compadre is between them, an enormous obstacle at the center of their silence. Juan sees him all of a sudden, sitting on the empty stool and eating with his eyes the tortillas the girl is preparing and eating up the girl, as well, whose back is turned and who pretends not to notice. Everything becomes more complicated those days, the coffee is more bitter and the room is smaller and the feel of their bodies more rough, which bump into each other and get in the way. The floor turns infinite again and he realizes that he will never finish laying the stone, because there aren't enough stones in the river, there aren't enough stones in the whole world, to erase the humbleness of her dirt floor. She spends the rest of the day in an old rocking chair, haughty in her silence, contemplating the dusty light that enters through the window. Who knows what she sees there. What she imagines or remembers. Perhaps she also sees the Compadre, Juan thinks as he takes his hat. Perhaps his return is the reason she sighs when she sighs. Then, from the dust of the road, he turns to look at the reflection of his face in the window. The girl's eyes pass through him like they pass through the glass, without noticing. One would say that she caresses the armrests of her rocking chair as if she felt on them the warmth of a man's hand.

For the rest of the day, Juan looks for someone to give him something to do, hat pressed to his chest. He works or doesn't work under the same inclement sun. He mucks corrals or hoes the dirt or drives the cattle of some landowner who is, like all landowners in recent years, also a revolutionary. Before returning home, he stops in the cantina to drink one or two glasses of aguardiente, with the Compadre still sitting behind him or helping him to down the drink. He remembers, suddenly, that first mezcal the two half-Indian half-brothers gave him to try in the badlands, in times so remote that one would say they had to be unearthed. He thinks about that, about cadavers unearthed. About men who aren't entirely dead, nor completely covered with dirt.

And then the return home. The return home and in it the Compadre's ghost and the girl waiting with her lamp held aloft. He hears his own voice asking about the Compadre, his breath muddied by the mezcal. His name breaking the silence, for the first time. He asks as if he had suddenly decided to resume his search, through the house's miniscule geography. Every unswept corner, every clay gourd, every pile of bedcovers, could be a place where his ghost lies in wait. He wants to know if this is the rocking chair where the Compadre usually sat. Which foods he preferred, which beverages, which side of the bed. He asks if sometimes the Compadre also sat, absorbed, looking at the window, contemplating, on the other side of the glass, everything and nothing all at once. If he ever named the land and the life he left behind, many leagues to the south. What were the things he said and the gestures he used and the things he touched; and among those things, the girl, because sometimes Juan imagines her like that, one more thing the Compadre kept clutched in his fist all the time, like a child who suffocates his favorite toy. Was it her, the girl, that the Compadre wanted most, what he wants most still? But those questions, perhaps the only ones that matter, remain unasked. And the girl resigns herself to answering all the others simply and with a hint of shame.

She says:

"He sat there."

Or:

"On this side."

"He drank mezcal until he dropped; rather, he drank mezcal until the others dropped around him, and he laughed."

"He liked to laugh."

"He liked lamb, when it was available."

"He liked killing."

And it seems she is about to say more, but no, she bites her lip and that is all, he liked killing, he liked killing, period, the girl who continues to wash odds and ends in the bucket of sand or scrubs at the table with the corner of her apron or sits in that rocking chair where, if her words are to be believed, it wasn't the Padrecito who sat.

Another day, intertwined in bed—her hand paused in a frozen caress over his hand; her head on his chest—he asks her what he was like. What was he like? she replies, knowing, perhaps, but still not wanting to know. What was he like, Juan repeats, in a monotone. How was it. What was the Compadre like, there. What was the Compadre like in that same place. In bed, it is understood. On top of her, under her, inside her. Behind her. The girl takes a long time to respond. Her body seems suddenly very faraway, though her caress is still there, her embrace, her hair spilling like a black jellyfish over his chest. He was different, she finally admits. How can she explain. It was, let's say, something that happened for a time and then left nothing. Like a seed that falls on unplowed earth. She's not sure if that explains it—no, no it doesn't explain. He fucked like a soldier, she acknowledges at last. And then, reconsidering: He fucked, sometimes, like a soldier, and other times like a priest.

"Like a priest?"

"Yes."

He won't ask anything else that night; but another day, a day of bitter coffee and the small room, the rocking chair at the window, a day he comes home with breath muddied by mezcal, he will take up the interrupted dialogue, like someone picks up the end of a string. How does a soldier fuck? How does a priest? She considers or pretends to consider. She says you can recognize a soldier because when they start they have a wild impulse, a certain fierce burst, like someone who gorges after they've long been hungry, and sometimes, that hunger hurts, how to explain it, a pain that one feels half in her body and half elsewhere; to fuck with a soldier is, at first, like not being there, they hardly look at you, as if the little soldier was fucking one of his compadres or his own rifle and that's it. But then, when the thing lasts—sometimes it lasts—or rather, when the thing ends and that other face of fucking that isn't fucking but simply being begins, a soldier can transform into something else. All of a sudden, they are children, children whom the war returns, if only for an instant, to their mother's arms. She has it on good authority that this is, most definitely, what soldiers think about; though they make themselves out to be macho and shout viva this and viva that, all they think about are their mothers, though they often don't realize until the moment they die, when life is escaping through their wound and they shout, delirious and impossible, it is then when they cry for their mothers, like children who hurt themselves from so much playing war. That is, more or less, how a soldier fucks, first like someone who eats and then like someone who cries, rather, first like someone who chews and then like someone who only wants Mama.

And how, if it can be known, do priests fuck?

Here the girl's face becomes bitter. Priests, she says, fuck differently, like one gropes a sacred thing, with the scent of perfume and incense and to prevent who knows what sort of things, with thoroughness, with a pleasure from being so pure it ends up having at the bottom of the affair something very dirty, something that rots a girl from the inside, no matter how much the priest in question smiles and strokes the top of your head and says a prayer for you both at the end. That's how the Compadre fucked, sometimes like a soldier and sometimes like a priest; in other words, sometimes like she was a whore and sometimes like she was a mother and other times like she was a saint.

"I understand," says Juan in the dark. But he doesn't actually. He understands so little that hardly a few minutes later, when they begin to undress and their bodies strain to take the same direction as every night, they cannot make it. The error is perhaps there, in the same striving; for the first time between them, the effort of something, the need to see things from outside, the tall order of looking at themselves from outside and from the dark. Their bodies lost in the landscape of the little bed, destined to never find each other or find each other with brutality or clumsiness. In Juan's movements, a voracity whose owner is unknown, or it is known but best not to say, not to remember; his hands that are suddenly claw-like, that cling to flesh, as if they too, the hands, were also prey to another's will. That is how he takes her that night, with another's hands, another's mouth, another's sex, and when he finishes she also seems other and is very distant and very quiet. A heavy and sad silence has set up camp between them, breaths that sound alien and like shame of they know not what.

And then, suddenly, he hears the girl sob. She begins to speak, shielded by the dark, so close and so far from Juan. Her voice is telling a story. In this story, there are revolutionaries who parade up and down the street, ramrod-straight in the saddles of their horses. They parade unnecessarily, only so the marriageable and un-marriageable girls can watch them. One of those men is the Compadre. One of those girls is the girl. And in the beginning, that's how it is, the Compadre who parades with his men and the girls who come out to meet them, uniformed in their Sunday best to battle for love's toy. Among all the girls, the Compadre focuses exclusively on her. As he passes by her, he ceremoniously touches the wide brim of his hat and even the horse turns his gaze to look at her. She, of course, looks at him too. He is so dashing among his men, with his dirty shirt and dirty boots, stained by the dust of the road. They never exchange a single word, but certainly the Compadre made his inquiries, and the next night she has him on her doorstep, a cigar stub between his lips. He has come to steal her, and the girl remembers that, on hearing his horse's trot on the stone entryway, she felt joy and sadness at the same time. But then her father. Her father bursting into the story. Seated in the rocking chair, standing up with his shotgun in his hands. There is a brief conversation between the men, which the girl doesn't hear or doesn't remember. What she does remember is that the shotgun shook in her father's hands and that he didn't even have time to cock it. The Compadre holstered his pistol in the very instant her father collapsed into the rocking chair. His hands died still gripping the shotgun so tightly that they had to bury him with it. The Compadre calmly finished smoking his cigar and told her that nothing could be done that night, he wasn't in the mood anymore, but he would be visiting her again. That she should be ready for that and for everything. He also said that if she had some brother who wanted revenge, he already knew where to find him: at the very heart of the war. But all she has left are two brothers whose mustaches are the only bit of man about them. They couldn't even tear the shotgun from their father's hands. Later the war would take them, too, cowards and all, each to die in the name of a different general.

And she stayed.

She is, still there, simultaneously inside and outside the story, lying in the bed the Compadre must have returned to so many times. Her father dead and her brothers cowards, he didn't even have to steal her. He simply came by when and as frequently as he wished, like a man who returns to the same cantina to get drunk. The Compadre was a monster. The Compadre, she says, her voice sloshing in tears, was wicked. If he knew how much the Compadre had hurt her, on that land and in that house. He had executed men who had wished him neither good nor bad and hanged peasants who never troubled anybody and set fire to churches just because he didn't like what their curate preached. And he had burned and executed her, as well, in a way, in that bed, without even granting her the grace of a blindfold. She is also a victim of the Revolution, she says. Until one day, and that day came later rather than sooner, the Compadre died. Did she see it? No; but I knew it in the instant, I felt it here—and in the darkness, Juan doesn't know if she touches her belly, her head, her heart. And then, after a time, she heard the trot of a horse on the stones out front, and the girl felt terror and hate at the same time. It was a stranger, and he brought the same horse and the same attitude with certain similarities in his restraint and his face. She saw him dismount, spurred by the dog's barking, and for a moment she feared it was him and that her gut had been mistaken. But then. Then what. Then you appeared, the girl says, her voice strangled by the memory. And then she falls silent.

Juan shares that silence for several moments. He tries to imagine it. The Compadre shooting an innocent man, hundreds of innocent men. The Compadre raping a girl. The Compadre, a villain. Those images produce in him both relief and fear. The fear of having traveled a path that wasn't worth it in the end—just a villain's trail. The relief that, in the end, that path led him to where he is, in that too-narrow bed, touching the girl deeper inside than the Compadre ever believed possible.

"And how do I fuck? Like a soldier or a priest?" he asks.

The girl has returned to herself. The girl, who was so far away, suddenly smiles. It is so dark that Juan can't even make out the tiny rectangle of the window and yet he knows this: the girl is smiling. He feels her smile a foot away and even closer the flight of her hand, which comes closer until grazing his face.

"You aren't like that," he hears the smile say. "You are good . . ."

Sometimes, after fucking like a soldier or a priest, the Compadre walked over to the window. Still naked or only half-dressed, but always with his revolver in hand. He pushed the curtain aside with the gun barrel and looked at length at the shadows that crept on the other side. What was he looking at? What was he waiting for? The Little Widow, who wasn't the Little Widow yet, couldn't have said. He seemed to be waiting for someone. At least that was his reply when the girl asked: I'm waiting for someone. Someone who had to arrive and never did.

"Was he waiting for you?" the Little Widow asks in the dark.

"I don't know."

"I think he was. He was waiting for you. Waiting to kill you."

"Maybe it was I who was coming to kill him," Juan replies, and his own voice sounds strange to him.

"Oh, no," she says bitterly. "You're not one of the ones who shoot. You're more like the ones who receive the bullets."

And Juan asks himself how he would have received the Compadre. Would he have been able to shoot after all? Would he have knelt at his feet, like one of his disciples?

Now it's Juan who sits in the rocking chair. Juan who looks out the window. Through the pane he sees snow fall, dry leaves, rain, evenings. He sees the horizon burn at sundown and the same fire swooping over the backs of the men as they reap and sow. Over his own back, too, over his hoe, over his hat. He sees the earth spit out ears of corn that men harvest and women strip of their kernels. He sees starving herds pass by, on their way to empty mangers. The government delegates pass by, as well, every year a different delegate but always the same mustache and the same suit from the capital; he waves in a sign of greeting from inside the car, never stepping out. The peasants run behind that car, in the wake of his promises. The land, our land, they say. All that land worn on their white clothes, in the form of the dust the delegate's car leaves behind. A done deal, waves the delegate's hand. A done deal, a matter of days, confirm the newspapers, the post offices, the knowledgeable. Experts are measuring and remeasuring the land to be distributed; it's a lot of land but they are also many men and they must be patient; just two short weeks of waiting. They toppled tyrants and proved themselves in battle; now, are they not men enough to have a little bit of patience?

Viva la Revolución, they reply.

Viva la Revolución, they plead.

Juan and the girl are patient but also very hungry. They sell the Compadre's horse to lease a scrap of land and a few hectoliters of grain. One day, when the government delegate's car stops, they'll have enough land to lose themselves on; but for the time being, they have only this, a small plot of depleted earth on which they plant a few rows of corn. Juan sees, from the window, the still-green ears. He sees the scarecrow that stands awkwardly among them, crooked and solitary as an actual human being. He sees himself clumsily wielding the hoe, scratching the dirt with implausible hope, like someone trying to shake awake a corpse. There was a time when Juan's clumsiness inspired the locals' laughter, something they even celebrated, perhaps. It inspires nothing now. If anything, a certain discomfiture; the sensation produced when watching a cripple go to great lengths to perform a movement that is commonplace but impossible. He sees himself as useless as a cripple, and the girl bringing him jugs of water, rakes, damp cloths. A wicker basket with the vestige of lunch languishing at its bottom. He sees himself alone again, at the evening Angelus, lighting a cigar—a new habit, picked up who knows where—and looking in the direction of his house, and in that house, his window, and in that window, his own face.

From that window, he also sees things that are not yet, but which might come to be, why not, in just a matter of two weeks. The delegate finally stopping. The government putting its eyes, its giant finger, on the tiny corner of the world that is his town. His little plot growing to encompass all that the eye can see, so vast that it can only be covered on horseback, and to that end, one horse, two horses, the damaged stables raised again and in them, a horse for him and a horse for her and a dozen horses for the foremen. The rows of corn fattening until they burst with kernels and the girl swelling, too, the girl's thin little body that seemed as dry as the dirt but no, neither the woman nor the land were desert, his harvest flourishes and so too does his son, something to see grow before life that stops. He sees that: life, which stops. His son a handsome man by now, with his own horse and his own purpose, giving orders here and there to one hundred, maybe two hundred, overseers. And sitting on the other side of the windowpane, him and her, still him and her, old but not, their eyes young and satisfied with seeing how it grows, the world they built by hand.

Would that be enough? If that was the destiny that awaited him from the beginning, would he have started the journey?

He sees everything from his window: everything except the Compadre. That is to say, he sees the Compadre's absence everywhere. And that absence is neither good nor bad: like the absence it is, it means nothing. It must be accepted without reproach, like one cannot question the night's duration or the desert's length. The Compadre converted into a question, or many questions, and Juan without a single answer. Sometimes he opens the book and contemplates the portrait at length, with the same amazement with which he contemplated the horizon. He recovers a few fragments of the past, scenes that must be laboriously exhumed, as if they came from another life or had happened to another person. He thinks of all the steps that have carried him here and he wonders at which point he lost his way, if there ever was a path to begin with. Is this life? Is this the world he belongs to, or has he arrived at it by chance, like someone who falls off a cliff believing that they are walking? He sees the body of the crucified Indian and a stone cathedral and a cotton factory purified by fire's light. The Compadre, who appeared good or bad by turns, or was, perhaps, good and bad at the same time, capable of setting fire to the world's injustices and of murdering the girl's father, his redeemer's hands digging under her skirt, inside her body. He looks before him—the land without hope, without grain; the peasants whispering long live the Revolution, like a person crying—and asks himself if this is the perfect world the Compadre hoped for. He looks behind him—the bed with its jumble of blankets; the girl kneeling at the stove to stoke the fire—and asks himself if this is the life he dreamed of for himself.

One day, the government delegate stops. Ceremoniously, he gets out of his car. He comes bearing good news which is in actuality a stack of papers no one in the town is capable of reading. They are maps and acts and deeds that must be signed here and here. But they are not just papers. Those papers represent something. Thousands and thousands of jugerum of land that as of today belong to the council; so many thousands that, upon hearing it, the peasants all look up at once, as if they don't fully understand. And they haven't fully understood. Because those thousands of jugerum do not correspond to irrigated land, nor the plains of good earth, nor is there, in all their expanse, a single creek or trickle of water to make them fertile. The Patrón, who wanted everything, had never wanted that land. Not just land, it's a desert: they are taking it from the desert and giving it to them. But not even the government can take from the desert what is hers.

The delegate says that he understands their concerns, while handing them a pen to sign with. What's more: he understands them very well. They have the right, of course, to present a written complaint. The government is always prepared to listen to its campesinos, or rather, it is always prepared to read what those who know how to write have to say. Meanwhile, he leaves them that little piece of desert, so they may pamper it and care for it and do with it what a campesino does with dirt. For the official response, he says, for the government to send their experts and surveyors and specialists, they'll have to wait a little longer, perhaps just two weeks, that's all; but courageous men like them, men who have bled from their wounds on so many hills, won't they be men enough, ah, to have just a little pinch of patience?

Some men turn out not to be men enough. They say viva la Revolución one last time, put on their hats, and take the road north. Juan sees them walk without looking back, with their straw mats and without their wives. They will never return, or they will return transfigured, looking at things from a different stature, a place that seems to sit just a little higher than what a man's life can reach. They bring with them new clothes and lordly ways. Strange machines that pick apart the cotton without using hands and that plow the earth without the need for oxen. Briefcases stuffed with green papers that, for as light as they look, are actually very heavy indeed; perhaps because they represent something else, like the delegate's papers were equal to a desert. The north, they say, the future is the north, which is to say that the rest of them are stuck in the past. And in that future, there are no longer Seven Cities, nor Thirteen Colonies, but no less than forty-eight, forty-eight states and each one of them richer than an entire country. They say there is hope there. They say there is work there. They say that the women there are prettier and easier; women with golden hair and blue eyes; women with skin so white that a man makes them blush just by looking at them, let alone touching them. Juan listens transfixed to the tales those emigrants bring back; stories that are hard to understand, because they are told in a strange accent, and even with new words, cultivated far from this land.

Later, in the too-narrow bed, holding the girl's naked body, he will repeat some of those stories out loud, embellished, perhaps, by his imagination or his hope. He speaks of distant directions where there are apparently no golden cities, as he'd once heard told, but cities of iron, cities of glass, cities made of lights that shine all night long, with no smoke or flame. A world where gold flourished, gold that couldn't be seen or touched but which was still gold and still grew, like the desert flourishes on these lands.

The girl listens to him speak of those wondrous, faraway places, saddened by premonition. She says nothing. She falls asleep rocked by those dreams that, she doesn't know why, behind her closed eyelids, take on the consistency of a nightmare. Juan doesn't sleep. On his side of the bed, the thoughts come so quickly that he is surprised that, on her side, the girl can even close her eyes. He keeps thinking about the gold, but also about everything that isn't gold, about the barren earth and the barren home, he thinks about hunger, the increasingly thin tortilla and increasingly less meaty meat and stretches of hunger that are increasingly long, a certainty that lasts the whole day and part of the night. To shake in bed in the middle of the night and feel the Compadre's absence in the stomach, as well. And to counter those thoughts, nothing or almost nothing: just a tiny, distant hope. Juan who, in order to fall asleep, tries to recapture the names of those fabulous realms, such as he remembers hearing them. Their names repeated like an antidote or spell; like sheep jumping the fence of his insomnia.

Arizona . . . Conéctica . . . Tejas . . . Oclajoma . . . Niu Yorc . . . Luisiana . . .

In his dream the Compadre is also dead. He appears to be moving, about to say or do something, but no: it is only the work of the wind that makes his clothes flutter. He is wearing his revolutionary dress coat, his cowboy hat, his boots, and metal spurs. Metal, too, the nails that keep him fixed to the wooden cross-piece. His arms spread in an embrace that never stops, like a god displaying his humanity to the world. He looks at his face masked by blood. He looks at his mouth, a mouth that will never open again, and inside it, the sharp-edged words that will never wound his ears. He looks at the hand, transformed into a mere grape-shoot of bones and shriveled ligaments. His hand, still nailed to the cross, still nailed, as well, in the act of pointing north.

It happens before the cock's crow. Before the Little Widow wakes to prepare the coffee with yesterday's grounds and warm the tortillas. The window is still a black rectangle, darkness inside and outside the house and Juan already up, shadow among shadows, slipping out of bed. Hands blindly searching and finding the book, his hat, his satchel already provisioned for the journey. Noiseless steps, muffled by the dirt floor—because the floor never stopped being dirt; just a few sections laid in a grid of rough white stone, as if Juan had, at some point, run out of gold or hope. Under the stove, the rusty can, and Juan opens it and removes just a handful of coins before returning it to its corner.

Juan on the threshold.

Juan turning for a moment to look for the last time at the woman's sleeping body, or rather the piece of darkness where the woman perhaps sleeps.

Juan raising his hand in that darkness, as if covering up a farewell.

Juan quietly pushing open the front door, which creaks drily. Juan fixed on the threshold for what feels like a vast length of time, concentrating on the night sounds.

Outside, the moon shines. Its light casts in white the tilled fields, the gravel path, the town's limewashed walls. Behind him, the garden's fruit trees throw ghostly shadows, like arrows that sail and land in a clear direction. Juan follows that course, that clear direction. While he walks, he seems to sense a weight on his back, the weight of a gaze already known to him, watching him from through the net curtains. A gaze that is no lighter for being familiar. He feels it as he moves away and as the sun peeks over the mountains and he feels it much later, too, when, at a bend in the road, the town, and with it the house, disappear.

At the bottom of his satchel, mixed up with the handful of nickel coins, is the Padre's book, and between its closed pages, among the apostle's ferocious drawings, are some passages underlined or crossed out or circled in ink with such fierceness that the paper is torn in some places. They are, they can be nothing else, the Padre's favorite passages. Places where the Padre's gaze came to rest. Ideas he touched, for a moment at least, with the tip of his thoughts.

He remembers: Your desire shall be to your husband, and he shall rule over you.

He remembers: And you see among the captives a beautiful woman, and desire her and would take her for your wife, then you shall bring her home to your house, and she shall shave her head and trim her nails. She shall put off the clothes of her captivity, remain in your house, and mourn her father and her mother for a full month; after that you may go to her and be her husband, and she shall be your wife. And it shall be, if you have no delight in her, then you shall set her free, but you certainly shall not sell her for money; you shall not treat her brutally, because you have humbled her.

He remembers: Woman is more bitter than death, because she is a tie, for her heart is a net and her hands are fetters. He who pleases God shall escape from her, but the sinner shall be trapped by her.

A town in the region, that same afternoon, when his journey has only just begun. He is seated at one of the tables, meticulously eating a bowl of vegetable stew. First he had asked the waiter for the price of each dish, one by one, and all the beers. The vegetable stew is the cheapest, the waiter replied, as he continued drying the crockery. And so vegetable stew it was, with the house beer.

At first, when he hears the voice, it takes him a moment to understand where it's coming from. In a poorly lit corner of the tavern, as if mummified in the gloom, waits an old man wearing a wool poncho. He is a blind guitarist, the emptiness of his eyes fixed on the wall opposite. A single movement: his right hand, sliding down to stroke the belly of his guitar.

"Where is it you're going, boy?" he shouts, his blind eyes fixed on a spot high above Juan's head. "To the States?"

Juan nods. Then he corrects himself.

"Yes."

"You're the gachupín, aren't you?"

"Yes."

"The one who moved in on the Compadre's widow."

Juan doesn't answer. He has finished his stew and drunk his beer, but he fiddles with the spoon, waiting for something.

"Tell me, boy, did you get scared the Compadre would come back and put three bullets in your belly?"

Juan drops his spoon. He stands up lazily, wiping his beard clean with a napkin. He speaks with his back to the blind man.

"The Compadre is dead."

"Ah, no, no, no . . . no sir, the Compadre is not dead. I've seen him, you know? I've seen him . . ."

Juan's hands shake as he puts down half a peso; as he puts on his hat and pushes through the cantina's swinging doors. Before he exits, he has time to hear, to see once more, the old man who points to his eyes wasted by white.

"With these eyes, you understand? With these eyes, I see him . . ."

XI

All cool, thank God – To ride a snake – An oil lamp goes out – Cities and stars –
Chinga tu madre – The kingdom's second apostle – Where I said I say I say Diego –
Journey from night to night

The train never comes on schedule. They warn him in the last town: he should
stock up on patience, and tequila. He doesn't have money for tequila. But he
does have patience, the whole day ahead of him to sit on a bench in the seemingly abandoned station. There is no one on the platform and no one in the
ticket booth and no one in the telegraph office. Not even a switchman. Just
the rails, sparkling like silver stitches. Above, a windmill's creaking blades. A
rusty water tank. Flies that come and go, and just his hat to shoo them away.
Overhead, a clock stopped at quarter past five, who knows when. And Juan, sitting there, sitting there shooing away the flies and the heat with the same hat,
waiting for the smoke from the locomotive to rise on the horizon.

And yet, there is no smoke. Noise, but no smoke. No smokestack. At last,
the train appears from around a curve in the track, not too fast but not slow
either. A strange train, a strange engine, a smokestack that isn't there. How does
it move, that train? He gets slowly to his feet, the bag on his back. Closer and
closer to the tracks, without knowing whether the train that doesn't look like a
train is going to stop. It doesn't stop. It passes slowly, but not too slow: he could
probably catch it if he ran a little. And then, on the roofs of the wagons, men,
women. Hundreds of people clambering all over, as if they had rained down
from the heavens, cheering him on, waving at him with open arms.

233

"Come on! Órale cabrón! Jump!"

Juan lets one car, two cars, three cars go by. He starts running to position himself alongside the fourth, the fifth. He doesn't think he can do it, but he does, he jumps, just in time to take hold of the last car, the last handle. Juan holding onto the little ladder on the last car of train with no smokestack, no smoke, but with people who urge him to climb. There's room for him on top, they say.

He hasn't felt afraid, up until then; he jumped without thinking or weighing the consequences. Now is when he senses the magnitude of his actions, the two hands that cling to life while his legs still hang, pedaling in the air. He feels the wind on his face, the promise of the fall, the railroad ties coming one after another with increasing speed, a vertiginous flickering. He finally manages to climb the ladder, without looking down. Up top, a crowd of smiling faces and clapping hands await him. They're strange, these men and women. They wear clothing like he has never seen before, garish colors everywhere and torn or partially torn pants, caps like sailors wear on land and shirts without sleeves and full of scribbles, shirts full of drawings, full of meaningless phrases or phrases whose meaning is obscure, as if they came dressed as shop signs or school chalkboards. When the heat gets uncomfortable, they remove their T-shirts and show their striped skin, smudged with more abstract messages, more drawings like cave art or tribal symbols that are in some ways reminiscent of the tattooed skin of the Chichimeca.

Someone whistles. Another pats his back. They find an empty spot on the roof and a young man hands him a bottle of water, surprisingly light.

"How's it going, man?"

The words they pronounce are also unclear, as if they were reading the claims on their shirts and torsos out loud to one another. Before answering, Juan takes a swig from the flimsy bottle. A long swig, unnecessary, because he doesn't know what to say. Just to do something, he smiles.

"And you all?"

"Cool, compa, everything's cool, thank God . . . nice and slow and real careful."

Also beside him is a girl, half-young and half-pretty, who squints at him, blinded by the bright sun.

"You're not from around here, are you?"

"No. I'm from Castilla."

"Castilla? What are you, gachupín?"

"Yes."

The girl exchanges surprised looks with the others.

"Wow, the crisis must've really hit you guys hard, too . . ."

Another man offers him a cigarette. He speaks loudly, raising his voice to be heard over the screech of metal and rail.

"Dude, you got up here so fast. I thought you fell . . . that the Beast squashed you . . ."

"The Beast?"

"Simon. Yeah man. Like, that the train got you, I mean."

Juan doesn't answer right away. His mind is like run-aground on the word "Beast," the word "Simon." But he catches hold of the word train, the only one he understands, or believes he understands.

"I thought it stopped there," he manages to say, pointing at the station left behind.

"Ah, yeah, no, it doesn't stop . . . It never stops here . . . they told you wrong. And farther back are the brakemen, who won't let you on, and up ahead too, brakemen, all of them, so you did good, grabbing it here . . ."

Then, taking advantage of the intimacy of the shared smoke, he warns him that, the next time, he has to be careful with how he jumps. He's obviously new with this boarding-the-moving-Beast thing, and he must be careful. Gotta respect the Beast, he says. Look: it's simple. You have to let the handles on the freight car hit your hands, to see how fast it's going, because this is something you have to feel, not just see. It's misleading. If he thinks he can, he must run about twenty meters or so, to catch its rhythm, holding on to a handle. Once he's taken its pulse, he has to lift himself with his arms, pull himself up just by the arms, to get his feet away from the wheels, and only then put the leg closest to the train on the rung. This, he explains, is extremely important: the leg that's next to the train, not the other one, so your body doesn't go against the car and mess you up and swallow you. Understood?

"Yes."

"Trust me, I'm an old dog and I've got my years and my old accounts with the Beast, okay?"

And then the man points to his left leg. What's left of his left leg: something that ends at the knee with nothing at all below that, the hollow pant leg, phantom, grazing the roof. Juan nods uncomfortably. Perhaps in order to ward off or mitigate the discovery, he decides to come up with a question. He turns to another man seated on his left, taciturn under his hat and mustache.

"What are they carrying?"

"Who said anything about carrying, cabrón? No one's carrying anything."

"I meant the boxcars."

"The boxcars?"

"Yes, what are they loaded with?"

The guy shrugs.

"Oh, I dunno ... They usually carry chemicals or minerals or cement and stuff like that. Stuff like that. Some of 'em don't carry anything."

"They're empty?"

"Some of 'em."

Juan stares, for several moments, into the man's mild eyes. He doesn't understand, he confesses at last. If they aren't carrying anything, what are they all doing there, up on the roof? If it's dangerous to board a moving train, then why doesn't the driver simply stop? Those around him look at one another in silence, feeling each other out. Then they break into laughter.

"Ah! You made us laugh, güey."

No one asks him where he's going. They are all headed for the same thing: the dollars, the gig, the grind, the good money. They're all going to the United States, which they sometimes call USA and other times América, or say to the gringos, to the north, and sometimes they don't call it anything; they just point to the horizon. They speak of the border, of getting to the border, as if the border was a place, a destination in and of itself, and not just a line that is crossed. There, on the other side, is where the money is. Prosperity. The future. And all are heading to that future, on the roof of a boxcar that travels empty, on a train that doesn't stop.

But the train must not be called a train: it doesn't take Juan long to learn this. Trains are the other ones, the ones people ride inside and not on top, people who buy a ticket and board at a specific time, when the whistle blows. This train is not a train but the Beast. They call it the Beast, they explain, because of its inexhaustible voracity. A monster that feeds solely on Central American flesh. If you listen carefully to the Beast, they tell him, if you pay attention to the squeals of iron, of hardware, underneath he'll be able to hear the moans of the men and women who lost their lives between its wheels. That's what can make you go deaf: not the thunder of the boxcars, not the whistle of the locomotive, not the hurricane of wind inside the tunnels, but that other hell that pulses below, those voices that continue to ask for help from those who can no longer give it. From his corner, Juan listens. Juan looks. He contemplates the Beast for what it is, an enormous snake slithering through the mountains and the plain, with its insatiable beast roar; that's what it looks like, yes, an insatiable beast, an enormous snake, and they are the scales, they are the rash, the tumors, the sores that the snake suffers, ugly like her, dirty like her, condemned to languish in the desert like her. They always seem about to fall, always in motion and always looking for a home that never comes, perched clumsily on life, rocked by the clatter of the rails and whipped by the wind and, sometimes, even lashed by the lowest tree branches, which warp to sweep the roof. They have to be very careful with that, with the branches, they say, because there are plenty who get knocked off or hurt themselves. But there are also plenty who get there in one piece and plenty who get there and still get nothing. They are left to wander along the border like sleepwalkers, or ghosts; like dead men condemned to watch life on the other side, powerless to touch it. This, in short, is the Beast: not just the train but the people who climb onto it, the danger that stalks them, the destination that is never reached or never reached entirely. The Beast is the route, the train that runs through desolation as well as the very desolation that train traverses, the journey with its stops and pauses, its stumbles; the women who throng alongside the rails to throw them fruit or bottles of water and the narcos who come to collect their harvest of the dead.

Squeezed in his corner, his pack between his knees, Juan watches, astonished, at what occurs right around him and what occurs in the distance. He sees four mustachioed men playing cards, oblivious to the train's sway, and a sierra comprised of tight ravines in whose many curves and twists the train's urgent speed calms a bit. He sees a succession of miserable shacks that sag low to touch the tracks and a woman next to him, cradling a baby, the baby rocked by the mother and the mother rocked by the clatter. He sees metal towers that seem to hold up the sky and smoke spirals busy on the horizon and gigantic, colorful photographs erected next to the tracks, so the men have no choice but to see them, and in those photographs there are semi-nude women and men in suits who promise México many things and smiling young people who drink a kind of dark black oil straight from the bottle. He sees men who urinated in the space between boxcars or who lie down with their backpacks as pillows or who fasten their belts to the train grille, so as not to fall off if they fall asleep. He sees the night spilling over the desert and over the men, boys who smoke cigarettes whose embers look like miniature cities floating on the horizon and cities floating on the horizon, their lights aglow like cigarettes. Rivers of black tar, dotted with red lights that come and yellow lights that go. He watches all of this in a state of perplexity, but also with a trace of fatigue, like someone reading a book in another tongue; a book he has given up on understanding, through which he allows himself to flow like a train crossing a foreign landscape.

Before, at some point in the evening, when the light still revealed where one body ended and another began, Juan opened his backpack and withdrew the book. It was a moment of weakness or nostalgia or clairvoyance. The whole way he had been asking himself whether this mysterious world he was traveling through looked more or less like the world the Padre had tried to create, and tired of asking himself, he asked the portrait. He asked it other questions, too, questions that weren't to do with the world itself but with the Little Widow, but the portrait either didn't answer or couldn't hear him. Just the words of God, of the Padre, underlined or crossed out or circled in ink, so fiercely that the paper is torn some spots. They, they can be nothing else, are the Padre's favorite passages. Places where the Padre's gaze came to rest. Ideas he touched, for a moment at least, with the tip of his thoughts.

He reads: Let servants be subject to their masters, and please them in all things without question.

He reads: Servants, be subject to your masters with all fear, not only to the good and courteous, but also to the harsh. For this is grace: anyone—for the sake of conscience toward God—enduring grief, suffering wrongly.

He reads: Why have you deceived us, saying: "Why have you deceived us, saying, 'We are from very far from you,' when you dwell among us? Now therefore, you are cursed, and none of you shall be freed from being slaves—wood-cutters and water carriers for the house of my God."

Someone, a man who comes midway through the journey talking about foot-ball squads and cable television and other farfetched concepts, looks over his shoulder at the Padre's likeness.

"That came out nice."

"Do you know him?" Juan asks, jolted by one last wish.

"Do I know him?"

"Yes."

Beneath the brim of the man's hat, a puzzled expression.

"Isn't it you?"

"No," Juan replies quickly, as if the question offended him. "It's the Com-padre."

"Who?"

"The Patrón. The Padrecito. The Padre."

"Your dad?"

"Juan the Indian."

"An Indian, you say?"

The man takes the book roughly.

Juan represses an attempt to resist while the man squints skeptically at the portrait, holding it close to his face, then far away. He returns it to Juan with the same brusqueness.

"There's nothing Indian about him here. He's güerito like you. Looks just like you."

"It's not me."

But he looks intently at the portrait again. It isn't him, of course isn't, how could it be, but it is true that the face doesn't look Indian, either. What it looks like isn't clear. And even less clear how he could have ever thought the likeness was of an Indian in the first place. There is something supremely imprecise in the features, something that might have to do with the colors of the evening's ebb, or the ragged paper, or the desire that eyes have to see movement in any motionless body, a trembling of a dead man's eyelids, life that returns. But feeling or not, be it an effect of the twilight or the paper or the imagination, the fact is that the portrait's expression seems, in effect, to be heading in another direction, to be partway through something, like an adolescent's features are only midway to the man he will become. His eyes, the curve of his mouth, the increasingly sharp jaw, the skin, whiter now, almost entirely white. It all gives the impression of a certain liquidity, of water-based paint, of motion written in that water's reflection, subject to tremors and shifts; to the accident of a pebble that suddenly falls, thrown by that same adolescent's hand, in an instant confusing the face in order to compose a different semblance in the stillness.

Later, it is the night that falls suddenly and all impressions vanish. This is how night falls in the desert, like someone puts out an oil lamp's flame.

All the colors of evening fade and only the sounds remain. During the day, one hears them without really listening, like background music or a sky no one notices. But at night, those same sounds swell with the desire to be heard, they have something of an echo, roots that grow inside, and then one steadily hears the rattle over every railroad tie, the whistle of the wind in one's face and a sound like a kind of waveless surf, a rumble both maritime and mechanical, of a sea without shore or harbor. Overhead one sees the black, star-studded sky and the earth below, also starred, but with cities, and feels overwhelmed by the magnitude of everything, and for the tiny scale of one's own purposes. Some-body yawns or stretches or stirs a bit, in their bed of backpacks and blankets, and that movement multiples and spreads all around, the bodies fitted together and connected like the rings of a snake that doesn't succumb to the night. Sleep won't come, and when it does is a multiplication of wakefulness, and it's unclear where sleep begins and memory ends, nor the sensation of what the body accommodates or rejects, all those chests that are like pillows and laps like nests and arms that retain you like lairs or traps. And at night all bodies are the same, all their flesh irrigated by the same blood, because the ground is the same distance away for all and the train shakes them all alike.

During the day, the travelers hardly talk. They make sure not to touch. They barely look at one another. Their closed mouths seem to chew on stories that no one knows or will ever know, shreds of past or future whose bitterness they savor in silence. They are one hundred, two hundred, maybe three hun-dred immigrants riding the same beast, and every one of them does it alone. Only occasionally is it possible to recognize the small domestic communion in a man who shares a cigarette or water jug. A child who cries and a man who hands him a piece of candy to distract him from the rigors of the trip. A voice that shouts: Branch! and then the one, two, or three hundred bodies bend at the same time, with unanimous will. The elements that become, for an instant, a piece of home. Otherwise, nobody speaks, nobody asks. Quiet trip, compa, they repeat as if to themselves. All cool, thank God: nice and slow and real careful. Then night falls, and the borders between bodies and consciences seem to dissipate with the last light. Now, amid the sounds of the tracks and ties, it is possible to hear a word here and there. Whole sentences. Closed mouths that suddenly open like nocturnal flowers to share lengthy stories that no one listens to, perhaps, like a child who tells himself a story with which to fall asleep. Those stories are faceless. They are hardly more than murmurs that travel from one lump to another, from night to the night. They could be told by people or by the Beast itself. Juan listens to those murmurs in the dozing of the trip. Or not Juan, exactly, because Juan is no longer sure of still being Juan; Juan's body and the migrants' bodies that press against his own have come to be the same thing. Their voices are mirrors or extensions or emissaries of Juan's voice. Their stories are one, as well. There is, in fact, just a single story, though they might seem many; a story repeated and multiplied up and down the boxcar's length, perhaps the length of the world. For the first time, they don't talk about dollars or work permits or that friend of a friend of a friend who will put them up in the United States, God willing, in just a couple of weeks. They settle for talking about the past, that is, about the remote corner of the world that saw them born. In their stories, that place seems to be the same: a miserable city in a poor country in which they lived a poor life, but in which they were, for a time at least, happy. And now, in the darkness of this wild land, they remember that happiness, which requires an entire world of distance to be considered. They talk about school playgrounds bathed in sunlight and nighttime parks where they had their first kiss or took their first hit of a joint. They talk about fields where they dreamed of being gringo sport stars and garages where they dreamed of being gringo rock stars and narrow teenage beds where they dreamed of this journey, gringo, as well. They talk about the pupusas in El Salvador, the most delicious corn tortillas in the world, and Panamanian sancocho and Honduran baleadas and the gallo pinto in Nicaragua. They talk about that house that they might never see again and the relatives waiting inside; little brothers and sisters who need new clothes and mothers who pray for our return and fathers who drink a bottomless bottle of beer. All those images are fixed on the date of their departure, like maps are fixed in a specific moment in time, in a specific corner of the world.

Juan doesn't add anything or ask any questions. His eyes are conveniently closed and, from the darkness behind his eyelids, he simply listens, in silence, to that collective life, incomprehensible as all lives are. Slowly, the migrants fall silent or asleep, rocked by the rhythm of the journey. Juan opens his eyes and looks again at their faces, or what of their faces the night permits him to see. They are men and women who have become twenty years younger, and by the lamppost light, their memories seem like solid things, real, upon which they could lie down to sleep.

Dawn arrives at last, or maybe they are the ones who arrive in a region where it is always morning, the sun eternally suspended on the horizon's edge. By that time, a while has passed since the migrants' voices broke off. The first rays set off bright glints on the rails and dazzle the men's precarious slumber, cradled by the Beast. It is suddenly impossible to imagine all those pilgrims confessing their fears, their histories, in the night. Silence, again; again, their expressions hardened by fatigue and suspicion. Juan tries and fails to associate the voices he has heard with the bodies rocking beside him. His head is still full of the stories that echoed while he drowsed; though now that those stories have been retrieved from the darkness, it is unclear whether they were dreams or something else. But then he remembers that those same stories are made of strange material, of many mysterious and foreign words, and it occurs to him that a man cannot dream of what he still doesn't know. The word television, the word pollero, the word narco, shuffling endlessly in his head, like cards with indecipherable numbers and pictures.

A short time later, they reach the city. Glimpsed in the distance, the station looks like a dismantled cathedral, with neither roof nor gods. The machine starts braking well before, on a track that runs into a kind of train cemetery. Before the locomotive has come to a complete stop, the migrants are already grabbing their backpacks and climbing down the ladders and jumping to the outer tracks, like sailors who can't wait for their boat to dock. Some ways off, two uniformed men smoke a slow and lazy cigarette. They watched the crowd spilling over the dead tracks like somebody observes a repeated scene, a horizon that never ends. Their cigarettes burn down in the same time it takes for the crowd to disperse.

Juan jumps with them, not knowing where he is going. Because everyone seems to be going in precise and opposite directions. They jump metal fences, cross tracks, board abandoned boxcars. Juan loiters on the crushed stone that lines the tracks, unsure of which direction to take. Before he knows it, the tracks are almost completely empty. Even the man with the missing leg is gone, flying on his crutches. There is no one or almost no one left beside him. A woman with a bundle that is a crying baby on her chest. Two kids who shake hands in a strange, complicated way, palms that meet and fists that do who knows what and hands that fly upward, then separate. Five young women, practically girls, who walk single file behind a young man inked in tattoos. Five women who do not take their eyes off their guide's back; who speed up when he speeds up and stop when he stops. And maybe that, Juan thinks, is a pollero: someone who shelters under his wing a cluster of still-tender creatures, who incubates them until they are ready to fly.

But fly to where. Where does that type of bird go and where will he go himself. Just to do something, he exits onto the street. He feels drunk with uncertainty and drowsiness, dazed by the early morning light emerging from behind a horizon of rooftops and brick walls. Growing confusedly on the roofs are some metal poles, tortured and twisted, as if someone had sown the buildings with iron cacti. What he sees around him is, has to be, a city, but to him it only looks like an enormous back patio, a jumble of cement and scrap metal, the rusty reverse side of some kind of dream. The city, so similar to a dilapidated factory or a crematorium, a factory that produces nothing, is good for nothing; just for festering with soot and oil and unbreathable, burnt air. He sees empty lots returned to the desert and fencing that looks like chicken coops and walls made of gray blocks and wooden or metal posts erected like gallows, with their cables and wires slicing up the sky. He sees some buildings of implausible height, as if the world, no longer able to grow northward, had seen itself forced to grow toward the sky. He sees automobiles pass by him, fleeing in all directions, automobiles that are fleeing, perhaps, their own city, so fast they seem to be made of nothing but air and noise. Because there are no people, at least no people he can see: just automobiles that come and automobiles that go and automobiles stopped on the side of the road, also waiting to run scared. Juan would also like to flee toward somewhere, perhaps, but what. He barely manages to cross the street; barely manages to discern the logic of those iron dwellers that stop just as quickly as they accelerate, that shout at him with their horns dodging and insulting him. His whole head is full of noise, besieged by the boom with which the machines' voices speak, by that clamor containing not a single vestige of humanity. From the walls, too, he is beset by all kinds of warnings and teachings that, in their own way, also shout and pierce his head without planting a single idea. He reads: Conchita Grocers. He reads: Pemex. He reads: Try the New Fanta. He reads, on a red disk, the word STOP in huge letters, letters that seem to shout over the motors' roar, and Juan, obedient, stops. An automobile stops with him so a human head can momentarily appear. The first human gesture.

"Chinga tu madre!" the man—or perhaps the automobile itself—shouts before speeding away.

It happens precisely at that very instant. The same moment when he rushes away from the road, giving up the idea of reaching the other side—Coca-Cola: Taste the Feeling, the neighboring wall blares. It is, at first, only a sensation: the certainty of being watched. He turns to encounter the eyes of a man who is, effectively, watching him. Under the visor of his cap, the man's gaze has something of an edge and something like the touch of steel. Nonetheless, this iron man is smiling at him; a smile so wide and so stiff that it seems to be vacillating between kindness and cruelty.

"Hell yes, man. I thought you weren't coming," he says simply.

Juan is slow to respond. In that pause, he has time to look in eyes of the man who knows him or says he knows him. His features are strange, yet familiar, like returning to one's childhood home. A home one doesn't remember.

"Who are you?"

"Definitely not the dude you're looking for," he says, and his smile intensifies, or perhaps it grows deeper.

"And who am I looking for?"

"You want the Padrote, cabrón. Why ask what you already know?"

"You mean Juan?"

"You know another fucking Padrote?"

Juan looks at the man's eyes. His smile, carved into his face by a knife. His hat with the visor backward, as if it had fallen on his head from the sky. His strange, mismatched clothes, that lend him a festive, minstrel-esque air. But he sees other things, too. He sees the Padre's many deaths, his many faces, his infinite signs and tracks, sown along way like shedded snakeskins. He sees the Padrecito's cell. The Patrón's factory in flames. The Compadre's grave. He sees himself, small and almost ridiculous, just one of many moths drawn to the Padre's fire, who knows whether to extinguish it or sacrifice himself in the flames. And lastly, he sees only this: the man looking at him, waiting for an answer.

"Yes," he admits. "I suppose I am looking for the Padrote."

"Knew it," the man says, broadening his smile. "I would have recognized you anywhere. You have his same expressions. Two of a kind, güey. The spitting image. You could be brothers or some shit."

"Something like that."

He nods, satisfied.

"Well, you know what he told me, your cabrón of a brother? Nothing. Or almost nothing. Just that someone was going to come and if that someone came, it was to find him. To keep my eyes open. But I'm sure he told you already."

"He didn't tell me anything."

"Ah! Fucking Padrote. You know him. The less words, the better. But he knew I was going to find you so why say more. But you took your time, cabrón. A shitload of time. I thought you weren't coming. All right, let's go."

The man sets off down the sidewalk. Juan follows, lagging somewhat behind, unsure whether he should stay behind the man or walk beside him. Then he sees the man come to a sudden stop again. He slaps his forehead hard, hard enough to hurt.

"Shit, I just realized I didn't introduce myself. Everybody calls me Navaja."

"Navaja," Juan says, as if dreaming, as remembering a flash of knife blade.

"Yeah. Navaja. What's your name?"

"Juan."

Navaja turns, a glint of suspicion in his eyes.

"Don't fucking tell me you've got the same name as your brother."

"We have the same mother, different fathers."

"Ah, I see. You still look so much alike. So similar. Two peas in a pod, you two."

He thinks a moment, then breaks into unprovoked laughter.

"Ah, cabrón! No matter how hard I try, I just can't imagine what the Padrote's father would've been like. Man's a devil, the Padrote. Pure dynamite. One of those dudes, you might say, who seem like they never had a father. Like he was his own father since he was in diapers, know what I mean?"

They've arrived at a black automobile, parked beside the entrance to the station. A very large automobile, bigger than Juan has ever seen. He opens the front door and motions to the empty seat with a gesture containing both a hint of courtesy and imperiousness. Juan hesitates.

"Are you going to take me to the Padrote?"

Navaja puts his hands companionably on Juan's shoulders. The contentment in his smile is still there.

"Ay, cabrón. So much to tell you."

His name was Diego. He always talks about himself that way, in the past tense. About a certain part of himself, at least. The man he was before he arrived here; before he met the Padrote. Because, back then, they called him Diego, or Die, or even Dieguito, but the Padrote decided that name lacked *punch*. He wasn't wrong, of course: in this business *el marketing* is everything. Being capable of something isn't enough: you have to prove you can do it. Even if you can't or can't completely. Would you respect a Dieguito, güey? Navaja asks, momentarily taking his eyes off the road. Would you do heavy business with a Dieguito? Of course not. So it was the Padrote who went with this Navaja thing, in spite of the fact that he's never carried a blade, just a .38. The kind with the sweet little cylinder. Who even uses a knife these days? Who is confident that he can get close enough to somebody who doesn't want him close? It doesn't matter.

Navaja is a good name. A nickname with an edge, with cachet, right? But he can call him whatever he wants. Call me Navaja, Navaja says. Or if you prefer, just call me Diego, Diego says. Diego or Navaja: the name thing isn't important between friends. The fact is, he owes a lot to the Padrote. Not just his name, obviously: he owes him . . . well, everything. When he met him, his shit was somewhere between messed up and totally messed up. If I told you where I come from, he says. In fact, he will tell him. He comes from shit itself. From a place so filthy shit would avoid it if it could. That's where he comes from. And, back then, he scraped by with this or that. His head down and his back prepared to take the blows. He accepted the cards he'd been dealt, you might say, and even came to believe that life consisted of those cards and nothing else. You were never dealt more than one hand. Everybody gets their own cards and they gotta be played no matter what, right? That's not true, obviously. The Padrote came to teach him that it isn't true, the world is full of opportunity and the rounds played in this game are infinite. Did Juan know what the Padrote did, the day they met? He showed him a dollar. That simple: a single dollar bill, old and battered like it had been through the fucking wash. He didn't let him touch it. He just passed it in front of his nose, first the side with the president and then the other, with the eagle and the pyramid. Where it said, like it does on all dollars, *In God We Trust*. Does he know English? It means: en Dios creemos. And he was like mesmerized by those little letters because, back then, he didn't know whether he believed in God or not. He's still not sure. Does the Padrote believe? Not sure on that, either. He definitely believes in something. At least he has the strength of somebody who believes in something: maybe in himself. If he doesn't believe in the God of dollars, as a minimum he believes in the dollars themselves. *In Gold We Trust*. Anyway, the Padrote showed him that dollar. You know what this is? he asked him, the bill so close he could smell the smell of money. It's a dollar, Navaja says that Navaja answered. The Padrote shook his head. It's a passport, he said. It's a beginning. It's my fucking baptism. The first dollar he earned over there, on the other side of the wall. He saved it because it reminded him of something. What did it remind him of? It reminded him of his humble beginnings, which were really tough, of course, but also happy, in their own way. These were those beginnings: a foreign country and him ready to conquer it. He alone with his dollar and nobody else to help him. And with that first dollar, he earned a second, and after that one, another, and now God knows how much money he's got, the cabrón. In the beginning, this is all I had, Navaja says the Padrote said, fingering the dollar bill for the last time; now I have the world. For a whole day and a whole night, the Padrote talked and talked. As he listened, Navaja forgot that something called sleep existed. He wishes he could remember his words: remember them with the same precision with which one looks at a picture. What he does remember is that first he asked him if he liked being a carwasher; washing the shit off other people's cars. Because at the time, he isn't ashamed to admit, he was doing exactly that, washing cars. But the Padrote didn't like that. Washing cars, he said, is for losers. He also told him that he needed to find out what his goals were and then later ask himself what obstacles were keeping him from those goals. He hesitated. Finally he replied that the answer to both questions was the same: money, fucking bread. That's what he said, and the Padrote nodded approvingly. That's right, he said. Money was the goal and the obstacle to reaching that goal was also money. He was finally starting to talk like a man who respected the three Cs: Conscientiousness, Conviction, and Courage. Until then, Navaja says the Padrote said, it hadn't been me talking, but self-pity. If I was a failure or in an unsuccessful situation—because that's failure, the place one is, but where one can always stop being—it was for precisely that reason. You get it, güey? If I was a failure, it was because I believed that I was. In his mind, he was already a loser! We are what we believe; what we make others believe. That's what the Padrote told him, in prettier and more exact words. Ah, so memorable, the words of the fucking Padrote. He knew them all, the simple and the convoluted, the ones only politicians and doctors say. And he liked repeating them in groups of three, words that always began with the same letter. He's forgotten some of them. Failure, that one he remembers, was a problem with the three Ds: Distraction. Decentering. Disarray. The path to success, curiously, also had three Ds: Define. Design. Deliver. Though if one preferred, one could also follow the three Bs: Brain. Boldness. Backbone. Did he happen to be doing any of that? Did he happen to do anything other than dunk a sponge in a bucket and scrub, scrub the windshield until all the shit came off? Was he anything more than the shit he cleaned? Because there'd always be kids to wash cars and drivers to drive them: he just had to decide if he wanted to be the owner or the asshole who cleaned it. Easy as that. Did he want to know the only thing separating him from success, from turning into the owner of the fucking car? the Padrote asked him, and he nodded repeatedly. It was like he was under a spell. The only thing separating you from success, the Padrote said, is yourself. Ah, shit. What does a person do in that case? What can you do when you are your own problem? But according to the Padrote, there was no problem. It was all there, in his head, and all he had to do was pull it out. It was a matter of putting the three As on the table: Attitude. Apprenticeship. Action. And also, of course, the three Cs: Constancy. Concentration. Confidence. Did he have Constancy, Concentration, Confidence? The Padrote talked like that, with a lot of initials, and he asked a lot of questions that, well, one already knew how to answer. But let's say that, by merely answering them, one took his first step: in a matter of speaking, one starts to walk just by opening his mouth to respond. He did, at least. He answered the questions and it was by answering the questions and leaving the carwash and getting into the party girl business that he helped out the Padrote with his dealings. Because back then the Padrote was still doing the grind with the girls, bringing them in and then taking them on to the US. That's where he got the name Padrote, obviously. Do you know what a padrote is, güey? Sure you do. I think they call them chulos in Spain. And it's a nasty word, to be honest, a real dirty word, kind of annoying, but the Padrote couldn't care less. The nickname might have hurt somebody else. Either pissed him off or embarrassed him. But the Padrote practically puffed out his chest when they said to him: Padrote. And that's how we were for a while, Navaja says, splitting the earnings, because business was booming and the Padrote needed a right-hand man. He was, for some time, that right hand. He learned everything there was to know about the business, which isn't all that much but is worth its weight in gold. It all consists in finding merchandise that fits the three Us—Umarried, Underage, Undocumented—and the three Cs—Compliant, Cute, Cheap. All to satisfy those other three Cs that explain any business's success: Customer, Customer, Customer. Of course, he was a real joker, your brother. He told that joke all the time: don't go forgetting the three Cs on me, young man: Customer, Customer, Customer. Or: apply yourself to the three Ws, kid, Work, Work, Work. Well. Truth is, in the blink of an eye I went from washing cars to driving them, and then giving orders for someone else to do it. How's that for you? It's all a question of desire, taking advantage of opportunities, and he grabbed them by the horns, as they say. Opportunity is a passing train and you either climb on or it climbs over you. That's just the way it is. Here, you either fuck or get fucked. Like I always say, says Diego, and I say it because the Padrote said it first, man is condemned to be free. That's the Padrote for you. Dude's a philosopher. Condemned to be free, he would say, and you can't blame your race or the crappy barrio you grew up in. Because we've all been through shit to get here. The Padrote himself was born in a piece of shit place, those were his exact words; but who better than Juan to confirm it. The Padrote told him that he grew up in a godforsaken corner of the world lost to God's memory, in the far south where there was no electricity or clean water. A place that was stuck in another time. Is it really like that? No water, no electricity? Did the fucking Padrote really come from somewhere so low? One expects anything from him. Anything seems possible. It's even hard to believe that he had a childhood. Anyway: it's a fact that we're all born into shit, Navaja says. And there are people who fight it and people who settle. The Padrote, obviously, isn't one for settling. A man who settles isn't a man but a fucking tree. Or rock. What was it the Padrote used to say, about settling? About the three Cs . . . Damn, he can't remember. Doesn't matter. The matter is clear: Never settle. Grow, always. Work a shit-ton because that—work, effort, drive—is what differentiates men from trees and rocks. What differentiates them from draught animals that walk when you say walk and stop when you say stop. Then the commies come and explain that you have to share your dollars with them. What one has earned with the sweat of their brow, split it down the middle with the lousy beggars. Ah! Why don't they ask to distribute the effort? Who worries about that, the effort? When are they going to come around asking for their share? One day—one night, actually; a night with a lot of weed and a lot of tequila—the Padrote told him that he had been a communist once, for a while. He explained that he was many things before being what he is now, and that all those things disappointed him to some degree, but Communism had disappointed him most of all. The Revolution! If they, the revolutionaries, applied the same determination to work as they did to their little class war, it would be a different story, right? Nowadays, every sleazy bum in Mexico, maybe every sleazy bum in the world, wants to blame you for making good dough. For getting your head above water, as if we should just drown, like them. For making it where your merits and your willpower take you: they don't like that, you see. And they don't want your apologies, nor do they have any interest in learning from you. All they want is your money! That's what the Padrote would tell him, and he was as right as a saint, the cabrón. I'm sure you understand these things, pal, you can tell how sharp you are just by your eyes, güey, but here it's like people can't get it through their heads. Like nobody wants to take charge, no one is responsible. They blame luck. They blame their parents' poverty or the filthiness of their neighborhood. They blame the government. Oh, the government! The government's good at being responsible for something. Wouldn't they like to have that much power, those assholes. No: here everyone has to carry their own little bit of guilt. And careful with trusting anybody. Because the world is a terrible place, a replica of hell: he learned that from the Padrote, as well. Lions kill to eat, but men kill for fun. People will always try to take you out, especially when you're on top. We all have friends who want everything we've got, Diego says. They want our money, business, house, car, wife, and dog. And those are our friends! Our enemies are worse! Understanding this isn't a matter of left or right: it's just good common sense. Having a pair of eyes is all you need. The fact is this is the world we live in: pure hell. And in this city more than any other. Maybe all borders are like this, he reflects; a place where the worst of both worlds meet. And he has seen the worst of those worlds. He thinks, for instance, about the issue of the girls. Because maybe Juan has heard some talk about that. Women dead by the hundreds, the thousands, as if some epidemic from the past was swallowing them up. A plague that only touches the females, right, most of them poor, because a poor female is like a female twice over, doesn't he think? Oh, those poor girls. He thinks about them so much. Because even though he lives off the business of women, fine, sure, and maybe he's overdone it with them on occasion, knocked them around a bit, just to soften them up, but everybody knows that he treats them decently. He doesn't ask more of them than they can give and some of them have even made good money thanks to him: by dint of their efforts on the pole and in bed they've been able to bring their kids here from Central America; some of the veterans even open their own small businesses. But the girls getting murdered in the desert is truly incomprehensible. Unforgivable. They fuck them and toss them out there, as if they were trash. Like lobster shells, thrown away after a good meal. Like a greasy taco wrapper, when the taco's gone. Exactly the same: like shells, like wrappers, like trash. As if the women weren't mothers, daughters, sisters. And sometimes, of course, whores. There has to be a little of everything, no? The point is, those fuckers beat them bad. They stuff them in trunks, rape them in all their holes, bite off their nipples. Sometimes they don't even have the basic decency to bury them. They leave them there, in the dirty dust for the desert to fuck. And it's truly an incomprehensible thing, because as far as he knows the narcos have always spoken loud and clear. If they torture you before they kill you, it means they needed you to give them certain information. If they shoot you in the back of the neck, out of the blue, it's because they want to teach a lesson: a lesson to the dead man and another for those still alive, right? If they wrap you in a blanket after killing you, well, that means that they had some respect for you when you were alive, maybe because you were a narco like them, and—rival and all—they respected you. If they pluck your eyes out, it means you betrayed the cartel, as a police informant, for example. But, what does a girl killed and raped and abandoned in the middle of the desert mean? Do they tell a story, those mangled, missing nipples? This is the question, Diego says: what's the message. Nothing we can understand. See that little hill out there, with that fucking billboard telling us to read the Bible? Well, they fuck them, who knows why. Maybe the murderers don't even know. Because we Mexicans aren't just enigmatic to others; we are to ourselves, as well. Our reality, Mexican reality, that is, only blooms in partying, alcohol, and death. Maybe that's why when it comes to a Mexican party, there's nothing more joyful. And nothing sadder. That's the murdered girls: the end of a party and the beginning of mourning. In short: somebody's whacking them, nobody knows why. He has his theories, of course. What theories? Oh, maybe it's no big thing, he isn't a learned man like the Padrote. Opinions are like asses: everybody has one. And my opinion, says Diego Navaja, that is, from the ass I sit on to give my opinion, the flesh throne from which one sees the world, is this: the Aztecs are to blame. Can you place the Aztecs, güey? Stupid, I know, of course you can place them: a gachupín sure as hell knows these things. After all, it was your ancestors who made short work of them. The ones who burned their cities and destroyed their temples and ripped them apart with their hunting dogs. They cleansed the country of Aztecs: as far as they could, at least. The Spanish back then, goddamn. Now they call it genocide, right? And fine: they can call it what they want. Though he has to say, he's not entirely convinced. Maybe the problem is precisely the opposite: that his ancestors, out of pure laziness, didn't take the cleansing seriously enough. Because it is proven fact that, somehow or another, the Aztecs survived. Even with the dogs and the conquistadors and the epidemics and slave plantations, the Aztecs are still here. And those dudes ate human flesh. While in Europe they were discussing whether the sun orbited the Earth, the Aztecs were discussing which part of the human body was tastiest. How to cook a human torso to make a nice pozole—because back then pozole, he must know, was prepared with the flesh of men, which other men ate. It's not that it didn't occur to them that the sun could turn: it's that, according to their view, they were the ones who made it spin with their human sacrifices. This is what they call culture. Ah! Now everything is culture. What the Aztecs did was as well, apparently. So maybe this is precisely the problem: that the Spaniards didn't finish what they started. Because those fuckers today, the narcos, some narcos at least, still carry the Indian inside them. The Aztec rotting inside their flesh, man. They get hard thinking about the black magic stuff the Aztecs did. And the women are their sacrifices. And the desert is their pyramid. And they, the fucking narcos, are the priests. A friend told him once that somebody else had told him that certain sicarios paid I don't know how many dollars to sacrifice a virgin. For their business. Can you believe that? They petition la Santa Muerte for their affairs and sacrifice little virgins. Oh! Is this also culture? What they do to those poor girls? I think that's what it's all about, Navaja says: for their sacrifices. Because a woman is a woman whether she likes it or not; but to be a man, to be a real machito, that's gotta be earned. And that's how they earn it. Maybe the women are nothing more than that to me: the waste, the trash left behind after a job. This city is fucked. This fucking city is, in fact, hell. Maybe Juan can't sense it, at least not at first sight, not from behind a car windshield, but the thing is, it is. Pure hell. And maybe for paradise to exist, well, hell also has to exist, nice and close by. Maybe it's as easy as that: if one wants to reach the paradise of the United States, first they have roast in the flames there awhile. Descend to the bottom before rising to the top. Because this thing with the hookers is just the tip of the iceberg, you get me? For every gram of ice that emerges above the water there's a fuckload more below. The dead women showing up are just the tip. Below the surface are the dead women who haven't turned up yet, who will never turn up, because the desert is really big and human curiosity very small. And even further below, worse things. And if that small tip of dead women is already heavy shit, something that makes one shudder, just imagine what remains in the depths. Because it's one thing to bump off the chick who's cheating on you, smack her around so she learns. Another thing is when one gets worked up and loses control of his hand or his bullet. Or give them a shove so they go work with the best thing they have, which is their body. But what's happening to those poor kids is something else completely different: truly incomprehensible. Anyway. The truth is, he never had the chance to discuss his theories with the Padrote. The Padrote didn't like to talk about ugly things. He said it was better to think positive. That one had to think big, and not about those teeny-weeny corpses. It just occurs to him that maybe that's why the Padrote left. He crossed the border and never came back because he realized that hell is fine for a little bit, but that's it. Who knows. Whatever it may be, he told him one day: that he was going to go and leave him everything. This biz-nass with no unions, no strikes, working with women: all fucking advantages, in other words. And yet, when the Padrote told him he was leaving, the first thing he felt wasn't gratitude, but a terrible fear. And keep in mind that the Padrote had warned him about fear: he used to say that fear was the excuse the weak used for not growing. That people were afraid of change, when what one should really fear are things that stay the same: only that which is willing to change can keep on living. That the best job was always ahead, just a step away, and never behind. The fact is, one day the Padrote left. That was when he told him about his brother—him, that is. Juan. Told him for the first and last time. He told him what Juan has already heard and nothing else: that he had been looking for him for a long time and that well he was going to find him soon. That's what he told him. He had to help him cross the border, because on the other side of that line waited the encounter. That and nothing else. And so that's what he's there for: to help him with the crossing, which gets harder every year. They'll do it as soon as possible. Tomorrow, if necessary. Tonight he'll stay with the girls at the club and tomorrow they'll see what's up with the crossing. From that point on, he doesn't know. It will be between the two of them: Juan and the Padrote. All he can say is that in El Past, and even further in, in the fucking heart of the United States, the Padrote has a lot of business. Stuff with hotels and value investments, he seems to remember. It's a strange thing, the investments: he's never entirely understood it. How one can make money with one's fucking imagination. He doesn't understand, but he respects it. He might not have been the smartest guy in the classroom, never the first to understand whatever the teacher said, but he knows something that others don't: he knows how to learn. He knows how to find his goals and recognize the obstacles in the way of those goals and how to beat the fear that stops him from confronting those obstacles. He knows a shitload of things. He knows how to adapt. And he owes all that, Diego says, to his brother. Don't forget to tell him when you see him: he made me a new man, a man he would be proud to meet again.

Juan nods. He nods the entire time. But does he really understand? At times he would say yes and other times it seems as if he is listening to the ravings of a lunatic. After a time, he isn't even attentive to the words. Just to how Navaja says them, like he's spitting them out or like they burned his mouth. As he talks, he keeps a firm hold on a kind of rudder that guides the automobile. On both sides of the road, Juan sees cantinas and back patios and sheet metal barracks and ramshackle yards, sown along the roadside with no clear plan unless it's a plan dedicated to madness. The entire city has the air of a caravan about to resume its march; a makeshift camp assembled with the desert's tools, which are dust and uncertainty and indolence. Only the enormous advertising notices towering everywhere look real: only those gorgeous women and those idyllic beaches and those bright and colorful claims seem to conserve something of the human, having been built with something that is reminiscent of love. At the foot of those billboards, like nightmares born in the shadow of those very dreams, sprout shanty towns made from zinc plates and sheets of tin. Juan can't help but compare their wretchedness with the humbleness of the wooden and adobe houses he left in the south. He asks himself where life is harder; which world is closer to the world the Padre dreamed of.

At some point, the horizon is broken by a range of bald peaks. The city trickles down the hillside, as if indecisive. Visible in the cracks between buildings and rooftops, fragments of sky, which slowly change tone until they acquire the color of blood, only to suddenly plunge into blackness. As if the conversation had lasted a whole day and now it was night again. Or as if in this city day never quite dawned and its borders resisted in never-ending dusk, a perpetual night with no limits save the desert. It is, in any case, nighttime. He sees the lights gradually turn on around him, flameless, smokeless fires burning through on the side of the windows, on the prows of the automobiles, at the top of the streetlamps. The city aflame with sickly light that makes the shadows more ominous and, everywhere, the poverty huddled in empty lots and unsound shacks and suburbs that seem as if erased by some kind of eclipse. The desert that embraces the city has been gradually dying out, until it no longer exists or acquires the blackness of an ocean, and by the streetlamp light, its boundaries appear like narrow dust beaches. He sees a square completely given over to the night, illuminated only by the coming and going of a cigarette's glow, cradled by an anonymous hand. He sees a woman who waits in a yellow pool cast by the streetlight. He sees a street vendor whose face is only visible when caught in the burner's flare. Then he sees nothing. The car gliding along the black artery of the highway, sinking deeper and deeper into the desert, and the headlights revealing, just for an instant, brick walls, and human bodies in front of them, bodies that move or converse or wait in stillness, faces darkened by mistrust, twisted intentions. In the dark, all the passersby look like victims or executioners, the momentary flash of their vaguely feline eyes, heads that harbor unconfessable crimes. The alleyways turned into mouths or drains or waste pipes rife with unbridled night and all the street corners like crossroads where something is about to happen or is happening already, in corners no light ever reaches. And Navaja talking with the same calm, as if his domain was precisely that, the night, words that sprout from the night to illuminate for an instant the things his brother thought, the things his brother said, that voice says with outlines of a nightmare, how much he knew, how many times he heard him relay his philosophies; relay, for example, the lives of those people the Padrote liked so much, guys who had grown up in shit and made it where no other man would have thought possible. Did you know that Einstein, the old guy who sticks out his tongue in pictures and invented so many things, flunked math in high school? And the dude who came up with Apple did it in his parents' garage, and when he was a kid, he used to collect empty Coke bottles just to earn a few cents. Ah, those stories were something. Really inspiring. The man who came up with the little apple, who's everywhere today, you know, picking up plastic like a fucking scavenger. And his brother chatted about that class of men all the time. He knew the histories and private affairs of each of them, like somebody learns the lives and miracles of saints. That's what Navaja says, or Navaja's shadow, Navaja's profile in the gloom, as the headlights sweep the ditches and the dusty flatlands and the by now deserted streets and a huge sign blazing with its own light. Bar Calipso, the sign says, and beside it, a red arrow that blinks and points to the exact spot where the car comes to a stop.

"Come on, cabrón, you're here," says Navaja's mouth from the gloom. "Make yourself at home."

XII

Contempt of women – To eat at the Padrote's table – A woman in twelve parts – Return to Tenochtitlan – A good man – Intercourse between two cities – Cuerpomático – The panty tree – The dead girl strips and then gets dressed

The house is an immense living room crowded with busy waitresses and robust mustachioed men who lean on the bar and drink bottles of beer. There's no light and at the same there's too much: a violent, volcanic brightness, which pulses in the obscurity and reddens the naked flesh of the women who dance. Because there are naked women everywhere: women who slither around metal poles that reach the ceiling. Poles that look like the bars of a prison cell. And the women seem to love those bars, they sway and rub against them, become passionate, lick them with rabid enjoyment, as the men whistle or throw bills or simply bob their heads to the music, transported by drunkenness or fatigue. There is no orchestra and yet there is music, an upbeat ranchera that comes from nowhere, bouncing off the concrete walls.

> Friend, what's wrong, you're crying
> I'm sure it's a woman's disdain
> there is no deadlier blow to men
> than the crying and scorn of those beings . . .

It smells like sweat, smells like booze, like tobacco. Through the haze of cigarettes, Juan barely manages to follow Navaja, who, determined, pushes through the patrons. When he passes, the men respectfully touch their hats or toast the air with their bottles. Some look at Juan himself with an expression of surprise: then they slowly turn their attention back to the dancing women, electric and smothered in the heat.

> Friend, I'm going to give you some good advice
> if you want to enjoy your pleasures
> get a pistol if you want
> or buy a knife if you prefer
> and become a murderer of women

The room is somehow reminiscent of a prison's madhouse basement. A cavern shaken by the tremor of ceremonial fire and tribal dances. Reminiscent of a castle's wine cellar where what ages isn't wine or liquor but human beings. That is exactly what it's like, a human wine cellar, tatters of women shrouded by the dense atmosphere and the makeup and the half-light: dozens of dancing bodies, violent or stupefied or sleepwalking, waiting for the moment to be uncorked and revealed in the sunlight. Juan looks at that cellar, that cavern, that prison, and realizes that had he burst onto that threshold on horseback he surely would've surely shouted—Flee! Come on! Flee! Can't you hear me? Escape!—and not a single one of those women would have followed him. Not one would have abandoned her pole. They wouldn't have because they can't. Or because they don't want to. Because they don't know. Because they understand that all is lost already or, on the contrary, they're scared of losing something that still belongs to them.

> Kill them
> with an overdose of tenderness
> suffocate them with kisses and sweet nothings
> contaminate them with all your craziness

Then he stops thinking. He simply follows Navaja to the other end of the room, asking no questions. A back door. A security guard who gives a slight nod. A woman haggard from something more than just age, leaning on her elbows behind a kind of sentry box. A staircase that leads to the rooms.

"This way," Navaja says.

Behind him, the heart of the music, beating ever more distant.

Kill them
with flowers, with songs, don't fail them
there is no woman in this world
who can resist a gift . . .

A room, among many identical rooms. A bed, a mirror, a narrow washroom. A vase in which a few yellow flowers languish. A sordid still life, hanging above the headboard. Tonight, this will be your room, Navaja says. Now make yourself comfortable and get some rest, because we leave early tomorrow and the trip will be tough. Juan nods mechanically.

Then Navaja leaves or appears to be leaving. Because at the very moment he steps out into the hall, hand still on the door, he remembers to turn back.

"Ah, cabrón, I forgot the most important thing. I have a present for you later tonight. The Padrote's favorite snack."

And before Juan can ask what he means, Navaja closes the door.

Juan lying in bed, the Padre's book in his hands. He doesn't look at the drawings, just the verses in tiny, cramped script. Some have been underlined or crossed out or circled in ink, so savagely that the paper has torn in some places. They are, they must be, the Padre's favorite passages. Places that held his gaze. Ideas he touched, for a moment at least, with the tip of his thoughts. Rapidly he turns the pages, letting his eyes jump from underlined word to underline word. He has followed the Padre's steps to this city where it is always night, to this room, this very bed, and now he follows the wake of his reading, lets himself slip inside the book in his hand as he falls asleep.

He reads: But if this thing be true, and the tokens of virginity be not found for the damsel, then they shall bring out the damsel to the door of her father's house, and the men of her city shall stone her with stones until she dies.

He reads: When a man consecrates a vow by certain persons to the Lord, according to your valuation, if your valuation is of a male from twenty years old up to sixty years old, then your valuation shall be fifty shekels of silver, according to the shekel of the sanctuary. If it is a female, then your valuation shall be thirty shekels; and if from five years old up to twenty years old, then your valuation for a male shall be twenty shekels, and for a female ten shekels; and if from a month old up to five years old, then your valuation for a male shall be five shekels of silver, and for a female your valuation shall be three shekels of silver; and if from sixty years old and above, if it is a male, then your valuation shall be fifteen shekels, and for a female ten shekels.

He reads: When he entered his house he took a knife, laid hold of his concubine, and divided her into twelve pieces, limb by limb, and spread her throughout all the territory of Israel.

Dead women. The dream is filled with them. Their bodies extend as far as the eye can see, disarranged and dirty, like dolls with either missing or extra pieces. A pyramid of corpses that rise from the sludge of the earth to the sludge of the sky, in all ways similar to an Aztec pyramid. Over the women, seated on a chair reminiscent of the throne of a minor king, the Padrote reigns. The Padrote's smile. His hand outstretched toward Juan, in a gesture of invitation or warning.

"Come," he says.

And then a hand, his hand, knocks on the door.

Juan opens his eyes in the dark, not waking completely. He stays like that for a time, on the edge of his dream. He's on the train, he thinks at first. And then: I've fallen off the train, the train has run over my legs, my arms, my head. He is surprised to be alive, if that darkness isn't actually death. I'm dreaming, he thinks. I'm in Navaja's car. I'm in the Chichimeca desert. On his horse. In the arms of the Little Widow. In the arms of my wife. Then he perceives the faint outline of square window, and on the other side, the red and yellow lights of automobiles speeding past on the highway. Much more slowly, memories return to him, in ambiguous waves. He feels along the wall until he encounters what turns out to be a switch and the light from the lamp blinds him like the flash of a gunshot. Gradually he comes into a heavy, viscous awareness of his surroundings. The lamp. The vase where the same withered flowers languish. The bed, his bed, immune to the train's violent jerking and his horse's trot. Finally, he remembers, or decides he remembers. Everything is calm. Only the same rhythmic sound persists; not the Beast's vibration, but a hand knocking on his door.

He stands to open that door.

He sees a very young woman on the other side. A girl whose childhood has been diligently erased, with deep red lipstick and dabs of makeup. She has a bottle of tequila in one hand and two small glasses in the other. A certain expression of neglect. Her eyes shine with a light that is at once familiar and remote.

"Can I come in, papaíto?"

She can. She does so, slowly, hesitant, with her too-short skirt, flesh-colored bra, and swing of her cheap earrings. She sets the bottle and glasses on the night table and then turns to him with something that isn't quite determination but aspires to be.

"You're not going to sit?"

Because she is already sitting on the bed, on the very edge of the bed, as if she would like to occupy as little space as possible. Juan is still standing, his hand on the doorhandle, looking at the girl's bare legs. Her hands, so small, as if created to hold a piece of art. Her white throat. In some ways, she reminds him of the women he saw advertised from the train, depicted on huge signs on both sides of the train track; women who were stunningly beautiful but also a little faded, mistreated by the elements.

"They call me the Güerita," the Güerita says.

"I'm Juan."

"I know. They told me you'd be waiting for me."

He waits a few moments before closing the door. Then he sits down beside the girl. He opens the bottle and fills both glasses. The girl accepts hers in silence; her hands don't meet around the glass. She isn't even looking at it. Her eyes have just discovered the book on the night table, open to the Padrote's page.

"You know him?"

The Güerita is about to reply, but in the end says nothing. Her eyes are fixed on him again, with an intensity that might be confused for fear. Eyes very open but simultaneously afraid, as if they were plumbing the depths of a well. At first, Juan doesn't catch the significance of that look.

"Am I so like him?"

She nods slightly. The glass doesn't quite make it to her lips.

"Navaja says you're brothers."

"Half-brothers."

They drink from their glasses at the same time. Between them, a silence has opened, made not only from a few centimeters of mattress, but from minutes or centuries of distance.

"He was the one who brought you here, right?" Juan asks.

"Yes."

Juan takes another drink, long and full, to decide what he needs to ask.

"Did he force you?"

purer they are. Well. They told her not to take anything and nothing was what she took. Nothing except a few hundred dollars in her socks, and a suitcase with a change of clothes and a Virgin of Guadalupe prayer card. She packed the prayer card face up, so the Virgen could breathe. And the journey had its setbacks and its small tragedies; not all of those who accompanied her had the same luck, but thanks to God nothing happened to her, the Beast was good to her, maybe it respected her because she prayed a lot to the Virgin or maybe— and it scares her to think this—it was nothing but chance, plain and simple. The fact is she reached the border in ten or twelve days, safe and sound and with most of the dollars still balled up in her left sock. But in the end, it turned out she didn't have enough for the crossing; the prices changed year to year, and in the previous eighteen months, the polleros' fees had gone up: supply and demand, sister, they told her, this is America, this is the free market. And so she tried—unsuccessfully— to climb the border wall, along with two guys who also didn't have the money to pay the pollero. And then they tried to swim across the Río Bravo—successfully, in a sense, because even though she didn't manage to reach the other side, she didn't drown either, not like one of the boys did. It was in that moment, soaked to the bone and shaking, when she decided to give up the dream, or a specific part of the dream, and settled down right here. In this city that kisses the border with El Paso and from that kiss, from that species of encounter or chat or intercourse between the two cities, nothing good is born. A city with a gentleman's name, but that was better suited to the name of a murdered female, and there are so many to choose from. Of course, back then she didn't know anything about this city, nothing about the murdered women, nothing, really, about almost anything. The worst thing about poverty, the girl says, is that it's not just your pockets that are empty, but your head, too. It costs money to know certain things. And she had nothing, knew nothing, just what was advertised on TV, that Coca-Cola is life and that it's a good time for the great taste of McDonald's; that Vicente Fox is the change you need and Felipe Calderón wants you to catch his passion for México and you know that Peña Nieto will deliver. Because advertising, the girl says, is free. It might be the only free thing in this world. Anyway. She arrived in this city whose name she doesn't want to remember with very little, with a couple hundred dollars and the address of her sister-in-law's friend written on the back of a flyer. Her sister-in-law's friend took her in as best she knew and could manage. The next day, that woman got her a job at one of the city's textile factories. Because sewing was among the few things the girl knew how to do. There, in that sort of stable or hothouse or mammoth cathedral, where all the people were women, bent over their sewing machines, strafing scraps of yellow canvas. It was so bright indoors that outside always looked like night. Very white light, like a highway gasworks. Or a hospital waiting room. Or the front window of a cafeteria open twenty-four hours. In fact, the factory was open twenty-fours a day, and inside you could eat lunch, shower, even work out in a kind of gym. When she earned enough, the girl told herself, she would cross the border. And that, earning enough, might still take a few months, because the pay was, shall we say, somewhere between low and really low, but her sister-in-law's friend told her no, they couldn't complain, especially considering what was going on. The girl, who knew nothing, nonetheless knew, or intuited, something, or rather she believed something in a blind and irrational way, a way she herself couldn't explain. She knew things had always been bad. And that they would continue to be bad. And that the poor would continue to find reasons not to complain. She was poor and—in accordance with her own theory—she didn't complain. Besides, what was there to complain about, what with the trimestral bonuses for employees and labor conventions, her sister-in-law's friend recited, impassioned; there were prizes for attendance and prizes for performance, employee of the month, employee of the week, social security, free uniform laundry service; they took out a life insurance policy for you while you were alive and paid for your funeral if, God forbid, you died. It was enough for the girl because the girl was going to leave. But between leaving and not leaving, while she machine-gunned scraps of yellow canvas in that stable or cathedral or hothouse, while she shared a mattress in a shared room in a shared apartment, while those things were happening, she says, other things were happening that she disregarded, at least in the beginning. There were tiny notices in the papers, between the crime section and the horoscopes. Flyers pasted on bus shelters or streetlights, and on them the faces and names of very young girls. Girls who weren't old enough. Old enough for what? What does she know, old enough to be alone, to be lost; to be, basically, all blurry in a black and white photograph, as if their own disappearance had caught them off guard. It's true that, in time, all or almost all of them turned up, poor things, mutilated and dirty with dust and blood, abandoned in the empty lots in Lomas de Poleo or the landfills of Santa Elena or the Cerro Bola hillside, under a jumbo inscription written in whitewash that said READ THE BIBLE. Just like that, in the imperative: Read the Bible. They turned up around there, and the newspaper devoted the same tiny space to them again, only now they were a female cadaver, and in the days following the press release someone, merciful or pragmatic, went around taking down the flyers with those photos that looked like they'd been taken for a First Communion. Other times, other bodies turned up, bodies no one identified or claimed, women for whom nobody had put up posters, and then the press release was even smaller. This is awful, I would say to my sister-in-law's friend, the girl says, although it's probably fairer to say that by that time she was not so much the sister-in-law's friend as her own. The girl's. What's awful? the friend would ask. Well, the stuff about those poor little girls. And she, the girl's friend, would gesture with whatever she had in her hand, a little scrap of yellow canvas, for example, she would make that gesture and say that it was sad, of course it was sad, but those little girls weren't little girls; most of them, in fact, were lost. The girl didn't understand: well of course they're lost, haven't you seen the posters? But her sister-in-law's friend, the girl's friend, didn't mean that. She meant that they worked in prostitution, did she get it? They took drugs or sold them or both. They went out alone at night or in bad company or tempting men in roadside bars. They were girls who paid for the trip north with their bodies, the body's ATM, the cuerpomático—and on saying this, cuerpomático—the sister-in-law's friend touched her breasts. Oh, the girl says she responded at the time. That was all. And she was left thinking about the pictures she'd seen on the posters, which looked like they were from a First Communion, or a quinceñera at most. She thought about that for a few days, about their First Communions, about where and how they had celebrated their fifteenth birthdays, and about how their parents must have suffered over the bad lives their daughters were living.

Word by word, drink by drink, the girl has drained her glass. Now she fills it again. Time for the second tequila has come and with it, the heaviest part of her story. Because the factory where the girl worked might have had labor agreements, and prizes for attendance and prizes for performance, and employee of the month, employee of the week, and social security, free laundry service for their uniforms, but it also had a very strict policy about punctuality. If you got to work late, even just a minute late, you didn't get in. Two minutes. That was how late the sister-in-law's friend was, the friend who was, by that time, the girl's friend. At least that's how the girl would remember her: as her friend. That's how she has been fossilized in her memory: the wee hours of one morning in some summer month in such-and-such a year. It was two minutes past midnight: that she can state with certainty. Two minutes late and they wouldn't let her in. That was as much as the girl knew and what she would later tell the police, when at eight o'clock in the morning she got home, never to see her friend again. She didn't actually tell the police right at that time, because first she wanted to be patient, wait a couple of hours, and then because the Mexican police have their procedures and protocols. One was required to wait so many hours, entire days, before filing a report. How many hours, how many days? The girl doesn't recall. What she does remember is that the commissioner who met with her was very gentlemanly, very polite, he pulled out a chair for her and even asked how she liked her coffee. She asked for it with a splash of milk because she'd heard that was a classy way to order, with a splash of milk, although she didn't even like milk and only sort of liked coffee; but she was weakened by her tears and intended to please the police every way she could. I-don't-know-what percentage of the muchachitas—that's what he called them, "muchachi-tas"—reappear within seventy-two hours of their own volition. That's what the commissioner said. The girl doesn't remember the figure: it was a high percentage. And the other percent? she asked, coffee cup trembling in her hand. The commissioner raised his eyebrows. A short time later, they called to tell her that her friend belonged to the small percentage, not the large group. It wasn't the norm: at least not according to the statistics. There were inquiries. There were witnesses who said they'd seen a black car stopped at the factory entrance, and also a white motorcycle, and a car that was a sort of a pistachio yellow. There was a small press release. There were posters with a blurry photograph. Her sister-in-law's friend was nineteen and in the only picture the girl had of her, she was smiling and winking at the camera. That was how the neighbors would see her, multiplied and laminated and cyclostyled by the city's streetlights and bus shelters. One afternoon, after posting a dozen leaflets around a block far from the apartment, she overheard a conversation between two boys who stopped to look at one of posters. The picture of her winking friend. She didn't hear or didn't recall hearing what the first kid said. But the second kid replied: One of those girls with the body's ATM, he said, grabbing his balls. She started to cry and the boys asked her if she needed help and she answered that she didn't need any help thank-you-very-much. But she didn't cry, however, when the police called her. Identifying the body wasn't as hard as she'd imagined, either: by then, she'd had lots of time to read plenty about the girls who got lost in that city. She knew what she could expect. She knew about ritualistic mutilations, nipples bitten off, rampageous rapes, the female cadavers—as they were called—that turned up with stiff arms, as if embracing the air; as if they were still embracing the last man who fucked them. In gynecologic positions, the experts said, which meant that the thing never ended, that, even dead, they looked like they were still getting fucked. As for her friend, the murder or murderers respected her, all things considered. Up to a certain point, at least. The deceased's demise was caused by strangulation, and most certainly occurred the same day as the kidnapping. She had been raped, yes, but only vaginally; no matter how thoroughly they explored her rectum, no signs of abrasion, tearing, or dilation were found. That, the absence of anal rape, was of great consternation to the medical examiner. The modus operandi, he said with a sigh, appears to have changed. But she, the girl, wasn't interested in the modus operandi. Over the preceding weeks she had read everything she could get her hands on about the wave of femicides, in the papers or online—because her factory, in addition to paying for your funeral if, God forbid, you died, also had a kind of employee internet café where they could call their relatives or play solitaire or do whatever they liked. She knew as much as could be known about the subject, which wasn't a lot. She knew the guilty party was a serial killer who mimicked other serial killers, imitators in theory but just as lethal in practice. She knew blame lay with the patriarchy. She knew blame lay with excess: an excess of women and an excess of desert. Blame lay with the gringos, who crossed the border like they were going on safari, hunters ready to claim their female trophies. Blame lay with the Mexicans, who no longer believed in the Virgin of Guadalupe with the intensity of yesteryear. Blame lay with the government. With the narcos. With the narco-government. Blame lay with the women, who walked alone. Blame lay with the women, who walked in bad company. Blame lay with the women, who were pretty. Blame lay with shamanic rituals and black magic and the Santa Muerte and the Aztecs. Blame lay with living like this, partway between the city and the desert, between Mexico and the United States, between Heaven and Hell, on that irresolute land between something and nothing. Blame lay with values, with a lack of values. Blame lay with poverty. Blame lay with the desert. That's what the girl read, and read, and read, like she'd read ads before, other claims, other highway signs and leaflets and billboards. Fuck it all. The factory, too: fuck it. As the deceased's next of kin—*her? she was her sister-in-law's friend's next of kin?*—she was left a bit of money. With that money, she bought what she had come to buy. Prices had gone up again—supply and demand, sister, free market—but still she had enough, she had enough, and when she went to hand over the bill to the pollero, the girl, who, until that moment, had known nothing, nonetheless knew, or intuited, something, or rather believed something blindly, irrationally, in a way she herself could not reasonably explain: that the price of her friend's cheap death meant that she'd have to pay so dearly for the passage.

The end of the story lives at the bottom of the third glass of tequila. The girl looks down at it, and looks again before she finishes. Suddenly, she is speaking in the third person again, as if describing someone else's life. Someone else's death. The death of one of those dead women. It was that very day, the girl says, her voice unusually grave. That exact pollero. That desert. The girl was part of a group of twenty or thirty migrants, all of them women—meaning, in other words, all of them on their own—and the pollero promised to get them over to the States at an unguarded point. There wasn't even a border wall: just the desert. And they were walking in that desert, seeing the dust and frayed clumps of grass and the skeletons of cattle gleaming in the sun, when they came upon the tree. It was a sad, awkward tree, parched from thirst. In its leafless branches fluttered little white and red and black rags, innocent as bunting at an open-air dance; like the final festivities of a village fête in Hell. Someone, maybe she herself, realized that the scraps of fabric were actually women's panties, tossed into the branches. Then they heard a whistle that came from the brush and another whistle answering from the opposite direction. The pollero stopped beside the tree and turned to the girls with a hint of a smile.

"Know what, girls? I think we'll stop here for a spell."

They saw them emerge from the brush in their black balaclavas. There weren't more than five of them, but they had automatic weapons and moved like soldiers. As they approached, the pollero warned the woman not to resist. If they ask for money, just give it to them, don't forget a single peso, and if they tell you to strip, well then, strip. By that time, the men were among them, looking at them through the white holes in the black balaclavas. The men asked for money and they gave it to them. The men ordered them to strip and they stripped. There were only five of them, the girl repeats, holding up the five fingers on her right hand, and they were many women; twenty, maybe thirty women, but taking the necessary pauses and delays, after many swigs of beer and moments of activity and rest, the men managed to fuck them all. The girls who were pretty and not so pretty, old women and young girls or almost girls—the men made no distinctions. They fucked them enthusiastically at first, then with growing indifference and increasingly marked effort, at times you might even say with an air of suffering, emitting snorts that didn't sound like pleasure, but distress. The girl remembers the big drops of sweat that soaked the balaclavas and dripped, like a wad of melted wax, onto the women's naked backs. They proceeded like an army carrying out orders that came from higher up; soldiers who storm whatever hill their officer points at, though neither their officers nor the hill matter much to them. They, the women, were the hill. And it was a very hot day, a day during which the women groaned under the weight of their bodies. And the men groaned as well, industrious and obliged, impugning, muttering filthy words that might just as well have been leveled against the migrants or themselves, against their shit job, against the fucking desert. There was a little old lady who was all years and all bones, and they didn't do much except grope her a bit, subdue her with a few apathetic thrusts, then shout at her to get dressed. They entertained themselves with the girl a little longer than necessary, much more than she deserved given the calculations of time and bodies. She was very young back then, just eighteen years old, the girl repeats, and they stripped her naked and rode her with a bit more frenzy, you might say they compensated for how hard it'd been for them to fuck some of the others—the old, the ugly, the really hideous—and the girl remembers how, in that moment, ground into the dirt, she perceived reality as multiplied or enhanced, the sensation and temperature of their cocks swelling inside of her, but also the exact asperity of a tiny stone against her cheek, the scent of every herb, the silent choreography of birds cawing in the sky, indifferent to them all, and meanwhile she was becoming conscious of parts of herself that until then hadn't been hers and which, since then, have always seemed like they belonged to someone else. She felt that other part was about to die. She felt she was her sister-in-law's friend, dying again. She died then and there, the girl says. They left her on her little scrap of desert, in the dust, bleeding out while the other women hurried to dress and get back in line. Now we're going to take you over, she heard the pollero say; they'd been promised the crossing and they were going to get them across, because they were men of their word, trustworthy men, did they or did they not understand? But first, they ordered the women to throw their panties up into the tree, making no distinctions there either, they just as soon hang a girl's thong as a pair of blood-stiff briefs or an old lady's underpants, big and embroidered like a tablecloth from yesteryear. Who knows why they did it: maybe to them, that tree meant something after all. She had been wearing a pair of panties with a picture of dinosaur on them and, as far as she knows, they must still be hanging from the same tree, the T-Rex dissolving in the sun. She felt that same sun dissolving her, as well, wiping her into the ground, and she couldn't stand up to rejoin the line, though she tried with all her might. She saw the women move away, bowed under the weight of their silence, as one of the men stood watching the pool of her blood spreading on the sand.

They loaded her back into a pick-up truck that suddenly appeared as if out of nowhere. She remembers that, on the side of the vehicle, someone had written in pink letters: Church of Love. And in that truck they applied gauze and a few drops of iodine that stung like the sun, a miniature sun that was still fucking her insides, and right then she wasn't herself, but her friend, and she wasn't in a truck, but on the table in the morgue, as they searched her rectum for signs of abrasion, tearing, or dilatation; the modus operandi appears to have changed, the medical examiner sighed, and then removed his rubber gloves and asked her how she liked her coffee. All those thoughts came very quickly, as the truck bumped down the dirt road, quickly with the clairvoyance present in those who are about to die. Only she didn't die. She didn't die because she was already dead. They left her, dead and all, on the side the of the road, very near to where she had begun her journey, and, still dead and bleeding, she stumbled a few steps into a vacant lot strewn with scrap metal and cigarette butts and crushed beer cans. She saw two trash-pickers pass by with their shopping carts, two men darkened by the sun who, for a few seconds, observed her with the same concentration with which they weighed the value of copper plumbing and aluminum sheets. But she was worth less than that, so they went away. She seems to recollect that immediately after, a woman brought her something to eat and drink, as well as some bandages and salves. She asked the girl whether she had a social security card and the dead girl told her nope, no card, and the woman gave her a tight, embarrassed smile. The hospitals are very expensive, she said, but the girl would see how, with the ointment and bandages, she'd be better soon. Don't die, my girl, the woman said before she disappeared forever; the girl said nothing: it would have been too arduous to explain how she was already dead. An indeterminate time passed during which the pain gradually eased and turned into hunger and, in order to quell it, she dug to the bottom of trashcans until she found wax paper containing the remains of a taco, a gordita, a cheeseless quesadilla. Then she saw a car stop and, through the window, the face of an elegant gentleman, well-dressed, watching her from behind the fog of his cigarette. That man asked if she needed help.

The Padrote, the girl repeats, is a good man.

She didn't work those first days: she simply convalesced in one of the bedrooms at the Bar Calipso. In a room that could just as well be this one. From her window, she saw many girls come and go, each on the arm of a different client, and she watched them with curiosity and shame. She doesn't remember doing anything else. Just watching the girls and watching cartoons on TV. Drinking a lot of cold Cokes, eating big spoonfuls of ice cream. She ate and drank what the Padrote brought her; she let herself be treated with surgical dressings and dressed in clothes that were too big for her. She said thank you with her lips or her thoughts. Some nights, she heard the girls' panting echo off the shared walls, and felt something that made her damp with fear and damp with desire. Be a good girl and get better soon, Güerita, the Padrote would say every time he came with ice cream and Coca-Colas. Because he had asked for her name the first day and she hadn't hesitated. I'm la Güerita, the girl said, though clearly she wasn't remotely blonde; she only said it because it was what people used to call her sister-in-law's friend. Now I'm la Güerita, la Güerita says. Then, when she was all better, dead but all better, the Padrote came back. That night, instead of dressing her, he began to take off her clothes. He was in no hurry. He touched her where the men had touched her and asked if it hurt. No, it didn't hurt. And it didn't hurt the way the Padrote did it to her the first time, with moves that were both firm and delicate, a potter who knows the secrets of flesh and clay. She was that clay, and the Padrote, the Padrote's hands, were patiently shaping her, explaining how she should position herself, which movements were expected of her, which moans, which silences, which words. That was it, at first: a lot of cartoons and a lot of Cokes and cups of ice cream and every night the Padrote's hands, the Padrote's lessons, the Padrote's hoarse pleasure when he came inside her. It was a strange thing, fucking the Padrote: sometimes she felt like she was fucking a priest and other times like she was fucking a soldier. She doesn't know if he, Juan, can understand that. I can, Juan says simply. Well. The fact is that one day, he came with another man and even then things didn't change much. The girl remembers the Padrote watching from his chair, counting bills like someone counting beads on a rosary, and the man on the bed, already naked, and in the end, what he did wasn't any different or any worse than what the Padrote had done to her first. And when the thing was over—because the thing, if one considers it coolly, never lasts very long—the Padrote took a handful of those pesos and handed them to her and told her she had been a good girl. She'd been a quick learner, she had a future in the business and she should go out and buy some clothes or jewelry or perfume of whatever she liked. Because the Padrote was always like that, always decent to her. That's how she remembers him: the handsome, elegant man who once looked at her through a car window. The only person that one summer day who didn't want her to die. What comes next doesn't matter. What comes next, the dead girl says, is a job like any other, and as far as she can judge, much more secure than trying to cross the border on her own or living alone in this fucking city. Because nobody has ever forced her to do anything: she wants to make that very clear. She is not a victim, nor is the Padrote a villain: if she's a prostitute, it's because she is willing, because she likes the money she makes on the pole and in bed and because what else could she do in this world. Sure, in this profession, sometimes bad or not entirely good things happened, but how was that the Padrote's fault. Sure, there are certain clients she would prefer to not deal with. Men who think they own you for the half hour they pay for and that the girls are like a rented house or hotel room or little broom closet that they can inhabit as they please. Sure, some of the girls are locked in the house, but that's because they're idiots and they fell into prostitution unwittingly and now they regret it. But she is no idiot. She came here with her five senses intact, and careful with calling her a victim, the victim of what. Victims are the girls who came to Calipso because they were tricked by boyfriends who said they loved them and victims are the women raped under the panty-tree in exchange for nothing; victims are the girls who still believe men's promises; victims are her mama and her papa, who never came back, and those who came back and didn't know what to do with what they learned away. Victims are the million women and men who die of disgust in this piece of shit city. Victim is la Güerita: the real Güerita. Victims, the dead girl says as she sets her thrice-emptied glass of tequila on the night stand, are the dead girls who still think they're alive, as if life consisted of swallowing air just to later spit it out. But she, what could she be a victim of, with her savings to spend on her whims, and her Mondays off, and her free beer. A victim? no way. And before she finishes speaking, she's already on her feet and lifting up her top and unclasping her bra, because with all that chatting it's gotten late and in this profession, like any other, there are deadlines to meet.

Juan watches the clothes drop silently to the floor. He watches the mouth grotesquely painted red, like a wound that will never heal. He watches her tiny breasts, narrow hips, her sex, atrociously bare, the white and trembling flesh revealed, suddenly, in the bulb's glare. He watches her porcelain-doll body that waits, the body the Padrote mounted so many times, like a horse.

"No," he says, and his own voice sounds strange to him.

The dead girl blinks, confused, her expression stalled between surrender and confusion. A body that has ceased to be sensual but now doesn't know what to be; a body that is, again, a girl's body, shivering with embarrassment and fear. She tries to control her voice, searching for the composure that appears to have fled her.

"You don't like me, papaíto? You want me to call another girl?"

But Juan shakes his head. No, he doesn't want her to call another girl. He doesn't want company. He doesn't want anything. Just sleep. That's what he says: I just need to sleep a little. And then, since the girl is still standing there, waiting for an explanation, Juan begins to talk incoherently about many things. He talks about fidelity. He talks about commitment. He talks about the desire to return home. He talks about a woman who waits for him somewhere, and he doesn't know if he is talking about his own wife, or the Little Widow he abandoned, or an indigenous woman who looks in horror at her people in one of Daga's cages, or a girl who looks in horror upon her own imprisonment, many leagues to the south.

"I understand," the girl says, with the look of someone who doesn't understand but does what she is trained to do: respect a man's will.

But she isn't going to put her clothes on. At least not yet. What the dead girl is going to do is come a little closer to Juan and extend, very slowly, one of her tiny hands to stroke his face.

"You're not so like him," she says.

She says it in a new voice, and it is unclear whether it contains gratitude or condemnation or simply surprise.

And that's how it all ends. Or not exactly. There is, still, the long process of bending to pick up her clothes, the long process of putting them on, the even longer process of silently stepping into her heels and adjusting her dress. And meanwhile, Juan, who still sits on the bed. Juan who watches her. Juan who knows he might never see her again. And he imagines her, for a moment, naked again, dead again, abandoned in the immensity of the desert. He imagines her body, beaten and humiliated and mutilated, illuminated, first by the glare of disappearing headlights and then by the moon's pale glow. He imagines a new day dawning over her dead body. He imagines what time, what the slowness of the desert, could do with all that withered flesh. And then he imagines days or weeks, eternities of sun and wind, and the sudden chance of a man walking the paths through Cerra Bola and finding, half-buried or not buried at all, a hand, or what is left of a hand, emerging from the sand to beg for help that no one can give her now. And if it isn't too late by then, if the vultures or vermin haven't had time to sack her flesh; if her face hasn't been dissolved or hollowed by worms or concealed by sand, he knows very well what that man will find. A pair of eyes that, even under the sand, still manage to look in a terrible way, as if they were looking at terrible things that have happened and the even more terrible things still to come; eyes divested of all will and all beauty, eyes that have seen horror and are full of it and therefore excruciating to see, or maybe they have seen horror and are empty for that very reason and that emptiness is even more intolerable. Eyes that reflect nothing now, eyes that are what remains of compassion when faith has been erased; freedom, when justice is withheld; will, when it lacks hands and voice. Hope minus hope.

XIII

A pipe shit would avoid if it could – God and the Padrote know – The final shedding of skin – The desert will make you free – The inside of a backpack and the inside of a thought – A scar on the earth – Pilgrims' lodge – In Gold We Trust – Drink water, eat bread – Old speech from a new pulpit – Communion and excommunion – Walking north, walking south – Sleep without dream – Easy women, pretty women – I JUAN TO BELIEVE – The beginning of the journey – This is how the world ends – This is how the world ends – This is how the world ends – Not with a bang, but a whimper

The wall is not a wall. Just a fence built from rusting metal sheets, partially consumed by the elements; a scar stitching the desert together in two equal and desolate tracts. The future is on the other side, Navaja said while they are still in the car, the dream of the United States, but that dream doesn't look all that different from the reality they leave behind. It too has a nightmare quality that reaches in all directions, an ocean of dust and bare hills where human will is dismantled until it is reduced to nothing.

They stop at some arbitrary point on the border. Only it isn't arbitrary. At the base of the fence, half-hidden behind brush and a pile of old tires, he makes out the dark mouth of a drainpipe linking desert with desert. Cautiously, Juan peers inside. A yawn of fetid waters reaches him from the blackness.

Behind him, Navaja smiles with certain discomfort. Yes; this is the path that will lead him to the Padrote. Juan hesitates a second then steps inside. The pipe is half a man's height. He will have to stoop to climb inside and then almost crawl along its mud-and-shit-stained walls. This is what Juan does now: allows himself to slip inside, like a piece of excrement striving to vanish from the face of the Earth.

A pipe shit itself would avoid touching if it could, he remembers.

Navaja makes no move to follow him. He's hardly moved at all, except to crouch down and wait next to the drainpipe opening. He holds out a very heavy black backpack, which Juan struggles to grab.

Is he not coming with him? Oh, no, Navaja says, the ever-present smile on his lips. Unfortunately, his journey ends here. He has done no more and less than what the Padrote asked of him: get Juan to the border. From there on, it's Juan's affair. There are certain roads, he says, that one must walk alone. Certain trips no one can take with us. This, he says in a voice the pipe's echo has made ominous, this is one of those trips. The Padrote told him and even repeated it, nice and clear: his brother had to find his trail on his own, without any more help than was strictly necessary. This is all Navaja has done: the strictly necessary and maybe a tad more. And now it is up to Juan to do the rest.

He gives a few more instructions before taking off. Because the United States are not at the other end of that pipe: at least not quite. First, he must come to a kind of no-man's land, defended by concertinas and barbed wire. On that ownerless tract, there are sometimes border patrol agents who travel the strip in jeeps or on bikes. Military helicopters that erase the dark with their floodlights. And if that happens, he'll have to wait, at least until the shift change. Because there is always, at some point, a shift change: a moment when even the border police take a breather or eat their sandwiches or drink their liters of beer. One instant when they let the night look after itself. That will be his moment. He must dash through the dark strip of desert, slosh through the water and the reeds, coat himself in sand. On the other side, he will find the opening to the other drainpipe, covered by a grille with bars as thick as a man's wrist. But not even those bars can stop him. He just has to give them a little shake to find that they've been carefully filed by other men who have traveled that same road before him. A grille that can be easily taken off and put on, as inoffensive as a bottle cap. On the other side, yes, this time he will find the dream that has been waiting for him forever. Only then will he be free: as free as a man can be when fleeing through the desert.

And what comes afterward? Only God and the Padrote know.

In the dream, the Padrote is not the Padrote. He wears a blue suit coat, meticulously ironed. A red necktie. A voice, his voice, so different, or maybe it's the same voice shouting new words; words Juan has never heard before. He no longer looms over a pyramid of dead women. The dead women are still dead, Juan knows that somehow, but they're gone now, or at least he can't see them. Only an enormous platform that hundreds, maybe thousands, of men bear on their backs, nearly crushed beneath its weight. Those men cheer for him. They shout. They clap. And Padrote sticks out his thumb, one appendage standing erect over their heads and their hopes. The Padre's smile. His thumb extended toward Juan in a gesture of invitation or warning.

"*Come here*," he says, using those new words.

And on hearing that voice echo off the pipe walls, Juan wakes, or believes he does.

He doesn't sleep the rest of the night. He is hardly more than a silent, motionless shape in the pipe opening. He hears the rumbling engines of cars that come and go and he sees the spotlight that patiently combs the frozen geometry of the border wall and hears voices the wind carries to and fro. Then he hears nothing, sees nothing. Only his panting breath. The beat of his pulse, his organs, silence buzzing in his ears. Time, or something Juan thinks must be time, goes by: a vague sense of opportunity, of urgency, of vertigo. Maybe this is the shift change Navaja told him about. Or maybe it is the silence that precedes a catastrophe. At first, he keeps his eyes closed when he finally jumps out onto the dirt. He senses that his every movement is accompanied by noise, by rattling; that his arms and legs and backpack are heavy as stone. High overhead shines an anemic moon, feeble, its light dripping down the metal of the fence and onto the puddle-filled earth. He sees the nightmares he is not dreaming gather before him; he sees cement watchtowers spying on him and he sees shifting shadows that are actually sheets of iron that detain human will, and over and over he imagines the many dangers that await him in the dark: the immigration police who will stop him, detain him, shoot him maybe. But no one detains him, no one stops him, no one shoots. The rest of the journey is exactly as Navaja described. Juan running through the swathe of darkness; Juan splashing through water and tufts of grass; Juan getting coated in sand. On the other side, the opening of the other drainpipe, covered by a grille with bars as thick as a man's wrist. But not even those bars can stop him. He just has to give them a little shake to find that they've been carefully filed by other men who have traveled that same road before him; who knows if by the Padrote himself. A grille that can be easily taken off and put on, as inoffensive as a bottle cap. Another pipe, fifty, maybe a hundred meters of horizontal anguish, and on the other side, yes, this time freedom; the dream that has always been waiting for him, as boundless and terrible as only the desert can be. Juan is free. Juan is free and he runs. Juan's body, Juan's shadow, shadow among shadows, finally running, finally free, a hope that rides night's bankless course; a horseless ride, but a ride all the same.

Inside the backpack: a jug of water, a sandwich wrapped in tinfoil, a plaid blanket. A stack of bills, so wrinkled they form a fat ball—*In God We Trust*, each one says. A compass that points vigorously north, with the obstinacy of which only machines are capable. Behind him, the unexpected dawn light, materializing with the shock of a thunderbolt. Before him, the vastness of the desert, so empty that his eyes and his imagination skate to the horizon's edge, never meeting a scrap of reality on which to cling.

Time is something we walk, he remembers. The past falls behind and the future draws near and the present is something we try to hold on to with both hands but can never quite grasp. Earth and dust and sky: that's all that exists.

He sees all that exists.

He walks on land, though everything that happens does so in the sky. He sees, on the always identical earth, the shadow of a cloud, the shadow of a bird. A flock of crows shaped like an arrow or the idea of an arrow.

He sees night fall and day break and night fall again. He sees dawns and dusks that, in his memory, are like immoveable landscapes, stations along a route that must be crossed like one fording a recollection.

At night, the frozen fire that burns in stars so close his fingers can almost touch them, and below, the dark earth on which another Juan before this Juan once tread.

In the distance he sees blue-tinged thunderbolts striking silently on the horizon, and he sees the scrawny shadows of coyotes, and stars that blaze for an instant and are extinguished, and others so bright they look like caldera conveying fire from another world. He sees all of this and more, but he does not see light from any houses. As if the gringos, too, were invaders in their own land and instead of inhabiting it, they lived fleeing it, frightened by its immensity or their own insignificance.

He sees his own insignificance. The smell of reality is the smell of sun-warmed rock and the smell of his own body cooking on that rock, and beyond that, nothing.

He sees the void. The bare peaks punished morning and night by sun and wind, without the consolation of a bit of shade, a gawky tree, a stunted cactus. He contemplates nature's resistance to being crossed, to being understood, and in this resistance, he sees the Padre's face.

He progresses northward as if guided by an arcane instinct, without making plans or weighing consequences, without rationing his food or water or deciding what he will do when he finds him. Finding him is all that matters. He wants to empty his head the way a desert traveler empties his canteen, sip by sip. He is that traveler and he is that canteen, too, the jug he carries in his backpack, less and less heavy. He is that traveler and that canteen and he is also the Padre.

Everything is simpler than we believe, Diego de Daga had said. Tomorrow comes, yesterday goes; all can be reduced to that. The savages, who have twenty-five words for their arrows, haven't required a single word to name such an essential, such an astonishing thing: time.

Around him, the earth pulses, vertiginous as a dreamscape. All the weight of humanity resides in his memories, ever smaller on the infinite horizon. Thoughts that dissipate with each step, as one strips off too-heavy clothes. Everything disappears. Everything except the women, who somehow remain. The dead women again. The secret that surrounds their disappearance, impenetrable, terrible, like a desert his memory cannot cross, a fence his memory cannot clear, a border his conscience will never, ever clear. The dead women and the living ones too, prisoners in that other jail of too-loud music and narrow bedrooms. If it was the Padrote who built that prison without bars, if he accepted or tolerated or even inspired that thing Juan saw happening inside, then what? But it wasn't the Padrote, he says, it couldn't be him. How could he? He, who came filled with so many beautiful dreams, wouldn't have been capable. Or, if he had done it, it was for the right reasons, in pursuit of ends not easily discernible today; not to lock them up, not to punish, not to torment all that withering flesh. Only Navaja could. It's men like Navaja who lay waste to the most magnificent aims: they are second fiddle, he thinks, emulators, mercenaries; they are the idiots, the satellites, the blind, the mediocre; the illuminated who do not shine with their own light but, like the moon, can only reflect the sun's splendor.

He sees the sun's splendor. He thinks about the weight of that sun on his head, a burden that is never finally relieved. He thinks about the weight in his backpack. He thinks about the weight of the water jug, increasingly light on his back and heavier on his conscience.

He sees tire tracks that crisscross in the dust, tracks that intersect and drive away and meet again, as if choreographed by a madman, and birds that patiently soar overhead, waiting, perhaps, for him to die, but he is not going to die, no sir, he is going to drink the water down to the last drop and lick the rough tinfoil that held the sandwich and he is also going to remove his T-shirt and knot it around his head, like a hat or a turban or a shroud, but he is not going to die, not a chance.

He sees the tinfoil that held the sandwich, empty.

He sees the jug without water, the empty shell of what was once a water jug. The jug abandoned at some point on the trail, like one abandons a plan.

He sees hunger, a country that stretches as far as the eye can see.

He sees thirst, a landscape of rough contours and concentric paths, like a thorn beating in his temples.

He sees his own shadow, long at daybreak and at dusk and reduced by the boiling heat of midday.

He sees his dead horse.

He sees death. Death right in front of him and what does it matter. Is this the last of the thousand deaths that await him?

Slowly he allows himself to succumb to the ground, as if he too had been turned into a handful of stones. He digs through his backpack in search of the impossible, a last sip of water where no water will be, water to fill a mouth that is all tongue and sand. He finds only a fistful of crumbs and the Padre's book. Lying in the dust, he opens the book. He tries to read, dazed by the sunlight. He doesn't observe the drawings: just the verses in tiny, cramped script. Some have been underlined or crossed out or circled in ink, so savagely that, in some places, the paper has torn. They are, they must be, the Padre's favorite passages. Places where his eyes came to rest. Ideas he touched, for a moment, with the tip of his thoughts. Rapidly he turns the pages, letting his eyes jump from underlined word to underlined word. He has followed the Padre's steps this far and now he follows the wake of his reading, lets himself slip inside the book in his hand.

He reads: It is not for you to know the times or dates the Father has set by his own authority.

He reads: I consider that our present sufferings are not worth comparing with the glory that will be revealed in us.

He reads: Then I said: Lord, how long? And He answered: Until the cities are laid waste and without inhabitants, the houses without a man, and the land utterly desolate.

He reads: Present your bodies a living sacrifice, holy, acceptable to God.

He reads: This is a hard word; who can hear it?

As he reads; as his cracked and arid lips separate to repeat Padre's words, the words of the Lord, overhead clouds and stars and twilights pass. Night falls, day breaks, and it's night again. The sky blinks and with each blink, new words emerge, scratched until the page bled.

He reads: And if the blind leads the blind, both will fall into a ditch.

He reads: I the Lord have said, I will surely do it unto all this evil congregation, that are gathered together against me: in this wilderness they shall be consumed, and there they shall die.

He reads: Put off the old man and put on the new man.

He reads: It is a fearful thing to fall into the hands of the living God.

He reads: I am coming soon.

At first, it looks like a second border: a black scar stitching the desert in two equal and desolate tracts. But with each step—the steps of a traveler unsure that he can keep moving forward; a traveler who drags the weight of the sun and the weight of thirst and the weight of memory—that border starts to become something else. There are no fences, no drainpipes or walls or barbwire or concrete watchtowers. Just a black highway that seems to writhe and melt in the distance, taking fire from the heat storm. A few more steps and Juan can make out the little dots moving over it, small as ants and silent. More steps and then, gradually, the noise: the drone of surf that comes to break on an ocean-less beach, a hum that grows, intensifies, is now the rumble of a car or many cars traveling over the desert's back.

Juan should ask for help, but there's not a single human to address. Just machines crossing the dust, thunderous and immediate; machines that want to spend as little time as possible in this hell.

Some cars head north.

Other cars head south.

For some time, Juan remains fixed on the roadside. Then he takes the way north.

The first thing he sees is a kind of slender tower, with blinking red digits. On top, an incomprehensible word and the image of a scallop shell not so different from those that pilgrims wear on their hats or cloaks. Is that shell a sign? Beside the little tower is a strange construction, all roof and no walls. Some cars are stopped in the shade of that roof. A man gets out from one of the cars to pull on a hose, elongating it, while another man walks toward a kind of cantina constructed of light and glass. The open door. Is that open door a sign? Painted clearly on the asphalted ground, a white arrow pointing to the place the man is headed. Is that arrow a sign, as well?

The interior is so bright that outside always looks like night. On seeing him enter, all those inside look up to watch him. The waiter, the families eating and drinking at the tables, the brown-skinned girl conscientiously sweeping the floor. They look at him because they know he has come from very far away. Or because he is coated in sweat and dust. Because he brings the desert with him. The waiter is speaking to him in an impossible language. He is staring at Juan's dirty hands, his dirty shirt. He says things or seems to say them and then waits for an answer. Juan croaks something that apparently cannot be understood; something the waiter might not understand even if he spoke Juan's language. His dry mouth is a vestige of the desert and his head spins and he holds on to the bar so as not to fall onto the floor.

"Are you okay, señor?"

The girl is suddenly at his side, still gripping the broom like a pilgrim holds his staff.

"Agua," Juan says.

"Pan," Juan says.

And then, with a final effort.

"Por favor."

The girl nods. She translates his words to the waiter, who is still studying him with a grave expression. But waiter does not appear inclined to fill any glass or serve him any crust of bread. He limits himself to posing another question, one which the girl, at first, hesitates to translate.

"Do you have money, señor?" she finally asks, her eyes on the end of her broom.

"Money," murmurs Juan.

"Money," the waiter repeats. "*Dollars.*"

"Dollars," the girl says.

"Dollars," Juan repeats, like an echo.

He rummages in the backpack. Inside he finds the plaid blanket. The last strips of tinfoil. A compass that points vigorously north, with an obstinacy of which only machines are capable. At last, the stack of bills, as wrinkled and useless as the tinfoil. He beings to lay them, one by one, on the bar.

In Gold We Trust.

In Gold We Trust.

In Gold We Trust.

The waiter takes one of the bills. He holds it up to the light, as if he wasn't sure what that bill might signify. Then he puts it away and hands the rest back, never meeting Juan's eye.

The girl smiles for the first time.

"Come with me, señor. I'll get your table ready."

Juan eats bread and drinks water. He eats bread of many shapes and flavors and water which is black and sweet and bubbles in his mouth. A big sandwich, round, which he barely manages to hold with two hands. He asks for more water, more bread. He asks to satiate his hunger; leave behind his thirst once and for all. The girl translates his words. Takes his bills one by one. She brings full plates that are soon empty, then she carries them away. More glass bottles, more round sandwiches—more bread with the taste of meat, cheese, onion; more water that fizzes with impossible flavor. The last dollar and the last bottle and the last sandwich and after that, nothing; hunger and thirst are finally calmed and, for the first time, Juan seems to have eyes capable of seeing the world around him. On the table, a jumble of crumpled napkins and crumbs. Nearby, men and women who study him, their faces severe or perplexed. Behind them, over their heads, a strange box which sounds and colors and lights synthesize. That box like a window behind which everchanging scenes take place. A man kisses a woman. A boy bites into a sandwich. A man looks into our eyes, a black artichoke in his hand. Juan lets himself sink into this square of reality, until nothing else exists. An automobile crosses the desert. A woman, almost nude, smiles at you and me, at all of us. An army of men with helmets but no weapons charge onto the grass to fight over some sort of treasured bladder. At some point, Juan looks away, dizzy and displaced. The men, the women, the children around him have tired of watching him; they too have turned, as if magnetized, toward that window open to the impossible. But now Juan isn't watching that window. He is watching their faces, their expressions of remote concentration. Parted lips. Eyes mesmerized by blue light. They look like orphans or exiles, like children who, for the first time, are watching fire burn.

And then, the Padre's voice.

He knows it is his voice well before he even looks. A voice Juan has never heard yet recognizes immediately, as surely as when we recognize our own image etched in a mirror. That, then, is the window open to the impossible: a black mirror into which we all peer with prophetic amazement. And inside that mirror, the Padre's voice at last. And though the Padre doesn't look like the Padre, not entirely, it is his voice. Stitched onto that voice, the Padre's face. The Padre's right hand, raised again and again in the air, like a puppet master who knows how to control his marionettes' will. He wears a blue suit coat, meticulously ironed. A red tie. His smile, the Padre's smile, a smile so wide and so stiff it seems to vacillate between kindness and cruelty. His movements simultaneously minstrel-esque and terrible, like a jester imitating his lord or like a carnival king who is obeyed in jest but obeyed all the same. He leans on a podium reminiscent of a plinth, of a sacred throne, a pulpit. Around him, hundreds, maybe thousands, of men and women rabidly cheer, holding small blue signs. They shout. They clap. And he sticks out his thumb, a single appendage standing erect over their hopes. His thumb held out to the world, in a gesture of invitation or warning. Behind that thumb, his eyes. The Padre's eyes. Eyes perpetually open, as if they lacked lids. As if they also lacked a gaze, if such a thing were possible. What do those eyes seek? They do not turn to the crowd below. They do not look at the blue signs. They look only ahead, always ahead, as if the Padre could see everything that hasn't yet happened except in his imagination; as if his eyes could pierce the glass separating him from the cantina and observe each and every one of his sons and daughters, in each and every home in America. And here, on this side of the glass, those sons and daughters, frozen in the act of biting into their sandwiches or finishing their pints of beer or completing a sentence; the waiter who stops washing glasses, the man in a hat who respectfully removes it, the girl who puts her spoon down beside her little plate of dessert. The mestiza girl who looks up in resignation, her chin resting on the end of the broom handle.

"Who is he? Juan asks, as if to himself.

"America's fucking papá," the girl replies. She hasn't looked away.

And America's fucking papá is speaking. Over the commotion raised by his subject, finally, the papá speaks. Can Juan understand him? the girl asks. Does he know what that papá says?

The girl says the papá says they are living in difficult times.

He says a terrible enemy waits outside and that inside terrible things are happening too.

He says some things are changing and many others will have to change.

He says the enemy assails them from their piece of shit countries; from countries shit would avoid having to touch if it could.

He says: Never again will those who sing the praises of democracy and then strike in the deepest regions of its heart hide out on our land.

He says: America first.

He says: America for Americans.

He says: Make America great again.

So says the papá. So says the jester. So says the carnival king who is never done; or at least that is what the girl says the papá is saying. The girl translates cautiously, her voice almost strangled, her right hand still gripping the broom. She says the papá says he's going to tell them a story. She says the papá says he's going to read them a poem. Do they want him to read them a poem? Does anybody wanna hear it again? You sure? Are you sure? They're sure, they shout his name with conviction that is almost frightening, and he's going to dedicate that poem to the Border Patrol *for doing such an incredible job*. Because at the border, he says, certain terrible things are happening, and they have to be smart; they have to be ready. So here it is: "The Snake." It's called "The Snake," the papá says. America's papá holds aloft a wrinkled sheet of paper. American's papá reads the wrinkled paper on which the poem is written. And in the poem there is, as is to be expected, a snake. The snake, as usually occurs in such cases, is wicked. The wicked snaked is half-dead from the cold when a woman on her way to work finds it agonizing in a field. The woman sheds tears of compassion and sadness, she wants to care for it, for the wicked snake, she wants to bring it into her home, the wicked snake, and the wicked snake begs, take me in oh tender woman, take me in for heaven's sake, take me in oh tender woman, the girl says the papá says the wicked snake says. So the woman gathers it up in her lap and wraps it in a blanket, even though it is her natural enemy, and brings it inside her cabin. She lights a fire for it. She cleans its cold-chapped skin. She spills drops of milk and honey onto its tongue—its forked snake tongue. From this part of the story on, the girl begins to get overwhelmed, she stutters, the poem is speeding up and she doesn't have time to translate everything the papá says; for some verses, she only manages to translate certain words—"fuego," "leche," "miel"—and repeats the others untranslated. Yet Juan doesn't need to listen, he doesn't need the words because they are all echoes of words he has already heard, he only need look in the Padre's eyes, the right hand raised like a cane or a scepter or a sword, the pulpit from which he exhorts his immobile troops, and meanwhile, inside the poem Juan doesn't hear, the snake is slowly revived, the woman kisses the snake, holds it to her breast—oh take me in tender woman take me in for heaven's sake take me in oh tender woman, says the vicious snake—and the surprise that comes next is no surprise to Juan, the surprise is in fact no surprise to anybody, not to the men or women or children who have come to hear the Padre; instead of saying thank you, the wicked snake chooses to give the woman a wicked bite. And after the bite, the death throes; the woman writhes on the floor and as she takes her final breath, she has time to ask why it bit her, for the love of God, why her, she who so freely offered aid, and then the reptile's smile, the Padre's smile, his subjects' smiles. Oh shut up, silly woman! says the snake with the Padre's mouth. You knew damn well who I was when you let me in!

The immigrants! says America's papá, thrusting away the paper that contains the poem.

The border! he says.

Mexico!

And then the roar. The world the Padre has built with his own hands clamoring as a single man—even the women, even the children, mimicking that one man's voice—the subjects get to their feet and shout, saying nothing, just shouting, and Juan comprehends that if a bark is a dog's voice and a trill a bird's voice, then this is man's original word, this is the seed of the human voice: a howl of rage that signifies nothing, a war cry echoing inside and outside the box, the waiter nodding his head, the man who has removed his hat listlessly applauding the air, the family returning to their interrupted conversation or their round sandwiches or their pints of beer, as if nothing has occurred. Only the girl remains stuck somewhere between the motion of sweeping and not sweeping, her gaze fossilized, her eyes wide open, and in the girl's eyes, Juan's eyes, and in Juan's eyes, the eyes of the girl, which seem to overflow and decant into the darkness of the box whose colors are suddenly extinguished, a ceding to the darkness in which there is no surprise, just the confirmation of something that is already known but no less intolerable for it. She doesn't look at the box. She doesn't look at the broom in her hand. She looks only at him. Inside him. Who knows if right through him. She looks in a terrible way, as one looks at the terrible things that have happened and the even more terrible things that are still to come; eyes from which all will and all beauty have evaporated, eyes that have seen horror and are full of it and therefore unbearable to look at, or maybe they have seen horror and they are empty for this very reason and that emptiness is even more unbearable. Eyes that reflect nothing, now; eyes that are what is left of compassion when faith is erased; freedom when justice is removed; will when it lacks hands and voice. Hope without hope.

At the back of the restaurant, a narrow hallway. At the end of the hallway, two doors. Behind one of the doors, a row of urinals. Two gleaming white privies, appointed with doors. Juan, on his knees and embracing one of those privies, like a monarch praying before the throne he will never again sit upon or a man revealing his secret to a sealed well. His hair tumbles down, spattered with the yellow paste of vomit. Because Juan is vomiting. He vomits the communion of bread and water; he vomits the desert and vomits the road and the things he has seen and the words he has heard. His hand half-rests on the door, and on that door, enlarged or distorted by dizziness, images like those that gestate in the womb of certain caves; obscure scribbles and drawings etched with child-like wonder and impossible dates and numbers, insults, anniversaries, rubrics, outlines of men stiff as scarecrows attached to penises of monstrous proportions, maps of implausible continents, a primitive alphabet, barbaric spells dedicated to the sun or the rain or the wind. Names in twisted, illegible letters, names whose only aim seems to be to not be read, not be recognized, not be understood. Only these hieroglyphs seem to bring Juan any consolation; only in them does he seem to find a vestige of faith or humanity, a reminder that something called humanity exists, flourishing in a desert of smooth tiles and mirrors that multiply his suffering in all directions; his colossal effort to reject a world.

Juan vomits a world and when he finishes, he rinses his head under a stream of water from a white baptismal font.

And then, suddenly, his face. In the mirror, the echo of his own face: a face he had almost completely forgotten. He sees his sopping hair and his beard, only partially clean. He sees his chapped lips and skin afire from the sun and eyes that are somehow feminine, or what Juan understands to be feminine: a gaze that is all pelt or hide; the hollow, the shadow, the imprint of a gaze; a casing emptied of desire and hope. A face that is not the Padre's, that looks nothing like the Padre at all. And from the mirror's depths, that unfamiliar face looks at him with surprise and something like tenderness.

Juan sitting on the asphalt, beside the cantina door. Juan waiting on the shores of the highway. Juan waiting on the banks of the desert.

What is he waiting for?

Machines cross the dust, thunderous and immediate; machines that want to spend as little time as possible in this hell.

One car, two cars that stop near him and drink from long, black hoses, like thirsty horses. First they stop and then they drink and then they go.

Some head north.

Others head south.

Juan sitting in the same spot, master only of his backpack and patch of ground.

The day and night, with no dusk in between. This is how night falls in the desert, like someone snuffs out an oil lamp's flame.

The cars are no longer cars. Just the night, and in it, pairs of lights, yellow as they approach and red when they move away.

Some lights head north.

Others head south.

Juan tries to sleep and finally he does.

There is no dream in his dream. In his dream there are no crucified Padres or Padres who pontificate or Padres who kill or Padres who reign. There are no crosses or signs or arrows. In his dream there is, at first, nothing. Just the dark of night; the same darkness before and behind his eyelids. Just his own body, walking blind down the riverbed of that darkness. And then, suddenly, a light that gleams, akin to a star. Juan, or the shadow that is Juan when he dreams, walking toward that light. A house that might be the image of home if something called home existed. The girl, a girl with no face or all the faces, waiting with her lamp in hand, its light like an outstretched hand in the dark. Juan trusts that hand in order to step through the door.

The night and day, with no dawn in between. This is how the sun rises in the desert, like fire swooping over the earth to ignite the world.

Juan wakes, still master of his backpack, of his little patch of asphalt. Beside him, someone has left a handful of scattered monies. A five-dollar bill, held down by a rock. Juan looks for a long time at the printed face. Then he carefully picks up the rock and puts it in his pocket.

A gust of wind and the bill skitters away, slow at first. The bill swallowed by the immensity of the desert.

Then, on the side of the road, he sees him. A kid with long black hair, a huge backpack at his feet. Brown-skinned, T-shirt wet with sweat. Boots almost completely worn by the bite of sand and dust. He expectantly watches the road like a fisherman contemplating a river's course. He is holding his arm out toward the passing cars, and at the end of that arm, a closed fist and raised thumb, as if imitating the Padre's gesture. His thumb held out to the world, in a sign of invitation or warning.

Juan stands next to him.

Eh, he says, simply, having carefully pondered what his first words would be.

Hey, the kid replies, not bothering to take his hand or eyes away from the road.

Juan asks what he is doing, and the kid says he's waiting.

Juan asks what he is waiting for, and the kid says he's waiting, obviously, for someone to pick him up.

Where do you want to go? Juan asks, and only now does the kid seem to take the time to consider his question.

"There," he says, pointing the way north. "Ahead, man, always ahead. Only go backward to pick up speed."

Juan nods, unsurprised, as if he expected such a reply. But then he asks:

"Why?"

"Why what?"

"Why go that way?"

For the first time, the kid looks up from the road.

"Why not?"

Juan doesn't answer. That reply, or lack of reply, makes the kid consider his own more slowly.

He says:

"They say there's a future there."

He says:

"They say there's work there."

He says:

"They say the girls are prettier and easier."

"I understand," Juan says.

But the kid still talks for some time about those pretty, easy women he'll find up north. Women with golden hair and blue eyes; women with such white skin that you make them blush by looking at them, friend; so white that, for a long time afterward, you can see the five red marks from your five fingers imprinted on their ass and titties. Women who study at college and carry leather briefcases and go to business meetings and talk all nice and professional, women who, in bed, just want to suck your cock. You can fuck them like actual whores. Those are the women he's talking about, the kid says as he puts his backpack in the trunk of the car that has just stopped; as he greets the driver and opens the door and allows the belly of that machine to swallow him up.

"You coming, man?" the kid asks, already inside.

Juan reflects for what feels like an excessively long moment.

"No," he says.

No, he repeats much later, like an echo, to the wake of dust the car has left behind.

Then he turns back to the road.

Some cars go north.

Others go south.

Juan turns southward.

He has hardly gone one hundred or two hundred steps when he hears the woman's voice. Hey, you, that voice yells from across the highway. Then he sees it: an old dirty truck, parked on the side of the road. The woman's arm hanging out the open window. Her straw-colored hair, pulled into a hasty bun. Her red visor. Her dark glasses.

"Where're you going?" the woman asks, not bothering to take the cigarette out of her mouth.

"I'm going home," Juan says.

"And where would that be?"

Juan points south. It is a weak gesture, hesitant. A gesture that is almost a question or an appeal.

"Mexico, huh?"

"Yes."

"Get in."

Juan hesitates. He takes another look at the truck. Its snout pointing rigorously north, with the obstinacy of which only compasses are capable.

"Are you going to Mexico too?"

"No," the woman says, tossing the cigarette butt. "I'm not going to Mexico."

And then, as if there were no contradiction at all, she repeats:

"Get in."

This woman is crazy, Juan thinks, or starts to think, because before he can give shape to that thought, something stops him. He has just noticed her clothes. She wears a black short-sleeved T-shirt, initialed with white scribbles that, from a distance, don't seem to transmit any meaning. But as he moves closer, those whimsical etchings begin to turn into something else; suddenly he recognizes the silhouette of a white cactus rising from the black desert of her shirt, and over that cactus, the drawing of a sombrero similar to the one the Compadre wore in his revolutionary days; a sombrero that appears suspended in air, like a sidereal disc or a bird surprised in mid-flight. Below, the mysterious letters:

I JUAN TO BELIEVE.

Juan studies those four words for a long time. The four letters that form the word Juan.

I JUAN TO BELIEVE.

Behind her dark glasses, the woman's eyes settle into an expression Juan cannot decipher. Her voice, suddenly, becomes a whisper.

"Get in," she pleads.

His hesitation lasts but another second. And in that second, Juan realizes that the woman isn't proposing to bring him back: the machine she drives, like all machines, is designed to be always driven ahead.

Out beyond, an expanse of plain peppered with sparse bushes and then a handful of cabins that come to kiss the road and still later the same plain again, the same bushes, the sky that, at the horizon line, takes on the color of the sand. Mexico behind him, Mexico further and further south, and still Juan hasn't asked any questions. Juan has suspended all will and limits himself to being present on his own trip, like one follows the course of a dream. A trip that isn't taking him back to any home, or maybe it is, he thinks, but a home he doesn't yet know: a home nobody has known. Then he doesn't think. He simply lets the desert air pummel his face and, with numbed consciousness, watching ranches, cars, fences go by, as one watches clouds float across the sky.

Otherwise, the sky is clear. Just blue signs appointed with names and numbers and arrows, lots of arrows that point ahead, always ahead. Behind her dark glasses, the woman's eyes might as well be glued in that direction. At a spot taking shape on the horizon or maybe the horizon itself.

At some point, Juan tires of looking at the scenery and looks, instead, at her. He looks at what the dark glasses let him see of her face and what her clothes let him see of her body. He looks at the shape of her lips, similar to other lips he has known. He looks at her hands on the steering wheel, chapped from who knows what kind of touch. He looks at the T-shirt flecked with highway dust—I JUAN TO BELIEVE—and the bare legs that occasionally tense to work the secret pedals. It looks like she, too, has come a very long way. I've come a very long way, she says, as if answering a question Juan hasn't dared to ask. She doesn't look at him at all. Her eyes are fixed on the road and she seems to be addressing herself. From where? Juan finally asks, and the woman makes a vague gesture that also seems directed at the asphalt, at the landscape slipping past through the windshield. Very far. Very far, she repeats. And she has been traveling this whole time, she adds, her voice hoarse: she has always been traveling, you could say. From the beginning.

"From the beginning of what?"

"From the beginning of the journey."

"I understand."

Only then does the woman turn to Juan. She smiles. She seems to smile. She studies him from the blind depths of her black glasses.

"Yeah? Do you really?"

For a time, Juan holds her pupilless, lidless gaze. A time full of blue signs that flash by, reflected in the dark lenses, full too of sun-bleached parcels of land, scrub withering in ditches, all converted by speed into a single dun-colored blur. Time full of himself as well, the tiny reflection of his own face.

"Where are we going?"

"You wanted to go home, didn't you?" she replies, turning her attention back to the road. "Well, that's what we're doing. We're going home."

"Home."

"Yeah. Home."

"And where is that home?"

"Close," she says. "Very close."

Juan doesn't appear satisfied.

"How much longer?" he insists, and there is a trace of impatience in his voice, of a child demanding that a trip come to an end. "Two weeks?"

The woman is smiling again.

"We'll be home today."

Home could be anywhere, the woman says. Here, for instance. This could be the place: as good a place as any to stop. They see a cluster of scattered cabins and barns clad in sheet metal and gardens enclosed with hedges or iron fencing. A row of trees planted along the roadside, maintaining the mirage that life is possible in the desert, too. Your house, the woman repeats, could be one of these. This, your garden. This, your neighborhood. Truth or Consequences, reads a metal sign presiding over the entrance to the town, and as they pass, the woman reads it out loud, in a voice that could just as well be admiration or reproach. Truth or Consequences. In other words, Verdad o Consecuencias. A town named Truth or Consequences, can he believe that? What truth can be found here, what consequences? There was a time when this place was called Hot Springs, the woman explains. A long time ago now. Sixty, seventy years? One day they simply decided to change the name. Only it wasn't so simple after all. Back then there was an American radio show called that, Truth or Consequences. It was a ridiculous program, the woman reflects, or maybe, with the passing of time, it seems ridiculous to us now. There were contestants and prizes and a repertoire of impossible questions. When the contestants didn't know the right answer to one of those questions—and they never knew; that was the gag: it was never possible to find the truth—there were consequences. The consequences were challenges or tests or dares that were also, at the time the show aired, ridiculous. Sometimes the contestants humiliated themselves to win money and other times, the majority, humiliated themselves and won nothing. That's America, the woman reasons: it was then and it is now. At some point, the host announced that the next show would air from the first city in the country to change its name to the name of the show. Hot Springs, or rather, Truth or Consequences, won the prize. They sold the truth of their name— though on the other hand, what sort of truth is there in a name, really—and they did it in exchange for something. In a certain sense, maybe it was a good deal for everybody. There are lots of Hot Springs in the United States—the woman has counted nine at least—but only one Truth or Consequences. In any case, the show has been off air for many years and Truth or Consequences the town still calls itself Truth or Consequences. The future, says the woman, the place where we will live out the rest of our days, could look like this one. A place where words no longer have meaning. A world in which nothing true is left: just its consequences. And they could form part of that world, she says; all they'd have to do is turn off the engine. That easy. We could simply stop here, she says, never reducing her speed for an instant; we could, she repeats, and keeps on driving.

We could stop here, too, the woman says. Put down roots in this place as easily as in any other. In Cuchillo. In Los Lunas. In Bosquecito. In one of those towns that still holds the memory of another world: Doña Ana, Las Cruces, Rincón, Oasis. Caballo, Polvadera, La Joya, Escondida. The journey could end here, she says again: inside a name. In another time or the memory of another time. Did he know that right here on this very land, maybe right below this very asphalt, once ran the Camino Real de Tierra Adentro, the so-called Silver Route? It linked Mexico City with Santa Fe and was the closest thing the Spanish ever had to a highway. That's why El Paso is called El Paso: because it passed right through there. He didn't know? Well, now he does. Human beings might forget, but names do not. Sometimes she dallies with remembering what cannot be remembered. She remembers this land when the conquistadors still roved. She imagines them covered by their breastplates or cuirasses, their notched sables, their arquebuses and skins of gunpowder, with their dogs and wives and packs of mules, with their dirty clothes and heads full of experiences minted in another world. Men who went from one night to another with their lamps and lanterns and torches, and in that torchlight, sustained the memory of another land. And that memory was about to ignite the world. Because it's customary to believe the Spaniards were the light and the savages the dark, the woman says, and mile by mile, her voice has become increasingly grave, until it acquires its own weight, casts its own shadow, is one more thing among the rest; it's customary, she repeats, to think their eyes were open and the Indians didn't see the world or only saw it just barely, but maybe it's exactly the opposite. Maybe the world is made to be seen that way, in semi-darkness, to be inhabited and loved and understood by feeling our way, barely glimpsed by the light cast by campfires or dreams. But the Spaniards brought their light. A light that was maybe not all light, not entirely. Fire that dimmed the shadows and maybe with it dimmed hope, too, the dreams they dreamed; more and more light and less and less space to dream in, light before their eyelids and behind them. Maybe, illuminated by that glow, the Spaniards saw something the Indians hadn't seen, but they also stopped seeing many other things the Indians saw or understood with the clairvoyance only the half-light provides. A new sun to reveal that the caves where they painted their bison and their doodles and their gods weren't the Earth's womb, that the Earth, in fact, doesn't have a womb; that the same earth they venerated wasn't a mother but an enemy, an obstacle, a limit. They came, in short, with their priests and their wares and their books and their certainties, they came to build prisons and hostelries and hermitages and ranches and barracks. Let's just say that she, the woman, remembers it. Let's just say that she, too, was there. That her journey began at the beginning and that beginning dates back to that time. That she inhabited the world when it was still young, fresh-baked, as we say; when anything was still possible. She's talking about those men forged on other continents, fed on the milk of other lands, ravaged by the sun and fatigue and the wreck of their bones in the dust; she is talking—and Juan shudders to hear it—about those men and women who left everything in exchange for nothing, or in exchange for something that didn't matter, or in exchange for something that did matter but not to themselves, not for them—for whom, then?—the woman wonders in her new-found voice. Men who came just so that Las Cruces would be called Las Cruces and not The Crosses. And now they—she and Juan, that is—could continue the route those men carved with their caravans. They could—why not?—stop right in Santa Fe, which must have been an important place, a destination worth suffering through fifteen hundred miles of desolation and vertigo and blisters. That could be their destination, the place in which to build a new house: Santa Fe. A curious name for a beginning. A curious name for a city, if one thinks about it. Back then, those were the names people gave the places where they were going to be born and die: saints' names, names from legends, names from dreams. That's all that's left of them. Names that speak of a time in which men didn't see rivers, mountain ranges, canyons, plains, but rather patron saint protectors and compassionate virgins and divine plans. Maybe the fact that those names haven't been lost has some significance or offers us some kind of lesson: the woman isn't sure. After all, does a name protect us? Does it provide warmth, offer some kind of comfort, leave a physical sensation? She can't say. The point is, back then men still believed in things. Things that might have been true or false, that doesn't matter, because they were as real as the ground they walked on. Realer than giving the name Rock Canyon to a rock canyon; or Elephant Butte to an elephant-shaped hill or New York to a city destined to replace England. The Spanish came with their swords and their horses and their dogs and their skins of gunpowder but they came, above all, with their words. Those words wounded more than any kind of iron. Because long before that, these lands undoubtedly had other names. Who remembers those names today? Who cares how an Apache saw the world when he looked at it? Moreover, who cares about the first colonist's eyes to open and close on this land, whether they saw dreams or hopes or nightmares under its sun or beneath its stars? All we have are their words. The skin they put on the world. Everything is left of Hot Springs, except its name. Of all those little villages, it's only the name that remains. There's Socorro, though not many know that's a way of asking for help. There's Lemitar, which sounds Spanish, the woman says, but damned if she has the faintest idea what it means. There's San Antonio, even if maybe nobody worships St. Anthony or any other saint, though not even the churches offer succor or a place to pray. Pray to whom? Pray for what? They could, in short, stop here, the woman says, without slowing down at all, without turning the wheel or applying the brake: they could settle inside a belief. She seems to remember hearing that very nearby, just a few miles away, the San Miguel mission still stands. The first building built on this land. Because the first building built on this land was a church, you see. What will be the last? Where would they stop, if they were to stop?

Or we could stop where no one ever has. Stop—why not?—in this desert. At no house, in no town. We would be that town. The desert, the woman says, would be our home. Death, our kingdom. Can Juan see it, the desert? It extends on both sides of the highway, an oceanless, boatless beach. The old conquistadors also gave a name to this patch of nothing: they called it Jornada del Muerto, surely because a man, or many men, died trying to cross it. But there had to be a first: someone who made Jornada del Muerto be called Jornada del Muerto. We don't know his name, we only know his suffering. The memory of his suffering. They could stop here and agonize where he agonized. They would inherit his thirst. They could be the last dead in Jornada del Muerto. And maybe their deliberate death, their refusal to advance, would be a metaphor for something. A symbol. They would die surrounded by life, because here, too, in this hell, there is a place for it. Somehow, enough water dribbles through for bushes and thistles to take root. But there was a time, the woman says in the voice that grows graver and more remote by the second, a time, she says, when even the most minute version of life was impossible. Doesn't he know? It was seventy-five years ago; just the other day, she says. Right before that time, the desert contained, briefly, more life than ever before. They came from all over: men and women who sawed boards and raised walls and built houses and shelters and observation decks and bunkers where before there had been nothing. They were men of science. They brought their trucks and their mathematics and their objectives. They also brought their names. They brought bottles of Coca-Cola and Lucky cigarettes and Heinz ketchup and Bazooka gum and Durex condoms. They brought their nightmares, their dreams, their certainties. They inhabited this land for but a moment, in order to destroy it for decades. They were, no doubt, men with good intentions. They were the best minds of their generation and I, says the woman, I was able to watch them shine and burn out before my very eyes. Because I was there too. We are, in fact, right here, right beside them—seventy-five years ago, she repeats; just the other day. They are men of science but they are also soldiers and they are prophets and they are children. They have dreamed of weapons beyond the reach of our imagination; weapons so lethal that, on witnessing their birth, the world can and must instantaneously age. The men are also, in their twisted way, gods, because one must be terrible, she says, one must, in a certain sense, be God, a diminished version of God, God's will made flesh, to go so far on the strength of their numbers and their bare hands alone. We see them build an iron tower one hundred feet high. We see them calculate, argue, dream. We see them believe—and this, says the woman, is maybe the last time mankind will believe in something. We see them create. They are about to give birth to a terrible and beautiful boy, like themselves. A son made for and of and against flesh. That boy is called Trinity, because someone has heard that name in a certain poem by a certain poet, and somebody else had said already that poetry will save the world. But in order to save the world, say the men of science, say the soldiers, the prophets, the children, first you must destroy it. And that's what they're about to do. We will join them—can't Juan see them, right there, just a few yards from the highway?—as they labor to raise their son up to the highest part of the tower and then move away. They shelter in their parapets and they put on their sunglasses, their sunscreen, their helmets and earplugs, their thermal suits. Before, like the children they are, they made their predictions and placed their bets. They want to guess how loud their firstborn will be. Some say that its voice won't make any sound at all, that the plutonium will fall, sterile, to the sand—plutonium valued at billions of dollars—and there are those who say it will raise many decibels, ten, one hundred, one thousand kilotons. There are even those who say its voice will deafen the world, that it will annihilate the whole state of New Mexico; that it will cause the atmosphere to ignite and with that the Earth's destruction. But we mustn't be afraid, the experts say, because such a possibility—the world's destruction—is a remote one, negligible. Negligible, the woman says, doesn't mean impossible. It means just what it says: a negligible risk. A risk worth taking. And finally, the exact day and time arrive, the chosen moment, and the world isn't destroyed after all. Or maybe it is destroyed, in a certain sense. Maybe the seconds and days and years that come after are nothing more than that: a countdown. The son will speak, ultimately, in a voice neither as low nor as high as was expected—eighteen kilotons will be the official estimate—and then there will be hugs and cheers and applause. There will also be a long silence. But many other things will come first. Ten million degrees for a tenth of a second, the woman says. A crater ten feet deep and more than a thousand feet wide. A shockwave that could be felt a hundred miles away: the wind of progress, which hasn't stopped blowing since; still it comes through the open window to whip the woman's hair and T-shirt. Light brighter than eight suns and a mushroom cloud seven miles high. All life, the meager desert life, destroyed within a five mile radius. Several tons of sand ejected and vaporized and crystallized. A light so bright it can be seen, they claim, from El Paso and Albuquerque—can't Juan see it shining now, reflected in the woman's dark glasses?—as if after centuries or millennia of indifference, God had decided to snap our photo. That light has no definite color; rather, it passes through many, from white to purple, from gray to blue, to yellow, to green, lights never before seen illuminating the plain, every hill and every crevice, and the scientists, the soldiers, the prophets, the children, see the world by the flare of that light and they don't like what they see, or maybe they like it too much; they like it enough to bring those colors to Hiroshima and Nagasaki, to the Marshall Islands, to Novaya Zemlya. They see that light for but an instant and now they can never forget it. They will reproduce it always and forever, in secret and not-so-secret shelters, in the atmosphere and on land, in the depths of the earth and the depths of the sea. A light so blinding that, beside it, the light the Spaniards brought was nothing but a humble campfire, fire's little brother, barely capable of wounding the night. And now one of those prophet-children, who maybe senses or intuits or knows what is going to happen, says: Now I am become Death, the destroyer of worlds. Another adds: it is one small step for life, one giant leap for death. And a last voice: Now we're all sons of bitches. And they are, of course: scientists and children and prophets and soldiers and sons of bitches, too. They've just seen how the bomb's first victim has been its own land, the country of its creators, like a child who, on learning to stand, knocks down his parents' house with a swipe of his hand, and maybe now they realize that what they've conceived is not a gift but a punishment, one that will rain indiscriminately on all, blacks and whites, enemies and allies and indifferent parties, a democratic bomb and its aftermath the equal wounding of humanity's flesh, with no distinction or amnesty for anyone. Those men, the children of those men, the children of the children of those men, are about to learn new words: "strontium," "nuclear radiation," "neutrons," "acid rain." The woman's hands tense tighter and tighter on the wheel, as if she wasn't driving a car but the destiny of humanity as a whole. "Atomic," "chain reaction," "uranium-235," "fusion," "fission." They will read pamphlets provided by their governments that explain, with simple instructions and colorful illustrations, what to do in the event of a nuclear warning, because in the event of a nuclear warning, the pamphlets say or suggest or insinuate between the lines, the blast will be so extreme that any insignificant object, a pencil, say, can pierce us straight through like shrapnel. In the event of a nuclear warning, the windows must be opened so the shattered glass doesn't kill us. In the event of a nuclear warning, we must be fifteen feet underground so the flash of deflagration doesn't melt our eyeballs. In the event of a nuclear warning, the pamphlet says, we must rid ourselves of all those objects we have accumulated in the belief that they would make our lives easier, because now they can turn against us. In the event of a nuclear warning, we need a bunker. In the event of a nuclear warning, we need to pray. But we've already said, the woman reminds him, that man has stopped praying. To God, at least. And so, in the event of a nuclear warning, there is just one thing that man can do: die. And death is the destiny that would await them if they were to stop the car then and there, to die at last—but she isn't going to stop; she won't end their journey yet. So the woman says in a voice increasingly pained and increasingly human. A voice that separates from the machine it drives; a voice much more than an iron will. And now the road goes on, the voice is saying, because those prolific parents still have more atrocious children to bear; grandchildren and great-grandchildren conceived to touch an ever-widening radius—a radius that might come to coincide, the woman says, with that of the world. New generations of memoryless children, raised to be increasingly benign with things and increasingly ruthless with mankind: bombs designed to destroy life wherever it may be found but respect our houses, our cathedrals, our highways. This is how the world ends, she says. This is how the world ends, she repeats. This is how the world ends. A future in which objects will reign: the books we write, the machines that gave us work or took it away, our satellites, our country homes, our toys, our schools. A future with a place for our works, but not for us. Maybe that's what we sought from the very beginning of the journey: a world without us. Things without their names. Names without their memory. No truth, no consequence. And that ultimate bomb, the daughter of all bombs, hasn't yet detonated. Or maybe she has, the woman admits after a silence filled with dust and asphalt. Maybe she's already detonated in a way we didn't expect; maybe she actually detonates every day, an explosion without flames or sound or hope. So often have we prayed to things, so often have we knelt before our machines, before our stuff, our screens; we have poured so much sweat and blood into them that now just one thing remains: to die in their name. The religion of capital outliving its faithful. Highways outliving their travelers. Borders outliving their immigrants. The future could look like that, the woman says, and her voice contains something of the many voices Juan has heard; a voice that unites known sufferings and sufferings yet to be known, but which still makes itself heard, still rises anyway, does not succumb to silence. This could be the future. This, she says, is the present. And it wouldn't take much to get there: we are, in fact, already so close. All we'd have to do is turn the wheel a little bit, barely a couple inches, and the future that awaits us, she says, would be the desert. Or we could simply continue ahead, always ahead, faster, always faster, and sooner or later the desert would come again. Or we could stop at any point and refuse to advance and then, of course, that's the desert too. All roads seem to lead to the desert. Maybe all roads are the desert. And yet, says the woman. Yet. We are here. Somehow, we continue the journey as if some hope remained. And who knows, she says, whether that hope isn't the journey itself.

The woman keeps talking about alternatives to the road that awaits them. She talks about secondary highways and dirt roads and even bridlepaths; routes that don't go exactly north but maybe to the northeast or northwest, a little to the right or left. She talks about detours that seem to double-back but which actually, one way or another, lead onward. She talks about service stations where it's possible to stop for a minute, to reprogram or confirm or delete the directions. But Juan has stopped listening by then. He's no longer there. He only has eyes for the horizon and ears for the silence of that land, its immeasurable vastness. He looks to verify that the woman's words have come to fruition: how the only thing left ahead is, in effect, desert. Earth and dust and sky: all that exists. He sees metal towers supporting cables that transport lights and sounds to no one. He sees a long stretch of asphalt ruled by machines that nobody seems to be driving, machines that push on, guided by their own intentions. He sees the horizon empty of human beings, as if they had already reached the epicenter of that explosion which had to come and, in the end, finally came. From now on, this is the world that awaits, Juan tells himself, startled and prescient, a world made by and for things; a world that must be seen and named and created anew. This is how it will happen, he realizes, over the course of miles or centuries; this is how it will happen, in short, for all time—might time ever end? This is what he thinks. The idea of eternity, contained in a single flash of his thought. But the instant passes and eternity endures and Juan turns to the woman. How could he not, if her hand, the woman's hand, has suddenly begun to speak louder than her words. The hand that seems to come alive, that suddenly rises to remove the dark glasses as if removing a blindfold; as if removing another blindfold from Juan's eyes. And then the woman's face, bare for the first time. The woman's eyes, open. Her gaze. Juan who both recognizes that gaze and does not, not at all: the same eyes, but they are not the same. Eyes that reflect everything, yes, eyes that are what remains of faith when one includes compassion, freedom when justice is present; will, when it possesses hands and a voice. The beautiful and the terrible in those eyes; horror and hope, together at last. A gaze that sees both yesterday and tomorrow without turning its head; that watches the ruins they leave behind in the rearview mirror and through the windshield, sees the future that awaits. And Juan, too, of course; in the woman's eyes, Juan's eyes, and in Juan's eyes, the woman's, which seem to overflow and decant until they arrive at some kind of common revelation. Or maybe there is no mystery, no revelation. Only this: the certainty that they are traveling together. The conviction of not going back and, at the same time, the promise not to continue pressing ahead; not at any price. Before them, the desert solitude, like an enormous answer or deferral or refutation of that hope. Though who knows if the desert is really empty, after all. Who can be sure the desert is a real desert. Juan suddenly recalls the woman's words: somehow, enough water dribbles through for bushes and thistles to take root. That's what she said. And now Juan looks at those bushes, those thistles, with something like faith. Occasionally, a teetering tree. A yellow shrub. Juan sees it everywhere through the car window, open seas of creosote, that plant they call gobernadora because that's exactly what it does, governs the environs human will has relinquished.

300

There are tumbleweeds that don't even need roots, living in the incessant drift of sand and dust, like how birds stay up in the air. Juan sees all of this and much more. He sees the creeping return of minute life. Life that returns after the detonation; life that maybe never left. And suddenly, in the midst of the yellow dirt, on that horizon with no foothold or resistance, a white dot growing bigger by the moment. A white dot that is—that is slowly becoming—a house, set on the side of the road. A normal house, no different in any way from any others, and beside it, waiting on the stoop, a black dot, a black dot that is in fact a human figure, man or woman, it doesn't matter, why should it, a human being in any case, an upright figure with a head to think and a mouth to speak, with two arms to do and undo and two legs to walk forward or backward, as needed. A future brother who simply sits and waits by the front door; a body increasingly real in the abstraction of the desert.

And then, only then, the car stops.

Acknowledgements

I first thought of Juan the Indian in 2009, in my classes at the Complutense University of Madrid with professors Alfonso Lacadena and José Luis de Rojas. Back then, the project was no more than a moderately-long story, which earned me an artist residency in Mexico. As often occurs in my case, during the residency I didn't write more than a handful of pages of the project in question: instead, I was able to finish *Los que duermen*, which would become my first book of stories. I wouldn't return to my frustrated attempt until another residency many years later, in 2016 at the Academia de España in Rome, where I was—of course—on a scholarship to write something else.

The current state of *Not Even the Dead* owes much to the writer Sara Barquinero, who believed in this book even when I did not. Her advice was vital, both during the research process and the actual writing: she fleshed out Juan's flesh, brought his wife into existence, and helped provide more conceptual grounds for his adventures. I also don't want to forget the invaluable aid from The International Writers' House in Graz, who gave me the space and, above all, the time to write some of the chapters in this novel. I owe the Donald Trump snake speech to the playwright and novelist Natascha Gangl; to Auxiliadora Ruiz Sánchez, the lending of certain crucial books; to Andrés de Arenal, manager of the Juan Rulfo bookstore, some pieces of good advice; to Professor David Bowles, the translation of the incipit to Nahuatl; to Juan Soto Ivars—and, of course, to Walter Benjamin—the choice of the title. Daniel Herrera and Daniela Suárez, with their invitation to the University of Long Beach in 2018, did more for this novel than they ever dreamed, and introduced me to valuable informants like Leydi Ahumada and Erika Tapia. Riki Blanco put a face to the original Spanish edition of this book (for the third time). I'd say the infinite discussions about the shape of the knife and the background color were worth it in the end. My thanks to the team at Sexto Piso, who believed in my literature once again. I've never had the opportunity to speak with the journalist Oscar Martínez, but I have read his powerful book *Los migrantes no importan*, full of real testimonies that filtered into different moments of this novel. I don't personally know Professor Johannes Schneider, to whom I owe a debt I could never repay. The numismatics scholar María Teresa Muñoz Serrulla gave me a few keys for resolving the slight historical inaccuracy that occurs in the first chapters, but I ended up persevering in my error because, by that time, I already loved my novel more and monies less. Also critical, as with all my projects, were readings by professionals and friends like Andrea Palaudarias, Víctor Balcells, Guillermo Aguirre, Daniel Arija, Ángel García Galiano, Alfonso Muñoz Corcuera, Ella Sher, Samir Mendoza, Lucía Martínez Pardo, Mercedes Bárcena, and Emilio Gómez, and the conversations with Viridiana Carrillo, Eduardo Ruiz Sosa, Florencia Sabaté, Desirée Rubio de Marzo, Javier Vicedo, Laura Jahn Scotte, Cristina Morales, María Laura Padrón, Edgar Straehle, María Zaragoza, Carla Martínez Nyman, Montxo Armendáriz, Puy Oria, Melca Pérez, Zita Arenillas, Meritxell Joan, Helena Ruiz, Silvia Pérez, Alejandro López, and Muriel Cuadros. And thanks, once again, to Marta Jiménez, to whom I also owe those readings and those conversations, and at the same time, much more.

JUAN GOMÉZ BÁRCENA (1984) holds degrees in literary theory, comparative literature, and history from the Complutense University of Madrid, and a degree in philosophy from Spain's National University of Distance Education. He's the author of numerous essay, short story, and poetry collections, for which he's received the José Hierro Prize for Poetry and Fiction, the International CRAPE Prize for stories, and the Ramón J. Sender Prize for Narrative, among others. He lives in Madrid.

KATIE WHITTEMORE translates from the Spanish. Her work has appeared in *Two Lines*, *The Arkansas International*, *The Common Online*, *Gulf Coast Magazine Online*, *The Brooklyn Rail*, and *InTranslation*. Current projects include novels by Spanish authors Sara Mesa, Javier Serena, Aliocha Coll, and Aroa Moreno Durán. She lives in Valencia.